PENGUIN CLASSI

THE SATASAĪ

Bihārī's date of birth and caste are shrouded in controversy, though his position as one of the foremost poets of the Rītikāla tradition (also called Śṛngārakāla tradition) of love poetry has never been in dispute.

Bihārī was probably born in 1595 in Gwalior to Keśavarāya and Mahāvidyā—a family of Gharawārī Mathura Caubeys, a Brahmin sub-caste. He got his early education from his father who was a Sanskrit scholar. When he was about eight years of age his mother died and the family moved to Ōrchā in Bundelkhaṅḍ after which they went to Vṛṅdāvana. At around this time Bihārī married and shifted to Mathurā with his wife. When Emperor Jehāngīr visited Mathurā with his son Shāh Jahān, the latter invited Bihārī to the Moghul court at Agra; Bihārī recited some of his poems there and was awarded an annuity by the princes present in recognition of his talents. During the political unrest after Jehāngīr's death Bihārī returned to Mathurā.

He was then invited to Amber by its ruler to his court. It was here, under Jayasiṅgha's patronage, that Bihāri wrote *The Satasaī*. After his wife's death Bihārī returned to Vṛṅdāvana, where he spent his last days of his life. He died in 1664 at the age of sixty-nine.

K. P. Bahadur was born in 1924 in Allahabad and took a post-graduate degree in English from the Allahabad University. He served the Uttar Pradesh government in various administrative assignments and retired as Commissioner in 1982.

A prolific writer, Bahadur has authored over forty books covering various subjects including philosophy, history, sociology and poetry. His writings include *The Wisdom of India Series* (7 volumes), *History of the Indian Civilization* (7 volumes), *History of the Freedom Movement* (5 volumes), and *Castes, Tribes and Cultures of India* (7 volumes). He has also contributed a section on Indian authors in *Major World Writers*.

K. P. Bahadur has received several honorary awards including the Vidya Visharada and the Vidya Ratnakara. He is currently working on three books – *World Religions*, *Women in Crime* and a translation of the *Bhagavad Gita*.

K. P. Bahadur is married and lives in Lucknow.

BIHĀRĪ

The Satasaī

Translated from the Hindi and
with an introduction by
Krishna P. Bahadur

PENGUIN BOOKS/UNESCO

PENGUIN BOOKS

Published by the Penguin Group
Penguin Books Ltd, 27 Wrights Lane, London W8 5TZ, England
Penguin Books USA Inc., 375 Hudson Street, New York, New York 10014, USA
Penguin Books Australia Ltd, Ringwood, Victoria, Australia
Penguin Books Canada Ltd, 10 Alcorn Avenue, Toronto, Ontario, Canada M4V 3B2
Penguin Books (NZ) Ltd, 182–190 Wairau Road, Auckland 10, New Zealand

Penguin Books Ltd, Registered Offices: Harmondsworth, Middlesex, England

Published in India in Penguin Classics 1990
Published in Great Britain and the USA in Penguin Classics 1992
1 3 5 7 9 10 8 6 4 2

Printed in England by Clays Ltd, St Ives plc

To Sandhya

Alas, that Spring should vanish with the Rose!
That Youth's sweet-scented Manuscript should close.

Ib. ed. i, lxxii
Omar Khyyām (Trans. Edward Fitzgerald)

CONTENTS

ACKNOWLEDGEMENTS

The author gratefully acknowledges the assistance of the following commentaries on *The Satasaī* of Bihārī, in this English verse translation.

Bihārī Bhāṣya, Dr Deśarājasiṅgha Bhāṭī, Delhi: Aśoka Prakāśan, 1978. (Hindi)
Bihārī-Bodhinī, Lālā Bhagawāna Dīna 'Dīna', Banāras: Sāhitya-Sevā-Sadan, 1978. (Hindi)
Bihārī-Satasaī, Śrī Rākeśa, Lucknow: Prakāśan Kendra. (Hindi)

The author is indebted to Bihārī Satasaī, (lālacandrikā ṭīkā), Lallūjī Lāl, Kāśī: Nāgarīpracāriṇī Sabhā. (Hindi), for Bihārī's portrait—Kavivar Bihārī.

Sources cited are referred to in the notes at the end of the book. Verses which bear no such source reference are the author's own translation.

INTRODUCTION

Bihārī's Times

Bihārī was born in an age when the barbarity of conquerors like Mahmūd Ghaznī and Tīmūr was spent and the puritanical iconoclasm of Aurangazīb had not yet begun. He also escaped the stormy uncertain years of the early Moghul emperors, Bābur and Humāyūn. Akbar's rule began on 14 February 1556, about thirty-nine years before Bihārī was born, and ended with the emperor's death on 25 October 1605 when the poet was only ten years old. By that time Akbar had consolidated his empire. He had also provided an atmosphere in which even a culture alien to his own, could flourish. By the time Akbar's successor, Jahāngīr, died (7 November 1627), Bihārī was thirty-three. Jahāngīr continued Akbar's liberal policy of universal toleration, having temples and churches built, and observing Hindu fasts as public holidays. But Bihārī's formative years were tied up with Jahāngīr's son and successor, Shāh Jahān, whose period (1628–58) is sometimes called the 'Golden Age' of Moghul history. Bihārī had only six years more to live after Shāh Jahān stepped down to make way for Aurangazīb. Shāh Jahān, the builder of the Tāj Mahal and several other masterpieces of architecture, encouraged music, dance and painting, had Sanskrit works translated into Persian, and patronized Hindu poets.

Naraharidāsa, who was to become Bihārī's spiritual guru, introduced him to Shāh Jahān when he was still a prince. The poet composed some verses in his praise which pleased Shāh Jahān so much that he invited Bihārī to Agra. That gave the poet an opportunity to learn Persian and to get acquainted with other scholars flocking to the Moghul court. Bihārī also became the favourite of Jayasiṅgha, ruler of Amber (near Jaipur) which was to become one of the most prominent states of Rājpūtāna. It was Jayasiṅgha who encouraged him to write the *Satasaī.*

Thus Bihārī came at the right time. Had he been born earlier, perhaps his poetic genius would not have blossomed so freely, for those were years of turmoil, persecution and bloodshed, and not favourable at all to art and culture. In other respects, however, Bihārī's times were not so happy. It was the age of social and spiritual decline. The middle class—merchants, doctors, men of letters and so forth—were almost extinct. There were either the very rich or the very poor; grandeur on one side, misery on the other. 'The peasantry,' says Bernier, a physician of those times, 'was completely crushed.' It was natural under these circumstances, that the vices and extravagance of courts should have been mirrored in the lives of the aristocracy—the class which really mattered—in manners, dress, pastime, food and drink. Abu'l Fazl, the chronicler of the times, tells us that one hundred dishes were served to Akbar at just one meal, and that he wasn't a gourmet! Drinking was quite common and though some of the emperors like, Jahāngīr (himself a drunkard) and Aurangazīb, tried to enforce prohibition, drinking had come to stay. Aurangazīb exclaimed in despair, 'In all Hindustān there can't be found more than two men who don't drink' (meaning himself and his chief *qāzī*, Abu'l Wahāb). And even about his *qāzī* he was wrong, because Manucci, commenting on what the emperor said, wrote, 'He was in error, for I myself sent Abu'l Wahāb a bottle of spirits which he drank in secret!' Women drank too, and some of Bihārī's heroines are shown not only drinking, but drunk.

About the jewellery worn by the ruler of Malabar, Marco Polo says, 'What this king wears between gold and gems and pearls, is worth more than a city's ransom.' Ornaments indeed were a craze, particularly with women. Abu'l Fazl mentions thirty-seven kinds. Complimenting the women for their beauty, Orme, the historian, says, 'Nature seems to have showered beauty on the fairer sex throughout Hindustan with a more lavish hand than in most other countries.' And of course when nature bestowed beauty on Indian women, they took good care to enhance it. They were very particular about their make-up. Eyelids were blackened with lamp-black on their inner edges, lips stained red with betel-juice (which women were fond of chewing), feet and palms with henna and the borders of the sole with lacquer dye. High class ladies blackened the crevices between their teeth with *missi* and darkened their eyelashes with antimony. Long hair was considered graceful, being often gathered into a bun in which a gold bodkin was stuck. Shoulders and breasts were anointed with a paste of sandalwood powder, camphor and other fragrant unguents. In dress too, women of the upper classes were fastidious. Hindu women wore saris and a small jacket beneath it called the *aṁgiyā.* About the *aṁgiyā,* Stavorinus wrote, 'They support their breasts and press them upwards by a piece of linen which passes under the arms and is made fast on the back.'[1] All these fashions are reflected in Bihārī's women. He rarely speaks of a village girl, and when he does so, the change in dress and ornaments from the ornate to the humble is very much in evidence.

Morals shared the inconsistencies of the age. Akbar noticed that Hindu women were 'flaming torches of love and fellowship'.[2] Jahāngīr said they would not 'let the hand of any unlawful person touch the skirt of their chastity'.[3] On the other hand all the ills of a degenerate society were also present—polygamy, prostitution and illicit sex. Although there were wantons among women then, as now (Bihārī mentions a few in his *Satasaī*), the fault lay more with the men than with the women. Manucci writes about 'wretched pretenders to holiness who satisfy their lust and avarice'.[4] Speaking of Mohammedans he says, 'They are very fond of women who are their principal relaxation and almost their only pleasure'.[5] There were child-marriages, dowry and widow-burning. Men kept many wives and mistresses. They had secret affairs. Concubines were on the increase. A number of women in the cities took to the veil.

All this was reflected in Bihārī's men and women, known as *nāyakas* and *nāyikās* in Hindi love poetry. Quite a few of the *nāyakas* were faithless to their wives or beloveds and returned from the arms of their mistresses boldly displaying the marks of their nightlong love-making in a devil-may-care manner. Then there was this further complication resulting from polygamy, in that almost every man had more than one wife (the woman being expected to be satisfied, on the contrary, with one husband). The man's affection kept shifting to the newest wife, making the others, her co-wives, naturally jealous.

The same atmosphere of conflict dominated religion also. On the one hand Hindus were willing to admit Muslim converts to their fold, on the other they kept up a stiff resistance and reaffirmed their conservatism. Those Hindus worshipping Viṣṇu were known as Vaiṣṇavas, and those worshipping Śiva, Śaivites. The Vaiṣṇavas predominated northern India and the other sect the south. Then there were the Tāṅtriks, the most renowned of them being Kṛṣṇānanda Āgamavāgiśa of Navadvīpa, who wrote the *Taṅtrasāra.* Certain sections of the Tāṅtriks of the *śakti* cult, however, took to sensual pleasures in the name of religion, while the Aghorapanthīs followed all kinds of horrible practices.

A significant development of Vaiṣṇavism was the Kṛṣṇa cult which grew round the love of Rādhā and Kṛṣṇa. Jayadeva, the court poet of Lakṣmaṇasena (twelfth century), gave a highly sensual account of this love in his poem, the *Gītagoviṅda.* An even more erotic narration was given in the *Brahma-Vaivarta Purāṇa.* Caitanya, the mystic saint of India, was also a Kṛṣṇa devotee, but of the spiritual kind. He attached no significance to caste or community, and one of his prominent disciples was a Muslim. There were many Vaiṣṇava saints in the south, for example Rāmānuja, Nimbārka, Mādhava, Vallabha, the Āḷvārs and the Kartabhajas. All of them were for the worship of a god with form. Rāma, another incarnation of Viṣṇu, also had worshippers, some of whom like Rāmasakhejī considered him as much as Jayadeva conceived of Kṛṣṇa. These devotees were known as *rasikas.*[6]

Of the Śaivites there were the Vīraśaivas who believed in the complete union of the soul with god through the power called *śaktī*, and the Śaivasiddhāntas who recognized the reality of the world and the plurality of souls. Midway between the monoism of Śankara and the dualism of Rāmānuja, there was Śrikaṇṭha who believed that *karma* (action) decided a man's fate, but it was subject to god's grace.

The *bhakti* (devotional) movement, which swept over the greater part of India at this time, also found many followers. Some of the *bhakti* sects, like the Rādhāvallabhas, gave Rādhā a position superior to Kṛṣṇa. They believed the only male in the universe was Kṛṣṇa (*puruṣa*), all the others being females (*prakṛtis*). The followers of the sect imagined they were friends of Rādhā. They put on a woman's dress, took feminine names and behaved like women. Some of them favoured extra-marital love too.

Others of the *bhakti* school, like Rāmānanda, Ravidāsa, Kabīr, Jñāneśvara, Nāmadeva, Ekanātha, Tukārāma and Rāmadāsa, most of them being of humble origin, were purely spiritual in their devotion.

The Sūfī Muslims believed in spiritual advancement, mystical ecstasy and public service. Their influence was all for the good. As Barnī remarked, 'Vices among men have been reduced by their teachings.' They also tried to bring the Hindus and Mohammedans together. The non-Hindu religions were Islam, the religion of the rulers, Buddhism, Jainism, Sikhism and Zoroastrianism.

Bihārī was a Kṛṣṇa devotee, and therefore, there are some couplets in the *Satasaī* about Kṛṣṇa in his divine aspect. But a majority of them depict him as the *rasika* lover of Rādhā and the milkmaids. Kṛṣṇa is the fickle lover, who can't stick to any one girl, and with whom all of them are enthralled. Rādhā is his favourite, but he can't resist a beautiful woman, and so makes love to all of them in his favourite haunt, the woods on the bank of the Yamunā river.

Bihārī's couplets also mention some of the games and pastimes prevalent then, as, for example polo (*caugāna*), blind-man's buff, chess, and so forth. His acquaintance with Persian and Arabic is reflected in the various words and phrases used, such as *kibalnumā*, *jāma*, *fānūs*, *āb*, *hamām*, *ahasān*, *adab*, *khuśahāl*, and so forth. His lovers were like the men of those times, pleasure-seekers lusting after girls, capricious, blatantly adulterous and dandies. His women heavily ornamented and gracefully adorned, ever ready to display their charms, slyly amorous, artlessly bashful in adolescence and subtly seductive in youth. They display the same inconsistent nature as of the women of the period, one moment peering secretly at their lover from behind curtains and casements, and sometimes throwing all shame to the winds, craftily revealing their limbs, bathing semi-nude, and on occasions even drunk. They seethe with inner fury at the misdemeanours of their lover, but are unable to check their longing. They remain faithful to him, ever ready to forgive and forget, fearing most his journey abroad which would leave them lonely and sad.

The influence of the court is unmistakable. It had to be. But Bihārī had his dig at those sychophants who managed to get undeserved position, power and wealth by fawning and flattery. His verses depict not only the glamour of court life but also its profligacy.

Life

As for other Indian writers, a lot of controversy exists about Bihārī's date of birth, his caste, and even about his patron.[1] According to some scholars he was not a Brāhmin as most of his biographers think, but of a mixed caste, a *mūrdhāvaṣika,* i.e., the son of a Kṣatriya mother by a Brāhmin father. But this does not seem to be correct and is apparently due to a misreading of '*dvijarāja kula*' in one of the verses of the *Satasaī* (verse 101) on which Grierson comments 'He (Bihārī) tells us himself that he was twice born by caste. . .'[2] The word '*dvijarāja*' means 'twice born' and signifies a Brāhmin, for, according to a legend, Brāhmins were created from the mouth of Puruṣa, apart from their natural human birth. It does not mean, as Grierson seems to think, 'born of parents of two different castes'. Besides, it is doubtful if this particular verse refers to Bihārī at all, for most commentators have taken it as meant for Kṛṣṇa.

Bihārī was born in Gwalior in 1595 in a family of Gharawārī Mathura Caubeys, a sub-caste of the Brāhmins. His father's name was Keśavarāya and his mother's Mahāvidyā. Bihārī got a good education for his father was a scholar of Sanskrit and himself taught the language to the boy.

In 1602–03, after Mahāvidyā's death, the family moved to Orchā, a state in Bundelakhaṇḍ, whose ruler, Indrajīt, a cultured man, patronized art and literature. Here Bihārī met the renowned poet, Keśavadāsa, and visited Naraharidāsa, a Vaiṣṇava savant, who lived in the village of Guḍau by the Dhasāna river. Soon, however, many of the poets and scholars frequenting Indrajīt's court, left, and Keśavarāya too departed for the Braja country (Vṛndāvana), along with Bihārī. There Bihārī met Sarasdeva, Naraharidāsa's guru, and made the acquaintance of a number of Vaiṣṇava devotees and poets.

About this time Bihārī married a girl belonging to a Caubey family of Mathurā. After his marriage, force of circumstances compelled him to live with his in-laws at Mathurā. Bihārī's father stayed on in Vṛndāvana. The *Tuzuk-i-Jahāngīrī* mentions that in 1618 the emperor Jahāngīr visited Mathurā and met a saint of the name of Cindrarūpa. Quite possibly prince Shāh Jahān, the emperor's son and future successor, came along too and met Naraharidāsa who was also there. Bihārī, who was close to Naraharidāsa, was introduced to the prince. According to Ratnākara, the poet recited some verses which pleased Shāh Jahān, and the prince invited him to Agra, the Moghul capital.

At Agra, Bihārī made the acquaintance of poets, artists, musicians and scholars who thronged the Moghul court, among them the illustrious poet Nawāb Abdur Rahīm Khānakhānā. When a son was born to Shāh Jahān, there was the usual royal celebration to which a number of princes were invited (fifty-two according to Ratnākara). Bihārī recited some of his poems in this august assembly and in recognition of his talents got an annuity from the princes. This assured the poet of a steady income. From 1621 to the year of Shāh Jahān's coronation in 1628, there was great political unrest, and the prince had to leave Agra. Consequently, Bihārī's connection with the Moghul court was severed and he began to live at Mathurā again, though it is possible he paid occasional visits to Agra as well. During these years he also went round to collect the annuities the various rulers had granted him. Shāh Jahān's coronation must have been hailed joyfully by Bihārī, for he already had the new emperor's favour. It is quite likely he paid a few visits to Agra to renew his connections with the court.

One of the princes who had promised Bihārī an annuity was Jayasiṅgha of Amber, an ambitious ruler who kept on the right side of the Moghuls and proved to be of great service to them. When Bihārī went to Amber to collect his annuity he found Jayasiṅgha so helplessly enamoured of a young girl that he gave her all his time and neglected his duties of state. His chief queen, Anaṅta Kumārī, known as Cauhānī

Rānī felt equally neglected. The harried ministers thought Bihārī's coming a good augury, for he was a man who counted, as well as a talented poet. So they approached him for setting things right. Bihārī did the trick by writing a couplet (verse 38) and having it introduced surreptitiously into the rajah's bedroom. That made Jayasiṅgha realize his fault, and he turned his attention to state matters. He also became Bihārī's enthusiastic patron and promised to give him a gold coin (*aśarfī*) for each couplet the poet composed.[3] The grateful queen appointed Bihārī poet of her chamber and made a grant to him of the village of Kālī Pahāḍī. Bihārī was tempted. The revenues of the village would yield him a steady income, and he would be assured of a generous reward for his labours. He decided to stay on in Amber along with his wife. But he had no son of his own, and adopted his nephew, Nirañjana Kṛṣṇa. When a son was born to Jayasiṅgha, Bihārī was entrusted with his education.

While at Amber, Bihārī wrote the *Satasaī* which he had begun at Jayasiṅgha's bidding. According to Ratnakāra, the work was most probably completed by the poet in 1647 and contained seven hundred odd couplets. Some time after the work had been finished, Bihārī's wife died. That caused him a great shock and he decided to leave Amber where he had spent the formative years of his life. He made a round of the various states from where he had to collect his annuity, and returned to his guru, Naraharidāsa at Vṛndāvana, where he spent the last days of his life. He died peacefully in 1664 at the age of sixty-nine.

The Rītikāla Tradition and Love in Bihārī's Poetry

The later medieval period of Hindi poetry (seventeenth and eighteenth centuries) was that of the *rītikāla* poets (also called *śṛngāra-kāla*, from *śṛngāra* meaning 'love' and *kāla* meaning 'age'). The poets of this period, of whom Bihārī was one, wrote mainly about love in all its aspects. Hindi poets of this period termed the lover as a *nāyaka* (literally 'an eminent person'), and the loved woman as a *nāyikā* (literally 'a beautiful woman'). But they made many minute classifications of the *nāyakas* and *nāyikās* they wrote about, particularly of the *nāyikās*. These were mainly on the basis of the woman's nature, condition and intensity of her passion. The poet Keśavadāsa mentions eight kinds of *nāyikās* and Bharatamuni fourteen. Broadly speaking, they were classified under three main heads, the *svakīyā*, the *parakīyā* and the *veśyā* or *sādhāraṇī*. Their characteristics were mentioned as follows:

(i) The *svakīyā* was the highest type of womanhood, sharing the yearnings, inclinations, pleasures and sorrows of her lover. She was spontaneously ready for love-making and had no fear of public censure because she observed all the social conventions in her love relations.

(ii) The *parakīyā*, on the contrary, had fear of being censured because she was unconventional. If a man loved a married woman who was not his own wife, that woman was called a *parakīyā*. Clearly the *parakīyā's* love was illicit, and the stronger her longing the greater was bound to be her fear of wagging tongues. Of the *parakīyās* there were two kinds—the *kanyā* who was younger, less experienced and more secretive about her love, and the *prauṛhā* who was older, adept in love-making, lustful and shameless, and carried on openly with her lover, caring little for what people might say. It wouldn't be wrong to call her a wanton.

(iii) The *veśyā* was practically a prostitute or a courtesan. She was available to any man who could spend money on her, and she was unmindful of all criticism.

Other *rītikāla* poets like Sūr, Naṅdadāsa, Kṛpārāma, Rahīm and Ghanānaṅda, had still more minute distinctions. These were on the basis of intensity of love, qualities, and moods. According to the intensity of love, women were classified as *jyeṣṭhā* and *kaniṣṭhā*, i.e., the former having intense love and the *kaniṣṭhā* kind somewhat less. On the basis of qualities the classification was three-fold, namely *uttama*, *madhyama* and *adhama* (good, middling and low). From the aspect of mood there were as many as eight kinds of *nāyikās*. It is beyond the scope of this brief introduction to go into the details of the characteristics of each of these.[1]

The *nāyakas* were not given much importance inasmuch as we do not find such a detailed classification of them in Hindi love poetry. The poet Keśavadāsa mentions just four types, viz. the agreeable, the dexterous, the deceitful and the brazen.

Bihārī exploited almost all the types of *nāyakas* and *nāyikās*, and followed the traditional divisions.

Rītikāla poetry was a departure from the devotional one which had become popular from the mid-fifteenth century to the mid-seventeenth, and of which Tulsī, Sūr, Kabīr and Mīrā were exponents. The *rītikāla* poets turned from the spiritual to the sensuous, from introspection to the pursuit of external beauty. It was not a break from the past, but rather a transformation of it. The love they wrote about was sublime, not coarse. Very few of their women were wantons. They glanced shyly at their lovers from behind casement windows. Very little of their love-making was narrated in all its details. It was suggestive and symbolic. The art of the *rītikāla* poets, however, was not only circumscribed—though within that limit they were superb—it was also short-lived. Spiritualism had been the soul of Indian culture right from the *Vedas*. To transform the spiritualist into the voluptuary was as vain as to erase an indelible ink mark. The *rītikāla* poets wrote in a characteristically ornate style, putting the entire battery of embellishment, figures of speech, metrical variations, rhetoric and poetic artifice to their task. But while they charmed the minds of their readers they could not tug at their heartstrings. In this the *bhakti* poets held their ground. So the *rītikāla* poets had to bring in Rādhā and Kṛṣṇa to sanctify their sensuality. That was not difficult, for Jayadeva's *Gītagovinda* and the *Bhāgavata Purāṇa* gave them a ready-made background.

The *rītikāla* poets are often criticized for being too sensual, sometimes even bordering on the obscene. That may be true for a few stray verses, but by and large they weren't. They were of course bound by their subject and wrote about the myriad aspects of love-making. But they remained within the bounds of decency. They refrained from writing about making love that seemed salacious. The *rītikāla* poets depicted a Victorian restraint in their attitude to love. Their women seldom kiss or are kissed. And when they do so, it is on the cheeks not on the lips![2] They show their longing, instead, by yawning and stretching and by covert glances and smiles, and only the wanton among them ogling and shamelessly baring their midriffs. They make love but are never shown doing it. We only know they have done so, by their limbs bearing love-bites and nail scratches, the marks of pearls and gems pressed between clinging bosoms, sleep-starved reddened eyes, tired listless bodies, tell-tale signs, like eyebrows stained with the lips' betel-juice or lips stained by the eyes' lamp-black, and perhaps a ring or a garland exchanged when the 'woman plays the man', and carelessly left where it was, afterwards.

Love, for the *rītikāla* poets meant the joy of union as well as the pangs of separation. Often it arose in the heart by the mere sight of the loved one, even before the lovers met. Thus there were three elements constituting it—love before union, meeting, and separation. Love before union may be born by hearing about the beloved, seeing her picture, or having a mere glimpse of her. In all these states the women messengers of lovers, or their companions, played a prominent role. They exchanged messages between lovers, extolled their qualities to attract them to each other and arranged meetings. Kalyāna Malla lists fifteen kinds of women who can act as the go-betweens (AR, pp. 206–8), while Vātsyāyana devotes a whole chapter to go-betweens in his noteworthy book on eroticism, and mentions eight types (KS, pp. 109–14). Some of them go on special errands like carrying presents or exchanging love-letters. Others undertake the entire task of bringing the lovers together. In rare cases the woman chosen as the messenger turns out to be so charming that the lover cannot resist the temptation of seducing her, and instead of a go-between she becomes his mistress!

Another characteristic of the *nāyikās* depicted by the *rītikāla* poets was what they called *mān* (literally 'arrogance'), a word which does not seem to have an exact equivalent in English. It is the 'chief cause of quarrels between lovers'. According to Bhūpāl, a Sanskrit writer, it may be of four kinds—produced by sight, by knowing about another woman's enjoyment, by hearing about another woman through the *nāyaka* himself, or by hearing about such a woman from a person other than the *nāyaka*. The *māninī* is the woman offended because she suspects her lover to be faithless to her or finds tell-tale signs of his guilt on him. The wronged woman's anger fluctuates between putting on a mere pretence and persistent sulking. Thus the amount of appeasement by the recalcitrant lover also varies. He may flatter her, ask her forgiveness, or even fall at her feet. In all this the girl's confidante or companion goads him on, for she is eager to bring about a reconciliation. But if the adulterous lover persists in denying his guilt with false excuses and keeps giving fictitious explanations for the love marks on his limbs, it enrages his girl the most and the making up becomes all the more difficult. It also provokes her to speak her mind about his false denials.

Bihārī strikes the entire gamut of *rītikāla* poetry, the ornateness of language and diction, the sensuous concept of beauty and the voluptousness of love. He describes the beauty of adolescent and youthful girls, and sometimes of middle-aged women. Occasionally it is a lovely rustic belle flaunting her robust charms, wearing a necklace of beads or of strikingly colourful seeds. The beauty of nature and of the seasons is also described by Bihārī with equal charm. But most of his verses are naturally about love and love-making and the bewitching charm of lovely women, for these form the backbone of *śṛṅgāra*. The *nāyikā* in all her moods—amorous in love-making, angry when wronged, sorrowful in separation and thrilled by the union with her lover—form the core of his love poetry.

Bihārī put love on a high pedestal. For him it did not mean just sex. He prized equally the sweet strains of music, the haunting melody of song, and the ecstasy of verse.[3] But the overpowering passion of youth, he believed, carried everything before it, like a river in flood.[4] Bihārī was what the Hindi poets call a *rasika*. This implies one who has a deep emotional response to beauty, not only in the human form, but in everything, as for example in nature or the arts, a moving strain of music, a haunting melody, or a glorious sunset. It is not only that which stirs the heart which is beautiful, but also that which elevates the mind and the soul. So was it with love also. In one of his verses he says, 'That sublime ocean which connoisseurs of beauty and love can't fathom, even after diving in it a thousand times, seems to be a mere ditch, easily crossed, to people with carnal minds'.[5] His object was to elevate love and beauty to a point where they turn from the coarse to the sublime, and this was not an easy task. It was, as Marlowe had said, next to impossible, for when everything had been written by the poets:

> Yet should there hover in their restless heads,
> One thought, one grace, one wonder at the least
> Which into words no virtue can digest.[6]

Indeed much like Marlowe, Bihārī says: 'The spoken words are of no account, because they are false. That's why perhaps Brahmā (the Creator) has made eyes for expressing what lies in the heart.'[7]

Despite his occasional lapses (even Homer nods), Bihārī fulfilled his object admirably. The love he narrates soars to sensuous and even spiritual heights. It is a love which knows no bounds, and which is indifferent to praise and blame: 'There are many virtuous married women in Gokul (the scene of Kṛṣṇa's amours),' he says, 'and each sermons the other on upright conduct. But who among them has not abandoned family honour on hearing the bewitching notes of Kṛṣṇa's flute?'[8] And when a girl spreads out her lovely tresses, the *nāyaka* is so enraptured that he cannot distinguish between right and wrong![9]

Bihārī conceived of love as a pure and healthy emotion. In this he followed the tradition of Hindu erotic writers like Vātsyāyana and Kalyāna Malla, who even went to the extent of developing love and love-making as an art in which all citizens ought to be properly trained! 'A beautiful person,' says Bihārī, 'is attractive only so long as there is love in the heart, as a lamp will give light only when there's oil in it'.[10] Separation does not diminish love, for love, as Shakespeare says, 'looks not with the eyes, but with the mind.'[11] Bihārī's *nāyikā* may be parted from her lover, but like a kite aloft in the sky, his love can't go away, for her mind is always joined to him as the string attached to the kite always stays in the flier's hands.[12] Beauty, too, is not something external. It is in the eye of the beholder. 'Nothing is intrinsically beautiful or inelegant in this world,' says the poet. 'It may seem lovely to one and plain to another, depending on the attraction one has for it.'[13]

Bihārī had of course to describe love in its physical aspect too, for otherwise he wouldn't be conforming to the requirement of *rītikāla* poetry. He had also to make many of his verses suit the tastes of kings in order to trigger their interest. But it wouldn't be fair to accuse him of not being able to 'rise above the limitations of his age and look into the depth of life,' or of not being able to cultivate 'the philosophic mind', as one critic says.[14] He could not be a diver moving on the ocean bed of philosophy—he couldn't then have been a *rītikāla* poet at all—but he certainly dived often enough to be a philosophical observer of life. His verses on 'wisdom' will surely prove that. He was all this, and more; for with him love was a kind of religion, something mundane and yet divine. It was almost like emancipation, as he says in one of his couplets.[15] He would have believed with Scott that

> Love rules the court, the camp, the grove,
> And men below, and saints above;
> For love is heaven, and heaven is love.[16]

The Concept of Beauty in Bihārī's Poetry

A notable feature of Bihārī's descriptions of human beauty is the quaintness of the imagery he uses. Describing the adolescent girl he says, 'Youth swells out some parts of her body at the cost of others which it makes slender, like a rapacious official depriving those who are not in his favour, of their wealth, to enrich his favourites.'[1] The ornaments a girl wears are 'as a doormat for onlookers to wipe their glances on, so that her body retains its shine'![2] The slightly raised breasts of an adolescent girl can be seen by peering carefully at them 'as the abstruse meaning of a poem revealed only by close study'.[3] The swelling breasts of a woman make men abandon their virtue as 'travellers avoiding a bandit-infested hill road'.[4] A woman's chin is so charming that strangled by the noose of her smile, her admirer lies dead in its hollow.[5]

Indian poets often describe a woman's beautiful limbs in exaggerated terms. Bihārī sometimes uses this device. About the slenderness of a woman's waist he says, 'People gather she must have a waist because they hear she has one. No one has actually seen it'![6] 'The glances of men who look at the slender waist of another woman described, remain stuck to it as birds stuck fast in birdlime'![7] 'The feet of a woman are so tender that blisters are liable to appear on them if they are rubbed clean with a brush of roses'![8] A barber's wife who comes to apply red lacquer dye on a girl's feet finds them so charming and rosy that she thinks it is pointless dyeing them red.[9]

Bihārī's *nāyikās*, like those described by other Hindi love poets, adorn themselves and wear ornaments on various parts of their body. Speaking of a girl's eyes darkened with lamp-black, he says 'who are these bandit-like eyes of yours about to rob?'[10] In another verse he eulogizes the crimson mark on a girl's forehead.[11] A girl's lover is fascinated by the tip of her little finger reddened with henna dye.[12] The usual traditional forms of adornments like the *bindī* (beauty mark on a girl's forehead), henna, and so forth, are frequently mentioned. All the various kinds of ornaments worn by Indian women are described, for example the ear ornament and the nose-ring.[13] Not infrequently the *nāyikā's* natural beauty is so great that ornaments are of no use in enhancing it; indeed they may even mar it, as the case of the girl on whose body they are 'as rust on a mirror's face'![14]

The *śṛṅgāra* poets were fascinated by the girl passing from childhood to adolescence. They wrote enthusiastically about such a girl's lengthening eyes, shy sidelong glances, budding breasts, slimming waist, and the three folds appearing below her navel. Bihārī, too, has many such descriptions.[15] Girls are also depicted bathing in ponds and rivers or sporting in the water in pools in their mansions, or swinging on a wooden plank suspended from the branch of a tree in their garden.[16]

With infinite charm and brevity, Bihārī depicts his women in various moods and situations like the woman lazying, anxious, pleased, excited, proud, sorrowful and so forth. A woman who has been lovemaking all night, walks proudly but with an unsteady gait.[17] Bashful girls keep timidly peering at their lover from behind casements, and one of them is so shy indeed that while doing so she dare not remove her veil![18] Celebrating the festival of Holī, a woman gracefully lifts her veil and turning slightly towards her lover without glancing at him, throws on him a fistful of *gulāl* (coloured powder), leaving him spellbound.[19] Conflicting emotions are sometimes displayed by his *nāyikā*, as for example the girl who, when she comes to know that her husband, ignoring her co-wives, has been making love to another woman, is glad, downcast, angry, amused, pleased and vexed, all in one moment.[20]

Although Bihārī's heroines generally stay sober, a few of them are soused with wine. One of them 'sways drunkenly, and laughing and mumbling, shamelessly embraces her lover again and again'.[21] When the flush of intoxication mounts on the face of another woman, her forehead's sandalwood paste mark which ordinarily blends into her complexion, stands out sharply.[22]

Charming as they are, the merit of Bihārī's descriptions of women lies more in their ingenuity than in their originality. He uses all the conventional comparisons for the various parts of a woman's body; the moon for the face, the wagtail, the deer, the fish and the lily for eyes, a bow for eyebrows, the trunk of a banana tree for thighs and so forth. The golden complexion, the triple folds above the waist, and rosy feet are all items in beauty's inventory.[23] He also follows the usual practice of Hindi love poets of describing a woman's beauty from head to foot (*nakhśikh varṇan: nakhśikh*= from head to foot, *varṇan*= description).

The handsome man is not described in such detail. Kṛṣṇa is often praised for his charm, as for example the verse in which his body is likened to 'the peak of a sapphire hill in the morning sun'.[24] In another verse a man is said to be so handsome that his girl's eyes keep glued to him for ever.[25]

Although there are some fascinating descriptions of beauty in the *Satasaī*, they are subordinate to the love element in it. The strands of beauty and love are twisted together, and quite often that of beauty is so slender that it can hardly be noticed!

Nevertheless Bihārī's concept of beauty was not skin-deep. He sought it in everything around him. A haunting melody or a thrilling strain, the ravishing beauty of nature and the grandeur of the seasons—all moved him. For him beauty was a kind of ecstatic revelation. It was indeed truth. And that, says Keats, 'is all ye know on earth and all ye need to know'.[26]

Nature in Bihārī's Poetry

Although Bihārī cannot be said to have a keen perception of nature in all its myriad charms, such as, for example, Wordsworth had, the stray verses in the *Satasaī* which describe natural beauty show his deep feeling for it. Some of his descriptions of nature are startlingly beautiful. Describing the parting of the clouds after a shower he says, 'The massed clouds have been scattered, and wayfarers can again move on the pathways happily'.[1] In quite a number of his descriptions he uses erotic imagery, as when he likens the breeze to a lover embracing his girl, or Summer grieved at parting from Spring, his beloved.

The cool breeze suddenly arising in the night is like 'a lover who remains inert all day but at midnight comes to caress his beloved's breasts'.[2] It comes 'laden with the perfume of flowers, like a newly-wed bride with faltering steps, tired and perspiring, and bashfully covering her limbs'.[3] The warm, nectar-laden, southern wind comes haltingly, 'like a tired wayfarer resting off and on under the shade of trees'.[4]

The Indian seasons are described in a picturesque and charming manner. Spring comes with the hum of black bees pleasing to the ears 'as the jingle of bells, and laden with the nectar of flowers as ichor dropped from the temples of elephants in rut'.[5] It is the season when 'black bees wander about intoxicated with the fragrance of mango blossoms and the Spanish jasmine'.[6] The heat of summer is so intense that even creatures which prey on each other take refuge from it at the same spot.[7] In the rainy season the blanket of dark clouds covers the earth so completely that the ruddy goose thinks night has come and starts calling to its mate![8] Autumn is likened to a charming girl who captivates everyone wherever she goes.[9] Just as the heat of the Indian summer is oppressive, the cold of its winters often becomes unbearable. Bihārī puts it figuratively: 'When warmth was scared away by winter's cold, it went and hid in the impregnable breasts of women'![10] The daylight in winter months when the sky is overcast, is so dim that the *cakor* bird (which is believed to be enamoured of the moon) mistakes the sun for the moon and keeps staring at it rapturously.[11] The bright full moon of *Aświn* (September–October) is so fascinating that it is believed to drop nectar! Bihārī describes it as 'the canopy of the love god scattering its brilliance on earth'.[12]

Flowers find place in Bihārī's descriptions, but rather than bring out their beauty, his purpose, primarily, is to accentuate the loveliness of his women. The jasmine and the *campā* serve to emphasize the yellow golden hue of a girl's complexion.[13] The crimson *gullālā* flower is mentioned to point out the state of sleep-starved eyes of a woman who has been making love all night.[14] When a woman with rosy feet walks, the poet fancies a red *dupahariyā* flower blossoming at each step she takes![15] A rare occasion when a flower's loveliness is described without serving such an end, is the verse in which the blossoming *palāśa* trees in a forest (bearing flaming red flowers) spread such a riot of colour that some travellers who have never seen such a sight before, think it is a forest fire and hurry off to escape its flames![16]

Very few of Bihārī's descriptions of nature are for their own sake. They were not an end in themselves, only the means to an end. He harnessed nature to heighten the loveliness of his women. His flowers seldom grow on trees. They are threaded on garlands dangling on the lovely breasts of his women. The seasons don't bestow beauty to the landscape. They serve to excite dormant passions. Nature, in Bihārī's verse, is only the bridesmaid. It is love and corporeal beauty which are the bridegroom and the bride.

Philosophy in the Satasai

It is sometimes said that Bihārī was so taken up with the aristocracy that he ignored the common people. Also that he 'looked down on the rustics' and 'rural ways at every level were only a laughing-stock with him'.[1] It is true that the society in which Bihārī moved was highly urbanized. The Moghuls neglected the villages and scruplously avoided them. The nobility and the intelligentsia was concentrated in the towns. Renowned poets, musicians and artists thronged the Moghul courts and the courts of Indian native rulers. For all this Bihārī could hardly be held responsible, for he, just as anyone else, had to move with the times. He painted village life as he found it, but nowhere does he speak unfavourably either of the common people or of the village folk.

The village women he describes are praised for their beauty in no uncertain words—the rustic girl with 'a mark of rice and turmeric on her brow', the village belle with dimpled cheeks, the big-breasted beauty tending her field, the radiant-faced housewife doing her chores, and the woman gracefully working the spinning wheel.[2] Bihārī disparages only those village people whom he finds to be fools and dunces, and who are too stupid to appreciate the finer things of life.[3]

Bihārī wasn't at all against the common man. It was his destiny which brought him into contact with those in power. But he could 'walk with kings—nor lose the common touch'.[4] In fact he was critical of 'kings who crush the weak' and bemoans that 'the faults of great men are often overlooked'.[5] No one knew more than him that power corrupts and greatness thrust on the unworthy does not sit at ease. He condemned men who turn vain by empty flattery.[6] He was aware that one had to surrender his self-respect if he craved for royal favour.[7] He knew that one liked to stick to a high office even though slighted.[8] But whatever a man's position, however wealthy he was, he could not achieve greatness if he was shallow-minded, and such homage to the undeserved was only for a while.[9] Power, Bihārī knew, was not only empty without worth, it was also shortlived. While one held a chair people flocked to him for favours, but forgot all about him when he was there no longer. Such a man was like a flashing garland of seeds, valued so long as it lay on a lovely woman's bosom, but of no account when cast away.[10] The nature of a man can't change, Bihārī believed, although he may 'try a million ways to change it'.[11] An ignorant man does not become learned merely because people call him so. He has to have real wisdom.[12] Even good company cannot reform the wicked.[13]

But the influence of the age in which one lives does have its effect. Even God becomes heartless in the sinful *Kali* age (when morality is at the lowest ebb).[14]

Bihārī's attitude to wealth was equally balanced. He did not despise wealth but believed it should be acquired by honest means. He knew that the intoxication of wealth was unbounded. However rich a man, he never abandoned his quest for amassing it, and even went round begging for money![15] The richer a man was the stingier he became.[16] In order to put a stop to the race for wealth, a man should restrict his desires and be content with simple food and plain clothes, and with one woman for his wife.[17] As for himself, the poet says, 'If I can get esteem along with wealth which is not tainted with evil, why should I hanker after money?'[18]

He was also aware of the evanescent nature of power, even though he had the protection of powerful men. He decried the pompous person who bragged about the homage paid to him for just a short while, and the man in power swollen with vanity.[19] He also condemned the depraved and the wicked and those who managed to get power even though they had no merit.[20] He bemoans the tendency to ignore the righteous man and honour the wicked.[21]

Knowing the falseness of worldly honour, the shallowness of power, and the depravity of the wicked, Bihārī was nonetheless a realist. He realized that it was the people of importance who could benefit others, not the resourceless man. He wasn't an opportunist, but believed in making the best use of opportunities. He would have agreed with Shakespeare that,

> There is a tide in the affairs of men,
> Which, taken at the flood, leads on to fortune;[22]

What counts is help, he says, irrespective of the source from where it comes.[23] A rich benefactor must not be given up, even though he may fall on evil days. Maybe there's a comeback, and then his favours will revive.[24] Although wealth was not meant to be squandered, one who had the means, would be a fool if he denied himself proper food and the necessities of life.[25] Sometimes even a petty thing was worth its weight in gold, if it could fulfil the need of the moment.[26]

All the pleasures of the world, Bihārī believed, are in the end of no consequence, for they are fraught, as the Buddhists would say, with pain. The shackles of worldly existence, cares and worries, are difficult to shake off. The more one tries to get free of them the more entangled he is.[27] One can't control his destiny, but it is within his power to be unhappy with his lot, or satisfied. 'If one could be content with his gains and reconciled to his losses' says Bihārī, 'he could achieve salvation in a moment'.[28] And in that again, he echoes Kipling's idealism:

> If you can meet with Triumph and Disaster
> And treat those two imposters just the same.[29]

The Devotional Element in Bihārī's Poetry

Bihārī was deeply religious, but the few devotional verses in the *Satasaī* (a little over fifty) were not intended to formulate any sectarian viewpoint. He was against any controversies about religion, and at one place says 'people fruitlessly wrangle over the various faiths'.[1] His favourite deity, however, seems to be Kṛṣṇa (though he mentions Rāma too in a couple of his verses).[2] Some scholars, picking on a stray verse of his in which he speaks of a formless god, think he was a Vedantist. But that does not appear to be reasonable, for he places emphasis on the devotional aspect and most of his verses are addressed to the God Kṛṣṇa.[3]

Resignation and acceptance of one's lot, are the keynotes of Bihārī's religious thinking, as indeed they are of all religion.[4] Meekness and humility win God's favour. The arrogant man can never achieve devotion.[5] It is only God's grace which can can bring a man relief, and God cares for the man who is helpless and throws himself completely on his mercy.[6] Sensual desires are an impediment to devotion, and should be cast off 'this very moment'.[7] Devotion is the only way to achieve salvation. It is that alone which can steer one across the ocean of worldly existence.[8] But it must be true devotion, not mere outward show like painting holy marks on the body, saying the rosary, going on pilgrimages and the like.[9]

A number of Bihārī's devotional verses are addressed to God as a kind of complaint or taunt (*upalambha*). In these he upbraids Kṛṣṇa for not listening to his prayers and for remaining indifferent to him.[10]

In accordance with the traditional views of the times about women, Bihārī, even though praising their beauty and grace, believes that they are an impediment to spiritual advancement. Strangely enough, though he portrays his youths as being the greater transgressors of morality, he calls a woman 'the temptress ever lying in wait to pounce upon the man striving for salvation'![11]

Bihārī's Poetic Art

Some scholars are of the view that Bihārī's poetry lacks depth, 'serenity of the soul', and 'seriousness of thought'. They feel it is neither dynamic nor original and inventive, and often just a clever manipulation of words: that it has no spontaneity, 'emotive quality', or sublimity of sentiments; that it fails to rise from mere eroticism to 'the heights of genuine love'. They disparage Bihārī as having 'no message to give' and 'having no plans to improve life or to bring about a change in the philosophical temper of the age'.[1]

On the contrary there are other scholars who are all praise for Bihārī. Professor Viśvanāth Prasāda Miśra writes that the excellence of his poetry is seldom to be found in Hindi poets.[2] George A. Grierson says, 'I have never failed to find fresh pleasures in its (the *Satasaī's*) study, and fresh beauties in the dainty word-colouring of the old master.'[3] F. E. Key praises Bihārī as being 'the most celebrated Hindi writer in connection with the art of poetry' and says about the *Satasaī* that 'it is a triumph of skill and felicity of expression'.[4] Another critic says about Bihārī, 'He is intellectual but not without emotion. He is sophisticated but not pedantic. He is fond of the dazzling magic of words but somehow manages to communicate from the plane of common experience. Perhaps his verse has not lost its lustre nor force all these centuries because of two not-so-common qualities—restraint over the devices of expression and balance between design and spontaneity.'[5] Āditya Nāth Jhā, an eminent scholar, remarks that 'most of Bihārī's poems find their way straight to the heart'.[6]

It should not be forgotten that Bihārī was a love poet of the *rītikāla* tradition. One could not expect such a poet to have a message to give or to be philosophical. The subject of *rītikāla* poetry was external life, the meeting and parting of lovers and their changing moods, and the beauty of youths and girls. It was, as one writer has said, 'very much a poetry of the world'.[7] To say that Bihārī lacked 'the philosophical temper', 'high seriousness of thought and serenity of the soul', is to expect from him what he never even tried for. Nor did he seek innovation. Indeed it was unnecessary for him to do so when he could express whatever he wanted by the simple couplet. The other things critics say he lacked were originality, spontaneity and 'pure emotive quality', and in addition he is accused of being just a juggler of words. Originality may be all right as a requisite of philosophy, politics and so forth, but in poetry there's nothing really new under the sun. Poets have from eternity been writing about love, beauty and nature and, to twist a cliché, it is all the same wine in different bottles. As regards jugglery with words, all writing, and poetry in particular, is that, to a certain extent. But the poet does not throw about his words as a magician doing his tricks. He carefully chooses them like a jeweller matching gems to make a perfect ornament. In this sense Bihārī was certainly a juggler with words, and one of the biggest ones born. He stringed words together making them seem as beautiful as the flowers in the garlands he decked his women with. Each one was put in its place to create the effect he wanted, as when he described the different kinds of breezes—the cool one which rises suddenly at midnight, the gentle fragrant one, and the hot oppressive breeze which haltingly blows from the south.[8]

The *rītikāla* poets had no truck with sermons on philosophy, and it would be as vain to search for these in them as to seek accounts of love-making in the writings of Kant. Bihārī was, in fact, an exception, inasmuch as he has a fair number of verses in the *Satasaī* on wisdom and devotion. Instead of being censured for not being able to put across a message on morals and so forth, he ought to be given credit for doing so well with such opposed tasks as depicting love and beauty and producing gems of wisdom.[9]

The idea that Bihārī's poetry is unemotional and not spontaneous enough, stems from the excessive ornateness of its language. The ornateness can't be denied. His poetry is like a woman over-decked with jewellery. In order to appreciate why Bihārī chose to be ornate rather than plain in his language, one has to take into account the kind of poetry he was writing. *Rītikāla* poetry was highly sophisticated, and the poets made copious use of verbal devices to bring about this effect. The foremost of these was *alaṅkāra* (literally 'ornamentation' or 'embellishment'). A Sanskrit writer declares this to be the soul of poetry. *Alaṅkāra* is a word which does not have any English equivalent. It is sometimes understood as 'figures of speech' but it is not exactly that, for it is something wider. It is defined as 'those devices which establish such a relation between word and meaning as adds to the charm of poetry'.[10] Other characteristics of *rītikāla* poetry are *śailī*, i.e. 'style of expression' and *hāva* (roughly 'blandishments') which implies the various ways in which women give expression to their longing to meet their lovers.[11] The *rītikāla* poets made very frequent use of various figures of speech, to a far greater extent than in any other kind of verse. Besides there is a difference between what 'figures of speech' imply in English and what they do in Hindi. In Hindi they are more complex, with finer shades of distinction. *Rītikāla* poets, and Bihārī too, exploited to the full all these devices, and among them also the ones used in English, like the metaphor, hyperbole, fancy (*utprekṣā*), double entendre (*śleṣa*), irony, innuendo, satire, oxymoron, onomatopoeia, pun, paronomasia and richness of imagery.

Bound as he was by the canons of *rītikāla* poetry Bihārī could hardly be an innovator. But despite this he was one in the sense that he enlarged the scope of Brajabhāṣā, the language in which he wrote. True he invented no new metre or style, but he borrowed words from different sources in writing his *Satasaī*, mainly Bundelī and Sanskrit, and those of foreign origin, Persian, Arabic and Turkish, thus enriching his language. Other devices for making it lively were the use of idioms and proverbs, personification and transferred epithet like 'smiling eyes', 'tired wind' and so forth. He also coined new words, for example *chamgira* 'shade-giving umbrella' (from the Prākṛta, *cham* meaning 'shade' and the Persian suffix *gira* meaning 'umbrella').

Bihārī was able to draw charming pictures with an economy of words that is amazing.[12] His verses have often a haunting onomatopoeic quality which gives them a musical lilt.[13] He injects variety in his language. For example he has forty different names for Kṛṣṇa and a number of them for the black bee (*ali, bhṛnga, bhouṁrā, madhukara, madhupa,* etc.).

Humour was almost unknown to the *rītikāla* poets, but Bihārī has it in quite a few of his verses.[14] His knowledge of *āyurveda* (the Hindu system of medicine), astrology, astronomy and so forth is also evident in many others. Being a court poet he was familiar with royal recreations and pastimes like polo (*caugān*), horse riding etc. In one of his verses he depicts his intimate knowledge of the training of horses.[15]

It can't be denied that there are verses in which Bihārī's genius suddenly seems to take a dip. In one of these he says the flames of separation so greatly scorch a woman that even on winter nights her companions can't go near her except by holding a wet cloth as a kind of shield![16] This is too much for the mind to take in. Then there is the verse which depicts a woman so frail that Death, who's after her can't spot her even with glasses on![17] The imagery used by the poet is not only strange but also crude. Very occasionally Bihārī also violates poetic convention, which in a *rītikāla* poet is unpardonable; as for example when he makes a black bee alight on a *campā* blossom.[18] Bihārī's craze for *alaṅkāra* sometimes makes him overdo it. In one of his verses an angry girl swears by her uncle, of all the persons![19] This, merely because he found the word for uncle, *kakā* (or *kākā*) more appropriate to the pattern of alliteration in the verse. But such lapses are few, and predominantly his poetry is never banal or commonplace.

Bihārī was pompous no doubt. His verses are profusely ornate, like an overdressed bride. Nonetheless his skill is amazing. He does stir the emotions, but of course primarily those of love and beauty because he was a poet of love. His verses are amazing in their variety and brevity, and have rightfully been likened to polished gems.

The Satasaī Tradition and Bihārī's Achievement

There were very few verse anthologies in early Hindi and Sanskrit literature. Books of stray verses, particularly of love poetry, were popular. The larger collections came later. The first large collection of love poetry was the *Sapta-Śatikā* or 'Seven Centuries' of Hāla, written at the beginning of the third century and containing about seven hundred verses in the Prākṛta.[1] It is notable that this was almost the same length as Bihārī's *Satasaī*. The *Sapta-Śatikā* was followed by other smaller anthologies of a hundred poems or less. The most outstanding among these was the *Vajjalagga*. Both these works began to attract Sanskrit writers. Amarūka wrote the *Amaru-Śataka* 'Century of Amaru' and Bhartrihari the *Vairāgya-Śataka* and *Śṛṅgāra-Śataka*. Almost every Sanskrit poet was busy writing an anthology in the sixth and seventh centuries. But the subjects were mostly religious. Some time after, Rahīm wrote his collection of seven hundred couplets of which only half have come down to us. Tulsīdāsa wrote a verse anthology at about the same time.

Although Bihārī was not the founder of the mode of writing *Satasaī* collections (*satasaī* meaning 'an anthology of seven hundred verses'), it was he who made this form of writing greatly popular. After him there was a flood of *Satasaīs*, which has continued even to this day, some of the prominent ones being *Vikrama Satasaī*, *Sṛṅgāra Satasaī*, *Matirāma Satasaī*, *Vṛnda Satasaī*, *Vīra Satasaī* and so forth. Every succeeding poet who wrote in this form, copied Biharī, and some of them tried to expand their anthologies to even greater lengths, writing collections of over a thousand verses.

Apart from the imitators, Bihārī's *Satasaī* found a host of commentators, about sixty in all. Commentaries were written for three hundred years after, and still new ones are coming up almost every year. The first commentary was by Kṛṣṇa Lāla in 1662, followed by one by Mān

Siṅgha of Udaipur between 1673 and 1677. The better known commentaries are those of Jagannātha Dāsa Ratnākara (*Bihārī-Ratnākara*) which came out in 1926, and Lālā Bhagawāna Dīna (*Bihārī-Bodhinī*), 1950. These commentators helped a great deal in the proper understanding of Bihārī's terse couplets. But often they did him a disservice too, reading all kinds of fancy meanings into them, and losing what the poet might have meant, in the maze of scholarship.

Scholars of Sanskrit, Persian, Urdu and Gujarātī wrote glosses and commentaries on the *Satasaī*, and made translations of it. Paṇḍita Hariprasāda translated the verses into Sanskrit in the Āryā metre. Another Sanskrit translation was made by Paṇḍita Parmānanda Bhaṭṭa. Ānadī Lāl Śarmā made a Persian rendering. Two translations in Urdu were Munśī Devī Prasāda's *Guladaste-e-Bihārī* and *Gulazāra-e-Bihārī* by an unknown writer.

Not content with mere translation, other scholars tried to recast Bihārī's *Satasaī* into different forms such as the *kuṇḍali*, *savaiyā* and *kavitta* metres. One of the scholars, Choṭū Rāma, even tried to interpret the verses of the *Satasaī* in terms of the Hindu system of medicine (*āyurveda*)!

Bihārī's *Satasaī* contains approximately seven hundred couplets in the Hindi verse form known as a *dohā* or *soraṭhā*. Neither the exact number of the verses nor their arrangement is uniform in the various recensions, of which there are as many as twenty-five, the most famous of these being the *Anwara-Candrikā* (1714) and the *Azamśāhī* (1724)—the latter prepared at the instance of Āzam Khān, the ruler of Āzamgaṛh, by a poet of Jaunpur called Harjū. Quite often even the wordings show minor differences.

Grierson has defined the *dohā* (in which most of the verses have been written) as having twenty-four *mātrās* or instants. Each line of the *dohā* has six feet (*gaṇas*), and the division of these in the first and second half of the line is respectively 6+4+3 and 6+4+1 *māṭrās*. The last foot of the three *mātrās* of the first part must be a tribrach (*nagaṇa*) or iambus (*dhvaja*), the last two syllables of the second part of the line must be a trochee (*tāla*). There are twenty-one varieties of the *dohā*.

Hindi poets, including Bihārī, have not kept strictly to the prescribed form.

The *sorathā* is just a *dohā* reversed. The second and fourth parts of the two lines of the *dohā* become in the *sorathā* the first and the third; and the first and third, the second and fourth. The scheme of the line is, therefore, 11+13 instead of 13+11, and the general method of scansion is 6+4+1, 6+4+3. An example of the *sorathā* verse form is verse 181. The *dohā* and *sorathā* are so closely linked that one version may consider a particular verse as a *dohā* and another the same verse as a *sorathā*, the two halves merely being transposed.[2]

Very few writers have achieved fame such as Bihārī's and that too just by a single work. The *Imperial Gazetteer* takes notice of only three Hindi poets, Tulsī, Sūr and Bihārī, and calls the *Satasaī* one of the daintiest pieces of writing in any Indian language. Grierson says, 'Each couplet in itself is a completely finished miniature description of a mood or phase of nature, in which every touch of the brush is exactly the one needed and no one is superfluous.'[3] The verses have aptly been likened to perfect jewels or to a bouquet of flowers. Indeed they compress in their condensed language, thoughts, moods and situations for which other poets would require several lines to express. As one critic puts it, 'The *Satasaī's* couplets seem short, but they affect the heart as greatly as tiny barbs deeply embedded.'

Bihārī occupies a unique place among medieval poets. He is the only one on whose work so much critical literature has been written. Ācārya Rāmacandra Śukla says, 'no book has received such great honour in the *śṛṅgāra-kāvya* as the *Satasaī*'.[4] His work is significant from the historical point of view also. It gives us much valuable information about the art, music, manners and pastimes of his age. Most scholars are agreed that Bihārī is the most renowned of the *rītikāla* poets. According to Paṇḍita Padmsiṅgha Śarmā, 'his place is the highest among them'.[5] This is also the view of Dr Haravaṅśa Lāl Śarmā, who counts Bihārī amongst the few great Hindi poets, and says, 'of writers of stray verses in the *śṛṅgāra* style he is beyond doubt the most distinguished'.[6]

Both as a representative of his age and as foremost among the *rītikāla* poets, Bihārī's place in medieval Hindi literature is unchallenged. He initiated a tradition in poetry which survived for long. Some puritan critics seem to think he was at times obscene. Grierson clears this misunderstanding when he says that as a whole Bihārī's *Satasaī* can by no stretch of the imagination be called 'an obscene work'.[7] He was erotic no doubt, but rarely obscene. Bihārī's poetry is timeless. Like gold its glint can never get dull. The haze of the centuries has not bedimmed its pristine brightness, and scholars still continue discovering new treasures in it.

A Note on Translation, Transliteration and the Arrangement of Verses

Bihārī's verses are difficult to translate into another language. Any translation would, because of their terseness, mean expansion. That of course takes away much of the lilting rhythm and the ornamentation from the original. But that is inevitable. It is not without reason that Grierson says, 'Twenty years ago I began to translate him (Bihārī) into English, and after all that time, I have only been convinced of the impossibility of the adequate performance of the task at my hands.'[1] That's why the transliteration of each couplet has been given along with its rendering into English verse. The reader will thus be able to appreciate what a translation might not be able to capture.

It is not difficult for a reader unfamiliar with Brajabhāṣā to get an idea of the original from the transliteration, provided some pitfalls are avoided. One of these is the pronunciation of the 'o', which is to be pronounced as *o* in 'more' (not as in 'lion'). This is emphasized as no diacritical mark has been used for 'o' in the transliteration. Another difficulty is about the '*ṛ*' mark used. There is no exact equivalent for this in English, and the reader is advised to pronounce the *ṛ* as 'r', but with the tip of the tongue higher up on the upper palate, and brushing it with a downward motion. The *ṁ* nasalizes and lengthens the preceding vowel, as *n* in bo*n* (French).

The *ch* sound is also not found in English. It is pronounced with the tip of the tongue placed slightly higher against the upper palate than in uttering the *c* sound (*ch* as in *ch*urch), and emphasizing the *h* sound.

Other marks are explained as follows:

a as *u* in b*u*t.
ā as *a* in rather.
i as *i* in f*i*t.
ī as *i* in mach*i*ne.
u as u in p*u*t.
ṛ as *ri* in *ri*vea
ū as *u* in r*u*le.
e as *ay* in s*ay*.
ṅ as ṇ in si*n*g.
ñ as *n* in hi*n*ge.
ś, ṣ as *s* in *s*ugar.
g as *g* in *g*oat.
ṭ as *t* in top.
t, d, n are dentals.
ḍ as *d* in *d*oor.
c as *ch* in *ch*urch.

Cerebrals (*ṭ, ṭh, ḍ, ḍh, ṇ*) are pronounced with the tongue retroflexed, i.e., turned up and back against the roof of the mouth.

The dentals (*t, th, d, dh, n*) are pronounced with the tip of the tongue against the back of the upper front teeth.

The verses have been grouped under broad heads, avoiding the too meticulous groupings of commentators like Lālā Bhagawāna Dīna. The context of the verses has been explained by the line in italics just above the translated version, as for example *'What her companion said'* or *'What one of her companions said to another'*. 'Her' means the *nāyikā*, and her companion (or confidante) who is invariably a woman, just as the *nāyaka's* friend, or confidant, is a man.

Jagannātha Dāsa Ratnākara's commentary (*Bihārī-Ratnākara*) which came out in 1926 is one of the celebrated ones. He tried to bring some rational order in the verses by introducing a verse dealing with wisdom or devotion after each ten on love. Despite this they were not classified any further. The present translation groups the verses of the *Satasaī* under various heads such as Love, Love-Making, Beauty, Wisdom and so forth (as given in the chapter headings). This has been thought to be a more rational classification. The verses in the text (this translation) have been numbered consecutively throughout. The corresponding number in Ratnākara's arrangement has been indicated in the key at the end of the book. The spelling of the vernacular words in the transliteration, however, does not strictly follow Ratnākara's version. The two outstanding versions, namely Ratnākara's and Bhagawāna Dīna's (BBL), have been consulted, and the one which seemed more rational has been adopted.

In the verses which lend themselves to two or more interpretations, the translation follows the one which seemed most likely, and the others are mentioned in the note to the verse. Verses which require further elaboration or the explanation of some reference in them, are marked with an asterisk. Even though every effort has been made to avoid reference to notes, many of Bihārī's verses are so terse that they need further elucidation.

The Satasaī

LOVE

1. *sani kajjala cakha jhakha lagan, upajau sudhina saneha* ।
kyoṁ na nṛpati hvai bhogavai, lahi sudesu saba deha ॥

What her messenger said

Love's child was born
when you met her
at an auspicious moment
and looked into her collyrium-filled eyes.
Enjoy her now, lover,
as a king
his domain.*

2. *bahake saba jiya kī kahat, ṭhaur kuṭhaur lakhaiṁ na* ।
china aurai china aura se, ye chabi chāke nain ॥

What she said to her companion

Drunk with his beauty
my wayward eyes
do not heed the occasion,
and forgetting themselves
boldly speak out my love
which I would rather
keep hid!

3. *phiri phiri cita utahīṁ rahat, ṭuṭī lāja kī lāva* ।
aṅga aṅga chabi jhauṁra maiṁ, bhayau bhauṁra kī nāva ॥

What she said to her confidante

The rope of my shyness
has snapped,
my mind's boat is caught

in the whirlpool of contemplation
of his lovely limbs.*

4. *citaī lalàcauhaiṁ cakhana, ḍaṭi ghūṁghaṭ paṭa māṁha* ।
chala soṁ calī chuvāi kai, chinaka chabīlī chāṁha ॥

What he said to her companion

That lovely woman
threw an inviting glance at me
from within her veil
for just one moment,
and then
tantalizingly turned away
brushing me merely
with her shadow!

5. *piya bichurana kau dusaha dukha, haraṣu jāta pyausāra* ।
durjoṁdhana lauṁ dekhiyat, tajat prāna ehi bāra ॥

What one of her companions said to another

Torn between the anguish
of parting
from her husband
and the joy
of meeting her parents,
that woman's tortured mind
is like Duryodhana's
on his deathbed.*

6. *kīnehūṁ koṭik jatan, ab kahi kāṛhai kaun* ।
bho mana mohān rūpa mili, pānī maiṁ kau laun ॥

What she said to her companion

As salt dissolved in water
my thoughts are now one
with his bewitching beauty:

a million ways will not
bring them apart.

7. *bedhak aniyāre nayan, bedhat kar na niṣedha* ।
barabaṭ bedhat mo hiyo, to nāsā kau bedha ॥

What he said

It is not surprising, dear beloved,
that your eyes
pierce my heart
for they are pointed:
the wonder is
that even the hole in your nose
which is pierced itself
should so grievously pierce it!*

8. *saba hī sauṁ samuhāti china, calat sabani dai pīṭhi* ।
vāhī tyauṁ ṭhaharāti yaha, kibalanumā lauṁ dīṭhi ॥

What one of her companions said to another

Her glance brushes others
only a moment,
hastening back
to her lover,
as a *kibalanumā* needle
vibrating
before it steadies
towards Mecca.*

9. *kahat naṭat rījhat khijat, milat khilat lajiyāt* ।
bharē bhaun meṁ karat haiṁ, nainan hīṁ soṁ bāt ॥

What one of her companions said to another

With pleading glance
he asked her to make love,
protesting

she shyly shook her head;
her coy denial
even then charmed him,
and seeing his face lit up
she was vexed;
won over the next moment
she nodded her consent,
but when he beamed with joy
she bashfully lowered her gaze.
Thus even in the crowded hall
the lovers spoke
merely with their eyes.*

10. *lakhi gurujan bic kamal sauṁ, sīsa chubāyau syām* ।
hari sanamukh kari ārasī, hiyaiṁ lagāī bām ॥

What Rādhā's companion said

When he saw Rādhā
sitting among the elders,
you know what the wily Kṛṣṇa did?
He brushed his forehead with a lily
implying
'say yes, dear beloved,
see, I'm even falling
at your lotus feet!'
Clever Rādhā
consenting,
flashed her mirrored ring
at the sun
and hid away her hand
in the mounds of her breasts
as though to say:
'When the sun sets under the hills
lover, I will come to you.'*

11. *tohīṁ niramohī lagyau, mo hi yahai subhāu* ।
anāyau āvai nahīṁ āyai āvatu āu ॥

What she wrote to her lover

Hasten to me, heartless lover,
you alone I adore;
but you shun me,
and it seems my thoughts too
take after your nature,
for deserting me
they also stay with you,
returning only
when you come!

12. *nahiṁ parāg nahiṁ madhura madhu, nahiṁ bikās ihiṁ kāla* ।
alī kalīṁ hī sauṁ baṁdhyau, āgaiṁ kauna havāl ॥

What he said to him

You are bewitched
by this slip of a girl,
as a black bee lured
by a mere bud
without pollen or nectar!
How will it be with you
when she blossoms out
in all her womanhood?*

13. *khelan sikhaye ali bhalaiṁ, catūra aherī māra* ।
kānancārī nain mṛga, nāgar naranu sikāra ॥

What her companion told him

Kāma, the wily huntsman,
has taught her so, dear lad,
that with her piercing glances
that fawn-eyed girl of elongated eyes

wounds gallants of the town,
turning the hunter hunted!*

14. *sāje mohana moha kauṁ, mohīṁ karī kuchain* ।
kahā karauṁ ulaṭe pare, ṭone lone nain ॥

What she said to her confidante

I had adorned my eyes
to cast a spell on Kṛṣṇa,
little did I know
he would turn it against me!
His very sight, friend,
now makes me restless.*

15. *ḍārī sārī nīla kī, oṭ acūk cukaiṁ na* ।
mo mana mṛga karabaṭ gahaiṁ, ahe aherī nain ॥

What he said

As a tiger pouncing
from behind the branches
seizes suddenly
the helpless deer,
her eyes glancing
from within her blue sari
have imprisoned me
in their gaze.

16. *lakhi lone loyanani kaiṁ, koinu hoi na āja* ।
kaun garību nivājibau, kit tūṭhyau ratirāja ॥

What her companion said

No one can resist
the charm of your vivacious eyes.
Who will be the poor victim
of your glance next?
Dear friend,

whom will Kāma
now grant his favour?*

17. *maiṁ tosauṁ kaibā kahyo, tū jin inhaiṁ patyāi* ।
lagālagī kari loinana, ur maiṁ lāī lāi ॥

What her companion said to her

How often did I tell you
not to trust your eyes
still you heeded me not
and let them dwell on him;
and now see the outcome,
it's your glance
which has collided with his
but what they've set afire
is your poor heart!*

18. *jau na juguti piya milan kī, dhūri mukuti muṁha dīna* ।
jau lahiye saṁg sajan tau, dharak narak hūṁ kīna ॥

What she said

I care not for liberation
if it does not lead me
to my lover.
Hell holds no fears for me
if I can have him there
by my side.*

19. *kañjnayani mañjana kiye, baiṭhī byaurati bāra* ।
kac aṁgurī bic ḍīṭhi dai, citavat naṁdakumāra ॥

What one of her comapnions said to another

While tidying her hair
after her bath
that lotus-eyed girl
made a peephole

of her fingers and her tresses
through which she kept shyly glancing
at her lover, Kṛṣṇa.*

20. *kahati na devar kī kumati, kula tiya kalaha ḍarāti* ।
pañjara gat mañjāra ḍhig, suka laum sūkati jāti ॥

What one of her companions said to another

Fearing a family feud
that virtuous woman
does not tell her husband
of his younger brother's
lasciviousness;
but like a caged parrot
in constant fear
of a marauding cat,
she silently withers
day after day.*

21. *tribalī nābhi dikhai kai, sir ḍhaki sakuci samāhi* ।
galī alī kī oṭ hvai, calī bhalī bidhi cāhi ॥

What he said to his friend

When she saw me
she raised her hand
and covered her head
with her sari end
as though from bashfulness,
purposely baring
her navel with its triple folds.
Then, eluding her companion
she gazed at me
long and lovingly
before she turned into the lane.*

22. *kahat sabai kabi kamal se, mo mati nain pakhānu* ।
nataruku kat in biya lagat, upajat birah-kṛsānu ॥

'Lily eyes'
say the poets,
I think they're more like stone;
or else
how can the fire of parting spring
after they've collided?

23. *yā anurāgī citta kī, gati samujhai nahiṁ koi* ।
jyauṁ jyauṁ būṛai syāma raṅga, tyauṁ tyauṁ ujjala hoi ॥

What she said to her companion

Wonderful indeed
is my love-lorn mind;
the more it's drenched
in Kṛṣṇa's dark blackness
the purer it emerges!*

24. *chalā chabīle lāl kau, naval neha lahi nāri* ।
cūmati cāhati lāi ur, pahirati dharati utāri ॥

What one of her companions said to another

That ring
her handsome lover sent her
as a token of their new love,
she ardently gazes on
fervently kisses
and tenderly hugs to her bosom
before wearing it.
And when she takes it off
she hides it away
from curious eyes.

25. *lāj gahau bekāj kat, gheri rahe ghari jāṁhi* ।
gorasa cāhat phirati hau, gorasa cāhati nāṁhi ॥

What she said to him

Have some decency
brazen lover,
why do you badger me
needlessly here?
Let me go home
for it's not curd or milk
you hunger for,
but love-making!*

26. *un harakī haṁsikai itai, in sauṁpī musikāi* ।
nain milaiṁ mana mili gaye, dōū milavat gāi ॥

What one of her companions said to another

Laughing
he stopped her cows
from mingling with his.
She surrendered hers
to his keeping
with a smile.
That moment
their glances met
and their hearts were united.*

27. *cāle kī bātaiṁ calīṁ, sunat sakhina kaiṁ ṭol* ।
goyeūṁ loyana haṁsat, bihaṁsat jāt kapol ॥

What her friend said

When her companions told her
the date of her *gaunā*
was being fixed
she did her best to hide her joy,
but her blossoming smile

and her cheek's glow
were a dead giveaway.*

28. *ḍagaku ḍagati sī calī ṭhiṭhuki, citaī calī nihāri* ।
liye jāti cit coraṭī, vahai goraṭī nāri ॥

What he said to his friend

Thrilled with longing
that fair girl
took a few unsteady steps,
then stopping
glanced at me covertly,
and went away
stealing my heart.

29. *pheru kachuk kari paur teṁ, phiri citaī musakāye* ।
āī jāvana lena hiya, nehaiṁ calī jamāi ॥

What he said to her companion

No sooner than
she reached her porch
she turned back
on some pretence,
and, glancing at me,
smiled.
She had come for sour curd
to cast into milk for curdling,
but instead
cast love in my heart!

30. *bana tana kauṁ nikasat lasat, haṁsat haṁsat it āi* ।
dṛga khañjana gahi lai calyau, citavani caiṁpu lagai ॥

What she said to her confidante

Out to the woods
for sport,

my lover of bewitching smiles
passed by my house,
ensnaring me in his glance
as a *khañjana* bird trapped
with birdlime!*

31. *kahā laṛaite dṛga kare, pare lāl behāla* ।
kahuṁ muralī kahuṁ pīt paṭ, kahūṁ mukuṭ banamāla ॥

What her messenger told her

Your bewitching
sidelong glance
has so dazed
poor Kṛṣṇa
that he lies in a swoon;
his flute,
yellow dress,
coronet and
garland,
all in disarray.*

32. *jasa apajasa dekhat nahīṁ, dekhat sāṁval gāt* ।
kahā karauṁ lālica bhare, capala nain cali jāt ॥

What she said to her companion

Thirsting for his sight
and braving reproach
my restless glance
goes to that dark handsome lad
again and again.
What can I do, friend,
he captivates me so.*

33. *nakh sikh rūpa bhare khare, tau māṁgat musukāni* ।
tajat na locan lālacī ye lalacauhīṁ bāni ॥

What she said to her companion

Although my eyes have drunk
the nectar of his beauty
they'll not shake off
their greed,
and still beg from him
a smile.*

34. *chavai chigunī pahuṁcau gahat, ati dīnatā dikhāi* ।
bali bāvan kau byauṁta suni, ko hari tumhaiṁ patyāi ॥

What she said

Why should I go with you
Kṛṣṇa?
You feign innocence
and exploit an opening
to the full.
After hearing how
as Vāman, you tricked Bali,
O handsome lad
who'll ever trust you!*

35. *nainā naiṁku na mānahiṁ, kitau kahyau samujhāi* ।
tana mana hāraiṁhūṁ haṁsaiṁ, tin sauṁ kahā basāi ॥

What she said to her companion

What can I do friend,
I've cautioned these eyes
time and again
but they pay no heed,
and even after gambling away everything
in love's game

they still keep smiling
impudently!

36. *laṭaki laṭaki laṭakat, calat, ḍaṭat mukuṭ kī chāṁha* ।
caṭak bharyau naṭ mili gayo, aṭakabhaṭak-ban māṁha ॥

What she told her companions

I got lost
in the winding forest pathways
when a gorgeous acrobat
wearing a coronet
came swinging and swaying.
Only with his help, friend,
could I find my way!*

37. *bilakhī ḍabkauṁhaiṁ cakhani, tiya lakhi gaman barāi* ।
piya gahabari āye gare, rākhī gare lagāi ॥

What one of her companions said to another

Seeing her distressed eyes
brimful of tears
his voice faltered,
and wordlessly
clasping her to his bosom
he put off
his departure.

38. *cit biṭ bacat na harata haṭhi, lālan dṛga barajora* ।
sāvadhān ke baṭaparā, ye jāgat ke cora ॥

What she said to her companion

How can my mind
remain with me
when my lover's eyes
stubbornly abduct it?
They're like thieves and dacoits

who rob a man's wealth
even though he's cautious
and wide awake.*

39. *pahuṁcati ḍaṭi rana subhaṭ lauṁ, rauki sakaiṁ saba nāṁhi* ।
lākhanuhūṁ kī bhīr maiṁ, āṁkhi uhīṁ cali jāṁhi ॥

What her companion said to her

How brazenly
you glance on your lover
singling him out
when he's in company.
It's as though
a warrior undaunted
would cut his way
across enemy soldiers
to challenge his adversary.

40. *saras sumil cit turaṁg kī, kari kari amit uthānā* ।
goi nibāhaiṁ jītiyai, kheli prema caugāna ॥

What the newly-wed woman's companion said to her

As a skilful polo player
riding a docile and sturdy horse
makes repeated dashes
and pirating the ball
wins the goal;
so dear girl
with heart steeped in love
you should win him over
with secret sallies.

41. *haṁsi haṁsi herati naval tiya, mad ke mad umadāti* ।
balaki balaki bolati bacana, lalaki lalaki lapaṭāti ॥

What one of her companions said to another

That young woman
drunkenly swayed,
laughed,
looked around, and
mumbling,
embraced her lover
shamelessly
over and over again.

42. *jahāṁ jahāṁ ṭhāṁhau lakhyau, syāma subhag siramauru* ।
binahūṁ un chin gahi rahat, dṛgana ajauṁ vaha ṭhauru ॥

What one Braj belle said to another

Even though Kṛṣṇa,
handsomest among men,
has gone,
for a moment it seems
to the mind's eye
he's there still
where he used to stand.*

43. *ḍīthi barat bāṁdhī aṭana, caṁhi dhāvat na ḍarāt* ।
it ut tai cit duhunu ke, naṭ lauṁ āvat jāt ॥

What one of her companions said to another

The lovers gazed
at each other
from their balconies.
Their glances
were like a rope
tied across,
on which acrobat-like

their hearts ran
to meet each other.

44. *jhamaki caṁhat utarati aṭā, naiṁku na thakāti deha* ।
bhaī rahaṭi naṭ kī baṭā, aṭakī nāgar neha ॥

What one of her companions said to another

She swiftly climbed her balcony
to glance at him
but fearing prying eyes
ran down the next minute
not tiring a bit,
as though she was a yoyo
in her sweetheart's hand
whirled up and down
on the string of love!

45. *lobh lage hari rūpa ke, karī sāṁṭ juri jāi* ।
hauṁ in bēcī bīc hīṁ, loin baṛī balāi ॥

What she said to her confidante

My vexatious eyes
irresistibly drawn
to handsome Kṛṣṇa,
are like a broker
striking a deal
without my consent
and selling me off
in return for the wealth of his beauty.*

46. *cilak cikanaī caṭak sauṁ, lafaṭi saṭak lauṁ āi* ।
nāri salonī sāṁvarī, nāgini lauṁ ḍasi jāi ॥

What he said to her messenger

Ever since I saw
that dark beauty,

vivacious, buoyant,
lustrous, sleek,
slender and sinuous;
longing for her
pains me
as the bite
of a she-cobra.

47. *jure duhun ke dṛga jhamaki, ruke na jhīne cīra* ।
halakī fauj haraul jyauṁ, parat gol par bhīra ॥

What one of her companions said to another

Like a sortie
penetrating the enemy's
weak vanguard
and pressing on to
the commander,
his eager glance
pierces her gossamer veil
and engages her eyes.

48. *dṛga mihacat mṛgalocanī, bharyau ulaṭi bhuj bāth* ।
jāni gaī tiya nāth ke, hāthi paras hīṁ hāth ॥

What one of her companions said to another

Standing behind her
he covered her eyes;
her hands went up to his
and knowing
by their very touch
'twas her lover
she stretched her arms back
to clasp him.*

49. *khin khin maiṁ khaṭakati su hiya, kharī bhīr maiṁ jāt* ।
kahi ju calī anahīṁ citai, oṭhana hīṁ bic bāt ॥

What he said to her companion

Though she did not glance my way
in the thick crowd
her lips moved silently
as if she was trying
to tell me something.
Ever since
I'm wondering each moment
what it was
she meant to say.*

50. *naī lagani kula ki sakuci, bikal bhaī akulāi* ।
duhūṁ ora aiṁcī phire, phirakī lauṁ dina jāi ॥

What one of her companions said to another

Her newborn love
makes her yearn for her sweetheart
and she sets out to meet him,
but fear of family dishonour
makes her turn back.
Thus pulled both ways
that tormented girl
keeps going back and forth
like a gyrating *phirakī*.*

51. *it taiṁ ut ut taiṁ itai, china na kahūṁ ṭhaharāi* ।
jak na parati cakaī bhaī, phiri āvasi phiri jāi ॥

What one of her companions said to another

She ventures out
to have a glimpse of him
but fearing censure
instantly returns,

going back and forth
restlessly
like a child's yoyo.

52. *nisi aṁdhiyārī nīla paṭ, pahiri calī piya geha* ।
kahau durāī kyoṁ durai, dīpasikhā sī deha ॥

What her companion said to her

You're going to your lover's house
on this dark night
dressed in blue
to remain inconspicuous;
but say, how can you hide
your body's splendour
which shines out
like a lamp?

53. *rahyau ḍhītha ḍhārasa gahe, sasihari gayau na sūr* ।
muryau na mana muravāni cubhi, bhau cūrana capi cūr ॥

What he said to her companion

When I saw her lovely ankles
my valiant heart
unfalteringly
remained transfixed to them
till it was crushed to powder
under her anklets!*

54. *kiya hāila cit cāi lagi, baji pāil tuva paī* ।
puni suni suni mukh madhura dhuni, kyoṁ na lāl lalacāi ॥

What her companion said to her

When even the jingle
of your ankle bells
makes him long
to meet you,

how much more
will his yearning be
when he hears
your sweet voice?*

55. *līne hū sāhas sahas, kīne jatan hajāra* ।
loin loin sindhu tana, pair na pāvat pāra ॥

What she said to her companion

Every time I look at him
he seems handsomer.
Like a venturesome swimmer
my glance has dived deep
into the ocean of his loveliness
again and again,
but it could never fathom it.*

56. *nāha garaji nāhar garaj, bol sunāyau ṭeri* ।
phaṁsī fauj maiṁ baṁdhi bic, haṁsī sabana tana heri ॥

Hearing her lover
Kṛṣṇa
roared like a lion
challenging those on the battlefield;
Rukmiṇī,
encircled by soldiers,
knew there was none
to oppose him;
and looking all round her
smiled triumphantly.*

57. *bāla beli sūkhī sukhad, ihiṁ rūkhī rukh ghāma* ।
pheri ḍahaḍahī kījiyai, suras sīṁci ghanasyāma ॥

What her companion said to him

Your indifference

Kṛṣṇa
has made that charming girl
lustreless.
Give her your love
and make her happy,
reviving her
as a cloud showers
and makes green again
a withering creeper.

58. *tajī saṅk sakucati na cit, bolati bāka kubāka* ।
din chanadā chākī rahati, chuṭat na chin chabi-chāka ॥

What one of her companions said to another

Drunk with his love
night and day,
his beauty's splendour
so haunts her mind
each moment,
that, heedless of her elders,
she keeps blurting out
words
she should not.

59. *phiri phiri būjhati kahi kahā, kahyau sāṁvare gāt* ।
kahā karat dekhe kahāṁ, alī calī kyauṁ bāt ॥

What her companion (who had returned after meeting Kṛṣṇa, her lover) said

She asked me eagerly
again and again,
'Where did you meet Kṛṣṇa?'
'What was he doing?'
'What made him talk about me, and
friend, what did he say?'

60. *rabi bandau kar jori kai, ye sunat syāma ke bain* ।
bhaye haṁsauṁhaiṁ sabani ke, ati anakhauṁhaiṁ nain ॥

When Kṛṣṇa,
who had stolen the clothes
of the cowherd girls
bathing in the nude,
said,
'Fold your hands
and raise them
to salute the sun',
they could no longer
keep feigning anger
and glanced at him
with smiling eyes.*

61. *sovat jāgat supana basa, rasa risa caina kucaina* ।
surati syāmaghan kī su rati, bisarāyehuṁ bisarai na ॥

What she said to her companion

Though I'm trying
to banish Kṛṣṇa's remembrance
from my mind, friend,
his sweet ways of love
perpetually haunt me,
sleeping or awake,
or dreaming;
in joy, anger,
repose, or agitation.*

62. *ḍhare ḍhāra tehiṁ dharat, dūje ḍhār ḍharaiṁ na* ।
kyaumhūṁ ānan ān sauṁ, nainā lāgat nai na ॥

What he told his friend

She alone captivates me
none else;

my love is constant,
how can I even glance
at another girl's face?*

63. *man na dharat mero kahyau, tu āpane sayāna* ।
ahe parani para prema kī, parahath pāri na prāna ॥

What her companion said

Dear girl,
drunk with the vanity
of your wisdom
you do not heed my counsel;
still I'll caution you
not to surrender your heart
to your lover
if he wants to seize it
by force.

64. *bhaumha umcai āmcara ulaṭi, mauri mori mumha mori* ।
nīṭhi nīṭhi bhītar gaī, ḍiṭhi ḍiṭhi saum jori ॥

What he said to his friend

Seeing me at her door
she coyly arched her brow
and with a toss of her head
threw back her sari end
baring her midriff.
Then, fearing censure,
she reluctantly went inside
turning her face towards me,
her eyes meeting mine
as she went.

65. *rahī dahem̐ṛī ḍhig dharī, bharī, mathaniyā bāri* ।
pherati kari ulaṭi raī, naī bilovanihāri ॥

What one of her companions said to another

Her lover's coming
so thrilled that milkmaid
that the pot of curd near her
remained as it was,
and she started churning
the water in the churning-pot
with the churning-stick
upside down!*

66. *devar phūl hane ju su, su uṭhe haraṣi aṅg phūli* ।
ham̐sī karati oṣad sakhinu, deha dadorana bhūli ॥

What one of her companions said to another

Wherever the flowers,
thrown playfully at her
by her husband's younger brother
who was her paramour,
struck her,
welts of joy
appeared on her limbs!
Mistaking them for insect-bites
I hastened
with the jar of ointment,
but when she smiled
I guessed the truth
and stayed my hands.

67. *phule phudakat lai pharī, pal kaṭāccha karavāra* ।
karat bacāvat biya nayan, pāyak ghāi hajāra ॥

What one of her companions said to another

Like nimble-foot soldiers

with sword and shield
attacking and parrying,
were the sweet insistence and denial
of the myriad oblique glances
the lovers threw each other
under cover of their eyelids.

68. *laī saumha sī sunani kī, taji muralī dhuni ān* ।
kie rahati nit rāti dina, kānan lāge kān ॥

What one of her companions said to another

It seems she has vowed
to listen to no other sound
except that of Kṛṣṇa's flute.
Day and night
she strains her ears
to catch their notes
when he's piping
in the forest.

69. *nīcī yai nīcī nipaṭ, dīṭhi kuhī laum dauri* ।
uṭhi ūmcai nīcau diyau, mana kulaṅg jhapi jhauri ॥

What he said to his friend

As a low flying hawk
seeing a cuckoo
rises aloft
and suddenly sweeps down
wringing his victim's neck;
she lifted
her lowered eyes
and glancing at me,
abashed, looked down again,
enslaving my poor heart
forever.*

70. *sveda salil romāñca kusa, gahi dulahī aru nāth* ।
hiyau diyau saṁg hāth kai, hathalemaiṁ hīṁ hāth ॥

What one of her companions said to another

When their hands joined
no sanctifying water was needed
nor *kuśa* grass.
By the sweat of their longing
and their bristling body hair
they sealed the union of their hearts
even before
they were man and wife.*

71. *cit tarasat milat na banat, basi parosa kai bās* ।
chātī phāṭī jāti suni, ṭāṭī oṭ usās ॥

What she said to her confidante

I pine for my lover
but, alas, I can't meet him
even though there's only
a straw partition
between our houses.
When I hear
his deep sighs of love
from behind it,
it seems as though
my heart will break.

72. *jālarandha mag aṁgan kau, kachu ujās sau pāi* ।
pīṭhi diye jagatyau rahyau, ḍīṭhi jharokhā lāi ॥

What his messenger said to her

Glancing
through your casement
when he chanced to see
your lovely limbs,

he kept awake
all night
his eyes glued
on the same spot
hoping to catch
another glimpse.*

73. *par tiya doṣa purāna suni, lakhi mulakī sukhdāni* ।
kasi kari rākhī miśrahuṁ, muṁha āī musakāni ॥

What a woman, in the assembly of the teller of Paurāṇic tales, told her friend

Sitting in the assembly
where her lover was telling
Paurāṇic tales,
she glanced at him
with a meaningful smile
when he began to relate
a woman's seduction.
Fearing a giveaway
he suppressed
the answering smile
upon his lips.*

74. *sahit saneh sakoc sukh, sveda kamp musikāni* ।
prān pāni kari āpane, pāni dhare mo pāni ॥

What he said to his friend

Quivering with ecstasy
ardent and loving,
that bashful girl
stole away my heart
when she placed the betels
in my hand.

75. *bhaye baṭāū nehu taji, bādi bakat bekāj* ।
ab ali det urāhanau, ur upajati ati lāj ॥

What she said to her companion

You're upbraiding him in vain
dear girl,
he loves me no longer,
and like a wayfarer
pays me flying visits only.
He's so little mine now
that he's almost a stranger,
and even to reproach him
embarrasses me.

76. *diyau ju piya lakhi cakhan maiṁ, khelat phagu khiyāl* ।
bāṛhathuṁ ati pīr su na, kāṛhat banaiṁ gulāl ॥

What one of her companions said to another

The red powder
which he playfully sprinkled
into her eyes
in the *Phāga* festival
made them smart greatly,
but out of love for him
she bore the agony
and would not wash it out.*

77. *āpu diyau mana pheri lai, palaṭe dīnhī pīṭhi* ।
kaun cāla yaha rāvarī, lāl lukāvati dīṭhi ॥

What she said to taunt her faithless lover

After yourself giving me your heart
lover,
you've taken it away
and turned your back on me!
What has come over you

that you do not now
even raise your eyes
to glance at me?

78. *gopina saṁg nisi sarad kī, ramat rasika rasarāsa* ।
lahācheha ati gatin kī, sabani lakhe saba pāsa ॥

What one of her companions said

Sporting with the milkmaids
on an autumnal night
Kṛṣṇa, the amorist,
dances the *rāsa* dance.
Dizzily he whirls
round and round
appearing to be with each girl
at the same moment!*

79. *syāma surati kari rādhika, takati taranijā tīra* ।
aṁsuvana karati tarauṁsa kauṁ, khinaku kharauṁ hauṁ nīra ॥

What one of Rādhā's companions said to another

When memory of her lover, Kṛṣṇa,
took Rādhā to the Yamunā bank
where they used to make love,
so great was the flood of her tears
that for a moment
the waters nearby
turned salty!*

80. *gopina ke aṁsuvana bharī, sadā asos apāra* ।
ḍagar ḍagar nai hvai rahī, bagar bagar kaiṁ bāra ॥

What Kṛṣṇa's friend told him on return from Mathurā

Grieved by your absence
the tears of the milkmaids
flow so copiously

that they form
a perennial stream
which flows through every lane
and past every doorstep!

81. *ducitaiṁ cit halati na calati, haṁsati na jhukati bicāri* ।
likhat citra piu lakhi citai, rahī citra lauṁ nāri ॥

What one of her companions said to another

Seeing him draw
a girl's figure
she came quietly along
calm and unsmiling
gazing uncertainly,
as though herself a picture,
and wondered,
'Is it me he draws
or another?'

82. *bhṛkuṭī-maṭakani pīt-paṭ, caṭak laṭakatī cāla* ।
cala cakh citavani cor cit, liyau bihārīlāla ॥

What one of the milkmaids said to her companion

Kṛṣṇa's coquettish eyebrows
his bright yellow garment
swinging gait
and bewitching eyes
have captivated my heart, friend.*

83. *citavani bhore bhāya kī, gore mukh musakāni* ।
lāgani laṭaki ālī garaiṁ, cit khaṭakati nit āni ॥

What he said to his friend

The memory of her guileless glance
and the smile on her fair face
as she threw her arms

around her companion
again and again,
fill me, dear friend,
with wistful yearning.

84. *hari-chabi-jala jabateṁ pare, tabateṁ chin bichuraiṁ na* ।
bharat ḍharat būṛat tarat, rahaṁta-gharī lauṁ nain ॥

What she told her confidante

Ever since I saw Kṛṣṇa
my eyes are drenched
in the waters of his love;
they keep filling with tears
shedding them
swimming and drowning in them,
like the pots of a water wheel
moving in and out of the well.*

85. *kyauṁhu saha māt na lagai, thāke bhed upāya* ।
haṭh dṛṛh gaṛh gaṛhbai su cali, lījai suraṁg lagāya ॥

What her companion said to him

I've tried many ways, dear lad,
to placate her,
but she'll not be appeased.
Now you should breach
the fortress of her obstinacy
by the ardour of your love
and take it by storm!

86. *gaṛh racanā barunī alak, citavani bhauṁha kamān* ।
ādhu baṁkāīhiṁ caṛhai, taruni turaṅgam tān ॥

What her companion said to her

The built of a fort
an archer's bow

eyelashes and eyebrows
waving tresses and
a woman's oblique glance
are best askew and arched,
a horse looks stately
when saddling raises his mane,
even so, dear girl,
don't bend too much
lest easy winning
make the prize seem light.

87. *aiṁcati sī citavani citai, bhaī oṭ alasāi* ।
phiri ujhakani kauṁ mṛganayani, dṛgani laganiyā lāi ॥

What he told his friend

Glancing at me bewitchingly
from her window
that fawn-eyed girl
lazily withdrew,
deliberately leaving me
standing at mine
in the vain hope
of catching her eyes again.

88. *chaṭan na paiyai chinaku basi, neha nagar yaha cāl* ।
māryau phiri phiri māriyai, khūnī phirai khusyāl ॥

What she said to her confidante

Strange are the rules
of love's land,
he who enters it
even for a moment
is enslaved forever!
Slain by killer Love
he dies a thousand deaths
while the slayer

wanders about merrily
unpunished!*

89. *jadapi cavāini cīkani, calati cahūṁ disi sain* ।
taū na chāṁrat duhun ke, haṁsī rasīle nain ॥

What one of her companions said to another

Although tongues wag
and eyebrows are raised
all around them,
they keep smiling at each other
brazenly
with ardent eyes
whenever they meet.

90. *dṛgana lagat bedhat hiyahiṁ, bikal karat aṁg ān* ।
ye tere saba taiṁ biṣaṁ, īchan tīchan bān ॥

What he said to her

Arrows wound
only where they strike,
but the pointed shafts
of your sidelong glance
though aimed at the eyes
pierce the heart
and pain every limb of mine
with the ache of longing.

91. *chuṭat muṭhin saṅghīṁ chuṭī, loka lāj kula cāl* ।
lagai duhun ik ber hī, cal cit nain gulāl ॥

What one of her companions said to another

Family honour
and fear of censure
flew from them
the moment the *gulāl*

flew from their fists.
And when it touched
their eyes
their glances met
and their restless hearts
rushed together
in blissful union.*

92. *tiya kit kamanaitī paṁhī, bina jihi bhauṁha kamāna* ।
cal cit bejhaiṁ cukati nahiṁ, baṅka bilokani bāna ॥

What he said in her praise

Dear girl,
from where have you learnt
such wonderful archery
that with the bow
stringed only by your eyebrows
you shoot arrows
of oblique glances
and with unerring aim
pierce restless hearts?

93. *dṛga urajhat ṭūṭat kuṭum, jurati catura cit prīti* ।
parati gāṁṭhi durajan hiyai, daī naī yaha rīti ॥

What she said to her confidante

Oh god
how strange are love's ways;
the eyes of lovers
entangle
but what snaps
are family ties!
Love's string joins
tender minds
but it's knotted

in hearts
wicked and jealous!*

94. *nipaṭ lajīlī naval tiya, bahaki bārunī sēi* ।
tyauṁ tyauṁ ati miṭhi lagati, jyauṁ jyauṁ ḍhīṭhyau dēi ॥

What her companion said to him

Her bashfulness
has flown away
on the fumes of
inebriation,
and her wantonness
makes her more charming
each moment.
Hasten to her, lad,
she'll receive you now
with open arms.

95. *nain lage tihiṁlagani ju, na chūtaiṁ chutaihūṁ prāna* ।
kāma na āvat ekahūṁ, tere sauk samāna ॥

What she said to her companion

Our eyes have met
and I dote on him, friend,
even death
can't part us now.
Your countless admonitions
though prudently given,
are to no avail.

96. *uṙati guṙi lakhi lalan kī, aṅganā aṅganā māṁha* ।
baurī lauṁ daurī phirati, chuvat chabīlī chāṁha ॥

What one of her companions said to another

She's enamoured
even of the shadow cast

in her courtyard
by the kite
her lover's flying,
and runs about frenziedly
chasing it!

97. *ūṁcaiṁ citai sarāhiyat, girah kabūtaru let* ।
jhalakit dṛga mulakit badan, tana pulakit kihiṁ het ॥

What her companion said

Gazing aloft
you're pointing out to me
how admirably
the pigeons are somersaulting
in their flight.
But by the sparkle in your eyes
the rapture on your face
and the thrills coursing through your body,
I know you're enthralled
not by the pigeons
but by your lover who's flying them!

98. *lāgat kuṭil kaṭaccha sar, kyauṁ na hohiṁ behāl* ।
kaṁhat ji hiyaiṁ dusāl kari, taū rahat naṭāsal ॥

What her messenger said to her

Why should not
your sidelong glance
torment him?
It's like an arrow
shot obliquely
which, even after piercing the heart
through and through,
leaves agonizing fragments
of its arrowhead.

99. *ve ṭhāṙhe umadāu ut, jala na bujhai baṙavāgi* ।
jāhiṁ sauṁ lāgyau hiyau, tāhī ke hiya lāgi ॥

What her companion said to her

Look!
there your lover stands
and it's he
who'll appease your longing.
Twine your arms
round him
with whose heart
your heart is twined,
what will you get
by hugging me?
Has water ever been known
to put out
a submarine fire?

100. *chinaku calati ṭhahṭhakati chinaku, bhuj prītam gal ḍāri* ।
caṙhī aṭā dekhati ghaṭā, bijjuchaṭā-sī nāri ॥

What one of her companions said to another

Her arms twined round
her lover's neck
she stands on her balcony
watching the rising clouds.
Rapturously
she moves a step one moment
and the next
coquettishly stops.

101. *larikā laibe kaiṁ misanu, laṅgaru mo dhig āī* ।
gayau acānak āṁguri, chatiyāṁ chail chuvāī ॥

What she said to her confidante

Pretending to take

the baby from my arms
that audacious lad
came up to me,
and craftily
brushing my breasts
with his fingers,
went away.

102. *kori jatan kijai taū, nāgar neha durai na* ।
kahai det cit cīkanau, naī rukhāī nain ॥

What her companion said to her

You may try a million ways
but you can't hide
your love for him;
friend, it reveals itself
despite
the feigned indifference
your glances
have suddenly acquired.

103. *kālabūt dūtī binā, jurai na ān upāya* ।
phiri tāke ṭāre banai, pāke prema ladāya ॥

An arch
cannot be built
without a substructure
for support
till it's strong enough
to stand on its own,
so love cannot germinate
without a go-between,
but when it has taken root
she's no longer needed.*

104. *nāsā mori nacāi dṛga, karī kakā kī sauṁha* ।
kāṁte sī kasakati hiya, gaṛī katīlī bhauṁha ॥

What he told his friend

Finding her alone
I made advances.
She knitted her brows
wrinkled her nose
and swore by her uncle
she'd not have me;
but her coquettish glances
were a giveaway.
Her sweet blandishments, friend,
fill me with aching desire
as the pain
of a thorn embedded.

105. *kyauṁ basiyai kyauṁ nibahiyai, nīti neha-pur nāhiṁ* ।
lagālāgi loin karaiṁ, nāhak mana baṁdhi jāhiṁ ॥

What he said to his friend

How can one live
how survive
in this lawless land of love,
where the eyes steal glances
but it is the innocent heart
which is shackled?

106. *tyauṁ tyauṁ pyāseī rahat, jyauṁ jyauṁ pivat aghāi* ।
saguna salone rūpa kī, ju na cakh tṛṣā bujhāi ॥

What her companion said to her

As drinking brackish water
makes one thirstier,
the more I look on my lover

the greater my longing
to keep on gazing.

107. *prītam dṛga mīcat priyā, pāni-paras sukh pāi* ।
jāni pichāni ajāna lauṁ, naika na hoti janāi ॥

What one of her companions said to another

He came from behind
and blindfolded her eyes
with his palms.
Though she knew 'twas him
by his caress,
she feigned ignorance
to prolong its pleasure.

108. *dekhyo jāgati vaisiyai, sāṁkar lagī kapāṭ* ।
kit hvai āvat jāt bhaji, ko jānai kihiṁ bāṭ ॥

What she told her companion

Dreaming of my lover
I took him for real, friend,
and bolted the door!
When 'twas morning
I found the bolt still on.
It makes me wonder
which is the way he came
and went!

109. *karu uṭhāye ghūṁghat karat, usarat paṭ-gujhroṭ* ।
sukh-moṭaiṁ lūṭīṁ lalan, lakhi lalanā kī loṭ ॥

What one of her companions said to another

Seeing her lover
when she raised her hand
and pulled her veil down,
her upper garment

shifted up.
Her triple folds
thus bared
were stolen pleasure
for his enraptured gaze.*

110. *veī kar byaurani vahai, byaurau kaun bicāra* ।
jinahīṁ urjhyau mo hiyau, tinahīṁ surajhe bāra ॥

What she thought in her mind

These hands
are like those
of the barber's wife
and so's the manner of their settling my hair,
but why do they thrill me
with their touch?
It seems he
with whom my heart is tangled
is untangling my tresses.*

111. *rahi na sakyau kasa kari rahyau, bas kari līnau māra* ।
bhedi dusāra kiyau hiyau, tana duti bhedīsāra ॥

What he said to her messenger

I tried my best
to hold myself back
but at last
Kāma has subdued me.
My poor heart
has been completely rent
by her body's splendour
as though pierced by an auger
through and through!

112. *khal baṛhaī bal kai thakai, kaṭai na kubat kuṭhāra* ।
ālabāla-ur jhālarī, kharī prema taru ḍāra ॥

What she told her confidante

As a woodcutter
vainly trying to chop
a spreading tree branch,
are the evil tongues
of those who revile me.
Despite this, friend,
his love implanted in my heart
grows each moment
more and more.

113. *unakau hita unahīṁ banai, koū kare aneka* ।
phirat kākagokul bhayau, duhūṁ deha jyauṁ eka ॥

What one of her companions said to another

Their love is more ardent
than anyone else's,
for though separate in body
their souls are one,
as the pupil of a crow's eyes
which keeps moving
from one socket to the other.*

114. *ali in loin saran kau, kharau viṣam saṅcāra* ।
lagaiṁ lagāiṁ eka se, duhuvan karat sumāra ॥

What she said to her companion

Wonderful must be
the arrows
of my glances, friend,
to wound
one who shoots them

as much
as the one they strike!*

115. *karat jāt jeti kaṭana, baṛhi rasa-saritā sot* ।
ālabāla-ur prema-taru, titau titau dṛṛha hot ॥

The counsel her companions gave her

Do not be so restless
to meet your lover, friend,
for as the river's waters
cutting the bank
nourish trees to sturdiness
with added vigour,
the waters of severance
will give strength
to love's plant
sprouting in the heart.

116. *mana na manāvat kauṁ karai, det ruṭhāi ruṭhāi* ।
kautik lāgyau pyau priyā, khijhahuṁ rijhavati āi ॥

What one of her companions said to another

Even her petulance
captivates him,
so instead of speaking
words of endearment
he keeps provoking her!

117. *calat ghairu ghar ghar taū, gharī na ghar ṭhaharāi* ।
samujhi uhīṁ ghar kauṁ calai, bhūl uhīṁ ghar jāi ॥

What one of her companions said to another

Although all her neighbours
frown on her
she does not care
and stays not a moment

at home;
on purpose
or of themselves
her feet always turn
towards her lover's house.

118. *māryau manuhārina bharī, gāryau kharī miṭhāhiṁ* ।
vākau ati anakhāhaṭau, musakāhaṭ bina nāhiṁ ॥

What he said to her companion

Her chastisement is captivating
her tirades honeyed words,
her angry frowns
are as bewitching
as her smiles!

119. *maiṁ yaha tohīṁ maiṁ lakhī, bhagati apūrab bāla* ।
lahi prasāda-mālā ju bhau, tana kadamba kī māla ॥

What the temple priest said to her

Lady,
what remarkable devotion
you have,
that your body thrills
with ecstasy
on receiving this garland
as *prasāda*!*

120. *batarasa-lālaca lāl kī, muralī dharī lukāi* ।
sauṁha karai bhauṁhana haṁsaiṁ, daina kahai naṭi jāi ॥

What one of her companions told another

She hid Kṛṣṇa's flute
and each time he asked her
she swore denial
with a twinkling eye

so that he'd ask again;
thus she made him speak on
just to savour the charm
of his sweet words!

121. *rahau guhī benī lakhyo, guhibe ke tyaunār* ।
lage nīra cucāna je, nīṭhi sukhāye bār ॥

What she said to him

Leave off lover,
look how you're braiding
my hair.
Your caressing hands
are making them perspiring wet
after all the trouble
I've taken
to dry them!

122. *rahyau moha milanau rahau, yauṁ kahi gahaiṁ maror* ।
ut dai sakhihiṁ urāhanau, it citaī mo or ॥

What he told his confidant

The moment I came
she began to bitterly chide
her companion, saying
'Your long absence, friend,
shows how much
you care for me!'
But by her covert glance
I knew
'twas me she meant.

123. *neku utai uṭhi baiṭhiyai, kahā rahe gahi gehu* ।
chuṭī jāti naṁhadī chinaku, maṁhadī sūkhan dehu ॥

What her companion said to him

What makes you
so housebound, lad?
When she sees you near
her ardour
makes her perspire
dampening again
the henna paste
on her nails.
Go and sit
somewhere else awhile
and give it a chance
to dry up.*

124. *hauṁ hiya rahati haī chaī, naī juguti jaga joya* ।
āṁkhini āṁkhi lage kharī, deha dūbarī hoya ॥

What she said to her confidante

How strange have turned
the ways of the world, friend,
'twas my eyes
which clashed with his
but what took the punishment
was my poor body
wasting away!

125. *jyauṁ jyauṁ ujhaki jhāṁpati badan, jhukati bihaṁsi satarāi* ।
tyauṁ tyauṁ gulāl-muṭhī jhuṭhī, jhajhākavat pyau jāi ॥

What one of her companions said to another

Though there was no *gulāl*
in his fist
he feigned there was,

and the more she fought shy of it—
stooping,
hiding her face in her sari,
looking annoyed—
the more he teased her,
pretending
to throw the powder
in her eyes!*

126. *aṁgurina uci bharu bhīti dai, ulaṭi citai cakh lol* ।
ruci sauṁ duhūṁ duhūṁna ke, cūme cāru kapol ॥

What one of her companions said to another

Standing on tiptoe
and throwing their weight
on the wall
between their balconies,
they glanced furtively all around
with restless eyes,
and leaning forward
kissed.*

127. *mosauṁ milavati cāturī, tuṁ nahiṁ bhānati bheu* ।
kahe det yaha pragaṭ hīṁ, pragaṭyau pūs paseu ॥

What her companion said to her

I won't be taken in
by your pretences,
for the sweat
glistening on your body
in this cold *Pūs* month
clearly reveals
your secret love for him.*

128. *rasa bhijaye doū duhuni, tau ṭiki rahe ṭaraiṁ na* ।
chabi sauṁ chirakat prema raṁg, bhari picakārī nain ॥

What one of her companions said to another

Though surfeited with love
they're exchanging covetous glances,
as though *Holī* revellers
even though soaked
should go on spraying
jets of coloured water
on each other
with their syringes!*

129. *kāre baran ḍarāvane, kat āvat ihiṁ geha* ।
kai vā lakhī sakhī lakhaiṁ, lage tharaharā deha ॥

What she told her companion

I wonder why
this hideous dark-hued man
comes to my house.
Friend, I've seen him often here,
and each time
the sight of him
makes me tremble.*

130. *citavati jitavati hita hiye, kiye tirīche nain* ।
bhīje tana doū kaṁpaiṁ, kyauṁhūṁ japa nibarai na ॥

What one of her companions said to another

While they stand in the river
offering prayers
they exchange oblique glances.
Even though they're soaked
and shivering,
they're so greedy

for each other's sight
that they keep on praying!

131. *kiyau ju cibuk uṭhāi kai, kampit kara bharatāra* ।
ṭeṛhiyaiṁ ṭeṛhī phirati, ṭeṛhaiṁ tilak lilāra ॥

What one of her companions said to another

He raised her chin
to adorn her brow
with a *tilak*,
but his ardour
made his hand tremble
and he could not put it straight.
She goes about now
proudly showing off
that crooked mark!*

132. *dhorī lāī sunan kī, kahi gorī musukāt* ।
thorī thorī sakuci sauṁ, bhorī bhorī bāt ॥

What her messenger said to him

When the artless talk
and the bashful smiles
of that fair girl
keep even me, a woman,
spellbound,
how much more, dear lad,
will they captivate you!*

133. *āj kachū aurai bhaye, naye chaye ṭhikaṭhain* ।
cit ke hita ke cugal ye, nit ke hohiṁ na nain ॥

What her companion said to her

The new gleam
of ecstasy
in your eyes today

eloquently reveals
the secret love
which has blossomed
in your heart.

134. *chuṭahi na lāj na lālacau, pyau lakhi naihar-geha* ।
saṭapaṭāt locana khare, bhare sakoc saneha ॥

What one of her companions said to another

When she saw her husband arrive
at her mother's house,
she was torn between
ardour and bashfulness,
and cast on him
an agitated glance.

135. *samarasa samara sakoc bas, bibasa na ṭhik ṭhaharāi* ।
phiri phiri ujhakati phiri durati, duri duri ujhakati āi ॥

What one of her companions said to another

Thirsting for his sight
she stood on tiptoe
to peer at him
from her casement window,
but her modesty
made her withdraw again.
Thus veering between
longing and bashfulness,
she kept glancing
and looking away
by turns.

136. *doū cora-mihīcanī, khela na kheli aghāt* ।
durat hiyaiṁ lapaṭāi kai, chuvat hiyaiṁ lapaṭāt ॥

What one of her companions said to another

She never tires
of playing blind man's buff
when her lover is there,
for every time they hide
or touch each other,
they can ardently embrace.*

137. *misi hīṁ misi ātap dusaha, daī aur baharāi* ।
cale lalan manabhāvatī, tana kī chāṁha chipāi ॥

What one of her companions told another

He excused himself, saying
'The sun is too hot';
and when the other girls had gone
he drew his sweetheart
into the mantle of his shadow
and took her to the woods.

138. *rahī acal sī hvai manau, likhī citra sī āhi* ।
tajai lāj ḍaru loka kau, kahau bilokati kāhi ॥

What her companion said

Who is that man, friend,
at whom you're staring
spellbound
as though rooted to the spot,
without a care
for what people around
might say?*

139. *pala na calaiṁ jaki sī rahī, thaki sī rahī usās* ।
abahiṁ tana ritayau kahau, mana paṭhayau kihiṁ pās ॥

What her companion said to her

You're staring fixedly at him
with startled eyes
and sighing ardently:
it almost seems
your heart is no longer
in your body.
If you are not infatuated
with this lad
say, to whom
have you surrendered
your heart?

140. *kare cāha sauṁ cuṭaki kai, kharai uṛauṁhaiṁ main* ।
lāj navāyaiṁ tarapharat, karat khūṁd sī nain ॥

What one of her companions said to another

As a whip's snap
drives a horse forward
but the rein's tug
restrains him,
so that he keeps restlessly prancing
where he is;
Kāma goads her glance
on to her lover
but her modesty holds it back:
thus torn between
desire and bashfulness
her eyes keep quivering
agitatedly.*

141. *jyauṁ jyauṁ āvati nikaṭ nisi, tyauṁ tyauṁ kharī utāla* ।
jhamaki jhamaki ṭahalaiṁ karai, lagī rahacaṭaiṁ bāla ॥

What one of her companions said to another

As night approaches
yearning for her lover
mounts,
and she hurries through
her chores,
so that she can hasten
to meet him.

142. *doū cāha bhare kachū, cāhat kahau kahaiṁ na* ।
nahiṁ jāṁcak suni sūma lauṁ, bāhir nikasat baina ॥

What one of her companions said to another

Bursting with desire
the lovers yearned to speak
but bashfulness stayed them,
and the words
froze on their lips
as a miser
rooted to his house
when he learns
a beggar's at the door!

143. *cit dai dekhi cakor tyauṁ, tījaiṁ bhajai na bhūkh* ।
cinagī cugaiṁ aṁgāra kī, cugaiṁ kī canda mayūkh ॥

What she said to her companion

Like the *cakor*
which, even when starving,
will only feast on moonbeams
or swallow embers,
I will keep gazing
on his moonlike face

or else burn away
in separation's fire;
but I can never love
another.*

144. *nakh-ruci-cūran ḍāri kai, ṭhag lagāi nij sāth* ।
rahyau rākhi haṭhi lai gayau, hathāhathī mana hāth ॥

What he said to his friend

Despite all my wariness
she enslaved me
with the fascinating beauty
of her hands.
Thug-like
she sprinkled on me
the powder of enchantment
and in a moment
took my heart away.*

145. *surati na tāla ru tāna kī, uṭhyau na suru ṭhaharāi* ।
ai rī rāga bigāri gau, bairī bola sunāi ॥

What she said to her confidante

As soon as I heard his voice
the melody froze on my lips
and I forgot
both the note and the tune.
The coming of my charming lover
arrested my song.*

146. *ur urajhau citacora saurṁ, guru gurujana kī lāja* ।
carhaiṁ hiṁḍoraiṁ saiṁ hiyaiṁ, kiyaiṁ banai gṛha kāja ॥

What one of her companions said to another

She yearns for him
but can't disclose her love

because of the elders
of the family.
As she goes about
doing her daily chores
she keeps wavering
between ardour and bashfulness
as though moving to and fro
on a swing.

147. *maiṁ lakhi nārī jñāna, kari rākhyau niradhāru yaha* ।
vahī roga nidhāna, vahai baida auṣadi vahai ॥

What her confidante said to her

As a *vaidya*
can find out the ailment
by just feeling the pulse,
I know you suffer
from the age-long disease of love.
Your lover alone
is your physician
and union with him
your only medicine!*

148. *bheṭat banai na bhāvatau, cit tarasat ati pyār* ।
dharat lagāi lagāi ur, bhūṣan basan hathyār ॥

What one of her companions said to another

She yearns for him
but her bashfulness
prevents her going
to where he sits
with the elders
of the family:
so she assuages her craving
by lovingly clasping
again and again

the ornaments
arms and dress
he has cast off.

149. *nāvak sara so lāikaiṁ, tilaku taruni it tāṁki* ı
pāvak jhar sī jhamaki kai, gaī jharokhā jhāṁki ıı

What he said to her companion

Flashing like a tongue of flame
that young woman
peeped through her casement window,
and wounding me
with the dart of her glance
turned away.*

150. *bāma bāhu pharakat milai, jau hari jīvanamūri* ı
tau tohīṁ sauṁ bheṭihauṁ, rākhi dāhinī dūri ıı

What she said

My right arm throbs
presaging the return
of Kṛṣṇa, my beloved.
I'll reward it
if he comes
by keeping my left arm away
when I embrace him!*

151. *ihiṁ basant na kharī arī, garam na sītal bāt* ı
kahi kyauṁ jhalake dekhiyat, pulaki pasīje gāt ıı

What her companion said to her

It's spring, dear girl,
when the breeze
is not too warm or cold:
it can only be
his presence

which thrills you,
so that all in a moment
you're shivering
and bathed in sweat!

152. *rahi mumha pheri ki heri it, hita samuhau cit nāri* ।
ḍīthi parasi uṭhi pīṭhi kai, pulakeṁ kahaiṁ pukāri ॥

What her companion said to her

It's no use
turning your face away, friend,
to hide your love,
for his ardent glance
makes even your back
tremble so uncontrollably
that it's plain as day!

153. *lahi sūnaiṁ ghar karu gahat, dikhādikhī kī īṭhi* ।
gaṛī sucit nāhiṁ karati, kari lalacauṁhīṁ ḍīṭhi ॥

What he told her companion

Though I hardly knew her,
when I found her alone one day
in her house
I caught her hand
and drew her to me.
She refused, saying 'no',
but her ardent eyes
and her seductive glance
are forever embedded
in my memory.

154. *piya kaiṁ dhyāna gahī gahī, rahī vahī hvai nāri* ।
āpu āpu hīṁ ārasī, lakhi rījhati rijhavāri ॥

What one of her companions said to another

She dotes on him so much
that when she looked into the mirror
the poor fool imagined
herself to be the lover,
and remained fascinated
with her own reflection!

155. *kab kī dhyāna lagī lakhyauṁ, yah gharu lāgihai kāhi* ।
ḍariyatu bhṛṅgī kīṭ lauṁ, jina vahaī hvai jāhi ॥

What her companion said to her

Your mind's always with your lover, friend,
if you keep on like this
who'll look after the household?
You remain so engrossed in him
I fear
one day you might,
like the *bhṛṅgī* insect,
cease being yourself
and take on his form!*

156. *jhuki jhuki jhapakauṁhaiṁ palani, phiri phiri juri jamuhāi* ।
bīṁdi piyāgam nīṁd misi, dīṁ saba alī uṭhāi ॥

What one of her companions said to another

As the moment
of her lover's arrival neared
she nodded sleepily
as though tired
and yawned and stretched
again and again,
so that, taking the hint,

all her companions left
leaving her alone.

157. *dukhahāini caracā nahīṁ, ānan ānan ān* ।
lagī phirati ḍhūkā diye, kānan kānan kān ॥

What she told her lover who wanted to take her to the woods

I fear to come with you, lover,
for these accursed
scandal-mongering women
have nothing else to talk about
save our affair.
They keep prying
even in the woods,
all eyes and ears
for something which can make
their tongues wag.

158. *gaṛī kuṭum kī bhīr maiṁ, rahī baiṭhi dai pīṭhi* ।
taū palak parijāti it, salaj hasauṁhīṁ dīṭhi ॥

What he said to her companion

Though she sat amidst
the members of her family
with her back to me,
she now and again
stole an abashed glance
and smiled.

159. *nauṁ sunat hīṁ hvai gayau, tana aurai mana aur* ।
dabai nahīṁ cit caṛhi rahyau, abai caṛhāyaiṁ tyaur ॥

What her companion said

His name acted like magic on you

and you were wholly transformed.
Your love, dear girl,
can't now be hid
however much
you knit your brows.

160. *ḍigat pāni ḍagulāti giri, lakhi saba braj behāl* ।
kampi kisorī darasi kai, kharaiṁ lajāne lāl ॥

While Kṛṣṇa held up the Goverdhana Mount

his glance fell on Rādhā,
and her sight so thrilled him
that his hand trembled
making the hill shake:
but when he saw
the alarmed faces of the Braj folk
he looked down with bashful eyes.*

161. *ihiṁ kāṁṭaiṁ mo pāi gaṛi, līnī marat jivāi* ।
prīti janāvat bhīti sauṁ, mīt ju kāṛhyau āi ॥

What she told her confidante

The thorn which got into my foot
became my life's saviour;
for just then
the lad whom I adored
came that way
and he took it out so fondly
that I knew
he returned my love
and I was saved
of dying of grief.*

162. *nāṁk caṛhai sībī karai, jitai chabīlī chail* ।
phiri phiri bhūli vahai gahai, pyau kaṁkarīlī gail ॥

What one of her companions said to another

That lovely belle
looked so charming
when she turned up her nose
and hissed her disapproval,
that the oftener she did it
the more he walked barefoot
on the rough gravelled path!*

163. *lāj lagām na mānahiṁ, nainā mau basa nāhiṁ* ।
ye muṁhajora turaṅg lauṁ, aiṁcatahūṁ cala jāhiṁ ॥

What she said to her companion who cautioned her not to look at him so often

My eyes are not in my control, friend;
throwing caution to the winds
they shamelessly keep glancing
at my lover
like runaway horses
which can't be curbed
however hard
the reins are pulled.

164. *kari muṁdarī kī arasī, pratibimbit pyau pāi* ।
pīṭhi diyaiṁ nidharak lakhai, ikaṭak ḍīṭhi lagāi ॥

What one of her companions said to another

Though her back
was towards him
that audacious girl
caught her lover's reflection
in the mirror

set in her ring
and kept staring at it fixedly.*

165. *itī bhīrahuṁ bhedi kai, kitaū hvai it āī* ।
phirai ḍīṭhi juri ḍīṭhi sauṁ, sabakī ḍīṭhi bacāi ॥

What he said to his confidant

Sweeping the crowd
her piercing glance
surreptitiously
joins mine
for a moment,
before it sweeps back
again.

166. *lāi lāl bilokiyai, jiya kī jīvan mūli* ।
rahī bhaun ke kona maiṁ, sonajuhī-sī phūli ॥

What his woman messenger said

Dear lad
I've brought you this charming girl
precious to you as life;
there she stands
in the corner of the house
resplendent
as a yellow jasmine flower.

167. *nekau uhi na judī karī, haraṣi ju dī tum māl* ।
ur taiṁ bās chuṭyau nahiṁ, bās chuṭai hū lāl ॥

What her messenger told him

She prizes so much
the garland
you fondly gave her, dear lad,
that it does not leave her bosom
though its perfume has left!

168. *bihaṁsi bulai biloki ut, prauṛha tiyā rasaghūmi* ।
pulaki pasījati pūt kau, piya cūmyau mukh cūmi ॥

What one of her companions said to another

Seeing her husband
who was sitting with elders
kiss his child,
that wanton woman
yearned for a kiss too,
and calling the child to her
kissed him instead;
and bathed with the sweat of longing,
bristling with desire,
she threw her husband
a meaningful glance.

169. *dekhyau anadekhyau kiyau, aṁga aṁga sabai dikhāi* ।
paiṭhati sī tana maiṁ sakuci, baiṭhī citai lajāi ॥

What he said to his confidant

Though she glanced at me
she feigned to take no notice,
but at the same time
bared her limbs to my sight,
and then sat shyly
as though shrinking from shame.

170. *suni paga dhuni citayau itai, nhāti diyaiṁ hī pīṭhi* ।
cakī jhukī sakucī ḍarī, haṁsī lajī sī ḍīṭhi ॥

What he said to his friend

When I chanced upon her
bathing in the pond
the sound of my footsteps
made her look back,
and when her startled gaze met mine

she stooped
to bashfully hide her breasts
and looked timorously all round:
then seeing
we were alone
she shyly glanced at me
and smiled.

171. *gayo kampi kachu kachu rahai, kar pasīji lapaṭāi* ।
laiyau muṭhī gulāl bhari, chuṭati jhuṭhī hvai jāi ॥

What one of her companions said to another

So greatly did they thrill and perspire
with the ardour of their love
that some of the *gulāl* powder
dropped from their trembling hands
and the rest got stuck
to their moist palms,
so that when they opened their fists
to throw it on each other
they found it all gone!*

172. *dekhat kachu kautuk itai, dekhau naiṁka nihāri* ।
kab kī ikaṭak ḍaṭi rahī, ṭaṭiyā aṁgurina phāri ॥

What her companion said to him

Do you see
this marvel, lad?
Just look!
Your beloved stands motionless
parting the curtain of her window
with her fingers,
staring fixedly at you
with ardent eyes.

173. *cakī jakī si hvai rahī, būjhaiṁ bolati nīṭhi* ।
kahūṁ ḍīṭhi lāgī lagi, kai kāhū kī ḍīṭhi ॥

What one of her companions said to another

She appears to be lost
to the world,
and startled;
and when one asks her
why she's so
she answers not a word:
it's evident she's in love,
or maybe
her bewitching beauty
has caught the evil eye.

174. *dūryau khare samīp kau, let māni mani mod* ।
hot duhun ke dṛgana hīṁ, batarasa haṁsī binod ॥

What one of her companions said to another

Even while standing
far apart
they're savouring
the bliss of nearness,
for their eyes
twinkling with joy
speak out
the ecstasy of their love.

175. *mukhi ughāri piu lakhi rahat, rahyau na gau misa sain* ।
pharake oṭha uṭhe pulak, gaye ughari juri nain ॥

What one of her companions said to another

Covering herself
she lay on the bed
her eyes closed,
feigning sleep:

but when he came
and uncovered her face
she was so transported with bliss
that her lips quivered,
and opening her eyes
she threw on him
a longing glance.

176. *nahiṁ anhāi nahiṁ jāi ghar, cit cihuṁṭyau taki tīr* ।
parasi phurahari lai phirati, bihaṁsati dhaṁsati na nīr ॥

What one of her companions said to another

While bathing in the pond
when she saw her lover come
to the water's edge
her eyes remained glued to him,
and she trembled
with the ecstasy of love:
but throwing him a smile
she pretended 'twas the cold
that made her shiver,
and waded across to join him
without taking a dip.

177. *saṭapaṭāti sī sasimukhī, mukh ghūṁghaṭ paṭ ḍhāṁki* ।
pāvak jhar sī jhamaki kai, gaī jharokhā jhāṁki ॥

What he said to her messenger

That moon-faced beauty
timidly drew her veil
and peering from within it
as a tongue of flame,
swiftly flashed me a quick smile
through her casement window.

178. *rūpa-sudhā-āsava chakyau, āsava piyat banai na* ।
pyālau oṭha priyā badan, rahyau lagāye nain ॥

What one of her companions said to another

When he saw her
the nectar of her beauty
so intoxicated him
that his lips stayed
on the cup of wine,
and he kept staring at her
spellbound.

179. *kitī na gokul kulabadhū, kāhi na ko sikh dīna* ।
kaunaiṁ tajī na kula-galī, hvai muralī sur līna ॥

What she said to her companion

Why preach at me alone?
Who's the virtuous woman
in Gokul
who has not thrown
family honour to the winds
on hearing
the enchanting notes
of Kṛṣṇa's flute?*

180. *jadapi suṁdara sughara puni, sagunau dīpak deha* ।
taū prakāsa karai titau, bhariyai jitai saneha ॥

What his woman messenger told the reluctant girl

You may be endowed
with loveliness and virtue
but without love
in your heart
you'll be devoid
of all splendour;
as an ornate lamp

with an excellent wick
can yet give no light
without oil.

181. *in dukhiyā aṁkhiyāna kauṁ, sukh sirajyauī nāṁhi* ।
dekhat banai na dekhatai, anadekhaiṁ akulāṁhi ॥

What she said to her confidante

Happiness
simply does not exist
for these wretched eyes of mine.
When he's before me
they can't look at him
for bashfulness,
and when he has gone
they're restless
for his sight!

182. *cirajīvau jorī jurai, kyauṁ na saneha gaṁbhīr* ।
ko ghaṭi ye vṛṣabhānujā, ve haladhar ke bīr ॥

What one of Rādhā's companions said to another

How can you expect
their love to last, friend,
for is not Rādhā
daughter of the fiery Sun
in Taurus;
and Kṛṣṇa
brother of Balarāma,
who's no other
than headstrong Śeṣanāga?*

183. *aurai gati aurai bacan, bhayau badan raṁg aur* ।
dyausak taiṁ piya cit caṁhi, kahaiṁ caṁhaiṁ huṁ tyaur ॥

What her companion said

I know he has started
returning your love
from a couple of days:
it's no use knitting your brows
to hide it from me, friend,
for the spring in your gait
the animation in your voice
and your face's sparkle
are a dead giveaway.

184. *puche kyauṁ rūkhī parati, sagibagi gaī saneha* ।
manamohana chabi par kaṭī, kahe kaṁṭyānī deha ॥

What her companion said to her

You may answer me dryly
when I ask you
why you're bathed with sweat,
but your body thrilling all over
clearly betrays
your rapture
on seeing that handsome lad.*

185. *muṁha dhovati eṁī ghasati, haṁsati anaṁgavati tīra* ।
dhaṁsati na indīvara-nayani, kālindī ke nīra ॥

What one of her companions said to another

Sitting by the Yamunā bank
that lotus-eyed girl
unhurriedly washed her face
and rubbed her heels clean,
but delayed to enter the river
to bathe,

so that she could gaze longer
at her lover
who was looking on.

186. *baṁhati nikasi kuc kor ruci, kaṁhat gaur bhujamūla* ।
mana luṭigau loṭan caṁhat, coṁaṭat ūṁce phūla ॥

What he said to her companion

While gathering flowers in the woods
when she raised her hands
to pick the topmost blossoms,
my glance was rivetted
to her nipples
spilling out of her bodice,
and her fair shoulders bared
from her mantle slipping down;
and when I saw
the triple folds above her waist
my heart was lost to her
forever.*

187. *parasat poṁchat lakhi rahat, lagi kapol kaiṁ dhyāna* ।
kar lai pyau pāṭal bimal, pyārī paṭhaye pān ॥

What her confidante told her companion

He took the rose sent by her
and calling to mind
her lovely cheeks
caressed it
wiped it carefully
and stared long at it.
In return
he sent her
betels.*

188. *kaibā āvat ihiṁ galī, rahauṁ calāi calaiṁ na* ।
darasan kī sādhai rahai, sūdhe rahaiṁ na nain ॥

What the shy girl told her confidante

My lover often passes
through this lane
but though I long for his sight
I can't see him;
for whenever my yearning glance
speeds on to him
bashfulness gets in the way
and stops it from reaching!

189. *besari motī dhani tuhīṁ, ko būjhai kula jāti* ।
pībau kari tiya oṭha kau, rasa nidharak dina rāti ॥

What he said

You alone are fortunate
O nose-ring pearl,
for even though you come
from the lowly oyster
you can dauntlessly caress
those lips of hers
which I,
despite my noble birth,
can't kiss even once!*

190. *tiya mukh lakhi hīrā jarī, beṁdī baṁhai binod* ।
suta saneha mānau liyau, bidhu pūran budhu god ॥

What her companion said to him

Go to her this moment lad,
you'll be enraptured
for she's wearing
her lovely *beṁdī*
with its diamonds sparkling

like Mercury
in the lap
of his doting father
the Full Moon!*

191. *jau laurn lakhaurn na kula kathā, tau laurn ṭhika ṭhaharāi* ।
dekhairn āvat dekhihūrn, kyaurnhūrn rahyau na jāi ॥

Her reply to her companion

Your counsel
about keeping the family honour
makes sense
while I do not see him.
But the moment
he comes within sight
I can only stare and stare,
and all circumspection
is thrown to the winds.

LOVE-MAKING

192. *lāj garab ālas umaṁg, bhare nain musukāt* ।
rāti ramī rati det kahi, aurai prabhā prabhāt ॥

What her companion said to her

Your eyes
bashful and languid
twinkling merrily
with yearning and elation,
have a different gleam
this morning;
they clearly reveal
you have been making love
all night.*

193. *pati rati kī batiyaṁ kahīṁ, sakhī lagī musakāi* ।
kai kai sabai ṭalāṭalī, alīṁ calīṁ sukh pāi ॥

What one of her companions said to another

When her husband's talk
turned amorous
she smiled suggestively
at her companions;
upon which
on one pretext or the other
they cheerfully departed.*

194. *camak tamak hāṁsi sasak, masak jhapaṭa lapaṭāni* ।
ye jiṁhi rati so rati mukuti, aur mukuti ati hāni ॥

What he told her

Startled delights,
rapturous throbs,
passionate hugs,
moans, laughter,
rubs and squeezes—
such love-making
is liberation for me,
I care for
no other.

195. *kuñj-bhavana taji bhavana kauṁ, caliye naṁdakisora* ।
phūlati kalī gulāba kī, caṭakāhaṭ cahuṁ or ॥

What her companion told Kṛṣṇa, who was making love

Kṛṣṇa,
see it's morning and
all around the rosebuds
open up with a crackle.
Leave the arbour now and
hasten home,
or what will people say?

196. *suduti durāye durati nahiṁ, pragaṭ karati rati rūpa* ।
chutaiṁ pīk aurai uthī, lālī oṭha anūpa ॥

What her companion said

However much you try, friend,
you cannot hide
the crimson-kissed bruises
upon your lips.
The red betel-juice on them
has faded away now

and their crushed rubefacience
shines out
all the more.*

197. *heri hiṁḍoraiṁ gagan taiṁ, parī parī-sī ṭūṭi* ।
dharī dhāī piya bīc hīṁ, karī kharī rasa lūṭī ॥

What one of her companions said to another

Seeing her lover come
she suddenly jumped off the swing
looking like
a heavenly nymph
falling from the sky.
He caught her in mid-air
and strained her to his bosom
stealing the fruits of love
before he released her.*

198. *paryau joru biparīt rati, rupī surati-ran dhīra* ।
karati kulāhala kiṅkinī, gahyau mauna mañjīra ॥

What one of her companions said to another

Friend, she's on top
I reckon,
resolute in love's combat,
for the bells of her girdle
jingle away,
while those of her anklets
are now mute.*

199. *binatī rati biparīt kī, karī parasi piya pāi* ।
haṁsi anabolaiṁ hīṁ diyau, ūtaru diyau batāi ॥

What one of her companions said to another

When he clasped her feet
begging her to play the lover,

she laughed
and put out the oil lamp,
wordlessly
signifying consent.*

200. *mere būjhat bāt tū, kat baharāvati bāla* ।
jaga jānī biparīt rati, lakhi binḍulī piya bhāla ॥

What her companion said

Why do you hedge, dear girl,
on my asking you,
when everyone can guess
by the round mark on your lover's brow
that you've exchanged clothes with him
and played the man.*

201. *rādhā hari hari rādhikā, bani āye saṅketa* ।
dampati rati biparīt sukha, sahaja suratahūṁ leta ॥

What one of her companions said to another

Exchanging clothes
Rādhā and Kṛṣṇa
came to the rendezvous
for love-making.
She was on top
but dressed as a man,
so they got the thrill
of novelty
even while seeming
to make love
in the normal way!

202. *raṁgī surat raṁg piya hiyaiṁ, lagī jagī saba rāti* ।
paiṁṫ paiṁṫ par ṭhaṭhaki kai, aiṁṫ bharī aiṁṫāti ॥

What one of her companions said to another

She has woken all night
twined to her lover
and now, steeped in the rapture
of her love-making,
she walks about
swaying with pride,
stopping at each step.*

203. *paṭ ki ḍhig kat ḍhāṁpiyati, sobhit subhag subesa* ।
hada radachada chabi det iha, sada rada-chada kī rekh ॥

What her companion said to her

The exquisite love-bites
newly made on your lips
by your sweetheart
look fascinating, dear girl,
why hide them
with your sari end?*

204. *raman kahyo haṭhi raman kauṁ, rati biparīt bilāsa* ।
citaī kari locana satar, salaj saros sahāsa ॥

What one of her companions said to another

His insistence
in asking her to play the lover
piqued her,
but with a bashful arch glance
she smiled her agreement.

205. *jadapi nāhiṁ nāhīṁ nahīṁ, badan lagī jaka jāti* ।
tadapi bhauṁha hāṁsī bharinu, hāṁ sīyai ṭhaharāti ॥

What her messenger said to him

What if she keeps saying
'no! no!' dear lad.
Don't you see
her smiling eyebrows
signify 'yes'?

206. *jyauṁ jyauṁ pāvak lapaṭ sī, tiya hiya sauṁ lapaṭāti* ।
tyauṁ tyauṁ chuhī gulāba sai, chatiyā ati siyarāti ॥

What he said

The more
that girl
like a flame of fire
twines around me,
the cooler my bosom feels,
as though sprinkled
with rosewater!

207. *saras kusum maṁḍarāt ali, na jhuki jhapaṭi lapaṭāi* ।
darasat ati sukumāru tana, parasat mana na patyāi ॥

What her companion said

She's tender, lad,
make love to her gently:
the black bee only hovers
over a lovely flower,
he does not pounce
and roughly clasp it
fearing it's too delicate
to stand his weight.

208. *ḍhiṭhyau dai bolati haṁsati, prauṛha-bilāsa apauṛha* ।
tyauṁ tyauṁ calat na piya nayan, chakaye chakī navoṛh ॥

What one of her companions said to another

As the intoxication
of the newly-wed
who had been plied with wine
mounted,
and she brazenly laughed and spoke to him
like a wanton
arousing him to make love;
she held him so spellbound
with her enchantment
that he just gazed and gazed.*

209. *dīpa ujerehū patihiṁ, harat basan rati-kāj* ।
rahī lapaṭi chabi kī chaṭani, naikau chuṭī na lāj ॥

What one of her companions said to another

When he undressed her
in the lamp's light
to make love,
he was so dazzled
by her body's splendour
that his eyes could not see
her nakedness,
and her shame was preserved!

210. *lakhi daurat piya-kara-kaṭak, bāsa churāvana kāj* ।
barunī ban gāṛhai dṛgana, rahī guṛhau kari lāj ॥

What one of her companions said to another

When his eager hands
advanced
to unclothe her
as an army bent

on conquest,
bashfulness hid
in the fortress of her eyes
fringed by the forest
of her eyelashes.*

211. *sakuci surati ārambha hīṁ, bichurī lāj lajāi* ।
ḍharaki ḍhāri ḍhuri ḍhig bhaī, ḍhīṭha ḍhiṭhāī āi ॥

What one of her companions said to another

As soon as he began
to make love,
all bashfulness fled:
and thrilling
with ecstasy
that audacious wanton
flew to his arms.

212. *sakuci saraki piya nikaṭ taiṁ, mulaki kachuk tana tori* ।
kara āṁcara kī oṭ kari, jamuhānī muṁha mori ॥

What her companion said about her

Longing to make love
she arose
and, provocatively smiling,
stretched her limbs;
then as if abashed
she raised her sari end
and turning her face aside
sleepily yawned.

213. *nahiṁ hari lauṁ hiyarā dharau, nahiṁ hari lauṁ aradhaṅga* ।
ekat hī kari rakhiyai, aṅga aṅga prati aṅga ॥

What her messenger said to him

Enshrining her in your heart

as Lakṣmī is in Viṣṇu's
will not appease her, dear lad,
nor an embrace
like Śiva's of Pārvatī:
the only way to gratify
this wanton
is to fold her tight
limb to limb!*

214. *sukh sauṁ bītī saba nisā, janu soye ik sāth* ।
mūkā meli gahe su chin, hāth na choṛe hāth ॥

What one of her companions said to another

Clasping each other's hand
through the hole
in the partition wall
between their houses
they spent the night in bliss
as though they had slept together!*

215. *dhyāna āni ḍhig prānapati, rahati mudit dina rāti* ।
palak kaṁpati pulakati palak, palak pasījati jāti ॥

What one of her companions told another

Making believe
her lover was with her
she savoured the bliss of union
all night and day:
tremulously quivering
deliriously thrilling
and bathed in sweat.

216. *haṁsi oṭhan bic kara ucai, kiyaiṁ nicauhaiṁ nain* ı
khare are piya ke priyā, birī lagī mukh dain ıı

What one of her companions said to another

Her lover
obstinately refused
again and again
the betels she offered him,
yet she raised her hand
and, with downcast eyes,
smilingly put them in his mouth.*

217. *lakhi lakhi aṁkhiyana adhakhulina, āṁga mori aṁgrāi* ı
ādhik uṭhi leṭati laṭaki, ālas bharī jamhāi ıı

What her companion said about her state after love-making

Looking all round
with tired half-open eyes
and languorously stretching and
twisting her limbs,
she raises herself a little,
but again lazily yawning
falls back on the bed.

218. *nāka mori nāhīṁ kahai, nāri nihoraiṁ lei* ı
chuvat oṭha biya āṁgurina, birī badan pyau dei ıı

What one of her companions said to another

Protesting indignantly
she said 'no! no!'
beseeching him
not to press betels on her;
but, brushing her lips
with eager fingers,
he placed them
in her mouth.*

219. *maiṁ misahā soyau samujhi, muṁha cūmyau ḍhig āi* ।
haṁsyau khisānī gala gahyau, rahī garaiṁ lapaṭai ॥

What she told her confidante

I was abashed
to see my wily lover,
whom I thought asleep,
smile
when I stooped
and kissed him.
Nothing daunted
he twined his arms round me,
so weakening my resolve
that I gave up all pretence
and clung fast to his neck.

220. *nīṭhi nīṭhi uṭhi baiṭhihūṁ, pyau pyārī parabhāt* ।
doū nīṁd bharaiṁ kharaiṁ, garai lāgi giri jāt ॥

What one of her companions said to another

Exhausted
after nightlong love-making
the lovers
sat up somehow,
but nodding sleepily
clung to each other,
and fell back listlessly again
upon the bed.

221. *tanak jhuṭ na savādilī, kaun bāt pari jāi* ।
tiya-mukh rati-ārambha kī, nahiṁ jhūṭiyai miṭhāi ॥

What he told his confidant

Even a little untruth
is bitter,
but a woman's 'no!'

at the start of love-making,
though false
is sweet!*

222. *yauṁ dalamiyat niradaī, daī kusum se gāt* ।
kara dhari dekhau dharadharā, ajauṁ na ur te jāt ॥

What one of her companions said to another in her presence

O god!
How cruelly
he has crushed this girl
of flower-like tenderness,
just place your hand
on her bosom
and see,
her heart is even now
palpitating!

223. *lahi rati sukh lagiyai hiyaiṁ, lakhī lajauṁhīṁ nīṭhi* ।
khulati na mo mana baṁdhi rahī, vahai adhakhulī ḍīṭhi ॥

What he told her confidante

The shy glance
she threw
from half-opened eyes
as she lay against my bosom
satiated with the rapture
of love-making,
is forever etched
in my memory.

224. *chinaka ughārati chin chavati, rākhati chinaka chipāi* ।
sab dina piya-khaṅḍita adhar, darapan dekhati jāi ॥

What one of her companions said to another

The whole day
she's at the mirror
looking at the bruise
left on her lips
in love-making;
exposing it,
staring at it fondly
and then covering it again.*

225. *bhauṁhani trāsati muṁha naṭati, āṁkhin sauṁ lapaṭāti* ।
aiṁci chuṛāvati kara iṁcī, āgaiṁ āvati jāti ॥

What one of her companions said to another

She turned to him
an angry brow
saying 'no!'
but her ardent gaze
clung to him.
She pretended
to wrench her hand away
from his hold
but kept pulling him
closer!

ANOTHER WOMAN

226. *kharī pātarī kāna kī, kaun bahāū* bāni ।
āk-kalī na ralī karai, alī alī jiya jāni ॥

What her companion said

Foolish girl,
why are you duped
by what people say?
Does the black bee
ever suck pollen
from a *madāra* bud?*

227. *palana pīk añjana adhara, dhare mahāvara bhāl* ।
āj mile su bhalī karī, bhale bane hau lāl ॥

What she said

Well have you done, indeed!
In meeting me today
with eyebrows reddened with betel-juice
lips stained with lamp-black
and your forehead streaked with lacquer dye.
Lover,
what a sight you look!*

228. *vāhī kī cit caṭapaṭī, dharat aṭapaṭe pāi* ।
lapaṭ bujhāvat birah kī, kapaṭ bharehū āi ॥

What she said

Your unsteady gait shows
your thoughts are still with that girl
you've made love to all night.

Despite your duplicity, lover,
your coming
puts out the flames
of my separation.

229. *gahaki gāṁsu aurai gahe, rahe adhakahe bain* ।
dekhi khisauṁhaiṁ piya-nayan, kiye risauṁhaiṁ nain ॥

What one of her companions said to another

She clasped him warmly
whispering endearments,
but seeing his abashed eyes
she guessed he had been making love
to another girl,
and the words froze on her lips
as she cast on him
a withering glance.

230. *pāvak so nayanana lagai, jāvak lāgyau bhāl* ।
mukura hohuge naiṁku maiṁ, mukura bilokahuṁ lāl ॥

What she said

Your lacquer stained forehead
inflames my eyes.
Here's a mirror,
now see the proof
of your guilt, lad;
once it's washed away
you'll never own up!*

231. *tarivana kanaka kapol-duti, bic bīc hīṁ bikāni* ।
lāl lāl camakata cunīṁ, caukā cinha samāni ॥

What she said to her messenger

The golden glow
of your ear ornament

is lost in your cheek's lustre;
but their gem's red gleam
vies with the love-bites on them
made by his teeth!*

232. *mohi dayau merau bhayo, rahat ju mili jiya sāth* ।
so mana bāṁdhi na sauṁpiyai, piya sautihi kaiṁ hāth ॥

What she said to her husband

When you gave me your heart
dear love,
it became one
with mine.
Now if you wrest it
from me
to give it
to my co-wives,
it will carry away
mine too, and
how will I survive?*

233. *veī gaṙi gāṙaiṁ parīṁ, upaṭyau hāra hiyaiṁ na* ।
ānyau mori mataṅga mana, māri gurerana maina ॥

What she said

These marks
have not been made
on your bosom
by that woman's necklace;
lover, it seems to me
Kāma
has pelted your elephant-like
wayward heart,
with stones from a catapult,
to drive you back here!*

234. *naiṁku haṁsauṁhīṁ bāni taji, lakhyau parat muṁha nīṭhi* ।
caukā camakani cauṁdha maiṁ, parit cauṁdhi sī ḍīṭhi ॥

What her companion said to her

Leave off laughing
a moment, friend,
the glimmer
of your front teeth
so dazzles his eyes
that he can hardly
look you
in the face!*

235. *teha tararau tyauru kari, kat kariyat dṛga lol* ।
līk nahīṁ yaha pīk kī, śruti-mani-jhalak kapol ॥

What her companion said to her

Why do you frown on him, friend?
That is not
a streak of betel-juice
on his cheek,
it's just the glow
cast by his ear ornament's ruby!*

236. *nabha lālī cālī nisā, caṭakālī dhuni kīna* ।
rati pālī ālī anat, āye banamāli na ॥

What she said to her companion

The eastern sky
glows red
slaying night's darkness:
swarms of sparrows
twitter:
yet Kṛṣṇa does not come.
I fear he's lying, friend,

in the arms of some woman
somewhere.

237. *biya sautina dekhat daī, apane hiya kī lāl* ।
phirati ḍahaḍahī sabana meṁ, uhaiṁ maragajī māla ॥

What her companion said to him

Remember, dear lad,
the garland
you took off your bosom
and gave her
in the presence of your co-wives?
Even though its flowers
have faded,
she goes about
happily sporting it
to taunt them!

238. *āye āpu bhalī karī, meṭan mān maror* ।
dūri karau yaha dekhihai, chalā chiguniyā-chor ॥

What her companion said to him

It's good you've come
to soothe away her haughty sulkiness,
but pray remove
that telltale ring
from your little finger
before she spots it.

239. *chirake nāha naboṛh dṛga, kara-picakī jala jora* ।
rocana raṁga lālī bhaī, biya-tiya locana-kora ॥

What one of her companions said to another

With her co-wives looking on
he cupped his hands
and playfully squeezed

a stream of water
into the eyes
of his newly-wed wife:
and wonderfully
all their eyes became red;
hers from soreness,
theirs from jealousy!*

240. *bāla kahā lālī bhaī, loin koin māṁha* ।
lāl tihāre dṛgana kī, parī dṛgana maiṁ chāṁha ॥

His question and her reply

'Why are the corners
of your eyes red, dear?'
he asked his girl
whose eyes had reddened with rage
on seeing him come crimson-eyed
from nightlong love-making
with another woman.
She pertly replied,
'Lover, they're only reflecting
the redness of *your* eyes!'*

241. *tarun kokanad baran bara, bhaye aruna nisi jāgi* ।
vāhī kaiṁ anurāga dṛga, rahai manau anurāgi ॥

What she said to him

Your eyes turned crimson
from nightlong waking
look like a full-blown
red lotus;
it seems they've been dyed
with the love of that woman
with whom you've dallied.

242. *lālan lahi pāī durai, corī sauṁha karaiṁ na* ।
sīsa caṛhe panihā pragaṭa, kahaiṁ pukāraiṁ nain ॥

What she said to him

Dear lad,
one may swear and swear
he's not a thief,
but when he is exposed
how can he deny it?
Your reddened eyes
cry out brazenly
that you have spent the night
in secret love-making.

243. *turat surat kaisaiṁ durat, murat nain juri nīṭhi* ।
ḍauṁṛī dai guna rāvare, kahati kanauṛī ḍīṭhi ॥

What she said to him

How can you hide
you've come here directly
after making love
to another woman?
Your sheepish eyes
fight shy of mine
and even if they meet
you look guiltily away
the next moment.
Your shame-faced glance
proclaims aloud
your wrongdoing.

244. *marakat-bhājana-salil-gat, indukalā kaiṁ bekh* ।
jhīna jhagā maiṁ jhalamalai, syāmagāt nakh-rekh ॥

What she said to her faithless lover

The nail mark

on your dark body
made by the woman
you've made love to,
shines out from within
your flimsy garment
as the new moon reflected
in a sapphire bowl
full of water.*

245. *bālama bāraiṁ sauti kaiṁ, suni paranāri-bihāra* ।
bho rasa anarasa risa ralī, rījha khījha ik bāra ॥

What one of her companions said to another

When she learnt
he had made love
to another woman
giving a miss
to her co-wife,
she was, in the same breath,
glad and downcast,
angry and amused,
pleased and vexed!*

246. *kesara kesari-kusuma ke, rahe aṅga lapaṭāi* ।
lage jāni nakh anakhulī, kat bolat anakhāi ॥

What her companion said

Why do you chide him
needlessly, dear girl?
These marks you see
are not nail scratches
made by his mistress,
but filaments of saffron flowers
that have got stuck
on his body.

247. *rahī pakari pāṭi su risa, bhare bhaumha cit nain* ।
lakhi sapanai piya āna rata, jagatahu lagat hiyai na ॥

What one of her companions said to another

Asleep
pressed to her lover's bosom
she dreamt
he was making love
to another woman.
Waking
she fumed, and
turned her back to him!

248. *nakh-rekhā sohaim naī, alasomhaim saba gāt* ।
saumhaim hota na nain ye, tuma saumhaim kat khāt ॥

What she said to him

You're looking spent,
the scratches made by her
on your body
are still fresh
and your guilty eyes
can't meet mine.
Why then
do you keep vainly swearing
your innocence
lover?

249. *tu mati mānai mukutaī, kiyai kapaṭ cit koṭi* ।
jau gunahī tau rākhiyai, āmkhina māmjha agoṭi ॥

Her accusation

You've been making love to
another woman
lover,
how can your vain excuses

ever hide
your guilt?

His answer

Even though you doubt me
sweetheart,
give me your love still;
keep my remembrance imprisoned
forever in your eyes.*

250. *dacchina piya hvai bāma basa, bisarāī tiya āna* ǀ
ekai bāsari kaiṁ biraha, lāge baras bihāna ǁ

His co-wives, complaint

Neglecting us all
our adulterous husband
unmindful of his vow
remains always
with that villainous
neighbour woman.
Though only a wall
separates him from us
we haven't seen him
for a whole year now!*

251. *sohat saṅg samān sauṁ, yahai kahai saba loga* ǀ
pān pīk oṭhan banai, kājar nainana joga ǁ

What she said to him

Like things
go with each other
as all men know:
red betel-juice
makes lips look lovelier,
lamp-black
gives charm to eyes.

But how come, lover,
your *brows* are betel-juice stained and
the lamp-black is on your *lips*!*

252. *maiṁ tapāi traya tāpa sauṁ, rākhyau hiyo hamām* ।
mati kabahuk āyeṁ ihāṁ, pulak pasīje syāma ॥

What she said to him

You've returned from your mistress
all spent up and perspiring,
come lover,
I'll chase away your tiredness
in the *hammām* of my heart
which I ever keep warmed up
with the triple heat
of passion, ardour and craving.*

253. *anat base nisi kī risani, ur bari rahī biseṣi* ।
taū lāj āī jhukat, khare lajauhaiṁ dekhi ॥

What one of her companions said to another

Though she inwardly fumed
when her lover returned
from his nightlong
secret love-making,
seeing him penitently remorseful
her heart softened
and she refrained from
chiding him.

254. *suraṁg mahāvara sauti paga, nirakhi rahī anakhāi* ।
piya aṁgurina lālī lakhe, kharī uṭhī lagī lāi ॥

What one of her companions said to another

She burned with jealousy
seeing her co-wife's

elegant lacquer-stained feet,
and when she saw
the same dye
on her husband's fingers too
she knew 'twas he
who had put it on and
her fury knew no bounds.

255. *kat sakucat nidharaka phirau, ratiyau khori tumhaiṁ na* ।
kahā karau jau jāṁhi ye, lagaiṁ lagauhaiṁ nain ॥

Her taunt to her faithless lover

Strange you feel abashed
after all your affairs, lover!
Need you fear reproach
when,
each time you're bewitched by a girl,
you can throw the blame
on your fickle eyes?

256. *nirakhi navauṛhā nāri tana, chuṭat larikaī lesa* ।
bhau pyārau prītam tiyan, manau calat paradesa ॥

What one of her companions said to another

Seeing the newly-wed wife
from whom childhood had slipped away
blossoming into a lovely girl,
her co-wives knew
she would get
all their husband's attention.
That made them warm up to him
as though he was going
on a long voyage!*

257. *prānapriyā hiya maiṁ basai, nakh-rekhā-sasi bhāl* ।
bhalau dikhāyauṁ āī yaha, hari-hara-rūpa rasāl ॥

What she said to her faithless lover

Your mistress' memory
is enshrined in your heart
like Lakṣmi's in Viṣṇu's
and her nail mark shines on your brow
as the crescent moon
on Śiva's forehead;
how well of you lad
to bless me with the sight
of both the gods
at the same time!*

258. *tīja parab sautina saje, bhūṣan basan sarīra* ।
sabai maragaje muṁha karī, ihī maragajai cīra ॥

What one of her companions said to another

On the *tīja* day
her co-wives gaily adorned themselves
with ornaments
and gorgeous dresses,
but when they saw her sari
rumpled and soiled
with nightlong love-making
they burned with jealousy
and their faces were crestfallen.*

259. *muṁha miṭhāsa dṛga cīkane, bhauhaiṁ saral subhāi* ।
taū kharaiṁ ādar kharau, khina khina hiyaiṁ sakāi ॥

What he said to her

Although you're speaking sweetly
gazing lovingly
and your eyebrows

are not knit with anger;
your affected deference, dear girl,
makes me more and more apprehensive
each moment!

260. *hyāṁ na calai bali raurī, caturāī kī cāl* ।
sanakh hiyaiṁ khina-khina naṭat, anakh baṛhāvat lāl ॥

What she said to her faithless lover

I admire your cleverness, dear lad,
but it won't work with me.
Your denial
of having made love to another girl
despite her nail scratches on your bosom
only raises my ire
still more.

261. *ur mānik kī urbasī, ḍaṭat ghaṭat dṛga-dāga* ।
chalakat bāhir bhari manau, tiya hiya kau anurāga ॥

What she said

The telltale ruby necklace
on your bosom
which you've forgotten to take off
shows you've exchanged dresses
with your mistress
making her play the lover.
Its flashing redness
which inflames my eyes,
is as though your deep love for her
had spilled out
from your heart.*

262. *sughara sauti basa piya sunat, dulahini duguna hulāsa* ।
lakhī sakhī tana dīṭhi kāri, sagaraba salaj sahāsa ॥

What one of her companions said to another

When that newly-wed girl
learnt that her co-wife
dominated her husband
by her shrewdness,
she was supremely happy
for she knew she could be shrewder,
and bashfully threw me, friend,
a triumphant smile.

263. *ṭunahāī saba ṭol maiṁ, rahī ju sauti kahāi* ।
su taiṁ aiṁci pyau āp tana, karī adhokhil āi ॥

What the newly-wed woman's companion said to her

When everyone saw him
irresistibly drawn
to that co-wife of his
they dubbed her an enchantress;
but ever since
you've snatched him away from her
she's rid of the infamy!

264. *vaisīyai jānī parati, jhagā ūjare māhiṁ* ।
mṛganainī lapaṭī ju yaha, benī upaṭī bāhiṁ ॥

What she said

All your pretences
are vain, dear lad;
the braid marks
of the girl
you had pressed to your bosom
show unmistakably

on the sleeve
of your white dress.

265. *chalā parosini hāth taiṁ, chala kari liyau pichāni* ।
piyahīṁ dikhāyau lakhi bilakhi, risa sūcaka musakāni ॥

What one of her companions said to another

She was grieved to see
her lover's ring
on her woman-neighbour's finger.
Taking it from her
on some pretext
she showed it to him,
veiling her wrath
with a knowing smile.

266. *haṭhi hita kari prītam liyau, kiyau ju sauti siṅgāru* ।
apanaiṁ kara motin guhyau, bhayo harā hara-hāru ॥

What one of her companions said to another

She herself stringed
a garland of pearls
for her husband to wear.
When her co-wife,
who had cajoled it out of him,
came adorned
with that same garland,
it seemed to her as fearful
as the serpent
round Śiva's neck!*

267. *ḍīṭhi parosini īṭhi hvai, kahe ju gahe sayāna* ॥
sabai saṁdese kahi kahyau, musukahaṭ meṁ māna ॥

What one of her companions said to another

Pretending to be her friend

her audacious woman-neighbour
who was her husband's sweetheart
gave her some messages for him.
Though she conveyed them
she made it known by her smiles
she had got wise
to their romance.

268. *lalan salone aru rahe, ati saneha soṁ pāgi* ।
tanak kacāī det dukh, sūran lauṁ muṁha lāgi ॥

What she said to her faithless lover

You're handsome, dear lad,
and loving too;
but your deceitful lies
are like the acrid taste
of *sūran* left uncooked.*

269. *na karu na ḍaru sab jaga kahat, kat bina kāj lajāt* ।
sauṁhaiṁ kīje nain jau, sāṁci sauṁhaiṁ khāt ॥

Everyone knows
he has nothing to fear
if he has done no wrong.
If you insist, dear lad,
you've not been making love
to another woman
why can't you look me
in the eye?

270. *rahyau cakit cahuṁdhā citai, cit merau mati bhūli* ।
sūra udaiṁ āye rahī, dṛgana sāṁjha sī phūli ॥

What she said to her faithless lover

I'm perplexed and amazed
to see you come at sunrise

after your night of love-making
with the sunset's glow
reflected
in your sleep-starved eyes!

271. *kat bekāj calāiyat, caturaī kī cāla* ।
kahe deti yaha rāvare, sab guna niraguna māla ॥

What she said to him

Your deceit
will not work with me
crafty lover,
the telltale curve
of bead marks
upon your bosom
eloquently betray
your clandestine love-making.*

272. *bāṁhat to ur uraj bharu, bhar tarunaī bikās* ।
bojhan sautina kaiṁ hiyaiṁ, āvat rūṁdhi usās ॥

What her friend said to her

Your breasts turn heavy
as your girlhood slips away,
but it seems they're burdening
the hearts of your jealous co-wives
so that their grieved breath
comes in short gasps!

273. *naye birah baṁhati bithā, kharī bikal jiya bāla* ।
bilakhī dekhi parosinyau, haraṣi haṁsī tihiṁ kāla ॥

What one of her companions said to another

Parted from her lover
for the first time
that young girl

was lamenting his absence,
when she saw
her woman-neighbour's tormented face;
and guessing
the secret affair between them
she heartily laughed.*

274. *phūlīphalī phūla-sī, phirati ju bimal bikās* ।
bhor taraiyāṁ hohute, calat tohiṁ piya pās ॥

What her companion said

Your co-wives
are swaggering about joyfully
their faces bright
as blossoming flowers,
but the moment they see you go
to meet your lover
they'll turn pale
like stars fading
in the morning light.

275. *deha lagyau ḍhig gehapati, taū neha nirabāhi* ।
ḍhīlī aṁkhiyan hī itai, gāī kanakhiyan cāhi ॥

What he said to his friend

Even though all the three of us—
she, her husband and I—
were sitting so close together
that our bodies almost touched;
she managed to slant her eyes
and ogle at me!

276. *duraiṁ na nigharaghaṭyauṁ diyaiṁ, ye rāvarī kucāl* ।
biṣu-sī lāgati hai burī, haṁsī khisī kī lāl ॥

What she said to her faithless lover

However much you try,
your shameless excuses
can't hide your wrongdoing;
your dissembling smiles, dear lad,
are like poison to me.

277. *pala sohaiṁ pagi pīk raṁg, chal sohaiṁ saba bain* ।
bala sauhaiṁ kat kījiyat, ye alasauṁhaiṁ nain ॥

What she said to him

Your eyebrows
kissed by her
are still stained
by red betel-juice,
all your words
smack of deceit.
Faithless lover,
why do you on purpose
turn your sleepy eyes
towards me?

278. *kat lapaṭaiyata mo garaiṁ, so na ju hī nisi sain* ।
jihiṁ campakabarani kiye, gullālā raṁg nain ॥

What she said to her faithless lover

Why are you clinging
to my neck, lover?
I'm not
that *campaka*-complexioned beauty
you've gone to bed with,
who has kept you awake
all night

so that your eyes are red
as the *gullālā* flower.*

279. *bithuryau jābaka sauti paga, nirakhi haṁsī gahi gāṁs* ।
salaj haṁsauṁhiṁ lakhi liyo, ādhī haṁsī usāṁs ॥

What one of her companions said to another

She chuckled to see
the clumsily applied
lacquer dye
on her co-wife's feet.
But when her co-wife
bashfully smiled
she knew 'twas her husband
who had put it on
with hands trembling with ardour,
and her smirk
turned into a sigh of grief!

280. *sahī raṁgīlaiṁ rati jagaiṁ, jagī pagī sukh cain* ।
alasauṁhaiṁ sauṁhaiṁ kiyaiṁ, kahaiṁ haṁsauṁhaiṁ nain ॥

What her confidante said to her

The merry twinkle
in your tired sleepy eyes
unmistakably testifies
to your having been awake
blissfully love-making;
not, as you would have us believe,
watching a show.

281. *kat kahiyat dukh dena kauṁ, raci raci bacan alīk* ।
sabai kahāu rahyau lakhaiṁ, lāl mahāvara-līk ॥

What she said to her faithless lover

Why do you vex me

dear lad
by your trumped up excuses?
The telltale streak
of lacquer dye
on your forehead
is a dead giveaway.

282. *phirat ju aṭakat kaṭani bina, rasika surasa na khiyāl* ।
anat anat nita-nita hitan, kat sakucāvat lāl ॥

What she said to him

You keep getting infatuated
with new girls each day
without being true to them
so that love
has become for you
a kind of sport.
Faithless lover,
your fickleness
puts Love to shame.*

283. *sadan sadan ke phiran kī, sada na chutai harirāi* ।
ruci titai biharat phirau, kat biharat it āi ॥

What she said to him

Gallivanting lover,
it seems you won't cease
roaming from house to house
to dally with your mistresses.
Well, go
where it pleases you;
but don't ever come here
to break *my* heart.

284. *subharu bharyau tuva guna-kanani, pakayau kapaṭ kucāl* ।
kyauṁ dhauṁ dāryau jyauṁ hiyau, darakat nāhiṁ na lāl ॥

What she said to her faithless lover

My heart is burdened
by your faults
as a pomegranate shell
by its seeds;
and as, turning juicy
they fill the fruit all the more,
till over-ripening
it cracks open;
your misdemeanours, dear lad,
have brought my heart
to the bursting point,
and it's a wonder
it does not burst!*

285. *calat det ābhāru suni, uhiṁ parosini nāha* ।
lasī tamāse kī dṛgana, hāṁsi āṁsuna māṁha ॥

What one of her companions said to another

Her eyes were brimming with tears
when the moment came
for her husband's departure,
but when he entrusted the house
to his neighbour
who was her secret lover,
she flashed a sudden smile.

286. *paṭ sauṁ poṁchi parī karau, kharī bhayānak bhekh* ।
nāgini hvai lāgati dṛgana, nāgabeli raṁg rekh ॥

What the angry girl said

The red streak
of betel-juice

left on your eyebrow
by her kiss
seems like a fearful serpent to me;
wipe it away
with the hem of your dress
and remove my torment.

287. *jo tiya tuvȧ manabhāvati, rākhī hiyaiṁ basāi* ।
mohiṁ jhukāvati dṛgani hvai, vahaī ujhakati āi ॥

What she said to him

The girl
whose name you've just uttered
and who's treasured in your heart
is your true beloved;
no wonder her image
is always before your eyes
so that you keep
mistaking me for her
and calling me by her name.

288. *vāhī dina taiṁ na miṭyau, māna kalah kau mūla* ।
bhale padhāre pāhune, hvai guṛhar kau phūla ॥

What her companion said to him

Discord is now
like a guest come to stay
ever since
the day you came home
like a *guṛhal* flower
after spending the night
with your mistress,
telltale love marks
all over you.*

289. *mauhūṁ sauṁ bātan lagaiṁ, lagī jībhi jihiṁ nāi* ।
soī lai ur lāiyai, lāl lāgiyat pāi ॥

What she said to him

Release me from your arms
I beg of you, dear lad,
and embrace that woman instead
whose name keeps lingering
on your lips!

290. *mohiṁ karat kat bāurī, karaiṁ durāu duraiṁ na* ।
kahe det raṁg rāti ke, raṁg-nicurat-se nain ॥

What she said to her faithless lover

Why are you trying to fool me
by your lies?
Despite all your endeavours
the truth can't be hid.
Your crimson eyes
proclaim aloud
your nightlong love-making.

291. *bilakhī lakhai kharī kharī, bharī anakh bairāga* ।
mṛganainī saina na bhajai, lakhi benī ke dāga ॥

What one of her companions said to another

Overwhelmed with rage and anguish
that antelope-eyed girl
stood staring
at the impress
of another woman's braid
upon the bedsheet,
and turning her heart away from him
she would not get on the bed.*

292. *gahyau abolau boli pyau, āpahiṁ paṭhai basīṭhi* ।
diṭhi curāī duhun kī, lakhi sakucauṁhīṁ diṭhi ॥

What one of her companions said to another

When the woman
she herself had sent
to fetch her lover
returned with him,
she guessed
by their abashed glances
that the two
had been making love
on the sly;
and turning away from him
she kept sullenly silent.

293. *dusaha sauti sālaiṁ su hiya, ganati na nāha-biyāha* ।
dhare rūpa guna kau garab, phirai acheha uchāha ॥

What one of her companions said to another

Though knowing
what unbearable anguish
a co-wife can cause,
she's not bothered,
but goes about self-assured
proudly flaunting her beauty.

294. *aur sabai haraṣī haṁsatiṁ, gāvatiṁ bharī uchāha* ।
tuṁhī bahū bilakhī phirai, kyauṁ devar kaiṁ byāha ॥

What an elderly woman neighbour said to her

Young woman,
why do you alone
wander about lamenting
when all others
are lustily singing

and gleefully making merry
in your brother-in-law's
wedding celebrations?
Is it because
you yourself are in love with him?

295. *naṭi na sīsa sābit bhaī, luṭī sukhan kī moṭ* ।
cup rahi ye cārī karat, sārī parī saloṭ ॥

What she said to her woman messenger

It's no use your denying it
for it's evident
you've stolen my pleasures
by making love to him
yourself.
Even though you don't own up
the creases in your sari
are enough
to prove your guilt.

296. *jihiṁ bhāmini bhūsana racyau, caran mahāvara bhāl* ।
tihīṁ manau aṁkhiyāṁ raṁgīṁ, oṭhan kaiṁ raṁg lāl ॥

What she said to her faithless lover

The same woman
who has adorned your forehead
with the lacquer dye of her feet
has also lent your eyes
dear lad,
the colour of her lips!*

297. *tūṁ mohan mana gaṛi rahī, gāṛhī gaṛani guvāli* ।
uṭhai sadā naṭasāla lauṁ, sauṁtini kaiṁ ur sāli ॥

What the cowherd girl's companion told her

Dear girl,

you're firmly embedded
in Kṛṣṇa's memory,
but it constantly pains
the hearts of your co-wives
as a chipped arrowhead
deep in the body.

298. *piya mana ruci hvaibau kaṭhin, tana ruci hou siṁgāra* ।
lākh karau āṁkhi na baṛhaiṁ, baṛhaiṁ baṛhāyaiṁ bāra ॥

What her companion said to her

Fear not, dear girl,
it's hard for your co-wife
to win his love
by mere adornment,
for how can she excel
your natural beauty
which alone can captivate him?
Hair can be made
to grow longer
but eyes can't become
any larger than they are!*

299. *khalit bacan anakhulit dṛga, lalit sveda-kana-joti* ।
aruna badan chabi madana kī, kharī chabīlī hoti ॥

What she said to her faithless lover

How charming you look, lover,
indeed
you're like Kāma himself!
Your words faltering
your slumberous eyes
half-open,
your face flushed crimson
and your limbs

glistening exquisitely
with beads of sweat.*

300. *bahaki na ihiṁ bahināpulī, jab tab bīr bināsa* ।
bacai na baṛī sabīlahuṁ, cīla-ghoṁsuvā māṁsa ॥

The advice her wise companion gave her

Despite all your caution,
your blind trust
in your sisterly neighbour
will, sooner or later,
prove disastrous,
for he'll surely succumb
to her charms.
Can a piece of meat
ever remain in a kite's nest
without being devoured?

301. *ayau mīta bidesa taiṁ, kāhū kahyau pukāri* ।
suni hulasiṁ bihaṁsi haṁsī, doū duhuni nihāri ॥

What the girls' companion said

Hearing someone exclaim
'Your lover has returned
from abroad',
both the girls
who were in love with him
beamed with joy;
but instantly guessing
each other's secret
they exchanged
a knowing smile!

302. *pāryau soru suhāga kau, in bin hīṁ piya neha* ।
unadauṁhīṁ aṁkhiyāṁ kakai, kai alasauṁhiṁ deha ॥

What her companion told her

Your co-wives
deliberately appear before you
sleepy-eyed and tired,
but I'm telling you, dear friend,
it's all make-believe
to put you off.
It's only so that you may
keep on taking airs
and at length
estrange him from yourself.

303. *nhāi pahiri paṭu ḍaṭi kiyau, beṁdī misi paranāma* ।
dṛga calāi ghar kauṁ calī, bidā kiye ghanasyāma ॥

What one of her companions said to another

She bathed in the river
and dressed up,
then making as if
to apply the *biṅdi* mark
on her forehead
folded her hands
in a farewell greeting
beseeching Kṛṣṇa with her eyes
to go home
for fear
that if he stayed longer
that fickle lover
might fall for some other girl
passing that way!*

THE WOMAN OFFENDED

304. *citavana rūkhe dr̥gani kī, hāṁsī bina musukāni* ।
mānu janāyau māninī, jāni liyau piya jāni ॥

What one of her companions said to another

Her discerning lover
could guess
by her indifferent glances
and her forced smiles
that she was putting on airs.

305. *kahā lehuge khel meṁ, tajau aṭapaṭī bāt* ।
naiṁku haṁsauṁhīṁ haiṁ bhaī, bhauṁhaiṁ sauṁhaiṁ khāt ॥

What her companion said to him

What will you gain
dear lad,
by your foolish banter?
After much coaxing
she has unknit somewhat
her brows,
if you annoy her again
she'll be hard to appease.*

306. *sakuci na rahiyai syāma suni, ye risarauṁhaiṁ bain* ।
det racauṁhaiṁ cit kahe, neha nacauṁhaiṁ nain ॥

What her confidante said

Don't be put off
Kr̥ṣṇa,
by her angry words,

see now
her ardent eyes
are pouring out
her heart's love.

307. *hama hāriṁ kai kai hahā, pāina pāryau pyauru* ।
lehu kahā ajahūṁ kiye, teha tarerau tyauru ॥

What her companion said

We humbly entreated you
to make up with your lover
and even persuaded him
to fall at your feet,
yet you still
knit your eyebrows
and cast angry glances.
What will you gain, friend,
by this obduracy?*

308. *satara bhauṁha rūkhe bacana, karit kaṭhina mana nīṭhi* ।
kahā karauṁ hvai jāi hari, heri haṁsauṁhīṁ ḍīṭhi ॥

What she said to her companion

How many times
have I resolved, friend,
to harden my heart
speak roughly
and frown
when I see Kṛṣṇa;
but all my efforts
are in vain;
the moment he comes
within my sight
my eyes of themselves
throw him a smile!

309. *sakat na tuva tāte bacana, mo rasa kau rasa khoi* ।
khina khina auṭe khīr lauṁ, kharo subādilu hoi ॥

What he said to her

Your harsh
anger-charged words
cannot turn my love for you
insipid.
Instead,
each moment they make it more delicious
like milk
boiling away!

310. *torasa rāṁcyau āna bas, kahau kuṭil mati kūra* ।
jībha nibaurī kyauṁ lagai, baurī cākhi aṁgūra ॥

What her companion said

Don't be taken in
by the harsh words
of thoughtless men.
He loves you alone
not another.
Foolish girl,
how can one who has tasted grape juice
ever long for the bitter fruit
of the *neem* tree?*

311. *sovat lakhi mana mānu dhari, ḍhiga soyau pyau āi* ।
rahī supana kī milani mili, piya hiya sauṁ lapaṭāi ॥

What one of her companions said to another

Her lover came
and quietly lay
beside that sulking girl
who was feigning sleep.
No longer able

to restrain herself
but keeping up the pretence,
she turned
as though sleepily,
and twined her arms
around him.

312. *rasa kī sī rukh sasimukhī, haṁsi haṁsi bolat bain* ।
gūṛh mānu mana kyauṁ rahai, bhaye būṛh-raṁg nain ॥

What her companion said to her

O moon-faced woman
your smiles and endearments
are all very well,
but your angry eyes
red as a ladybird
are a giveaway.

313. *maiṁ barajī kai bāra tūṁ, it kat leti karauṭ* ।
paṅkhurī gaṛai gulāba kī, parihaiṁ gāt kharauṭ ॥

What her confidante said to her

How often have I told you, friend,
not to turn your face away
from your lover in bed
lest the rose petals strewn
near the pillow
scratch your tender cheeks!

314. *mān karat barajati na hauṁ, ulaṭi divāvati sauṁha* ।
karī risauṁhīṁ jayigī, sahaj haṁsauṁhīṁ bhauṁha ॥

What her companion said

Far from stopping you
I'll make you swear
to be cross with him;

but say, dear girl,
can those eyebrows of yours
which are always smiling
ever frown?

315. *ahe kahai na kahā kahyau, to soṁ naṁdakisora* ।
baṙabolī kat hot bali, baṙe dṛgani ke jora ॥

What her companion said

Tell me, dear girl,
what Kṛṣṇa has said
to make you so angry?
Don't revile him so
I beseech you,
for his rage
can't last long.
Your large bewitching eyes
will soon
bring him back.

316. *to hī ko chuṭ mān gau, dekhat hīṁ brajarāja* ।
rahī gharik lauṁ mān sī, mān kiyai kī lāja ॥

What her companion said to her

Just a glimpse of Kṛṣṇa
has won you over;
but still
you're keeping up the pretence
of being annoyed.
I'm sure, dear girl,
it's just to hide
the embarrassment
of your surrender!

317. *haṁsi haṁsāi ur lāi uṭhi, kahi na rukhauṁhaiṁ baina* ।
jakita thakita hvai taki rahe, takati tirīche nain ॥

What her companion said to her

Your irate glance
has awed and dazed him.
Leave off your sulking
and harsh words,
chase away his gloom
with smiles;
arise dear friend
and clasp him to your bosom.

318. *anarasahūṁ rasa pāiyatu, rasika rasīlī pās* ।
jaisaiṁ sāṁṭhe kī kaṭhina, gāṁṭhe bharī miṭhās ॥

What her companion said to him

Go to her, dear lad,
the harsh anger
of that ravishing girl
will be no hindrance
to your pleasure:
even the hard knots
of sugarcane
taste sweet!

319. *tapan-teja tapa-tāpi tapi, atula tulāī māṁha* ।
sisir sīta kyauṁhuṁ na miṭai, bina lapaṭaiṁ tiya nāṁha ॥

What the sulking girl's companion told her

You can't beat
winter's cold
by the warmth of the sun
or of the fire,
or by covering yourself
with a thick quilt.

The only way, dear girl,
is to go and lie
twined to your lover.

320. *kharaiṁ adab iṭhalāhaṭī, ur upajāvati trāsa* ।
dusaha saṅk bisa kau karaiṁ, jaisaiṁ soṁṭhi miṭhāsa ॥

What he said to her

I know you're acting proud
dear girl,
your affected deference
makes me highly suspicious,
as one would be
of sweet dry ginger
which though tasting good
is poisonous.*

321. *nahiṁ nacāi citavati dṛgana, nahiṁ bolati musakāi* ।
jyauṁ jyauṁ rūkhī rukh karati, tyauṁ tyauṁ cit cikanāi ॥

What he said to his sulking beloved

You neither throw
a loving glance my way
nor smile at me
nor speak;
yet the greater
your indifference, dear,
the tenderer
is my heart
for you.

322. *niradaya neha nayau nirakhi, bhayau jagat bhayabhīt* ।
yaha na kahūṁ ab lauṁ sunī, mari māriyai ju mīt ॥

What her companion said to her

Stubborn girl,

your love has just blossomed
don't alarm us all
by sulking;
what will you profit
by tormenting yourself
and being a kill-joy
to your loved one too?

323. *kuḍhaṅg kopa taji raṅgaralī, karat jubati jaga joi* ।
pāvasa gūṛh na bāt iha, būṛhanahūṁ raṅg hoi ॥

What her companion said to her

This is the rainy season
when young girls
no longer able to put on airs
rush to their lovers' arms.
Everyone knows
that it makes even old women
turn amorous
like ladybirds
taking on a reddish hue.
So your sulking
won't work now, dear girl,
better hasten
to your sweetheart.

324. *apanī garajani boliyat, kahā nihorau tohiṁ* ।
tū pyarau mo jīya kauṁ, mo jiya pyārau mohiṁ ॥

What she said to him

I love you so dearly, lad,
that your grief at my silence
saddens me even more.
So I'm making up
for my own sake

to end my misery,
'tis no obligation on you!

325. *kapaṭ satara bhauṁhaiṁ karīṁ, mukh manakhauṁhaiṁ bain* ।
sahaj haṁsauṁhaiṁ jāni kari, sauṁhaiṁ karati na nain ॥

What one of her companion said to another

Feigning anger
she knitted her brows
and spoke to him harshly,
but fearing
the twinkle in her eyes
would be a giveaway,
she kept looking down.

326. *rukh rūkhī misa-roṣa mukh, kahati rukhauṁhaiṁ bain* ।
rukhe kaisaiṁ hota ye, neha cīkane nain ॥

What her companion said to her

Though you are pretending anger
and speaking to him harshly,
how can your eyes
softened by love
showunconcern?

327. *pati ritu avaguna guna baṛhat, mān māha kau sīta* ।
jāt kaṭhin hvai ati mṛdau, ramanī mana navanīta ॥

What her companion told him

You have yourself to blame
dear lad,
for as soft butter
hardens
in the cold *Māgh* month
a woman's tender mind

is turned harsh
by her husband's vices.*

328. *rāti divasa hause rahai, mān na ṭhiku ṭhaharāya।*
jetauṁ auguna ḍhūṁḍhiyai, gunhai hāth pari jāya॥

What she said to her companion

Each moment
I'm eager
to put on airs,
but it's no use, friend,
for the more faults
I seek in him
the more virtues
I discover!

329. *disi disi kusumiti dekhiyat, upavana vipin samāja।*
manau biyogini kauṁ kiyau, sarapañjara riturāja॥

What her companion said to her

Leave off sulking
and hasten to your lover's arms
dear girl,
the forests and groves
in bloom
are like Spring's
arrowhead-walled cages
to torture women
parted from their lovers!*

330. *tiya tarasauṁhaiṁ mana kiye, kari sarasauṁ haiṁ neha।*
dhar parasauṁhaiṁ hvai rahe, jhar barasauṁhaiṁ meha॥

What her companion said to her sulking lover

How can you keep away from her
dear lad,

when the rain-filled clouds
eager to caress the earth
pour all around
making lovers' hearts
overflow
with longing?*

331. *kiyau sabai jaga kāma-bas, jīte jite ajeya* ।
kusumasarahiṁ sara-dhanuṣa kara, agahan gahan na deya ॥

What her companion said to her

You can't pretend indifference
dear girl
even if you want to,
for in this cold *Agahan* month
lovers rush to each others' arms
of themselves.
It unsettles the minds
even of austere sages
so that Kāma
has no need to shoot
his flower-tipped arrows!*

332. *chaki rasāl saurabha sane, madhura mādhurī gaṁdha* ।
ṭhaur ṭhaur jhauṁrat jhaṁpat, bhauṁra-jhaur madhu aṁdha ॥

What her companion said to her

It is spring, dear girl,
when even swarms of black bees
wander about
drunk with the fragrance
of mango blossoms
and go surfeited
with the sweet nectar
of *mādhurī* creepers:

how can *you* keep away
from your lover's arms?*

333. *mili biharat bichurat marat, dampati ati rati līna* ।
nūtan bidhi hemaṅta saba, jagat jurāfā kīna ॥

What her companion said to her

Stop puṭting on airs
dear girl,
when couples
lie cuddled together
and lovers embrace.
Don't you know
in winter's new regime
keeping away from your lover
may prove as fatal
as for a *jurāfā*
separation from its mate?*

334. *sauṁhaiṁhuṁ heryau na taiṁ, ketī dyāī sauṁha* ।
eho kyauṁ baiṭhī kiye, aiṁthī gvaiṁṭhī bhauṁha ॥

What her companion said

How many times
we urged you
to give up sulking
but you never so much
as glanced at him.
Why do you sit now
knitting your brows
when he
whom you wish to show your anger
has gone?

335. *calau calaiṁ chaṭi jāhigau, haṭh rāvaraiṁ saṁkoca* ।
khare caṛhāye he ti ab, āye locana loca ॥

What her messenger said to him

Now's the time, dear lad,
to win over that indignant girl
for her wrathful glances
have softened somewhat,
and your presence
will no longer provoke her.

336. *mānu tamasau kari rahī, bibasa bārunī sei* ।
jhukati haṁsati haṁsi haṁsi jhukati, jhuki jhuki haṁsi haṁsi dei ॥

What one of her companions said to another

She's so drunk
that she is not in her senses
and keeps scolding him
and laughing
by turns,
so that even her sulking
has become
a mockery!

337. *tuhūṁ kahati hauṁ āpu hūṁ, samajhati sabai sayānu* ।
lakhi mohanu jau manu rahai, tauṁ mana rākhauṁ mānu ॥

What she told her companion

Pretending unconcern
might, as you say,
thaw that charming lad,
but when he steals away my heart
the moment I see him,
with what, friend,
should I show indifference?

338. *ḍoū adhikāī bhare, ekai gauṁ gaharāi* ।
kaun manāvai kau manai, māne sana ṭhaharāi ॥

What one of her companions said to another

The lovers are sitting
drowned in conceit:
each thinks
'let the other appease me first',
and so they keep
putting on airs,
each trying to outdo the other!

339. *haṭh na haṭhīlī kari sakaiṁ, yaha pāvasa ṛta pāi* ।
āni gāṁṭhi ghuṭi jāti jyauṁ, māna gāṁṭhi chuṭi jāi ॥

What her companion said to her

The rains are here
filling all hearts with desire;
it's no use sulking, dear girl,
for even the most obdurate woman
can't pretend indifference now.
It's the season
when hemp knots
get tighter
and those of standoffishness
loosen.

340. *mohiṁ lajāvat nilaj ye, hulasi milat saba gāt* ।
bhānu udai kī os lauṁ, mān na jānati jāt ॥

What she said to her companion

Pining for his embrace
my love-starved limbs
put me to shame,
for the moment he comes
they make me cling to him

and my indifference flies away
as dew-drops vanishing
before the rising sun.

341. *rahaiṁ nigoṛe nain gaṛi, gahaiṁ na ceta aceta* ।
hauṁ kasa kai risa ke karauṁ, ye nisuke haṁsi deta ॥

What she said to her companion

My wretched eyes
are so bewitched by him
that they'll not be admonished.
Although I counsel them
to feign anger,
the moment they see him
they smile!

342. *erī yaha terī daī, kyauṁhūṁ prakṛti na jāi* ।
neha bharaiṁ hiya rākhiyai, tau rūkhayai lakhāi ॥

What her companion said to her

Oh god,
why do you keep pretending
indifference?
You're treasured
in his heart and
steeped in his love,
yet you remain unmoved;
as though an oil-filled urn
should stay dry!

343. *prema aḍola ḍulai nahīṁ, muṁha bolaiṁ anakhāi* ।
cita unakī mūrati basī, citavani māṁhi lakhāi ॥

What her companion said to her

Your love
steadfast and unwavering

can't be hid, dear girl,
by a show of rage,
for your ardent glances
clearly reveal
that his image
is enshrined in your memory.

344. *khiṁcaiṁ mān aparādhahūṁ, caligai baṛhaiṁ acaina* ।
jurati ḍiṭhi taji risa khisī, haṁse duhuna ke nain ॥

What one of her companions said to another

They could not look
each other in the eye,
he from shame
at his wrongdoing,
she to keep up the pretence
of indifference,
but their ardent love
weakened their resolve
and gazing at each other
they burst out laughing!*

345. *bidhi bidhi kauni karai ṭarai, nahīṁ parehū pān* ।
citai kitai taiṁ lai dharyau, itau itai tana mān ॥

What her companion said to her

Your lover
has beseeched you
in all ways,
even falling at your feet,
but you're still unmoved.
Oh god,
what enormous vanity
in a puny body!

346. *jadapi lauṁg lalitau taū, tū na pahiri ik āṁk* ।
sadā sāṁk baṛhiyai rahai, rahai caṛhī sī nāṁk ॥

What her lover said to her

Though this nose ornament
looks charming on you,
don't wear it on purpose
dear girl.
As it is
you're always
wrinkling your nose at me
and the ornament
makes me feel
all the more
that you're putting on airs!*

MEETING

347. *lagyo sumanu hvai hai saphala, ātapa ros nivāri* ।
baurī bārī āpanī, sīṁci suhridatā bāri ॥

What her companion said to her

Leave off your anger
foolish woman,
You'll have your pleasure
if you heap endearments on him
when he comes;
for a plant
is sure to bear fruit
if the gardener
keeps watering it.*

348. *dvaija sudhādīdhiti kalā, vaha lakhi ḍiṭhi lagāi* ।
manau akāsa agastiyā, ekai kalī lakhāi ॥

What her messenger said to remind her of her promise to meet him near the agastya tree

Feast your eyes
dear girl,
on the new moon
which in the sky
is captivating
as a lone blossom
on the *agastya* tree.*

349. *sovat sapanai syāmaghana, hilimili harat biyoga* ।
tabahīṁ ṭari kitahūṁ gaī, nīṁdahuṁ nīṁdana joga ॥

What she said to her confidante

Asleep
I dreamt Kṛṣṇa clasped me
driving off
my parting's grief.
Just then
I know not where
this wretched sleep vanished,
leaving me
forlorn again!*

350. *ghāma gharīka nivāriyai, kalit lalit ali puñj* ।
jamunā tīra tamāla taru, militi mālatī kuñj ॥

What she told him

Wait for me, lover,
by the Yamunā bank
where *mālatī* creepers twine
round *tamāla* trees.
The sun is hot
but I won't be long,
and in that bower
away from prying eyes
where the black bees swarm
we'll make love.*

351. *sanu sūkyau bītyau banau, ūkhau laī ukhāri* ।
arī harī arahari ajauṁ, dhara dharihari hiya nāri ॥

What her confidante said

The fields of hemp,
cotton and sugarcane
are bare

but do not lose heart,
the green *arahar*
still stands
where you can meet
your lover.*

352. *phiri phiri bilakhī hvai lakhati, phiri phiri leti usās* ।
sāiṁ sira kaca seta lauṁ, bītyau cunati kapās ॥

What one of her companions said to another

As an old man
despondently
pulling out his grey hair,
she plucks the cotton
at the final pick
looking on in anguish
sighing mournfully
again and again;
recalling
those rapturous meetings
which will be no more
once the field is bare.*

353. *jadapi teja rauhāla bala, palakau lagī na bāra* ।
tau gvaiṁṛau ghar kau bhayo, paiṁṛau kos hajāra ॥

What he said to her

Though it took me
not a moment, love,
to reach you
on the swift horse;
as I neared the house
it seemed I had gone
a thousand *kos*!*

354. *harași na bolī lakhi lalana, nirakhi amila saṁg sāth* ।
aṁkhiyani hī maiṁ haṁsi dharyau, sīsa hiyaiṁ dhari hāth ॥

What one of her companions said to another

She was overjoyed
to find him
but could not speak her message
for he sat in the company
of strangers.
Her smiling glance
spoke her love,
and placing her hand
on her bosom
and then on her head
she disclosed to him
by signs alone
the rendezvous.*

355. *gopa athāina taiṁ uṭhe, goraj chāī gail* ।
cali bali ati abhisāra kī, kharī saṁjhaukaiṁ sail ॥

What her confidante told her

The cowherds have left
the village assembly
the dust raised by
cows returning
fills the pathways;
I beseech you, dear girl,
go now to meet your lover
for dusk is the time for
love-making.

356. *uyau sarada rākī sasī, karati na kyauṁ cit ceta* ।
manau madana chitipāla kau, chāṁhagīra chabi deta ॥

What her messenger said to her

Aświn's full moon
is up
as Kāma's royal canopy
scattering brilliance
on earth.
It should remind you
dear girl,
of a promise.*

357. *galī aṁdherī sāṁkarī, bhau bhaṭabherau āni* ।
pare pichāne parasapara, doū parasi pichāni ॥

What one of her companions said to another

They chanced upon each other
in the narrow lane;
though 'twas too dark to see
she could know
it was her lover
by his very touch
as she brushed against him.

358. *kahi paṭhaī mana bhavatī, piya āvana kī bāt* ।
phūlī āṁgana maiṁ phirai, āṁga na āṁgi samāt ॥

What one of her companions said to another

Learning of her lover's homecoming
she walks about her courtyard
thrilled,
her breasts
so swollen with pleasure
that her bodice
can't contain them!

359. *arī kharī saṭapaṭa parī, bidhu ādhaiṁ maga heri* ।
saṅg lagaiṁ madhupana laī, bhāgana galī aṁdheri ॥

What she said to her confidante

Back from meeting my lover
on a dark night
I was unnerved
to see the moon come out
when I was only halfway:
but by my good fortune, friend,
drawn by my body's fragrance
black bees
so swarmed around me
as I went along
that I remained hid
from prying eyes!

360. *nāci acānak hīṁ uṭhe, bina pāvasa bana mora* ।
jānati hauṁ naṁdit karī, ihi disi naṁdakisora ॥

What her companion said to her

The peacocks are dancing gleefully
even though the rainy season
is not here:
friend, it seems
your lover, Kṛṣṇa,
is coming to end your separation
and they're mistaking him
for a dark cloud!

361. *pāvasa nisi aṁdhiyāra maiṁ, rahyau bheda nahiṁ āna* ।
rāti dyaus jānī parat, lakhi cakaī cakavāna ॥

What her companion said to her

'Tis the rainy season
when the blanket of thick clouds

lends the day night's darkness
so that deceived
the ruddy goose
calls to his mate.
No one can see you now
go with an easy mind, dear girl,
to meet your lover.*

362. *rahī paija kīnī ju maiṁ, dīnī tumaiṁ milāi* ।
rākhahu campakamāla lauṁ, lāl hiyaiṁ lapaṭāi ॥

What her messenger said to him

I swore I'd unite you
to this precious girl and
I've redeemed my promise.
Now keep her
twined to your bosom
as you would
a *campā* garland.*

363. *ur līne ati caṭapaṭī, suni muralī dhuni dhāi* ।
hauṁ hulasī nikasī su tau, gau hula sī hiya lāi ॥

What she said to her confidante

The moment I heard
the sound of his pipe
I joyfully rushed
to the rendezvous
my heart yearning
for love:
but he had gone
leaving me agonized
as though pierced
by a lance.

364. *bichuraiṁ jiye sakoca ihiṁ, bolat banat na bain* ।
doū dauri lage hiyaim, kiye lajauṁhaiṁ nain ॥

What one of her companions said to another

Embarrassed
at being still alive
even though they had avowed
separation would kill them,
they spoke not a word
but with downcast eyes
rushed into each other's arms.

365. *kiyau sayānī sakhina sauṁ, nahiṁ sayāna yaha bhūl* ।
durai durāī phūl lauṁ, kyauṁ piya āgama phūl ॥

What her companion said to her

Smart girl,
you're mistaken
if you think you can hide
from your shrewd companions
your joy at his homecoming,
for it suffuses your face
as perfume
in a full-blown flower.

366. *rukyau sāṁkare kuñja maga, karat jhāṁjhi jhukarāt* ।
maṅd maṅd mārut turaṅg, khūṁdita āvat jāt ॥

What she told her confidante when she did not find her lover at the rendezvous

Even the gentle breeze
seems to lash at me, friend,
like a wayward horse
which scampers along

a narrow garden path
crushing the flowers.

367. *uṭhi ṭhaka ṭhaka yetau kahā, pāvasa kaiṁ abhisāra* ।
jāni paraigī dekhiyauṁ, dāmini ghana aṁdhiyāra ॥

What his messenger told her

Hasten dear girl,
fear not,
the rains are here
and the gleam of your body
is so like a flash of lightning
in the dark clouds,
that no busybody'll
notice you!

SEPARATION

368. *neha na nainanu kauṁ kachū, upajī baṛī balāi* ı
nīra bhare nita prati rahaiṁ, taū na pyāsa bujhāi ıı

What she said to her confidante

This is not love;
it seems my eyes are plagued
by some vexatious malady
so that my tears flow
perennially:
even then
they do not relieve
the thirst of my longing.

369. *lal tihāre viraha kī, agani anūpa apāra* ı
sarasai barasaiṁ nīrahuṁ, jharahūṁ miṭai na jhāra ıı

What her messenger told him

How strange is
the never-dying fire
of her parting
which all her tears
cannot put out.
Even the hot wind
increases her agony
instead of soothing her.

370. *yākaiṁ ur aurai kachū, lagī virah kī lāi* ।
pajaraīnīra gulaba kaiṁ, priya kī bāt bujhāi ॥

What one of her companions said to another

Wonderful are the flames
of her separation;
they rise more
when sprinkled with rosewater,
and die out
with the gust-shaped talks
about her lover!*

371. *homati sukha kari kāmanā, tumahiṁ milan kī lāl* ।
jvālāmukhī sī jarati lakhi, lagani agani kī jvāl ॥

What her confidante said to him

You should see, dear lad,
how the flames of love's fire
consume her.
Longing for you alone
she surrenders all her pleasures
as oblations made in a sacrifice,
and like an erupting volcano
smoulders
with the grief of your parting.

372. *marī ḍarī ki tarī bithā, khari kahā cali cāhi* ।
rahī karāhi ati, karāhi ab muṁha āhi na āhi ॥

What one of her companions said to another

Why do you delay friend?
Come and see
if that poor girl is dead,
or has she got over
the grief of her separation;
for she was moaning incessantly till now

but now her moans
have ceased.

373. *kahā bhayau jau bīchure, mo mana to mana sāth* ।
uṛī jāhu kita hūṁ taū, guṛī uṛāyaka hāth ॥

What he wrote in his letter to her

What if we are apart
dear girl?
You are ever in my thoughts
as wherever a kite may fly
the string always remains
in the flier's hands.*

374. *kagad par likhat na banai, kahat saṁdesu lajāta* ।
kahihai saba terau hiyo, mere hiya kī bāta ॥

Her message to him

My tears of grief
will not let me write
what I feel
and I am too shy
to speak out my love;
but your heart knows
my heart's secret
and that will reveal
all I'd like to say.

375. *jab jab vai sudhi kījiyai tabai sabai sudhi jāṁhi* ।
āṁkhina āṁkhi lagī rahaiṁ, ākhaiṁ lāgati nāṁhi ॥

What she said to her confidante

The memory of my absent lover
makes me swoon with grief
dear friend;
his charming image

is so much in my eyes
that sleep eludes them.

376. *kauna sunai kāsauṁ kahauṁ, surati bisārī nāha* ।
badābadī jiya leta haiṁ, ye badarā badarāha ॥

What she said to her confidante

To whom shall I tell my sorrow now
when even my lover
has forsaken me?
These malicious clouds
hovering overhead
thunder out their rancour
and agonize me
all the more.

377. *maiṁ ho jānyau loinana, jurat bāṛhi hai joti* ।
ko ho jānata dīṭhi kauṁ, dīthi karakaṭī hoti ॥

What he said to his friend

I had thought
when I gazed into her eyes
my eyes would gain brilliance;
but friend, it seems
they have instead
become afflicted
as though by a mote.

378. *basi sakoca dasabadan bas, sāṁcu dikhāvat bāla* ।
siya jyoṁ sodhati tiya tanahiṁ, lagani agani kī jvāla ॥

What her companion said

Bashfulness,
like the ten-headed Rāvaṇa
had deterred her
from showing her love;

but now, dear lad,
it is made manifest
by the purifying fire
of separation.*

379. *mohū saum̐ taji mohu dṛga, cale lāgi uhi gail* ।
chinaka chāi chabi gur-ḍarī, chale chabīlaim̐ chail ॥

What she said to her confidante

As one who lures
a child with a lump of molasses,
that handsome lad
beguiled me
with just a glimpse
and then
went away.
Ever since
my eyes no more befriend me,
for they too
remain with him.*

380. *aurai bhām̐ti bhaye ab ye, causara cam̐dana cam̐da* ।
pati bina ati pārat vipati, mārat mārut mam̐da ॥

What she said to her confidante

Contrary to their nature
my four-stringed garland
moonbeams and sandalwood paste
afflict me greatly
ever since he went.
Friend,
even the gentle soothing breeze
seems to stifle me!*

381. *dekhat vurai kapūr laurh, upai jāi jina lāl* ।
china china jāti pari kharī, chīna chabīlī bāla ॥

What her companion told him

Ever since you've gone
that lovely girl
grows thinner each moment,
like camphor
vapourizing.
Go to her soon, lad,
lest she withers away
and dies.

382. *haṁsi utāri ur taiṁ daī, tum ju tihi dinā lāl* ।
rākhati prāna kapūr lauṁ, vahai cihuṭinī māla ॥

What her companion said

The *ghuṁghacī* garland
you took off your bosom and
in jest placed
round her neck,
has saved her life, dear lad,
or else
as camphor evaporating,
her soul
would have departed.*

383. *naiṁka na jhursī biraha-jhar, neha latā kumhlāi* ।
china china hoti harī harī, kharī jhāhalati jāi ॥

What her messenger told him

The creeper of her love
does not sear and wither at all
with the flames
of her separation,
rather it turns

each moment greener
and more luxuriant.*

384. *kahā kahaum̐ vākī dasā, piya prānana ke īsa* ı
biraha jvāla jaribo lakhaim̐, maribau bhaī asīsa ॥

What her companion said to her lover, Kṛṣṇa

How should I tell you
her condition
O lord of her life,
Kṛṣṇa;
the blaze of her parting
now burns her so grievously that
death
would be a blessing.*

385. *naim̐ku na jānī parati yaum̐, paryau birāha tana chāma* ı
uṭhati diyaim̐ laum̐ nām̐di hari, liyaim̐ tihārom̐ nāma ॥

What her companion said

Parting's grief
has made the poor girl
almost a skeleton;
but when she hears your name
Kṛṣṇa,
she rallies somewhat
as a lamp's flame
flaring up once
before it dies.

386. *hari hari bari bari uṭhati hai, kari kari thakī upāi* ı
vākau juru bali baid jau, to rasa jāi tu jāi ॥

What her companion said to him

Raving suddenly
she mumbles 'Hari! Hari!'

I have tried all remedies
but in vain.
I beseech you
by my oath,
hasten, dear lad,
for only the elixir
of your love
can cure the fever
of her parting.*

387. *yaha binasata naga rākhikai, jagat bařau jasa lehu ।*
jarī visam jura jyāiye, āi sudarasana dehu ॥

What her companion wrote to him

Do not let this precious girl
of gem-like loveliness
die
of the burning fever
of separation.
If you hasten, lad,
you may save her
even now
by your life-giving presence
and earn
everybody's esteem.*

388. *nit sañsau hañsau bacat, manau su ihiṁ anumāna ।*
biraha agini lapaṭani sakata, jhapaṭi na mīcu sicāna ॥

What her companion said to him

Her parting's grief
is like a preying hawk
constantly sweeping down
to stifle
her feeble swan-like life-breath.
She's saved each time

only because
he can't get through
the wall-like flames
of her separation!

389. *thākī jatan aneka kari, naiṁku na chāṁrati gail* ǀ
karī kharī dubarī su lagi, terī cāha curail ǁ

What her companion said to him

She wastes away
pining for you
as though seized by a witch.
I'm tired out
trying and trying,
yet the evil spell
will not for a moment
leave her.

390. *kari viraha aisī taū, gail na chāṁrata nīcu* ǀ
dīnaiṁ hūṁ casamā cakhanu, cahai lahai na mīcu ǁ

What her companion told him

She has turned so frail
that Death
who's after her
can't spot her
even with glasses!
Despite this
villainous Separation
keeps pursuing her.

391. *jo vāke tana kī dasā, dekhyau cāhat āp* ǀ
tau bali naiku bilokiyai, cali acakāṁ cupacāp ǁ

What her confidante said

If you wish to know

for yourself, precious lad,
what parting has made of her;
come on the quiet
I entreat you
and see her unawares.*

392. *pūs māsa suni sakhina maiṁ, sāīṁ calat savāra* ।
laiṁ kar bīna prabīna tiya, ṛāgyau rāga malāra ॥

What one of her companions said to another

Learning from her friends
in the *Pūs* month
her lover
was to go abroad
next morning,
that girl
expert on the *vīṇā*
played the *malhāra* tune
causing such a downpour
that he couldn't go!*

393. *marana bhalau baru biraha taiṁ, yaha nihacaya kari joi* ।
marana miṭai dukh eka kau, biraha duhūṁ dukh hoi ॥

What one of her companions said to another

Know for sure
death's better for her
than the distressing sorrow
of her separation.
If she dies
at least grief will be hers no longer,
or else
it will keep tormenting
both her and her lover.*

394. *ko jānai hvai hai kahā, jaga upajī atī āgi* ।
mana lāgai nainana lagai, calai na maga laga lāgi ॥

What she said to her companion

Who can say
what'll happen
when the fire of separation
burns so strangely.
It's ignited
by the clash of soft eyes
but flares up
in the heart!
I caution you, dear friend,
not to go
anywhere near it.*

395. *malin deha veī basan, malin biraha kaiṁ rūpa* ।
piya āgama aurai baṛhī, ānan op anūpa ॥

What one of her companions said to another

Listless with the grief
of separation
her body was lustreless
her clothes unkempt;
but when she heard her lover was coming
her face glowed
with surpassing splendour.

396. *raṁgarātī rātaiṁ hiyaiṁ, priyatama likhī banāi* ।
pātī kātī biraha kī, chātī rahī lagāi ॥

What one of her companions said to another

She ardently clasped
to her bosom
the letter
full of sweet endearments

he fondly sent
to console her;
looking upon it as a sword
to slay
the sorrow of her separation.

397. *tajata aṭhān na haṭh paryau, saṭhmati āṭhau jāma* ।
bhayau bāma vā bāma kauṁ, rahai kāma bekāma ॥

What her messenger told him

Kāma, the villain,
does not relent one bit,
he obstinately persists
in tormenting that parted girl
day and night.*

398. *calat calat lauṁ lai calai, sab sukh saṅg lagāi* ।
grīṣma bāsar sisir-nisi, pyau mo pās basāi ॥

What she said to her companion

Though he's still here
the thought of his going
has taken away my joys.
With his departure
my lover will leave me
oppressive days
recalling
summer's ṣultriness
and weary wintry nights.

399. *bikasit navamallī kusum, nikasit parimal pāi* ।
parasi pajārati birahi hiya, barasi rahe kī bāi ॥

What she said to her companion

When in the rains
the cool breeze

laden with the perfume
of new jasmine blossoms
brushes my bosom,
it heightens the grief
of my separation
and burns me
all the more.

400. *ajauṁ na āye sahaj raṅg, biraha-dūbare gāt* ।
abahīṁ kahā calāiyati, lalan calan kī bāt ॥

What her companion said to him

Dear lad,
why are you talking
from now
of leaving again,
when even today
her body,
emaciated by the grief of parting
has not regained
its former loveliness?*

401. *auṁdhāī sīsī su lakhi, biraha barani bilalāt* ।
bica hī sūkhi gulāba gau, chiṭau chuī na gāt ॥

What her companion said to him

Hearing her moan
with the burning pain
of parting
I emptied a whole bottle
of rosewater on her;
but the flames of his separation
vapourized it in mid-air
and not a drop
fell on her!

402. *mṛganainī dṛga kī pharak, ur uchaha tana phūl* ।
binahīṁ piya āgama umagi, palaṭan lagī dukūl ॥

What one of her companions said to another

There was no news
of his coming
yet her longing made
her bosom heave
her left eyelid flicker;
and hopefully
that gazelle-eyed girl
changed her dress
all ready to
receive him!*

403. *rahe baroṭhe maiṁ milat, piya prānana ke īsu* ।
āvat āvat kī bhaī, bidhi kī gharī gharī su ॥

What one of her companions said to another

Returning from abroad
when her lover stopped awhile
in the vestibule
to greet his elders
and near friends,
those few minutes
seemed to that expectant girl
as long as
Brahmā's epoch!*

404. *hauṁ hīṁ baurī biraha basa, kai baurī saba gāuṁ* ।
kahā jāni ye kahat haiṁ, sasihiṁ sītakara nāuṁ ॥

What she said to her companion

Either the grief of my parting
has deranged my mind
or the village people

have turned crazy,
or else
why should they call the moonbeams cool
when they scorch me so?*

405. *kaurā ām̐su būm̐d, kasi sām̐kara barunī sajal* ।
kīne badan nimūm̐d, dṛga-malaṅga ḍāre rahat ॥

What her companion said to him

She sits tight-lipped
silently grieving for you, lover,
like a *malaṅga* fakir
in quiet meditation.
Her moist eyelids
are as iron chains
hackling his limbs
and the tear-drops
imprisoned
are like his string
of cowries.*

406. *jonha nahīm̐ yaha tama vahai, kiye ju jagat niketa* ।
hot udai sasi ke bhayau, mānahu sasihari ṣeta ॥

What she said to her companion

This is not moonlight friend,
it seems
the eternal darkness
enveloping the earth
has turned yellow with fear
on seeing the moon arise!

407. *jihiṁ nidāgh dupahara rahai, bhaī māha kī rāti* ।
so usīr kī rāvaṭī, kharī āvaṭī jāti ॥

What her messenger told him

So great is the fire
of her separation
that even the *khas* curtains
which give the coolness of *Māgh* nights
to hot summer noons,
seem to burn her!*

408. *sīraiṁ jatanani sisir ritu, sahi birahini-tana-tāpa* ।
basibe kauṁ grīsam dinana, paryau parosina pāpa ॥

What her messenger told him

In winter
by using cooling devices
her neighbours
somehow saved themselves
from being scorched
by the flames of separation
which arose from her;
but in summer
their sizzling heat
became unbearable!*

409. *ganatī ganibe taiṁ rahe, chat hūṁ achat samāna* ।
ab patrā tithi aum lauṁ, pare rahau tana prāna ॥

What she said to her companion

The grief of separation
has so exhausted me friend,
that though living
I'm as good as dead,
as the *avam* lunar day

which remains in the almanac
but is of no consequence.*

410. *jāti marī bichurī gharī, jala safarī kī rīti* ।
china china hoti kharī kharī, arī jarī yaha prīti ॥

What she said to her confidante

This accursed parting
so torments me, friend,
that each moment
I writhe with pain
as a fish without water.
Even then my wretched infatuation
keeps mounting
more and more!

411. *piya prānan kī pāharū, karat jatan ati āp* ।
jākī dusaha dasā paryau, sautinhūṁ santāp ॥

What one of her companions said to another

Her co-wives know
that if she dies
of the grief of parting
their husband too can't live,
so distressed by her condition
they themselves try all ways
to save her.

412. *āṙe dai āle basan, jāṙehūṁ kī rāti* ।
sāhasa kakai saneha bas, sakhī sabai ḍhiga jāti ॥

What her messenger said to him

So fiercely does she burn
with the flames of separation
that even on winter nights
her fond companions

have to take courage to go near her,
and that too
by holding a wet cloth before them
to shield them from the scorching heat!

413. *saba aṅga kari rākhī sughara, nāik neha sikhāi* ।
rasajut leti anaṁta gati, putarī pāturarāi ॥

What one of her companions said to another

The pupils of her eyes
moving restlessly
as she oft glances
on the path of his coming,
are like accomplished dancers
trained by his love
skilfully adopting
many poses.

414. *sunat pathik muṁha māha nisi, calati luvaiṁ uhiṁ gāma* ।
bina bujhe binahī kahe, jiyat bicarī bāma ॥

What one of her companions said to another

When a wayfarer
come from his village said
'Even in the chilly *Māgh* nights
the scorching *lū* winds blow there',
he guessed without being told
that his wife
though burning with the grief of parting
was still alive.*

415. *tiya nija hiya ju lagī calat, piya nakh rekh khaṁroṭ* ।
sūkhan deti na sarasaī, khoṁṭi khoṁṭi khat khoṁṭ ॥

What one of her companions said to another

She keeps removing the scales

from the nail scratches
made by her lover on her breasts
when he ardently hugged her
before going abroad,
and keeps them fresh
to treasure in her mind
the memory of his embrace.

416. *māra su māra karī kharī, marī marihi na māri* ।
sīṁci gulāba gharī gharī, arī barihi na bāri ॥

What she said to her companion

Kāma has greatly vexed me
leaving me almost dead,
pray do not increase my agony
by sprinkling rosewater on me
for it only causes
the fire of separation
to flare up all the more!

417. *it āvat caḷi jāt ut, calī chasātak hāth* ।
caṁhī hiṁdoraiṁ sī rahai, lagī usāsanu ṣath ॥

What one of her companions said to another

She has turned so frail
with the grief of her separation
that her deep sighs
throw her back and forth
six or seven cubits
as though she was going
to and fro
on a swing!

418. *tar jharasī ūpar garī, kajjal jala chirakāi* ।
piya pātī binahīṁ likhī bāṁcī biraha balāi ॥

What one of her companions said to another

When he got her letter
charredbeneath
by her burning fingers
and smudged with tears
from her collyrium-filled eyes
he could know the grief
of her separation
even though she wrote
not a word about it.

419. *biraha sukhāī deha, neha kiyau ati ḍahaḍaho* ।
jaise barase meha, jarai javaso jyau jamai ॥

What her companion said to him

As the rain
shrivels up the stems
of the *jawāsa* plant
but makes its roots firm,
her parting's grief
has emaciated her body
but made strong her love.*

420. *lalana calana suni palana maiṁ, aṁsuvā jhalake āi* ।
bhaī lakhāi na sakhina hūṁ, jhūṭhaihūṁ jamuhāi ॥

What one of her companions said to another

When she heard
her lover was going abroad
tears welled in her eyes,
but not wishing to reveal
to her friends
her love for him

she forced a yawn,
pretending it was that
which had brought them on!

421. *tacyau āṁca ab biraha kī, rahyau prema rasa bhīji* ।
nainan kaiṁ maga jala bahai, hiyau pasīji pasīji ॥

What her companion said

Those are not tears
flowing from her eyes, dear lad,
to me it seems
separation's fire
has so heated up
her love-juice soaked heart
that it's oozing out
drop by drop!

422. *rahihaiṁ cancala prāna ye, kahi kaun kī agoṭ* ।
lalan calan kī cit dharī, kala na palan kī oṭ ॥

What she said to her companion

When I can't bear
to part from him
even for a moment,
what's there to keep me alive
now that my lover
has decided to go abroad?

423. *rahyo aiṁci aṅta na lahyau, avadhi dusāsana bīru* ।
ālī bāṛhat biraha jyauṁ, pancālī ko cīru ॥

What she said to her companion

As the hour of his return nears
my parting's grief grows more;
dear friend,
it seems to be endless

as Draupadī's sari
pulled by Duhaśāsana.*

424. *pāvaka jhara ta meha jhara, dāhaka dusaha bisekhi* ।
dahai deha vākauṁ parasi, yāhi dṛgana hī dekhi ॥

What she said to her companion

Without my lover, friend,
this pouring rain
torments me more
than flames of fire.
They burn only by their touch
but this
by its mere sight!

425. *na jak dharat hari hiya dharat, nājuk kamalā bāla* ।
bhajat bhār bhayabhīt hvai, ghana caṅdana banamāla ॥

What Kṛṣṇa's messenger said to her

Dear girl
delicate as Lakṣmi,
Kṛṣṇa has stopped
smearing his bosom
with camphor-and-sandal paste
fearing it will be a burden
to your tender image
enshrined in his heart!
Go to him
and remove
the grief of his parting.

426. *lalan calan suni cup̐a rahī, boḷī āpu na īṭhi* ।
gāṙhe gahi rākhyauṁ garau, manau galagalī ḍīṭhi ॥

What one of her companions said to another

Hearing her lover

was going abroad
she became speechless,
as though throttled
by her tearful eyes
her throat
had lost its voice!

427. *biraha-bithā jala parasa bina, basiyat mo hiya-tāl* ।
kachu jānat jalathambha-bidhi, durajodhana lauṁ lāl ॥

What she wrote in her letter to him

Though enshrined in my heart, lover,
you're untouched
by the grief
of my separation,
as Duryodhana
who could stay under water
and yet remain unharmed.*

428. *syauṁ bijurī mana meha, āi ihāṁ birahā dhare* ।
āṭhaṁ jāma acheha, dṛga ju barat barasat rahat ॥

What she said to her confidante

Day and night
my eyes keep burning
and at the same time
shedding tears,
it seems as though
parting has brought them
lightning as well as rain.*

429. *biraha bipat dina paratạhīṁ, taje sukhana saba aṅga* ।
rahi abalauṃ ab dukhau bhaye, calācalī jiya-saṅga ॥

What she wrote in her letter

When you went, lover,

all pleasures forsook my limbs,
and now this separation
has become so grievous
that my soul too is preparing
to bid adieu.

430. *chayau neha kāgad hiyaiṁ, bhaī lakhāi na ṭāṁka* ।
biraha tacaiṁ ugharayau su ab, seṁhuṛa kaiso āṁka ॥

What one of her companions said to another

The fire of separation
has revealed the love
hid in her heart
as letters written
with invisible ink
standing out
when parched by heat.*

431. *bana-bātan pik-baṭaparā, lakhi birahani mat main* ।
kuhū kuhū kahi kahi uṭhaiṁ, kari kari rāte nain ॥

What she said to her lover about to go on a voyage

As a wayfarer
done to death
on a forest pathway,
I'll be slain
by the plaintive calls
of the cuckoo,
if leaving me
you go abroad.

432. *ghana gherā chuṭi gau harasi, calī cahūṁ disi rāha* ।
kiyau sucainau āi jaga, sarada-sūra naranāha ॥

What her companion said to her

Like bandits fleeing

a dreaded ruler's realm
the encircling clouds have been scattered
by King Autumn;
wayfarers can once again
move happily on pathways:
he'll come any moment now
dear girl,
to end your separation.

433. *nāhina ye pāvak prabal, luvaiṁ calaiṁ cahuṁ pās* ।
manahu biraha basant kaiṁ, grīṣam let usās ॥

What the parted girl's companion said

These gusts of wind
searing as tongues of fire
are not the *lū*, dear girl,
it seems they are
the sighs of Summer
sorrowing on being separated
from Spring his beloved!*

434. *hiya aurai sī hvai gaī, ṭarī audhi kai nāma* ।
dūjaiṁ kai ḍārī kharī, baurī bauraiṁ āma ॥

What one of her companions said to another

She was dismayed to learn
that her lover's arrival
had been put off,
and the grief of her separation
became so unbearable
that even the sight
of the new mango blossoms
maddened her.

435. *pahirati hīṁ goraiṁ garaiṁ, yauṁ daurī duti lāl* ।
manau parasi pulakit bhaī, maulasirī kī māla ॥

What her companion told him

When she put the *maulaśirī* garland
sent by you, dear lad,
round her neck
it seemed to her
you yourself
had clasped her!
and thrilling with joy
her pale limbs
shone with a new splendour.*

436. *kar ke mīre kusuma lauṁ, gaī biraha kumhilāi* ।
sadā samīpini sakhina hūṁ, nīṭhi pichānī jāi ॥

What one of her companions said to another

Parting's grief
has made her pale
as a crushed flower
so that even her companions
who are with her all the time
find it hard
to recognize her!

437. *bhau yaha aisoī samau, jahāṁ sukhad dukh det* ।
caitra cāṁda kī cāṁdanī, ḍārati kiye aceta ॥

What she said to her companion

So grievous is this parting
that things which should delight
torment me;
friend,
even the serene moonlight

of *Caitra*
agitates me!*

438. *lope kope indra laurṁ, rope pralaya akāla* ।
giridhārī rākhe sabai, go gopī gopāla ॥

What Rādhā's messenger said to Kṛṣṇa

Grieved by your separation
Rādhā, who adores you,
is shedding streams of tears
which threaten to cause
the world's dissolution
before its time!
O Kṛṣṇa,
even as you lifted a hill
to protect the cowherds
from Indra's wrath,
go to her now
and caressing her expansive breasts,
save the world.*

439. *hyāṁ taiṁ hvāṁ hvāṁ taiṁ ihāṁ, naiko dharat na dhīra* ।
nisi dina ḍāṛhī sī phirati, bāṛhī gāṛhī pīra ॥

What her companion told him

Burning constantly
with the grief of separation
she restlessly wanders
back and forth
and does not know
a moment's rest.

440. *biraha bikal bina hī likhī, pātī daī paṭhāi* ।
aṅk bihūnīyau sucita, sūnaiṁ bāṁcati jāi ॥

What one of her companions said to another

The grief of separation
so tormented her
that she could not write a word
and sent him a blank sheet!
Even that
he pretends to read attentively
when he's by himself!

441. *araiṁ parai na karai hiyau, kharai jaraiṁ par jāra* ।
lāvati ghori gulāba sauṁ, bhalai milai ghanasāra ॥

What she said to her companion

Do not persist
in applying this unguent
of sandalwood paste
camphor
and rosewater
on my bosom
burning with separation's grief,
for it makes it burn
all the more!

442. *maiṁ lai dayau layau su kara, chuata chanaki gau nīra* ।
lāl tiharau aragajā, ur hvai lagyau abīra ॥

What her companion told him

So greatly does she burn
with the grief of separation, dear lad,
that the moment I placed
the perfume you sent
in her hands
it sizzled away,

and by the time
she applied it to her bosom
it had turned into
useless powder!*

443. *kahe ju bacana biyoginī, biraha bikal bilalāi* ।
kiye na ko aṁsuvā sahit, suvā su bola sunāi ॥

What one of her companions said to another

Her tame parrot had learnt
what she had said
in the deep anguish of her separation,
and when he repeats
those pathetic words
whose eyes
can remain dry?*

444. *dhuravā hohiṁ na ali uṭhai, dhuvāṁa dharani cahuṁ koda* ।
jārata āvat jagat kauṁ, pāvasa prathama payoda ॥

What the parted girl said to her confidante

This is not drizzle, friend,
but smoke billowing all round;
to me it seems
the first clouds of the rains come
scorching the earth
as they move along!

445. *pajarau āgi biyoga kī, bahyau bilocana nīra* ।
āṭhauṁ jāma diyau rahai, uṛyau usās samīra ॥

What her messenger told him

She's scorched
in separation's fire
and drenched by tears;
her heart seems to float away

dear lad,
on her endless sighs
as a kite
meandering.*

446. *veī cirajīvī amar, nidharaka phirau kahāi* ।
china bichure jinakī na yahi, pāvasa āyu sirāi ॥

What she said to her lover to persuade him not to go abroad

Only he has long life
assuredly,
who is not parted
from his beloved
even for a moment
in this ravishing rainy season.*

447. *maribai kau sāhasa kakaiṁ, barhaiṁ biraha kī pīra* ।
daurati hvai samuhe sasī, sarasija surabhi samīra ॥

What her companion told him

The moon
the lotus flower and
the perfumed breeze
seem to scorch her,
and she rushes after them
so that she may be burnt to death
and end
the unbearable anguish
of her separation.

448. *hita kari tum paṭhayau lagaiṁ, vā bijanā kī bāi* ।
ṭalī tapati tana kī taū, calī pasīnā nhāi ॥

What her messenger told him

The fan which you sent her
as a gift of love

fanned away the heat
from her body
burning with the grief of separation,
but so thrilled her
with your fond remembrance
that she was bathed with sweat!

449. *sakai satāya na tamu biraha, nisi dina sarasa saneha* ।
rahai uhī lāgī dṛgana, dīpasikhā sī deha ॥

What he told her messenger

The darkness of separation
is powerless to cause me gloom,
for day and night
her charming adorable image
shining like the flame of a lamp
is treasured in my memory.

450. *biraha jarī lakhi jīganani, kahyau na ḍahi kai bāra* ।
arī jāhi bhaji bhītarī, barasat āj aṁgāra ॥

What one of her companions said to another

Seeing the glow-worms blink
how many times
has that girl
burning with the anguish of separation
not said to me,
'Hasten inside, friend,
the sky is raining embers!'

451. *jo tab hot dikhādikhī, bhaī amī ik āṁk* ।
lagai tirīchī ḍīṭhi ab, hvai bīchī ko dāṁk ॥

What the parted girl said to her companion

Those sidelong glances
we exchanged

when love began
were assuredly
sweet as nectar,
but now that he's gone
their memory
has a scorpion's sting.

452. *cāha bharīṁ ati rasa bharīṁ, biraha bharīṁ saba bāt* ।
kori saṁdese duhuna ke, cale pauri lauṁ jāt ॥

What one of her companions said to another

By the time they reached
the outer door of the house
they had exchanged
a million messages,
which spoke their ardour
their tender yearnings and
the poignant grief
of their parting.*

453. *mili cali cali mili mili mili calat, aṁganā athayau bhān* ।
bhayau muhūrat bhor kau, paurihiṁ pratham milān ॥

What one of her companions said to another

The auspicious time
for him to go
was in the morning,
but he could not tear himself
from his beloved,
and he stopped
to bid her farewell
again and again
till the day passed
ere he reached his doorstep!

454. *kara lai cūmi caṁhāi sir, ur lagāi bhuj bheṭi* ।
lahi pātī piya kī lakhati, bāṁcati dharati sameṭi ॥

What one of her companions said to another

Beside herself with joy
to get her husband's letter
she read it
and on an impulse
pressed it to her bosom
and hugged it lovingly.
She often glances at it ardently
and scans it again and again
before she carefully
keeps it away.

455. *palani pragaṭi baruninī baṁhi, nahiṁ kapol ṭhaharāt* ।
aṁsuvā pari chatiyā chinaka, chanachanāi chipi jāt ॥

What her messenger told him

The fire of separation
blazes so fiercely in her
that the tears
which gather in her eyes,
and overflowing
roll past her burning cheeks,
fall on her scalding bosom
and sizzling
evaporate!

456. *phiri sudhi dai sudhi dyāī pyau, ihiṁ niradaī nirāsa* ।
naī naī bahuryau daī, daī usāsi usāsa ॥

What one of her companions said to another

This cruel sparrow-hawk
calls out *'pi! pi!'*
awaking in her

memories of her beloved
and making her sigh again
with grief.*

457. *koṭi jatan koū karau, tana kī tapana na jāi* ।
jauṁ lauṁ bhījai cīra lauṁ, rahe na pyau lapaṭāi ॥

What the parted girl said to her confidante

Even though I try
a million ways
the fire of separation's grief
will not go out
until my lover
hugs me close
as a wet garment
clinging to the body.

458. *dusaha biraha dārun dasā, rahai na aur upāi* ।
jāt jāt jyau rākhiyai, piya kau nāuṁ sunāi ॥

What one of her companions said to another

See the miserable state
to which
the unbearable grief of separation
has reduced her, friend.
The only way now
to save her from death
is to repeat to her
her lover's name.

459. *ab taji nāuṁ upaya kau, āyau pāvasa māsa* ।
khela na rahibau khema sauṁ, kema kusuma kī bāsa ॥

What his messenger said

She'll need no persuasion now, lad,
and come to you of herself
for the heart-stirring rains

are here
bringing with them
the voluptuous fragrance
of the *kadamba* flower.*

460. *saghan kuñj chāyā sukhad, sītal surabhi samīra* ।
manu hvai jāt ajauṁ vahai, uhi jamunā ke tīra ॥

What one milkmaid said to another

When Kṛṣṇa's remembrance
takes me
to the lonely Yamunā bank
where we made love,
the pleasing shade
of the thick woods
and the gentle breeze
cool and fragrant
fills my heart
with yearning.*

461. *bāmā bhāmā kāminī, kahi bolau prānesa* ।
pyārī kahat khisāt nahiṁ, pābas calat bidesa ॥

What she said to her lover who was going abroad

You call me 'beloved'
while saying goodbye,
but if I had been your true love
you wouldn't be so heartless
as to leave me alone
in this exciting rainy season.
Your callousness
makes me feel
you rather take me to be
a vixen,
shrew,
or a wanton!

BEAUTY

462. *appane aṅga ke jānikai, jobana nṛpati prabīna* ।
stana mana nain nitamba kau, baṛau ijāfā kīna ॥

What her companion told him

King Adolescence
now rules that pliant girl
swelling out
her breasts and loins
enlarging her eyes and
filling her mind
with love's longing.

463. *ar teṁ ṭarat na bara pare, daī marak manu main* ।
hoṛīhoṛā baṛhi cale, citu caturāī nain ॥

What her companion said to him

Her glance's ardour and
her mind's longing
have bet on a race.
Spurred by Kāma
each is bent on
making the winning post!*

464. *aurai op kanīnikani, ganī ghani siratāja* ।
manī dhanī ke neha kī, banī chanī paṭa lāja ॥

What her companion said to her

Dear girl
of beauty nonpareil,
your glances

have now turned ardent;
and even though veiled
by your bashfulness
the pupils of your eyes,
glinting with a new light,
shine out as gems
proclaiming your love for him.

465. *sālati hai naṭasāla sī, kauṁhūṁ nikasati nāhiṁ* ।
manamatha nejā nok sī, khubhī khubhī mana māhiṁ ॥

What he said to her confidante

My girl's
clove-shaped ear ornament
has pierced my heart
like Kāma's arrowhead;
its memory pains me
as an embedded barb.*

466. *juvati jonha maiṁ mili gaī, naiṁka na hoti lakhāī* ।
sauṁdhe kaiṁ doraiṁ lagī, alī calī saṁga jāī ॥

What her companion said

Her bright radiance
was so like moonlight
that it was impossible to spot her;
her friend could keep up with her
only by the string
of her fragrance!*

467. *hauṁ rījhī lakhi rījhihau, chabihiṁ chabīle lāl* ।
sonajuhī sī hoti duti, milat mālatī māla ॥

What her messenger said to him

You will be spellbound
by her loveliness

even as I was, dear lad:
the radiance of her limbs
makes the white *mālatī* flowers
in her garland
glow golden
as the *sonajūhī*!

468. *joga jugati sikhae sabai, manau mahāmuni maina* ।
cāhat piya advaitatā, kānanu sevat nain ॥

What her companion said

As sages adept in meditation
go to the forest
to seek union with god,
so, instructed by Kāma
the great teacher,
her eyes
greedy for love,
stretch out to her ears
proclaiming
she is restless
to meet her lover.*

469. *jhinai paṭa maiṁ jhilamilī, jhalakati op apāra* ।
surataru kī manu sindhu maiṁ, lasati sapallava ḍāra ॥

What he said about her

Her dazzling splendour
shining through her flimsy dress
is breathtaking,
as a *kalpa* tree
reflected leaf and branch
in the waters
of the placid ocean.*

470. *ḍāre ṭhoṛī-gāṛa gahi, nain baṭohī māri* ।
cilaka cauṁdha meṁ rūpa ṭhag, hāṁsī phāṁsī ḍāri ॥

What he said to her companion

As a wayfarer
mistaking brilliant starlight for day
moves on;
and smothered by a thug's noose
is cast in a pit:
so her dazzling radiance
led me onwards
till
strangled with the noose of her smile
I lay
in the hollow of her chin's dimple!*

471. *to para barāuṁ urabasī, suni rādhikā sujāna* ।
tu mohana kaiṁ ur basī, hvai urabasī samāna ॥

What Rādhā's companion said

Gifted Rādha,
your beauty
puts Uravaśī's
into the shade.
You ever dwell
in Kṛṣṇa's heart
like a necklace of gold
dangling
between the breasts.*

472. *kuca-giri caṛhi ati thakit hvai, calī ḍīṭhi muṁha cāra* ।
phiri na ṭarī pariyai rahī, parī cibuka kī gāṛa ॥

What he said

Exhausted with climbing
her steep breasts,

my gaze yet moved on
craving to see
her face's ravishing beauty;
but in between
it tumbled
into the hollow of her chin
and there it remained stuck!

473. *lone mumhu ḍīṭhi na lagai, yaum kahi dīnau īṭhi* ।
dūnī hvai lāgana lagī, diyaim diṭhaunā dīṭhi ॥

What one of her companions said to another

The black mark
her friend put on her cheek
to guard her from the evil eye
heightened her charm so greatly
that men's gazes turned to her
all the more!*

474. *pāi mahāvara dena kaum, nāini baiṭhī āi* ।
phiri phiri jāni mahāvarī, eṛī mījata jāi ॥

What one of her companions said to another

Her heels were so rosy
that when the barber's wife
sat down to paint her feet
instead of squeezing
the lacquer-soaked cotton
she kept pressing her heels
again and again!*

475. *deha dulahiyā kī caṙhai, jyauṁ jyauṁ jobana joti* ।
tyauṁ tyauṁ lakhi sautyauṁ sabai, malin badan duti hoti ॥

What one of the companions of the newly-wed wife said to another

The more her youthful splendour
blossoms out
taking on a new lustre,
the paler turn
her jealous co-wives!*

476. *maṅgala biṅdu suraṅga, mukha sasi kesara āṙa guru* ।
ik nārī lahi saṅga, rasamaya kiya locana jagat ॥

What he said to her confidante

As Mars, Jupiter and the Moon
combine
to revive the parched earth
with life-giving rain,
her forehead marks
of red and yellow
make lovelier
her moonlike face
and relieve the thirst
of my eyes.*

477. *piya tiya sauṁ haṁsikai kahyau, lakhaiṁ diṭhaunā dīna* ।
caṅdramukhī mukhacaṅdu taiṁ, bhalau caṅda sama kīna ॥

What he said to her

Seeing her put on
the round black mark
to keep off the evil eye
he smiled and said
'Your moon-like face darling

now really looks
like the spotted moon!*

478. *kauṁhara-sī eṛīna kī, lālī dekhi subhāi* ।
pāi mahavara dei ko, āpa bhaī bepāi ॥

What one of her companions said to another

When the barber's wife
came to dye her heels
with the lacquer dye
she found their ruddiness
matching the red gourd;
perplexed
she stayed her hands,
not knowing what to do.*

479. *rasa siṁgāra mañjanu kiye, kañjanu bhañjanu dain* ।
añjanu rañjanu hūṁ binā, khañjanu gañjanu nain ॥

What her companion said

Though collyriumless
the coquettish eyes
of that girl
adept in the art of love-making
have put to shame
those of the *khañjana* bird;
even the lotus
pales before their loveliness!*

480. *baiṭhi rahī ati saghan bana, paiṭhi sadan mana māhiṁ* ।
dekhi dupaharī jeṭh kī, chāṁhauṁ cāhati chāṁhi ॥

So oppressive
is *Jeṭh's* midday sun
that even the Shade
seeks shelter under forest trees

and dare not venture beyond
the four walls of houses!*

481. *hā hā badan ughāri dṛga, suphal karaiṁ sab kou* ।
roja sarojana kaim parai, haṁsī sasī kī hou ॥

What her companion said

O! O! dear girl
unveil yourself
so that men may feast their eyes
upon your face
whose beauty
grieves the envious lilies
and puts the moon to shame!*

482. *sāyaka sama māyaka nayan, raṁge tribidha raṁga gāta* ।
jhakau bilakhi duri jāt jala, lakhi jalajāta lajāta ॥

What her messenger said to him

Mistaking
her crimson-streaked
coquettish eyes
for twilight
fishes regretfully hid
in the deep waters;
and, put to shame,
the water-lilies
closed up their petals!*

483. *bar jīte sar main ke, aise dekhe maiṁ na* ।
harinī ke naināna taiṁ, hari nīke ye nain ॥

What her companion told Kṛṣṇa

I never saw such eyes
with glances more piercing
than Kāma's arrows;

O Kṛṣṇa,
their loveliness
indeed surpasses
the eyes of a gazelle.*

484. *aṅga aṅga naga jagamagāta, dīpasikhā sī deha* ।
diyā baṛhāye hū rahai, baṛau ujārau geha ॥

What her companion said

All over
her flame-like body
gleam
the gems of her ornaments.
Their flashing brilliance
lights up her house
even after she puts out
the oil lamp!*

485. *chuṭi na sisutā kī jhalak, jhalakyau jobaṇa aṅga* ।
dīpati ḍeha duhūna mili, dipati tāfatā raṅga ॥

What her companion said

Ere childhood has left
youth sparkles in her
as though the flames
of the two had met.
Her body's lustre
glimmers now
as double-tinted silk.*

486. *patrā hīṁ tithi pāiyai, vā ghar kaiṁ cahuṁ pās* ।
nitaprati pūnyauīṁ rahai, ānana op ujās ॥

What her companion said

Around her house
the phases of the moon

can be known only
by the almanac;
for when the full moon
of her face is ever there
how can one know
when the moon rises?

487. *calan na pāvat nigam maga, jaga upajau ati trāsa* ।
kuca utaṅga giribara gahyau, mainā maina mavāsa ॥

What he said about her

As travellers shun
a hill-road
ravaged by a Mainā bandit;
those who glance on
her swelling breasts
where Kāma reigns,
abandon virtue.*

488. *gadarāne tana goraṭī aipana āṛa lilāra* ।
hūṭhyau dai iṭhalāi dṛga, karai gaṁvāri sumāra ॥

What he said

How captivating are
the banter
and the coquettish glances
of that fair rustic girl
in the bloom of youth,
who stands akimbo,
an oblique beauty mark
of rice and turmeric
adorning her brow!*

489. *sahaja sacikkana syāma ruci, suci sugandha sukumāra* ।
ganata na mana patha apatha lakhi, bithure suthare bāra ॥

What he said to his confidant

When she spreads out
her naturally glistening
smooth unsullied
fragrant black
tresses,
my mind remains
so entangled in them
that it cares not
for propriety.

490. *kesari kai sari kyauṁ sakai, campaka kitika anūpa* ।
gāt rūpa lakhi jāta duri, jātarūpa kau rūpa ॥

What her companion told him

Saffron can't equal
her loveliness
nor the *campā* flower
her splendour;
even the lustre of gold
pales before her!*

491. *makarākṛti gopāla kaiṁ, sohat kuṇḍala kāna* ।
manau dharyau hiya dhara samaru, ḍyauṛhī lasat nisāna ॥

What her companion said to her

Kṛṣṇa's
fish-shaped ornament
is resplendent in his ears
as though Kāma,
winning over his heart,
had planted his standard on the
entranceway!*

492. *khauri panica bhṛkuṭi dhanuṣa, badhika samara taji kāni* ।
hanata taruna mṛga tilak sara, suraka bhāli bhari tāni ॥

What he said to her confidante

Hereyebrows
are as a bow,
her forehead's auspicious mark
its bowstring,
and the ornamental line
extending to her nose's bridge
the shaft's pointed barb
with which Kāma,
bow full-stretched
pierces the hearts
of her youthful admirers,
as a huntsman
shooting gazelles.*

493. *nīkau lasata lilāra par, ṭīkau jaṭil jarāi* ।
chabihiṁ baṛhāvata ravi manau, sasi maṇḍala maiṁ āi ॥

What her companion said

The gem-studded pendant
on her forehead
flashes
as though the sun
had entered the moon's orbit
to heighten its splendour.
And wonderfully
her moon-like face
does not pale
in the sun-like radiance
but rather shines
all the more!*

494. *lasata seta sārī dhapyau, taral taryaunā kāna* ।
paryau manau surasari salila, rabi pratibimba bihāna ॥

What her companion said to him

Her ear ornament
quivering in her white sari
when she thrills with love,
seems as the golden ripples
of the rising sun
reflected in the Gaṅgā waters.

495. *vāhi lakhaiṁ loin lagai, kauna juvatī kī joti* ।
jākaiṁ tana kī chāṁha ḍhiga, jonha chāṁha sī hoti ॥

What her companion told him

After seeing her
who is the girl
whose splendour can catch
the eye?
Even her shadow
makes the moonlight
seem as shade!

496. *jyauṁ jyauṁ jobana jeṭh dina, kuca miti ati adhikāti* ।
tyauṁ tyauṁ china china kaṭi chapā, chīna parati sī jāti ॥

What her companion said to him

As *Jeṭh*
gives the days more hours
and the nights fewer,
adolescence
swells out her breasts and
makes her waist
more slender.*

497. *kahi lahi kauna sakai durī, saunajāi maiṁ jāi* ।
tana kī sahaja subāsa ban, detī jau na batāi ॥

What one of her companions said to another

Say, who could have spotted her
amidst the yellow jasmine creepers
if it wasn't for
the natural fragrance
of her limbs?

498. *jaṭita nīlamani jagamagati, sīṁk suhāī nāṁka* ।
manau alī campaka-kalī, basi rasa leta nisāṁka ॥

What her companion said to him

Fascinating, dear lad,
is the glimmer
of the sapphire
in her nose-pin;
it seems as though
a meandering black bee
alighting for once
on a *campā* flower
were fearlessly sucking
its nectar.*

499. *lai cubhakī cali jāti jita,* jita *jala keli adhīra* ।
kījat kesari nīra se, tita tita ke sari nīra ॥

What her companion said to him

Wherever that girl
skilled in the water sport
swiftly plunges,
the river's water
shimmers
saffron yellow.*

500. *lāl alaukika larikaī, lakhi lakhi sakhī sihāṁti* ॥
ājakālahi maiṁ dekhiyat, ur uksauṁhīṁ bhāṁti ॥

What her messenger told him

Dear lad,
seeing the peerless charm
of that girl's youth
even her companions
envy her;
her breasts
are about to swell
any time now.

501. *besari motī dutī jhalaka, parī oṭha par āi* ।
cūnau hoi na catura tiya, kyauṁ paṭa poṁchayau jāi ॥

What her companion said

That's not lime
O foolish woman
which you're trying to wipe off
with your sari-end,
it's only the glimmer
cast on you lips
by the pearl
in your nose-ring!*

502. *mili candana beṁdī rahī, goraiṁ mukha na lakhāi* ।
jyoṁ jyoṁ mada lālī caṛhai, tyauṁ tyauṁ ugharati jāi ॥

What her messenger said to him

She's so fair, lad,
that her forehead's
white sandalwood paste mark
can't be spotted!
But it stands out clearly

when her face is flushed
with wine.*

503. *durati na kuca bica kañcukī, cuparī sādī seta* ।
kabi āṁkanu ke aratha laum, pragaṭa dikhāī deta ॥

What her companion told him

Her blossoming breasts
can be seen now
beneath her plain white
perfumed bodice
but by peering eyes alone,
as the abstruse meaning
of a poem
is revealed only by
close study!*

504. *rahī ju tana chabi basan mili, barani sakaiṁ su na baina* ।
āṁga op āṁgī durī, āṁgī āṁga durai na ॥

What her messenger told him

Words can't describe
the splendour of her limbs
clothed in a dress
of shade perfectly matching
her complexion;
so much so
that despite her bodice
her breasts seem bare!

505. *sonajuhī sī jagamagai, aṁga aṁga jobana joti* ।
suraṅga kusūṁbhī kañcukī, duraṅga deha-duti hoti ॥

What her confidante said to him

Her bodice
red as *kusuma* flowers

seems to take on a dual hue
when seen
against her youthful limbs
glistening
like yellow jasmine.*

506. *apane kara guhi āp haṭhi, hiya pahirāī lāl* ।
naula sirī aurai caṁhī, maulasirī kī māla ॥

What one of her companions said to another

The garland of *maulasirī* flowers
he threaded himself
and urged her
to put round her neck
has made that lovely girl
look lovelier still.*

507. *sohat aṁguṭhā paikai, anavaṭa jaryau jarāi* ।
jītyau tarivana duti su ḍhari, paryau tarani manu pāi ॥

What her companion said to him

Her gem-studded toe-ring
shines so brilliantly
that it seems
the sun
humbled by the splendour
of her ear ornament
had fallen at her feet!*

508. *jaṅgha jugala loin nire, kare manau bidhi maina* ।
keli-taruna dukhadaina ye, keli taruna sukhadaina ॥

What her companion said to him

It seems Creator Kāma
fashioned her thighs
from the essence of pure beauty—

from the essence of pure beauty—
thighs which outvie
the plantain tree trunk
and give her lover
great pleasure
in love-making.*

509. *nava nāgari tana muluka lahi, jobana āmira jaura* ।
ghaṭi baṛhi taiṁ baṛhi ghaṭi rakam, karīṁ aura kī aura ॥

What her messenger said to him

Youth holds sway
over her body
transforming it wholly,
swelling out some parts
slenderizing others,
like a rapacious official
dispossessing the disfavoured
of their wealth
to enrich his favourites!

510. *baṛai kahāvat āpa sauṁ, garuvai gopīnātha* ।
tau badihauṁ jau rākhihau, hāthana mana lakhi hātha ॥

What her messenger said

You're so sure of yourself
Kṛṣṇa,
but let me see
if you can stay calm
when once you've seen
her lovely hands!

511. *tana bhūṣana añjana dṛgana, pagani mahāvara raṅga* ।
nahiṁ sobhā kauṁ sājiyata, kahibai hīṁ kauṁ aṅga ॥

What her companion said to him

her adornments,
when her body
is brighter than her jewellery,
her eyes blacker
than lamp-black
and her feet redder
than lacquer dye!

512. *pahulā hāra hiyaiṁ lasat, sana kī beṁdī bhāla* ।
rākhati khet kharī kharī, khare urojani bāla ॥

What he said to his friend

Her bosom resplendent
with a garland of lilies,
a hemp flower dangling
from her braid
upon her forehead,
and her taut breasts
jutting out;
that charming village girl
stands
looking after her field.*

513. *bhāvaka umarauṁhauṁ bhayau, kacuka paryau bharu āi* ।
sīpa harā kaiṁ misa hiyau, nisadina herat jāi ॥

What her messenger told him

Her blossoming youth
has made her breasts heavy;
on the pretext
of looking at her string of shells
she keeps glancing at them
often now.

514. *sūra uditahūṁ mudita mana, mukha sukhamā kī or* ।
citai rahat cahuṁ or taiṁ, nihacala cakhanu cakor ॥

What her companion told him

Even though it's day
the *cakors,*
seeing her lovely face,
think it's the moon come out
and keep gazing at it
raptly!*

515. *tū rahi sakhi hauṁ hīṁ lakhau, caṙhi na aṭā bali bāla* ।
saba hī binu sasi hī udai, daihaiṁ araghu akāla ॥

What her companion said

Dear girl,
do not climb the balcony
I implore you;
I'll go instead
and find out if the moon's up;
for if the other women see your face
they'll think it's the moon
and break their fast
untimely!*

516. *diyau araghu nīcai calau, saṅkaṭa bhānaiṁ jāi* ।
sucitī hvai aurau sabai, sasihīṁ bilokau āi ॥

What her companion said to her

You've made your moon-oblation
dear girl,
now let's come down
and end the pangs of hunger
or other fasting women
who're gazing on your face

will be perplexed to see two moons
and go on fasting!*

517. *lalit syāma līlā lalan baṁhau cibuka chabi dūna* ।
madhu chākyau madhukara paryau, manau gulāba prasūna ॥

What her companion told him

The round black tattoo mark on her chin
makes it doubly charming.
It's as though a black bee
drunk with nectar
were lolling on a rose.

518. *sabai suhayeī lagai, basaiṁ suhāiṁ ṭhāma* ।
goraiṁ muṁha beṁdī lasat, aruna pīta sita syāma ॥

All things look charming
at the right place,
as on a fair woman's brow
her red turmeric
yellow saffron and
black musk
marks.*

519. *tiya tithi taruna kisorabaya, punyakāla sama dauna* ।
kāhūṁ punyana paiyat, baisa saṁdhi saṅkrauna ॥

What her companion said

Her childhood's
blending into youth
as the auspicious passing
of the sun
from one zodiac sign
to another.
Now's the time, clever lad,
to seek her love.*

520. *mānahu mumha dikharāvanī, dulahini kari anurāga* ।
sāsu sadan mana lalana hūm, sautina diyau suhāga ॥

What one of her companions said to another

The beautiful newly-wed wife
charmed everybody
and got
as though gifts at her face-seeing ceremony,
from her mother-in-law
the right of being the lady of the house,
from her co-wives
precedence in conjugal love,
and from her husband
his heart's surrender.*

521. *kana debo saumpyau sasura, bahū thurahathī jāni* ।
rūpa rahacataim lagi lagyau, saba jaga māmgana āni ॥

What an observer said

That frugal man
asked his daughter-in-law
having small hands
to distribute charity,
hoping thereby
to seem bountiful
yet give less.
But thirsting to see the girl's beauty
it seemed as though the whole world
came begging
at his door!

522. *saghan kuñj ghana ghanatimira, adhika amdherī rāti* ।
taū na durihai syāma vaha, dīpasikhā sī jāti ॥

What her messenger said to Kṛṣṇa

The darkness of the woods

is increased by the black clouds
hovering overhead,
the night too is pitch dark;
just the opportunity for her
to hasten to you, Kṛṣṇa;
but alas,
her flame-like body
will be a giveaway!

523. *jarī kori gore badan, baṛhī kharī chabi dekha* ।
lasati manau bijurī kiye, sārada sasi paribekha ॥

What her messenger told him

The gold-embroidered border
of her sari
framing her fair face
makes it shine
with redoubled splendour,
like an orb of lighting
round the full moon
of the *śarada* night.*

524. *ihi dvaihīṁ motī sugatha, tū natha garabi nisāṁka* ।
jihi pahire jagadṛga grasati, lasati haṁsati sī nāṁka ॥

What he said about her nose ornament

Darling girl
you're rightly proud of
your nose-ring
with its twin pearls,
for it so enhances
the beauty of your comely nose
that all men glance on it
spellbound.

525. *sakhi sohati gopāla kaiṁ, ur guñjana kī māla* ।
bāhari lasati manau piye, dāvānala kī jvāla ॥

What she said to her confidante

Dear friend,
the *guñjana* garland
resplendent on Kṛṣṇa's bosom
is as though
the flames of the forest fire
swallowed by him
had burst out!*

526. *ur na ṭarai nīṁda na parai, harai na kāla bipāka* ।
chinaka chāki uchakai na phiri, khare viṣama chabi chāka ॥

What her companion said

Beauty's intoxication is strong,
even a little of it
makes one drunk;
fear does not drive it out
nor sleep pacify it,
it does not wear away with time;
its inebriation
is everlasting.

527. *bhūṣana bhāru saṁbhārihai, kyauṁ ihiṁ tana sukumāra* ।
sūdhe pāi na dhara parat, sobhā hī kaiṁ bhāra ॥

What her companion said

Ornaments, dear girl,
are surely an encumbrance
for your delicate limbs,
when even the burden
of your own beauty
makes you totter!*

528. *cunarī syāma satāra nabha, mumha sasi kī unahāri* ।
neha dabavata nīmḍa laum, nirakhi nisā sī nāri ॥

What he said to her friend

Within her black apparel
tucked with silvery stars
her face,
like the moon
in the night sky,
overpowers me
with love's slumber.

529. *kahat sabai bemdī diyaim, āmka dasaguno hot* ।
tiya lilāra bemdī diyaim, aginita baṛhat udot ॥

What he said to his friend

Everyone knows
that a zero
makes a figure
ten times more;
but there's no bound
to the increase in her beauty
when she puts
a round mark
on her brow!

530. *dekhat sonajuhī phirati, sonajuhī se aṅga* ।
duti lapaṭana paṭa seta hū, karat banauṭī raṅga ॥

What her companion said

Do you see that girl, dear lad,
wandering amid the jasmine flowers
in her garden?
The splendour of her limbs
matching their blossoming yellowness

makes her white sari
seem to take on a yellowish hue.

531. *dīṭhi na parat samāna duti, kanaka kanaka-seṁ gāta* ।
bhūṣana kara karakasa lagat, parasa pichāne jāta ॥

What her messenger told him

Her gold ornaments
blend so well
with her golden complexion
that one can know she wears them
only by feeling
their hardness!

532. *karat malina āchī chabihiṁ, harat su sahaja vikāsa* ।
aṅgarāga aṅgana lagai, jyoṁ ārasī usāsa ॥

What one of her companions said to another

Her body's natural sheen
is dimmed
instead of taking on brilliance
by the scented *aṅgarāga* paste
she put on;
as a mirror
blurred
by breathing deeply on it.*

533. *pahiri na bhūṣana kanaka ke, kahi āvat ihiṁ heta* ।
darpana ke se morace, deha dikhāī deta ॥

What her companion said

Listen to me, dear girl,
wear no gold ornaments
for on your body
they're as rust
on a mirror!*

534. *gorī chigunī nakh aruna, chalā syāma chabi dei* ।
lahat mukati rati palaka yaha, nain tribenī sei ॥

What he said to his confidant

Even a glimpse
of her fair little finger
with rosy nail,
resplendent with a black ring
set with sapphire,
enraptures my soul;
as though
it had got salvation
by looking on Triveṇī!*

535. *sahaja seta pacatoriyā, pahirati ati duti hoti* ।
jalacādara ke dīpa lauṁ, jagamagāti tana joti ॥

What her messenger said to him

From under her plain white
gossamer sari
her body's brilliance
shines out
as oil lamps glimmering
behind a thin water spray.*

536. *lagat subhaga sītala kirana, nisi dina sukha avagāhi* ।
māha sasī bhrama sūra tyauṁ, rahat cakorī cāhi ॥

In the *Māgh* month
the daylight is so dim
that the *cakor*
gleefully thinks it's night
and mistaking the sun for the moon
keeps staring at it rapturously!*

537. *likhana baiṭhi jākī sabī, gahi gahi garaba garūra* ।
bhaye na kete jagata ke, catura citere kūra ॥

What her companion said to him

Who's the vain artist
who has not essayed
to paint her elusive beauty,
and failing
given up in despair?*

538. *pīṭhi diye hīṁ naika muri, kari ghūṁghaṭ paṭa ṭāri* ।
bhari gulāl kī mūṭhi sauṁ, gaī mūṭhi sī mari ॥

What he told his confidant

Without glancing at me
she slightly turned
and lifting her veil
showered on me
a fistful of *gulāl,*
leaving me bound
in the spell of her enchantment.*

539. *jyauṁ jyauṁ paṭa jhaṭakati haṭhati, haṁsati nacāvati nain*
tyauṁ tyauṁ nipaṭa udārahūṁ, phaguvā deta banai na ॥

What one of her companions said to another

As she tugged at his dress
smiling with coquettish glances
insisting on her gifts
for playing *phāga;*
though large-hearted
he kept putting her off
to savour her charm
a little longer!*

540. *bhāla lāl bemdī diyaiṁ, chuṭe bāra chabi deta* ।
gahyau rāhu ati āhu kari, manu sasi sūra sameta ॥

What her companion said to him

Her scattered tresses
and the round red beauty mark
upon her brow
look so fascinating
that it seems as though Rāhu
had courageously challenged
the sun as well as the moon
and swallowed both of them!*

541. *kañcana tana dhana baran bar, rahyau raṅga mili raṅga* ।
jānī jāti subāsa hīṁ, kesari lāgī aṅga ॥

What her messenger told him

The saffron paste
she has applied
blends so perfectly
with her superb golden complexion
that one can know it's there
only by its fragrance!

542. *hvai kapūramanimaya rahī, mili tana duti mukatāli* ।
china china kharī bicacchanau, lakhati chvāi tinu āli ॥

What her companion said to him

The pearls in her necklace
reflecting the splendour
of her golden complexion
seem so like *kapūramaṇī*
that her puzzled friend
keeps testing them again and again
with a piece of straw!*

543. *ḋhani yaha dvaija jahāṁa lakhyau, tajyau dṛgana dukha daṅda* ।
tuma bhāgani pūraba uyau, aho apūraba caṅda ॥

What her companion told her

Dear girl I went
on the balcony
to see the moon
of the second night
of the lunar month's bright half,
when I chanced
by your good fortune
on the moon of your lover's face
wonderfully aloft in the east
which will gratify your eyes
and dispel your sorrows.*

544. *ranita bhṛṅga ghaṅṭāvalī, jharata dāna madhu nīru* ।
mañda mañda āvata calau, kuñjaru kuñja samīru ॥

Spring comes
with the hum of black bees
melodious as the jingle
of bells stringed
round an elephant's neck,
and flowers dropping nectar
as ichor oozing
from the temples
of elephants in rut.

545. *rahī rukī kyauṁhūṁ su calī, ādhika rāti padhāri* ।
harata tāpa sab dyaus kau, ur lagi yāri bahāri ॥

'That loved one' he said,
'who was quiescent all day,
came at midnight
and caressing my breast
dispelled all my grief.'

'Your sweetheart?' his friend asked,
'Ah no!' he lied, 'the breeze!'*

546. *cuvata sveda makaraṁda kana, taru taru tara biramāi* ।
āvata dacchina deśa taiṁ, thakyauṁ baṭohī bāi ॥

Like a tired
perspiring traveller
resting in the shade,
pausing under trees,
comes
the southern wind
laden
with the nectar
spilled
from flowers.

547. *lapaṭī puhupa parāga paṭa, sanī sveda makaraṁda* ।
āvata nāri navauṛha lauṁ, sukhad vāyu gati maṁda ॥

The pleasing breeze comes gently
swathed in the pollen of flowers
bathed with their nectar,
like a newly-wed bride
with faltering steps
tired and perspiring,
bashfully covering
her limbs.

548. *lāl tumhāre rūpa kī, kahau rīti yaha kauna* ।
jāsauṁ lāgat palak dṛga, lāgat palak palau na ॥

What her companion said

What a spell
have you cast on her
handsome!
If she glances at you

just once
she keeps staring and staring
and how can the poor girl
sleep?

549. *calata lalit śrama sveda kana, kalit aruna mukha taiṁ na* ।
bana bihāra thākī taruni, khare thakāye nain ॥

What one of her companions said to another

Exhausted
from wandering in the woods
with her lover,
the flushed face
of that young girl
glistening with beads of perspiration
looks so captivating
that though his eyes tire
with gazing
he cannot take them off her
even for a moment!

550. *mānahu bidhi tana accha chabi, swaccha rākhibaiṁ kāja* ।
dṛga-paga pochana kaum kiye, bhūsana pāyandāja ॥

What her companion said to him

To preserve her body's brightness
it seems god has fashioned
her ornaments
as a doormat
to wipe the feet
of Eyes which glance at her!

551. *aruna baran tarunī carana, aṁgurī ati sukumāra* ।
cuvati suraṅga raṅga manau, capi bichiyana kaiṁ bhāra ॥

What her companion said to him

This is not the rosiness
of her tender feet, dear lad,
it seems to me
it's the lacquer dye
being squeezed out
by the weight
of her toe ornament!*

552. *mora mukuta kī caṅdrakani, yauṁ rājat naṁdanaṅda* ।
manu sasisekhara kī akasa, kiya sata sekhara caṅda ॥

What his woman messenger said to her

The spots of colour
on Kṛṣṇa's crown of peacock feathers
flame so brilliantly, dear girl,
that it seems he were
jealous Kāma
who, to outvie Śiva,
had decked his head
with a hundred moons!*

553. *adhara dharat hari kaiṁ parat, oṭha ḍīṭhi paṭa joti* ।
harita bāṁsa kī bāṁsurī, indradhanuṣa raṁga hoti ॥

What her companion said to her

The gleam
of Kṛṣṇa's
red lips
yellow dress and
dark eyes,
falling

on his green bamboo flute
gives it the colourful radiance
of a rainbow.

554. *kharī lasati goraiṁ garaiṁ, dhaṁsati pān kī pīka* ।
manau gulubaṁdha lāl kī, lāl lāl duti-līka ॥

What her messenger said to him

Her throat is so fair, dear lad,
that the betel-juice she swallows
gives it a rosy tinge,
which makes it look
as though it was decked with
her neck ornament
and its string of rubies!

555. *kuṭila alaka chuṭi parat mukha, baṛhigau itau udot* ।
baṅka bakārī deta jyauṁ, dāma rupaiyā hot ॥

What her messenger said to him

The curly lock
lying on her face
enhances her splendour
as greatly
as an oblique mark
turning a mere *daṁṛī*
into a rupee.*

556. *gaṛe baṛe chabi-chāka chaki, chiṁgurī-chora chuṭaiṁ na* ।
rahe suraṅga raṁga raṁga uhīṁ, naha-do mehṁdī nain ॥

What he said to her

My eyes are so drunk
with the splendour
of your little finger's tip
reddened with henna dye

that they can't tear themselves away
even for a moment.
It seems, dear girl,
they too have been coloured
with its hue!

557. *gāṛhe ṭhāṛhe kucana ṭhili, piya hiya ko ṭhaharāi* ।
ukasauṁhaiṁ hīṁ tau hiyaiṁ, sabai daī ukasāi ॥

What her companion said to her

Your hard budding breasts
pushing against your lover's bosom
have already made him forget
all your co-wives.
What havoc
they'll play with them
when they fully blossom!

558. *rahī laṭū hvai lāl hauṁ, lakhi vaha bāla anūpa* ।
kitau miṭhāsa dyau daī, itau salono rūpa ॥

What her woman messenger said to him

Heavens!
How much beauty
has god given her!
Even I am bewitched by it
dear lad,
how much more
you!

559. *ṭaṭakī dhoī dhovatī, caṭakīlī mukha-joti* ।
lasata rasoī kaiṁ bagara, jagara-magara duti hoti ॥

What one of her companions said to another

Wearing a sari
come straight from the wash

when that girl
of radiant face
moves about
working outside her kitchen,
the whole veranda
in which she sits
seems to blaze
with her splendour!

560. *sohati dhotī seta maiṁ, kanaka barana tana bāla* ।
sārada bārada bījurī, bhā rada kījata lāl ॥

What her messenger told him

When she drapes
her golden-hued body
in a white sari
dear lad,
her splendour
puts to shame
the flash of lightning
in autumnal clouds!

561. *chāle paribe kaiṁ ḍarana, sakai na hātha chuvāi* ।
jhajhakata hiyaiṁ gulāba kaiṁ, jhaṁvā jhaṁvaiyata pāi ॥

What her companion said to him

Her feet are so tender
that the barber's wife
can't touch them
for fear of causing blisters!
And even when she rubs them clean
with roses for a brush
she does it
with a faltering heart!

562. *aruna saroruha-kara-carana, dṛga khañjana mukhā̇ caṅda* ।
samai āi suṅdari sarada, kāhi na karati anaṅda ॥

As autumn comes
bringing joy,
that moon-faced girl
of lotus-like hands and feet
and eyes as *khañjana* bird's,
captivates everyone
wherever she goes.*

563. *paga paga maga agamana parat, carana aruna duti jhūli* ।
ṭhaura ṭhaura lakhiyat uṭhe, dupahariyā se phūli ॥

What her messenger said to him

Her ruby feet
seem to shed
red dust
as she goes along,
as though
a *dupahariyā* flower
had blossomed
at each step she takes!*

564. *chinaka chabile lāl vaha, nahiṁ jau laga batarāti* ।
ūkhạ mayūkha piyūkha kī, tau lagi bhūkha na jāti ॥

What her messenger said to him

Her voice is so sweet
handsome lad,
that if you hear it
even for a moment
you'll consider
the sweetness
of sugarcane
honey and

nectar
of no account!*

565. *kahā kumuda kaha kaumudī, kitika ārasī joti* ।
jākī ujarāī lakhaiṁ, āṁkhi ūjarī hoti ॥

What her companion said to him

The brilliance of her body
dazzles the eyes.
What is the mirror's gleam,
moonlight's glimmer
or the lustre of the white lily
before it?

566. *lahalahāti tana taru naī, laci laga lauṁ lafi jāye* ।
lagaiṁ lāṁka loin bharī, loin leti lagāye ॥

What he said to her companion

The spellbound eyes
of those who glance
at her slender waist
bending with the burden of youth,
remain glued to it
as birds
stuck fast in birdlime!

567. *chapyau chabīlau muṁha khasai, nīlaiṁ aṅcara cīra* ।
manau kalānidhi jhalamalai, kālindī kaiṁ nīra ॥

What her companion said to him

The glimmer of her face
from within her blue sari's end
vies with the shimmering moon
reflected in the waters
of the Yamunā.*

568. *to lakhi mo mana jo lahī, so gati kahī na jāti* ।
ṭhoṛī-gāṛa gaṛyau taū, uṛyau rahai dina rāti ॥

What he said to her

How should I relate
the strange condition
of my mind
dear girl,
though imprisoned
in your chin's charming dimple
it still keeps flying
on the wings of its loveliness!

569. *to tana avadhi anūpa, rūpa lagyau sab jagat kau* ।
mo dṛga lāge rūpa, dṛgani lagī ati catapatī ॥

What he said to her

Your body
is the ultimate in perfection
dear girl.
It seems the Creator
has exhausted
all the world's beauty
in fashioning it!
My fascinated eyes
remain ever restless
to behold you.

570. *chuṭe chuṭāvat jagat taiṁ, saṭakāre sukumāra* ।
manu bāṁdhat beni baṁdhe, nīla chabīle bāra ॥

What he said to her messenger

When she binds
her long black glossy hair
whose heart does she not bind
with its loveliness?

And when she loosens it
whose enraptured mind
is not lost
to the world?

571. *camacamāta caṅcala nayana, bica ghūṁghaṭa paṭa jhīna* ।
manahu sūra saritā vimala, jala ucharata juga mīna ॥

What her messenger said to him

The sparkle
of her tremulous eyes
beneath her gossamer veil
is as the glint
of fishes leaping aslant
in the limpid Gaṅgā waters.

572. *chipaiṁ chapākara chiti chayau, tama sasihari na saṁbhāri* ।
haṁsati haṁsati cali sasimukhī, mukha taiṁ āṁcaru ṭāri ॥

What the messenger accompanying the girl going to meet her lover said

Though we're only halfway
and the moon has gone down
wrapping the earth
in the cloak of darkness,
fear not, my beauty,
go along happily beaming
for if you just remove your veil
our path will be lit up
by the moon of your face
and the flashes of your smiles!

573. *phiri ghara kauṁ nūtan pathik, cale cakita cita bhāgi* ।
phūlyau dekhi palāsa bana, samujhī samujhi davāgi ॥

When the inexperienced wayfarers
saw the *palāśa* blossoms
a blaze of red,
they mistook them
for a forest fire
and fled back home!*

574. *bāla chabīlī tiyana maiṁ, baiṭhī āp chipāi* ।
aragaṭahūṁ yānūsa sī, paragaṭa hoi lakhāi ॥

What her companion said

When she sits
in the assembly of young women
her face outshines
those of all others;
its ravishing radiance
glows from beneath her veil
like the flame
in a chandelier.

575. *oṁṭha ucai hāṁsī bharī, dṛga bhauṁhana kī cāla* ।
mo mana kahā na pī liyau, piyat tamākū lāl ॥

What she told her confidante

The dear lad
bewitched me
when moving his eyebrows seductively
and twinkling with delight
he raised his lips
to smoke his *hookah.**

576. *pacaraṁga raṁga beṁdī kharī, uthe ūgi mukha joti* ।
pahiraiṁ cīra cinauṭiyā, caṭaka caugunī hoti ॥

What her messenger said to him

Her forehead ornament
set with gems of five colours
adds to the dazzle
of her face,
and when she wears
her colourful wrap
it shines with redoubled brilliance.

577. *vārauṁ bali to dṛgana par, ali khañjana mṛga mīna* ।
ādhī ḍīṭhi citauni jihiṁ, kiye lāl ādhīna ॥

What her companion said to her

Upon my word, dear girl,
your ravishing eyes
dark as black bees
put to shame
those of the fish
the deer
and the wagtail,
for they can bewitch your lover
with just one glance!*

578. *jāt sayāna ayāna hvai, vai ṭhaga kāhi ṭhagaiṁ na* ।
ko lalacāi na lāl ke, lakhi lalacauhaiṁ nain ॥

What she said to her companion

How can I help
looking at him, friend?
His eyes are like cheats
tricking away
all prudence.

Who can remain unmoved
by their bewitching glance?

579. *jyauṁ kara tyauṁ cikuṭī calati, jyauṁ cikuṭī tyauṁ nāri* ।
chabi sauṁ gatī sī lai calati, cātura kātanihāri ॥

What he said about the woman at the spinning wheel

One hand of hers
skilfully turns the wheel
with lightning swiftness,
the other nimbly
pushes along the yarn,
while her neck
moves up and down
in unison.
Her rhythmic motions
are more like those
of a graceful dancer
than of a woman spinning!

580. *budhi anumāna pramāna śruti, kiyeṁ nīṭhi ṭhaharāi* ।
sūchima kati para brahma kī, alakha lakhī nahiṁ jāi ॥

What he said to her messenger

As Brahma's existence is known
by persistent reasoning
and by the testimony
of the scriptures,
so people gather
she must have a waist
between her upper and
lower limbs,
and because they hear
she has one;
but none
has really seen it!*

581. *lagī analagī sī ju bidhi, karī kharī kaṭi khīna* ।
kiye manau vehīṁ kasari, kuca nitamba ati pīna ॥

What her companion said to him

Brahmā has made her waist
so exceedingly slender
that though she has it
it seems it's not there at all!
And to make up for its slimness
he has filled out
her hips and breasts!*

582. *muṁha pakhāri muṛaharu bhijai, sīsa sajala kara chvāi* ।
mauru ucai ghūṭena taiṁ, nāri sarovara nhāi ॥

What he said to his confidant when he saw her bathing

See that charming girl
with uplifted head
squatting on the pond's edge
to bathe.
She scoops water
with her hand
souses her head
and washes her face,
wetting the hanging border
of her sari.*

583. *phiri phiri daurata dekhiyat, nicale naiṁka rahaiṁ na* ।
ye kajarāre kauna par, karat kajākī nain ॥

What her companion said

Never at rest,
your glance
keeps straying each moment.
Say, dear girl,
whose equanimity

are these collyrium-filled
bandit-like eyes of yours
about to plunder?

584. *lase murāsā tiya sravana, yauṁ mukatā duti pāi* ।
mānahu parasȧ kapol kaiṁ, rahe sveda-kana chāi ॥

What her companion said to him

There are not pearls, dear lad,
with which her ear ornament is set,
it seems
thrilled by brushing her cheeks
it's exuding
beads of perspiration!*

585. *mili parachāṁhīṁ jonha maiṁ, rahe duhuna ke gāt* ।
hari rādhā ik saṅga hīṁ, cale galī mahiṁ jāt ॥

What one of Rādhā's companions said to another

Is this a wonder I see
dearfriend?
Both Rādhā and Kṛṣṇa
in the moonlight-streaked lane,
two, but seeming one;
her golden-hued form
merging with the moonlight,
his dark one
with the night's blackness!*

586. *beṁdī bhāla taṁbola mukha, sīsa silasile bāra* ।
dṛga āṁje rājai kharī, sājaiṁ sahaja siṁgāra ॥

What her companion said to her

What need have you
of ornate adornments?
You look charming as it is,

your brow marked
with just a *bindī*
your lips stained
with red betel-juice,
your eyes darkened
with lamp-black
and your hair glistening
with perfumed oil.*

587. *aṅga aṅga pratibimba pari, darpana se sab gāt* ।
duhare tihare cauhare, bhūṣana jāne jāt ॥

What her messenger said to him

Her brilliant limbs
are like so many mirrors
reflecting
her ornaments
twofold
threefold and
even fourfold!

588. *mohiṁ bharosau rījhihai, ujhaki jhāṁki ik bāra* ।
rūpa rijhāvanahāru vaha, ye nainā rijhavāra ॥

What her companion said to her

Stand on tiptoe, dear girl,
and glance just once at him
from your window,
I'm sure you'll be captivated
for you are a worshipper of beauty
and he's Prince Charming!

589. *barajai dūnī haṭh caṁhai, na sakucai na sakāi* ।
ṭūṭati kaṭi dumaci macaki, lacaki lacaki baci jāi ॥

What her messenger told him

She does not heed
her companions
but swings on
more vigorously
neither fearing
to fall off
nor ashamed
of her dress billowing out
leaving her limbs bare.
When she works the swing
to and fro
her tender waist bends so alarmingly
that it seems
it's about to break!

590. *kara sameṭa kaca bhuja ulaṭi, khaye sīsa paṭa ḍāri* ।
kākau mana bāṁdhe na yaha, jūrau bāṁdhani hāri ॥

What one of her admirers said

Gathering her tresses
in her hands
her arms upturned,
her mantle dropping
from her head to her shoulders,
whose heart does she not bind
when she binds her hair?

591. *sohat oṛhai pīta paṭa, syāma salone gāt* ।
manau nīlamani saila par, ātapa paryau prabhāt ॥

What her companion said

Enveloped in a yellow mantle

dark Kṛṣṇa's handsome body
glinting with splendour
seems like the peak
of a sapphire hill
flashing
in the morning sun.

592. *bhāla lāl beṁdī lalan, ākhat rahe birāji* ।
iṅdukalā kuja maiṁ durī, manau rāhu bhaya bhāji ॥

What her messenger told him

When she painted
a crimson mark
over the sanctified rice grains
put on by the temple priest,
it seemed, dear lad,
as though the moon
had, out of Rāhu's fear,
parted with its lustre
and hid it in the orbit
of blood-red Mars!*

593. *aṅga aṅga chabi kī lapaṭa, upaṭati jāti acheha* ।
kharī pātarīū taū, lagai bharī sī deha ॥

What her messenger said to him

The brilliance
of her lovely limbs
increases day by day,
making her slim body
swell out
in all its fullness.

594. *bihaṁsati sakucati sī hiyai, kuca āṁcara bica bāṁha* ।
bhījai paṭa taṭa ko calī, nhāi sarovara māṁha ॥

What he told his confidant

After bathing in the pond
she went laughing
towards the bank
her wet garments clinging to her,
shyly cupping her hands
under her revealing
sari end.

595. *barana bāsa sukumāratā, sab bidhi rahī samāi* ।
pāṁkhurī lagī gulāba kī, gāla na jānī jāi ॥

What her companion said to him

Her pinkish cheek
is so tender
and fragrant
that the rose petal
which got stuck to it
could not be distinguished!*

596. *raṅca na lakhiyata pahiri yauṁ, kaṅcana se tana bāla* ।
kumhilāne jānī parati, ur campe kī māla ॥

What her companion said

How perfectly
the yellow *campā* garland
blends
with your golden hue
dear girl!
It can be seen
only when its flowers
fade!*

597. *ahe dahemrī jina dharai, jina tū lehi utāri* ।
nīkai hai chīmkai chavaī, aisaihī rahi nāri ॥

What he said to her

How charming you look
when you raise your arms
to put the butter pot
in the sling net!
Don't place it
nor yet take it down,
just stay as you are
dear girl,
that I may gaze and gaze
at your bewitching beauty!*

598. *gorī gaḍakārau parai, hamsati kapolana gāṛa* ।
kaisī lasati gamvāri iha, sunakirabā kī āṛa ॥

What he said when he saw the village girl

How gorgeous looks
that smiling rustic belle
with dimpled cheeks
and a flashing
sunakīrā's wing
stuck obliquely
on her forehead!*

WISDOM

599. *sītalatā aru subāsa kī, ghaṭai na mahimā mūra* ।
pīnasavāraiṁ jyoṁ tajyau, sorā jāni kapūra ॥

Camphor does not lose
its coolness and fragrance
merely because a man
diseased by *pīnasa*,
who has lost his sense of smell,
can't tell it from
saltpetre.*

600. *taṅtrīnāda kabitta rasa, sarasa rāga rati raṅga* ।
anabūṛe būṛe, tire, je būṛe saba aṅga ॥

Those who dive deep
in the ocean of
haunting music and song,
poignant poetry
and rapturous love-making,
are not drowned;
it's they who are sunk
who keep away!

601. *jetī sampati kṛpana kaiṁ, tetī sūmati jora* ।
baṛhat jāta jyoṁ jyoṁ uraja, tyauṁ tyauṁ hota kaṭhora ॥

The greater
a miser's wealth
the stingier he is,
as the more
a girl's breasts grow

the harder
they become!

602. *sampati kesa sudesa nara, namat duhuni ik bāni* ।
vibhava satara kuca nīca nara, narama vibhava kī hāni ॥

As a girl's hair
softening and
cascading down
the more it grows,
the wealthier
a virtuous man is
the gentler and lowlier
he becomes.
But as her breasts which,
rising proud and hard,
soon turn flabby,
is the vile man,
arrogant when in power and
humbled when shorn of it.

603. *kaisaiṁ choṭe narana taiṁ, hota baṛana kai kāma* ।
maṛhyau damāmau jāta kyoṁ, kahi cūhe kai cāma ॥

Of what use
can the small fry be
to people
of importance?
Can a rat's skin
make a mount
for the face
of a kettledrum?

604. *ghara ghara ḍolat dīna hvai, jana jana jācata jāi* ।
diyaiṁ lobha-casamā cakhani, laghu hūṁ baṛau lakhāi ॥

Feigning poverty
the avaricious man
wears the glasses of greed
which make even paupers
seem rich to him!
Thus he wanders
from house to house
shamelessly
begging.

605. *baṛe na hūjata gunana bina, birada baṛāī pāi* ।
kahat dhatūre sauṁ kanaka, gahanau gaṛhyau na jāi ॥

Greatness is attained
by noble qualities
not by empty praise,
as *dhatūrā* bears
the name of gold
but ornaments
can't be made from it.*

606. *kanaka kanaka taiṁ saugunau, mādakatā adhikāi* ।
uhiṁ khāyaiṁ baurāta hai, ihiṁ pāyaiṁ baurāi ॥

The intoxication
of *dhatūrā*
is only for a while,
but that of gold
is a hundred times greater,
for it turns one's head
and lasts for ever.*

607. *saṅgati sumati na pāvahīṁ, pare kumati kaiṁ dhaṅdh.*
rākhau meli kapūra maiṁ, hīṁga na hota sugaṅdha ॥

Even good company
cannot make
the wicked
virtuous,
as asafoetida
does not turn fragrant
though kept long
with camphor.

608. *jāta jāta bita hota hai, jyauṁ jiya maiṁ saṅtoṣu* ।
hota hota tyauṁ hoi tau, hoi gharī maṁhi moṣu ॥

If one could be content
with his gains
just as he's reconciled
to his losses,
he could achieve salvation
in a moment.*

609. *pāi taruni kuca ucca pada, ciramai ṭhagyau saba gāuṁ* ।
chuṭaiṁ ṭhauru rahihai vahai, ju ho mola chabi nāuṁ ॥

As village folk
prizing a *ghuṁghacī* garland
on the uprising breasts
of a woman,
which discarded
is a mere trifle;
so is a worthless man
given a high place
when he's on it
no longer.*

610. *jina dina dekhe ve kusuma, gaī so bīta bahāra* ।
ab ali rahī gulāba maiṁ, apat kaṁṭīlī ḍāra ॥

Spring has gone
O black bee,
taking away
its perfumed roses!
All that's left now
are the branches
bare and thorny.

611. *sabai haṁsat karatāri dai, nāgaratā kai nāṁva* ।
gayau garaba guna ko sabai, base gaṁvāre gāṁva ॥

What the town-dweller said

These ignorant village people
clap their hands and laugh
deriding my knowledge.
My stay in this village
has cured me
of the vanity of wisdom!

612. *bahaki baṛāī āpanī, kat rāṁcati mati-bhūla* ।
bina madhu madhukara kai hiyai, gaṛai na guṛahara phūla ॥

Foolish man
why are you conceited
by empty adulation,
as a nectarless *guṛahala* flower
ignored by the black bee
yet blossoming out
with haughty redness?*

613. *saṅgati doṣa lagai sabana, kahe ju sāṁce baina* ।
kuṭila baṅka bhru saṅga bhaye, kuṭila baṅka gati nain ॥

Crooked things
go together
in truth;
it is from under
arched eyebrows
that girls send
sidelong glances!

614. *na ye bisasiye lakhi naye, durjana dusaha subhāi* ।
āṁṭaiṁ pari pānanu harata, kāṁṭaiṁ lauṁ lagi pāi ॥

Never trust a vile man
however meek he seems,
for whenever he gets the chance
he'll be like a thorn in the feet
and be after
your very life!

615. *gahilī garaba na kījiye, samai sohāgahiṁ pāi* ।
jiya kī jīvani jeṭh jo, māṁha na chāṁha sohāi ॥

What her companion said

O foolish woman
don't be conceited
with your youth.
You please your husband now
but when you're no longer young
you'll not;
as the shade
which is pleasant in summer's *Jeṭh*
is vexatious
in wintry *Māgh.**

616. *nara kī aru nala nīra kī, gati ekai kari joi* ।
jètau nīcau hvai calai, tetau ūṁcau hoi ॥

It's humility
which makes a man noble,
as the lower a fountain
the higher
its water spouts.

617. *baṛhat baṛhat sampati salilu, mana saroju baṛhi jāi* ।
ghaṭat ghaṭat su na phiri ghaṭai, baru samūla kumhilāi ॥

The more a lake fills with water
the longer the lotus stem grows,
but when it's dry
it does not shorten
and shrivelling up
dies.
So desires increase
with a man's wealth
but do not get less
when it wanes,
even though he's ruined.*

618. *kori jatana koū karo, parai na prakṛtihiṁ bīca* ।
nala bala jala ūṁce caṛhaiṁ, taū nīca ko nīca ॥

One may try a million ways
but he can't change his nature
as water flowing low
rises in the pipe,
but pouring out
flows low again.

619. *gunī gunī sabakaiṁ kahaiṁ, ni̇gunī gunī na hota* ।
sunyau kahūṁ taru araka taiṁ, araka samāna udota ॥

An ignorant man
does not become learned
merely because
everyone calls him so.
The *madāra* tree
is known as *'arka'*
and so's the sun
but whoever saw it shine
with the sun's light?*

620. *dusaha durāja prajāna kauṁ, kyauṁ na baṛhai dukha daṅda* ।
adhika aṁdherau jaga karat, mili māvasa rabi caṅda ॥

Why should not
sorrows unbearably increase
in the kingdom
where two kings reign
at the same time?
Is not the darkness greatest
when the sun and the moon
are in the same House
on *amāvasya*?*

621. *pyāse dupahara jeṭh ke, phire sabai jala sodhi* ।
marudhara pāi matīruhīṁ, mārū kahat payodhi ॥

Searching in vain
for water to drink
in the hot *Jeṭh* noons
of barren Mārwaṛa
if one chances on
even a watermelon
he's as happy

as though he has found
the ocean!*

622. *viṣam vṛṣādita kī tṛṣā, jiye matīrana sodhi* ।
amita apāra agādha jala, mārauṁ mūṛha payodhi ॥

Watermelons
keep the people of Mārwaṛa alive
by allaying their burning thirst
in summer;
of what use
would the salty ocean be to them
even with its endless expanse
of unfathomable water?

623. *jagama jaladhi pānipa bimala, bhau jaga ādha apāru* ।
rahe gunī hvai gara paryau, bhalaiṁ na mukatāharu ॥

One who is gifted
and of noble birth,
when dishonoured
is like the lustrous costly pearl
taken out from the immeasurable ocean
only to be stringed
into a paltry necklace.

624. *gahai na nekau guna garaba, haṁsai sabai saṅsāra* ।
luca ucapada lālaca rahai, garaiṁ paraiṁhūṁ hāra ॥

The greed of high office
makes one stick to it
even though slighted,
as a necklace proudly lies
on a woman's swelling breasts
braving scornful glances.*

625. *basai burāī jāsu tana, tāhī ko sanamāna* ।
khalau bhalau kahi choṁiyai, khoṭaiṁ graha japu dāna ॥

The wicked man is honoured
the righteous ignored,
as when their stars are good
men do not bother,
but when vexed by evil ones
they pray and give charity.

626. *jau cāhat caṭaka na ghaṭai, mailo hoi na mitta* ।
raja rājasu na chuvāi tau, neha cīkanauṁ citta ॥

If you desire, friend,
your love-smeared mind
not to lose
its pristine radiance,
do not let the dust
of vice
settle on it.*

627. *ati agādha ati autharau, nadī kūpa sara bāi* ।
so tāko sāgara jahāṁ, jākī pyāsa bujhāi ॥

River, well, pond or tank,
even if shallow
is like the sea for one
whose thirst it can slake.
So what counts is help
whether it comes from those in power
or from the powerless.

628. *tau aneka auguna bharahiṁ, cāhai yāhi balāi* ।
jau pati samptihūṁ binā, jadupati rākheṁ jāi ॥

If I can get esteem
by Kṛṣṇa's grace

and wealth
which is not tainted with evil,
why should I needlessly hanker
after money?*

629. *kahai yahai śruti subhratyau, yahai sayāne loga* ।
tīna dabāvat nisakahī, pātak rājā roga ॥

There are three agencies
which crush the weak,
so say the wise
and the scriptures too.
Kings oppress them
diseases afflict them
and, exploiting their misery,
sins assail them.*

630. *jo sira dhari mahimā mahī, lahiyata rājā rāi* ।
pragaṭata jaṛatā āpanī, mukuṭa su pahirata pāi ॥

One who scorns
a person of high repute
only reveals
his folly;
he's like a king or chieftain
who wears his diadem
on his feet!

631. *ko kahi sakai baṛena saurn, lakhaim baṛī hū bhūla* ।
dīne daī gulāba ko, ina ḍārana ve phūla ॥

A great man's faults
are overlooked.
No one blames
god the almighty
for placing the lovely rose
on a thorny branch!

632. *samai samai sundara sabai, rūpa kurūpa na koi* ।
mana kī ruci jetī jitai, titī titai ruci hoi ॥

Nothing is beautiful or ugly
in itself,
beauty lies
in the beholder's eye.
The more a thing attracts
the lovelier it seems.

633. *dina dasa ādara paikai, kara lai āpu bakhāna* ।
jau laum̐ kāga sarādhapakha, tau lagi tau sanamāna ॥

Pompous man,
bragging
about the homage paid
to you
for a short while,
you're like the wretched crow
to whom
people toss a morsel
in the *śrādha* fortnight!*

634. *marata pyāsa piṅjarā paro, suvā dinana ke phera* ।
ādara dai dai boliyata, bāyasa bali kī bera ॥

There are times
when an honoured person
is disgraced
and one despised
esteemed;
as in the *śrādha* fortnight
the prized parrot
lies in his cage
languishing with thirst,
while the miserable crow

is coaxed
to accept the offering!*

635. *ihī āsa aṭakau rahata, ali gulāba kaiṁ mūla* ।
havaihaiṁ pheri basanta ṛta, in ḍārana ve phūla ॥

Even when the rose tree is bare
the nectar-sucking black bee
hovers round its roots
in the hope
that spring will return
bringing back its roses.*

636. *ve na ihāṁa nāgara baṛhi, jina ādara to āba* ।
phūlyau unaphūlyau bhayau, gavaṁaī gāṁva gulāba ॥

Who can be aware
of your virtues
in this village of ignoramuses?
Friend, you're like a rose tree
nurtured by an outsider
and left here
uncared for.

637. *calyau jāi hyāṁ ko karai, hāthina ko vyapāra* ।
nahiṁ jānata ihiṁ pura basaiṁ, dhobi oṛa kumhāra ॥

Try your trading talents
elsewhere friend,
who'll buy your elephants here?
Don't you know
only washermen,
labourers and
potters
live in this wretched town,
and their need is
donkeys?*

638. *pāila pāi lagī rahai, lage amolika lāl* ।
bhoḍarahūṁ kī bhasihai, beṁdī bhāmini-bhāl ॥

A vile man
however ostentatious
is despised,
one eminent
though simple
extolled;
as a woman's anklet
is set with priceless gems
yet its place is
on her feet,
while the plain talc mark
proudly adorns her brow.

639. *mūṙha caṙhāyai hūṁ rahai, paryau pīṭhi kaca bhāru* ।
rahai garaiṁ pari rākhiyai, taū hiyaiṁ par hāru ॥

However much he's honoured
an unworthy person
can't rise,
while one who has merit
prospers;
as tresses
even though brushed up
fall down the back,
while the garland
round the neck
proudly lies on the bosom.

640. *ik bhījaiṁ cahalaiṁ paraiṁ, būṙaiṁ bahaiṁ hajāra* ।
kitai na auguna jaga karaiṁ, bai-nai caṙhatī bāra ॥

As thousands are drowned
or swept away
by a river in flood

and others trapped in swamps
or drenched;
so some are soused
with youth's enjoyment
some trapped in its bonds
and for many
it is the speedy way
to perdition.

641. *nahiṁ pāvasa ṛturāja yaha, taji taravara cita bhūla* ।
apatu bhayaiṁ bina pāihai, kyoṁ nava dala phala phūla ॥

As in spring
a tree must shed
its old leaves
to get new ones,
a man has to forsake
his self-respect
to win the favour
of kings.

642. *mīta na nīti galīta hvai, jo dhariyai dhana jora* ।
khayaiṁ kharacaiṁ jau jurai, tau joriyai karora ॥

Advice by a man to his miserly friend

You shouldn't starve
to hoard wealth;
your savings, friend,
even if they are in millions
ought to be
what remains
after spending
on food and necessities.

643. *nīca hiyaiṁ hulase rahaiṁ, gahe geṁda ko pota* ।
jete māthe māriyata, tete ūṁce hota ॥

Effront
elates a vile man
all the more,
as the harder
one throws a ball,
the higher
it rises.

644. *burau burāī jau tajai, tauṁ cita kharau ḍarāta* ।
jyauṁ nilaṅka mayaṁka lakhi, ganaiṁ loka utapātā ॥

It's the spotless moon
which presages disaster.
Just so
the wicked man
who forsakes evil
is to be feared all the more
for one can never know
what new mischief
he's scheming!*

645. *oche baṛe na hvai sakaiṁ, lagyau satara hvai gaina* ।
dīragh hohiṁ na naiṁkahuṁ, phāri nihāre nain ॥

A shallow-minded person
can never achieve greatness
even though, in his vanity,
he thinks he can reach the sky;
as however wide open
the eyes may be
they do not, because of that,
become any larger.

646. *paṭa pāṁkhai bhakha kāṁkarai, sapara pareī saṅga* ।
sukhī parevā puhumi maiṁ, ekai tuhī bihaṅga ॥

To be contented
one must bridle his desires—
simple food,
plain clothes
and one wife
to share his pleasures.
See the homely pigeon
whose raiments are his feathers
grit his fare
and who's happy
with just his mate.

647. *are parekhau ko karai, tuhīṁ biloki bicāri* ।
kahiṁ nara kahiṁ sara rākhiyaiṁ, kharaiṁ baṛhaiṁ paripāri ॥

Why probe, O mind,
into that
which is plain as day?
Where's the pond
which does not overflow its banks
when flooded,
and who's the man
who, with surfeit of wealth,
will not break
the bounds of righteousness?

648. *kara lai sūṁghi sarahi ke, rahe sabai gahi mauna* ।
gaṅdhī aṅdha gulaba kau, gaiṁvaī gāhaka kauna ॥

How can you expect
these stupid people
to prize your virtues?
You're like a foolish perfumer
whose rare rose scent

the country bumpkins
rub on their hands and smell
and also praise,
but do not buy!

649. *bhāvira anabhāvira bhare, karau koṭi bakavāda* ।
apanī apanī bhāṁti kau, chuṭai na sahaja savāda ॥

Whether it pleases people
or annoys them
or is denounced
in a million ways;
a man's nature
does not change.*

650. *caṭaka na chāṁrata ghaṭatahūṁ, sajjana neha gaṁbhīra* ।
phīkau parai na ḅaru phaṭai, raṁgyau cola raṁga cīra ॥

The deep friendship
of a good and faithful friend
remains constant
even in adversity,
as cloth
coloured with the *cola* wood dye
may tear
but will not fade.*

651. *ko chūṭyau ihiṁ jāla pari, kat kuraṅga akulāta* ।
jyauṁ jyauṁ surajhi bhajyau cahat, tyauṁ tyauṁ arujhati jāta ॥

Who's not caught
in the meshes of worldly existence?
The more he tries
to free himself from them
the more he's entangled,
like a deer
struggling in a net.

652. *moracandrikā syāma sira, caṁhi kat dharati gumān* ।
lakhivī paina par luṭhati, suniyata rādhā mān ॥

What Rādhā's companion said

O peacock feather,
you're puffed up with vanity
because you adorn
Kṛṣṇa's head;
but soon you'll be trampled
underfoot,
for Rādhā is sulking
and Kṛṣṇa will appease her
by falling at her feet!*

653. *godhana tū hāraṣyau hiyaiṁ, gharīka lehi pujāi* ।
samujhi paraigī sīsa par, parata pasuna ke pāi ॥

A man's conceit
at the undeserved honour
given to him
can last
only a little while,
as the cow-dung *godhana*
worshipped one moment
and the next
left to be crushed
underfoot
by beasts.*

DEVOTION

654. *merī bhavabādhā harau, rādhā nāgari soi* ı
jā tana kī jhāīṁ paraiṁ, syāma harita duti hoi ıı

The poet's prayer to Rādhā

Gifted Rādhā,
even a glimpse of you
delights Kṛṣṇa;
dispel
my worldly sorrows
I pray you.*

655. *nīkaiṁ daī anākanī, phīkī parī guhāri* ı
tajyau manau tārana-birada, bāraka bārana tāri ıı

A devotee's complaint

My prayer
does not move you
O lord.
You once saved an elephant
who invoked your help,
thereafter
it seems you have ceased
redeeming your devotees!*

656. *ajauṁ tarauna hī rahyau, śruti sevat ik raṅga* ı
nāka-bāsa besari lahyau, basi mukutana kaiṁ saṅga ıı

In haughty isolation
a woman's ear ornament
adorns the humble ear

but her nose-ring
conjoining with pearls
proudly glitters on the nose;
even so, deliverance
is not obtained
by one, who all by himself
keeps reciting the *Vedas*:
but even the vilest soul
gets heaven
by association with god-knowers.*

657. *jama-kari mumha tarihari paryau, ihim dharihari cita lāva* ।
viṣaya tṛṣā parihari ajaum, narahari ke guna gāva ॥

Knowing for certain
you always lie
beneath the Yama-shaped elephant's mouth,
leave off sensual desires
this very moment
and sing the praises
of Lord Nṛsiṅgha.*

658. *kauna bhāṁti rahihai birada, ab dekhibī murāri* ।
bīdhe mosauṁ ānikai, gīdhe gīdhaiṁ tāri ॥

What a devotee said

It is now to be seen
O Kṛṣṇa,
how you will keep your repute
as a saviour;
it was easy to redeem
vultures
like Jaṭāyu,
but now you are faced with
the vilest of sinners!*

659. *jagata janāyau jihiṁ sakala, so hari jānyau nāṁhi* ।
jyauṁ āṁkhina jaga dekhiyai, aṁkhi na dekhī jāṁhi ॥

The entire world
is revealed to you by god
yet him
you do not see;
as the eyes
which gaze on all things
cannot gaze
on themselves.

660. *dīragha sāṁsa na lehu dukha, sukha sāīṁ nahiṁ bhūli* ।
daī daī kyauṁ karata hai, daī daī su kabūli ॥

Sigh not in your sorrow
nor forget god in your joy.
Why do you lament
'O god, O god'?
Accept cheerfully
what he has given you.

661. *bandhu bhaye kā dīna ke, ko taryau raghurāi* ।
tūṭhe tūṭhe phirata hau, jhūṭhe birada kahāi ॥

What a devotee said

O Rāma,
you go about elated
pretending to befriend
the distressed!
Whose grief have you ever removed,
whom have you emancipated?
When you cannot help even me
lowliest of the low,
how shall I know you
as a redeemer?*

662. *thoraiṁ hī guna rījhate, basarāī vaha bāni ।*
tumahūṁ kānha manau bhaye, āja kāliha ke dāni ॥

What a devotee said

O Kṛṣṇa,
you used to be won over
by even a little goodness;
but now it seems
like the reluctant philanthropists
of our days
you are hard to please!

663. *kaba ko ṭerata dīna raṭa, hota na syāma sahāi ।*
tumahūṁ lāgī jagata guru, jaga nāyaka jaga bāi ॥

What a devotee said

Kṛṣṇa,
master of the world
supreme guide;
I have been calling on you
plaintively
for long,
yet you do not favour me.
Has the callousness
of the people of the world
entered you too?

664. *diyau su sīsa caṛhai lai, āchī bhāṁti aeri ।*
jāpaiṁ sukha cāhata liyau, tāke dukhahīṁ na pheri ॥

Be resigned
to the grief god gives you
and accept it
cheerfully;
when you desire
happiness from him,

grudge not your share
of sorrows.*

665. *koū korik sangrahau, koū lākh hazāra* ।
mo sampatti jadupati sadā, bipati bidāranahāra ॥

What a devotee said

Some people collect
crores of rupees
some lakhs
some thousands.
My only wealth
is Kṛṣṇa,
destroyer of sorrows.

666. *pragaṭa bhaye dvijarāja kula, subasa base braja āi* ।
mere harau kalesa saba, kesava kesavarāi ॥

What a devotee said

Born in the Candra clan
O Kṛṣṇa,
you chose Braja
to live in.
Be a father to me
I beseech you
and remove
my sorrows.*

667. *japamālā chāpā tilak, sarai na ekau kāma* ।
kāṁcai mana mācaiṁ bṛthā, sāṁcai rāṁcai rāma ॥

Nothing is gained
by an impious man
engrossed in worldly things
though he may say the rosary
and paint his limbs

with holy marks;
for god is pleased
only by true devotion.*

668. *mohani mūrati syāma kī, ati adbhuta gati joi* ।
basati sucita antara taū, pratibimbita jaga hoi ॥

What a Kṛṣṇa devotee said

See how marvellous
is Kṛṣṇa's image:
though enshrined
only within the pure heart,
it's reflected
all over the world!

669. *maiṁ samujhyau niradhāra, yaha jaga kāṁco kāṁca sau* ।
ekai rūpa apāra, pratibimbita lakhiyata jahāṁ ॥

The world is surely false,
only the One Reality
exists as a mirror
reflecting
all shapes and forms.*

670. *taji tīratha hari rādhikā, tana duti kari anurāga* ।
jihiṁ braja keli nikuṅja maga, paga paga hota prayāga ॥

One who's steeped
in the love of Rādhā and Kṛṣṇa
need not go on pilgrimages,
for in the woods of Braja
where dark Kṛṣṇa
twined round fair Rādhā
as though the silvery Gaṅgā
had joined the blue Yamunā,
each step
has the sanctity of Prayāga.*

671. *kījai cita soī tare, jina patitana ke sāth* ।
mere guna auguna ganana, ganau na gopīnāth ॥

A devotee's prayer to Kṛṣṇa

Weigh not my faults
against my virtues
Kṛṣṇa,
but even as you've given salvation,
to countless fallen souls
forgiving their sins,
redeem me too.

672. *nita prati ekat hīṁ rahat, baisa barana mana eka* ।
cahiyata jugalakisora lakhi, locana jugala aneka ॥

What a Kṛṣṇa devotee said

Of the same name,
age and thinking,
Rādhā and Kṛṣṇa
are eternally united.
Wonderful
is their celestial beauty,
beyond the reach
of human eyes.*

673. *hari kījati binatī yahai, tumasauṁ bāra hajāra* ।
jihiṁ tihiṁ bhāṁti ḍaryau rahyau, paryau rahauṁ darabāra ॥

What a Kṛṣṇa devotee said

O Hari,
this is my only prayer to you
a thousand times over—
let me anyhow remain
in your divine presence.*

674. *mohūṁ dījai moṣu, jyauṁ aneka adhamanu diyau* ।
jau bāṁdhaiṁ hī toṣu, tau bāṁdhau apanaiṁ gunanu ॥

A devotee's prayer

Liberate me lord
even as you've liberated
many sinners.
Release me from the bonds
of worldly existence:
and if it pleases you
to keep me bound,
bind me with the rope
of your devotion.*

675. *sīsa mukuṭa kaṭi kāchinī, kara muralī ur māla* ।
ihiṁ bānaka mo mana basau, sadā bihārīlal ॥

A devotee's prayer

May your divine form
with a crown of peacock feathers,
girdle on waist,
flute in hand
and on your bosom
a *vaijayantī* garland,
ever dwell in my heart
O Kṛṣṇa.*

676. *tau laga yā mana sadan maiṁ, hari āvahiṁ kihi bāṭa* ।
bikaṭa jaṭe jau laga nipaṭa, khuṭaiṁ na kapaṭa kapāṭa ॥

How can the mind's mansion
become god's abode
while its gateway
remains barred
by the strong portals
of deceit?

677. *bhajana kahyau tātaiṁ bhajyau, bhajyau na ekau bāra* ।
dūri bhajana jātaiṁ kahyau, so taiṁ bhajyau gaṁvāra ॥

O foolish mind,
you shunned that god
whom you were told to worship,
you did not pray to him
even once,
instead you adored
worldly things
you were asked to renounce.

678. *patavārī mālā pakari, aur na kachū upāu* ।
tari saṅsāra payodhi kauṁ, hari nāvaiṁ ko nāu ॥

God's name is the boat, friend,
your rosary its rudder
which will steer you across
the ocean of this world.
There is no other way
to salvation.

679. *yaha biriyā nahiṁ aur kī, tū kariyā vaha sodhi* ।
pāhana nāva caṛhāi jihiṁ, kīne pāra payodhi ॥

What a devotee of Rāma said

You can find salvation now
only by seeking Rāma
by whose grace
a bridge of floating stones was made
to span the ocean
and take his army across.*

680. *karau kubat jaga kuṭilatā, tajauṁ na dīnadayāl* ।
dukhī hohuge saral hiya, basat tribhaṅgī lāl ॥

What a Kṛṣṇa devotee said

I'll bear the world's reproach
but I'll not abandon
my crookedness, Kṛṣṇa,
for then, with your askew form
of triple undulations,
you'd have trouble
dwelling
in my straight heart!*

681. *nija karanī sakucehiṁ kat, sakucāvat ihiṁ cāla* ।
mohūṁ se nita bimukha sauṁ, sanamukha rahi gopāla ॥

What a Kṛṣṇa devotee said

I'm myself repenting, Kṛṣṇa,
I have never been devoted to you,
why do you add to my embarrassment
by still being gracious to me?

682. *mohiṁ tumahiṁ bāṛhi bahasi, ko jīte jadurāja* ।
apanaiṁ apanaiṁ birada kī, duhūṁ nibāhana lāja ॥

What a Kṛṣṇa devotee said

Both you and I, Kṛṣṇa,
are struggling
to keep our reputation,
you as a redeemer
of sinners like me,
and I of the fallen
by showing you'll redeem us!

683. *dūri bhajata prabhu pīṭhi dai, guna bistārana kāla* ।
pragaṭata nirguna nikaṭa hvai, caṅga raṅga bhūpāla ॥

God turns away
from the arrogant
but is drawn
towards the meek,
as a kite soars higher
the more string it's given
and comes closer
when pulled.*

684. *jākaiṁ ekāekahūṁ, jaga byausāi na koi* ।
so nidāgha phūlai phalai, āka ḍahaḍaho hoi ॥

As it is only
the untended
swallow wort plant
which remains green
and bears fruits and flowers
in the exacting summer—
so god cares
for the man who's helpless.

685. *laṭuvā lauṁ prabhu kara gahaiṁ, nigunī guna lapaṭāi* ।
vahai gunī kara taiṁ chuṭaiṁ, nigunīpaiṁ hvai jāi ॥

As when a spinner
holds his top
it has the string wrapped round it
and when he flings it on the ground
it's stringless;
one who has god's grace
has all virtues
even though virtueless,
and one who hasn't

is wretched
despite all good qualities.

686. *pralaya karan barasana lage, juri jaladhara ik sātha ।*
surapati garaba haryau haraṣi, giradhara giri dhari hātha ॥

When the assemblage of clouds
began to pour
by Indra's command
as though they would cause
the world's dissolution,
Kṛṣṇa lifted the Goverdhana mount
on his hands
and destroyed
Indra's arrogance.*

687. *brajabāsina kau ucita dhana, jo dhana rucita na koi ।*
su cita na āyau sucitaī, kahau kahāṁ taiṁ hoi ॥

What a Kṛṣṇa devotee said

to a worldly-minded Braja-dweller

How can your mind
be tranquil
without Kṛṣṇa's love
which the unfortunate
do not prize,
but which
for Braja-dwellers
is all the wealth they have.*

688. *apanaiṁ apanaiṁ mata lage, bādi macāvata sora ।*
jyauṁ tyauṁ sabakauṁ seibau, ekai naṁdakisora ॥

What a Kṛṣṇa devotee said

Votaries of diverse faiths
needlessly wrangle,

for in his own way
each is worshipping
Kṛṣṇa
the supreme god.

689. *tau baliyai bhaliyai banī, nāgara naṁdakisora* ।
jau tuma nīkaiṁ kai lakhyau, mo karanī kī ora ॥

What a Kṛṣṇa devotee said

Much good will it do me
benign Kṛṣṇa,
if you look at my deeds
minutely!
Be gracious to me, I beseech you,
without sifting
the good from the bad.

690. *manamohana sauṁ moha kari, tū ghanasyāma nihāri* ।
kuñjabihārī sauṁ bihari, giradhārī ur dhāri ॥

O mind,
adoreKṛṣṇa
who steals all hearts,
meditate on his form
dark as a cloud,
linger with him where he sports
with the milkmaids in the woods,
and get your strength
from the saviour of Braja
who held aloft
the Goverdhana mount.*

691. samai palaṭi palaṭai prakṛta, ko na tajai nija cāla ।
bhau akaruna karunākarau, ihiṁ kapūta kalikāla ॥

A devotee's complaint

Whose nature does not change
with time?
Even god,
who is the ocean of mercy
has turned heartless
in this Kali age!*

692. *jyauṁ hvai hauṁ tyauṁ houṁgau, hauṁ hari apanī cāla ।*
haṭha na karau ati kaṭhina hai, mo tāribau gopāla ॥

What a Kṛṣṇa devotee said

Suffering punishment
for my evil deeds
I'll remain accursed
O Kṛṣṇa,
do not persist
in redeeming me,
for all your efforts
will be in vain!

IN PRAISE OF JAYASINGHA

693. *rahati na rana jayāsahi mukha, lākhi lākhana kī fauja* ।
jāṁci nirākharahū calai, lai lākhana kī mauja ॥

As soon as you took the field
valorous Jayasiṅgha,
Lākhana's troops
fled in awe.
And who can match
your generosity?
Even fools
are rewarded
lakhs of rupees
on the mere asking!*

694. *calata pāi nigunī gunī, dhana mani muktā māla* ।
bheṁṭa hota jayasāha sauṁ, bhāgya cāhiyata bhāla ॥

Scholar
or blockhead,
everyone,
gets as gifts from Jayasiṅgha
gold or gems
or a string of pearls,
if only he's lucky enough
to meet him.

695. *pratibimbita jayasāhi-duti, dīpati darapana-dhāma* ।
saba jaga jītana kauṁ karyau, kāma-byūhu manu kāma ॥

The splendour
of Jayasiṅgha
reflected
in the hall of mirrors
is as though
Kāma had arrayed his army
to vanquish the world.*

696. *anī baṛī umaṛī lakhauṁ, asi bāhaka bhaṭa bhūta* ।
maṅgala kari mānyau hiyaiṁ, bho muṁha maṅgala rūpa ॥

Seeing
the valiant sword-bearing kings
in the army
arrayed for battle,
Jayasiṅgha
considered it an honour
to oppose them,
and his face
flushing an angry red
seemed like ruddy Mars.*

697. *svāratha sukṛta na srama bṛthā, dekhi bihaṅga bicāri* ।
bāja parāyaiṁ pāni pari, tūṁ panchīhi na māri ॥

O Jayasiṅgha,
in vain you fight
your Rājpūt brothers
to add to Shāh Jahān's domain
reaping yourself
no advantage or merit,
as though a hawk
would prey upon innocent birds
to feed others.*

698. *sāmāṁ sena sayāna kī, sabai sāhi kaiṁ sāth* ।
bāhubalī jayasāhijū, fatai tihāre hāth ॥

Though Shāh Jahān
is a skilled warrior
and has all the weapons of war,
without you
O mighty Jayasiṅgha
how can he achieve
victory?*

699. *yauṁ dala kāṛhe balaka taiṁ, tai jayasiṅgha bhuvāla* ।
udara adhāsura kaiṁ paraiṁ, jyau hari gāi guvāla ॥

'Twas you
Maharaja Jayasiṅgha
who rescued
Shāh Jahān's army
beseiged in the Balkh country
as valiantly
as Kṛṣṅa,
ripping open the belly
of the demon, Adhāsura,
freed
the cowherds and their cows.*

700. *ghara ghara turakini hiṅdunī, deti asīsa sarāhi* ।
patina rākhi cādara curī, taiṁ rākhī jayasāhi ॥

You brought back alive
from Balkh
both Hindu and Muslim soldiers;
their wives
sing your praises
Jayasiṅgha,
from house to house

for having saved them
from cruel widowhood.*

701. *hukum paī jayasāhī kāu, hari rādhikā prasāda* ।
karī bihārī satasaī, bharī aneka savāda ॥

At the command of Jayasiṅgha
and blessed
with the grace
of Rādhā and Kṛṣṅa
I, Bihārī
composed the *Satasaī*
to cater
to diverse tastes and fancies.*

MISCELLANEOUS

702. *āvata jāta na jāniye, tejahiṁ taji siyarāna* ।
gharahiṁ jaṁvāī lauṁ ghaṭyau, kharo pūs dinamāna ॥

As the short days
of the *Pūs* month
denuded of warmth
and hardly noticed,
is the welcome made
to the man
who stays with his in-laws!*

703. *giri taiṁ ūṁce rasika mana, būṛe jahāṁ hajāra* ।
uhai sadā pasu narana kau, prema payodhi pagāra ॥

To the connoisseurs
with minds more elevated
than the highest mountains,
love and beauty
are an ocean unfathomed
even after a thousand dives;
but to ignorant fools
they seem to be
a shallow ditch
easily crossed.

704. *rahi na sakī sab jagata maiṁ, sisir sīta kaiṁ trāsa* ।
garama bhāji gaṛhavai gaī, tiya kuca acala mavāsa ॥

Scared by winter's cold
when warmth
could not find a place

in all the world,
it fled for refuge
to the firm impregnable breasts
of women!

705. *jhūṭhe jāni na saṅgrahe, mana muṁha nikase baina* ।
yāhī taiṁ mānahu kiye, bātana kauṁ bidhi nain ॥

The spoken words
are often false
and do not reveal
what's in the mind.
That's why it seems
god has given eyes
to unmistakably reveal
what's in it.

706. *yā bhava pārāvāra kauṁ, ulaṁghi pāra ko jāi* ।
tiya-chabi-chāyāgrāhinī, grahati bīca hīṁ āi ॥

Where is the man
who can get across
the ocean of worldly existence
when woman, the temptress,
lies in wait
ever ready
to pounce upon him?*

707. *bahu dhana lai ahasāna kari, pārau deta sarāhi* ।
baida-badhū haṁsi bheda sauṁ, rahī nāha-muṁha cāhi ॥

What a physician's friend said to his acquaintance

When that impotent physician
took a large fee
from a patient
and gave him mercury ash
to cure him of impotence too,

the doctor's wife
stared at her husband
amazed,
and gave him a sly smile!

708. *kahalāne ekat basat, ahi mayūra mṛga bāgha* ।
jagata tapobana sau kiyau, dīragha dāgha nidāgha ॥

Agitated
by the sizzling heat,
serpent and peacock
gazelle and lion
have taken refuge together,
as though summer has turned
their forced resting place
into a sanctuary!*

709. *jyauṁ jyauṁ baṛhati bibhāvarī, tyauṁ tyauṁ baṛhat ananta* ।
oka oka sab loka sukha, koka soka hemanta ॥

The lengthening winter nights
bring immeasurable joy
to every couple,
but to the ruddy geese pair
they give
boundless grief.*

710. *nāgari bibidha bilāsa taji, basī gavaṁlina māṁhi* ।
mūṛhani maiṁ ganabī ki tūṁ, hūṭhyau dai iṭhalāṁhi ॥

Gifted girl,
forsaking the comforts of the city
you've settled
in this backward village;
if you do not put on airs
as the women here do
they'll think you stupid!*

711. *cita pitumāraka joga guni, bhayau bhayaiṁ suta soga* ।
ati hulasyau jiya joisī, samujhaiṁ jāraja joga ॥

When the astrologer
read his newborn son's horoscope
he was grieved
it heralded the father's death,
but on deeper scrutiny
he was overjoyed to learn
the child was fathered
by his wife's lover!*

712. *aniyāre dīragha dṛgana, kitī na taruni samāna* ।
vaha citavani aurai kachū, jihiṁ basa hota sujāna ॥

Countless young women
are endowed
with large and pointed eyes,
but the glance that can enslave
men of virtue
is given only to some.*

713. *dṛga thirakauṁhaiṁ adhakhule, deha thakauṁhaiṁ ḍhāra* ।
surati sukhit sī dekhiyat, dukhit garabha kaiṁ bhāra ॥

What one of her companions said to another

When the old woman
who came to meet her
saw her tired and weary-eyed,
she said
'Maybe she has been love-making
and is still intoxicated
with its rapture,

that's why perhaps
she has sent you to receive me
instead of coming out herself.'
'Ah no' I said, 'you're mistaken,
she's heavy with a child
and it's that which makes her listless.'

NOTES

Abbreviations Used

AL W.G. Archer, *The Loves of Krishna*, London: George Allen & Unwin Limited, 1957.

AR *The Ananga Ranga of Kalyana Malla* (Trans. Sir Richard Burton and F.F. Arbuthnot), London: William Kimber and Company Limited, 1963.

BAH Mulk Raj Anand and Krishna Hutheesingh, *The Bride's Book of Beauty*, Bombay: Kutub Publishers Limited.

BBB *Bihārī Bhāṣya* (Commentary, Dr Desarājasiṇgha Bhātī), Delhi: Aśoka Prakāśan, 1978. (Hindi)

BBL *Bihārī-Bodhinī* (Commentary, Lālā Bhagawāna Dīna 'Dīna'), Banāras: Sāhitya-Sevā-Sadan, 1978. (Hindi)

BBP Dr Śakuntalā Pāñcāla, *Bihārī kī Bhāṣa*, Kānpur, Sāhitya Ratnālaya, 1979. (Hindi)

BSL *Bihārī-Satasaī* (*lālacandrikā ṭikā*) (Commentary and Editing, Lallūjī 'Lāl'), Kāśī: Nāgarīpracāriṇī Sabhā. (Hindi)

BSR *Bihārī-Satasaī* (Commentary, Śrī Rākeśa), Lucknow: Prakāśana Kendra. (Hindi)

BSS *Bigārī-Satasaī* (Commentary, Śarmā, Devendra 'Indra'), Agra: Vinod Pustak Mandir, 1978. (Hindi)

GBS *Bihārī-Satasaī* (Commentary, Śukla, Girijādatta), 1934. (Hindi)

HWB Benjamin Walker, *Hindu World*, 2 vols., London: George Allen & Unwin Limited, 1968.

KS *Vatsyayana's Kama Sutra* (Trans., Sir Richard Burton and F.F. Arbuthnot) London: Luxor Press, 1963.

SPI *Sanskrit Poetry* (Trans. Ingalls, Daniel H.H.), Cambridge and Massachusetts: Havard University Press, 1965.

Introduction

Bihārī's Times

1. *Voyages to the East Indies* (trans., Willcocke), vol. 1, p. 415.
2. Abu'l Fazl, *Ain-i-Akbarī*, vol. 3, p. 256.
3. *Tazuk-i-Jahangirī* (trans., Rogers & Bereridge), vol. 2, p. 268.
4. Manucci, *Storia do Mogor*, vol. 2, pp. 13–14; vol. 3, pp. 267–8.
5. ibid., vol. 2, p. 342.
6. For example the *Bṛhat-kausala Khaṅḍa* (cantos ix–xv) depicted Rāma as performing the *rāsalīlā* dance with heavenly nymphs and human princesses, even after he married Sītā.

Life

1. The version followed here is based generally on the one accepted by Jagannātha Dāsa Ratnākara, Bihārī's celebrated commentator.
2. George A. Grierson, *Indian Lyric Poetry and Bihārī-Satasaī*, in *Bihārī, an Anthology*, ed., Dr Nagendra, Delhi: Bansal & Co., 1981, p. 56.
3. Lallūjī 'Lāl' (*Bihārī-Satasaī, lālacandrikā ṭīkā*, commentary and editing by Lallūjī 'Lāl', Kāśī: Nāgarīpracārinī Sabhā, p. 8, Hindi), thinks it was not the Amber ruler who was Bihārī's patron, but Jayasiṅgha Sawāi (1693–1743). But the mention of the Balkh campaign in verse 699 could refer only to Jayasiṅgha, the Amber rajah.

The Rītikāla Tradition and Love in Bihārī's Poetry

1. A detailed account has been given in *Bihārī-Satasaī* (Commentary, Devendra Śarmā, 'Indra'), Agra: Vinod Pustak Mandir, 1978, pp. 103–119. (Hindi)
2. *Satasaī* (text), verse 126 (Note—All verses of the *Satasaī* quoted are from this translation. The numbers are those of the text.)
3. *Satasaī*, verse 600.
4. ibid., 640.
5. ibid., 703.
6. Christopher Marlowe, *Tamburlaine*, II.v.1.
7. *Satasaī*, verse 705.
8. ibid., 145.
9. ibid., 489.
10. ibid., 180.
11. *A Midsummer Night's Dream*, I.i.234.

12. *Satasaī,* verse 373.
13. ibid., 632.
14. K.K. Śarmā, *Bihārī: Philosophy of Life* (in *Bihārī, an Anthology,* ed. Dr Nagendra, Delhi: Bansal & Co., 1981, p. 171).
15. *Satasaī,* verse 194.
16. Sir Walter Scott, *The Lay of the Last Minstrel,* ii.10.

The Concept of Beauty in Bihārī's Poetry

1. *Satasaī,* verse 509.
2. ibid., 550.
3. ibid., 503.
4. ibid., 487.
5. ibid., 470.
6. ibid., 580. See also verse 581.
7. ibid., 566.
8. ibid., 561.
9. ibid., 478.
10. ibid., 583.
11. ibid., 592.
12. ibid., 556.
13. ibid., 494, 498, 501, 524 and 584.
14. ibid., 533. See also verses 527 and 586.
15. ibid., 462, 463, 464, 485, 496 and 513.
16. ibid., 499, 176, 582 and 594.
17. ibid., 202.
18. ibid., 135 and 177.
19. ibid., 538.
20. ibid., 245.
21. ibid., 41.
22. ibid., 502.
23. ibid., 466, 4, 468, 479, 482, 483, 21, 492, 508, 64, 541, 551, 563 and 596.
24. ibid., 591.
25. ibid., 545.
26. *Ode on a Grecian Urn,* 5.

Nature in Bihārī's Poetry

1. *Satasaī,* verse 432.
2. ibid., 545.
3. ibid., 547.
4. ibid., 546.
5. ibid., 544.
6. ibid., 332.
7. ibid., 708.
8. ibid., 361.
9. ibid., 562.
10. ibid., 704.
11. ibid., 536.
12. ibid., 356.
13. ibid., 505 and 278.
14. ibid., 278.
15. ibid., 563.
16. ibid., 573.

Philosophy in the Satasaī

1. *Bihārī, an Anthology* (ed., Dr Nagendra), Delhi: Bansal & Co., 1981, pp. 162 and 171.
2. *Satasaī,* verses 488, 512, 559, 597 and 598.
3. ibid., 611, 636, 710 and 648.
4. Rudyard Kipling, *If.*
5. *Satasaī,* verse 631.
6. ibid., 612.
7. ibid., 641.
8. ibid., 624.
9. ibid., 653.
10. ibid., 609.
11. ibid., 618.
12. ibid., 619.
13. ibid., 608.
14. ibid., 691.
15. ibid., 604.
16. ibid., 601.
17. ibid., 646.

18. ibid., 628.
19. ibid., 602 and 633.
20. ibid., 614, 626, 638 and 644.
21. ibid., 625.
22. *Julius Caesar,* IV. iii. 212–3.
23. *Satasaī,* verse 627.
24. ibid., 635.
25. ibid., 642.
26. ibid., 621.
27. ibid., 651.
28. ibid., 608.
29. Rudyard Kipling, *If.*

The Devotional Element in Bihārī's Poetry

1. *Satasaī,* verse 688.
2. ibid., 661 and 679.
3. ibid., 658, 662, 663, 665, 666, etc. The controversial verse is 669 in which Bihārī speaks of a formless god.
4. ibid., 660 and 664.
5. ibid., 683.
6. ibid., 684 and 685.
7. ibid., 657.
8. ibid., 678.
9. ibid., 667 and 670.
10. ibid., 655, 658, 662, 682 and 691.

Bihārī's Poetic Art

1. *Bihārī, an Anthology,* ed., Dr Nagendra, Delhi: Bansal & Co, 1981, pp. 77–97 and 199.
2. Rājeśvaraprasāda Chaturvedī, *Mahākavi Bihārīlāl,* Delhi: Bhāratī Sāhītya Mandir, p. 125, op. cit.
3. *Bihārī, an Anthology,* ed., Dr Nagendra, Delhi: Bansal & Co., 1981, pp. 62–3.
4. Rājeṣvaraprasāda Chaturvedī, *Mahākavi Bihārīlāl,* Delhi: Bhārati Sāhitya Mandir, pp. 145–6, op. cit.
5. *Bihārī, an Anthology,* ed., Dr Nagendra, Delhi: Bansal & Co., 1981, p. 112.
6. ibid., p. 194.

7. ibid., p. 99.
8. *Satasaī*, verses 545, 546 and 547.
9. See for example *Satasaī*, verses 657, 618 and 643.
10. *Viśāla Śabda Sāgara* (Hindi Dictionary), ed., Sri Navalaji, Delhi: New India Book Depot.
11. These are said to be of eleven kinds, namely *līlā, vilāsa, vicchita, vibhrama, kilakiṅcita, moṭṭāyita, vivvoka, vihṛta, kuṭṭamita, lalita and helā.*
12. *Satasaī*, verse 9.
13. As for example, *Satasaī*, verses 479, 544 and 551, q.v.
14. *Satasaī*, verses 73, 119, 273, 707, 711 and 301.
15. ibid., 140.
16. ibid., 412.
17. ibid., 390.
18. ibid., 498 (*campā* is a fragrant yellow flower)
19. ibid., 104.

The Satasaī Tradition and Bihārī's Achievement

1. According to Grierson the *Sapta-Śatika* belongs to the fifth century. Dr Randhir Sinhā (*Kavivara Bihārī aur unkā Yuga,* Kanpur: Anusandhāna Prakāśan, 1964, p. 232) gives the date as AD 200.
2. George A. Grierson, *Indian Lyric Poetry and Bihārī-Satasaī* in *Bihārī, an Anthology*, ed., Dr Nagendra, Delhi: Bansal & Co., 1981, pp. 64–66.
3. *Bihārī, an Anthology,* ed., Dr Nagendra, Delhi: Bansal & Co., 1981, p. 85.
4. *Hindi Sāhitya kā Itihāsa.* (Hindi)
5. *Bihārī kī Satasaī.* (Hindi)
6. *Bihārī aur unkā Sāhitya.* (Hindi)
7. *Bihārī, an Anthology,* ed., Dr Nagendra, Delhi: Bansal & Co., 1981, p. 62.

A Note on the Translation, Transliteration and Arrangement of the Verses

1. *Bihārī, an Anthology*, ed., Dr Nagendra, Delhi: Based & Co., 1981, p. 63.

Love

1. According to Hindu astrology a child born at the moment Saturn is in the House of Pisces will become a king. The *nāyaka* has met his beloved on a

Saturday, which is Saturn's day, and so the 'lucky child of love' is born. The woman's messenger tells the *nāyaka,* 'As this child will become a king and enjoy his domain so should you enjoy your girl.'

Indian women apply collyrium (lamp-black) to the edges of their eyelids to make the eyes look lovelier.

3. When there is a whirlpool, boatmen tie a rope to one end of their boat and hold the other fast from the river bank to prevent the boat being caught in it. Here the poet likens the girl's bashfulness to the rope and the boat to her thoughts about her lover.

Expressing a similar thought the *Āryāsaptaśatī* says, 'Going round and round in your love-shaped waters, this girl, abandoning propriety, remains caught in a whirlpool.'

5. Duryodhana, Dhṛtaraṣṭra's eldest son, was the leader of the Kauravas, in the great war of the Mahābhārata between the Kauravas and the Pāṇḍavas. According to legend there was a curse on Duryodhana that his death would take place when he was joyful and sorrowful at one and the same moment. While he lay mortally wounded on the battlefield, still thirsting for revenge, he was visited by Aśvatthāmā, son of Droṇa, and two other warriors, the only survivors of his army. He asked them to slay all the Pāṇḍavas, and particularly to bring him the head of Bhīma, who had struck him foully below the waist. Duryodhana's warriors went to the Pāṇḍava camp and, after killing five young sons of the Pāṇḍavas, brought their heads to him. Duryodhana was not able to distinguish the features, but was very happy that revenge had been taken. He asked that Bhīma's head be placed in his hands, and that having been done, pressed on it with his dwindling strength. When he found he could not crush it, he knew it was not Bhīma's head. He found out the deception and was filled with deep remorse for having been instrumental in the slaying of five innocent boys. These contrary feelings of joy and sorrow at the same time, fulfilled the condition of the curse, and he died.

The poet likens the conflicting emotions of joy and sorrow in the mind of the woman going to her mother's house, to Duryodhana's condition. Having experienced the pleasure of love-making with her husband she is now so enamoured of him that even a few days of separation causes her unbearable anguish. At the same time she is happy to go home and meet her parents.

7. Indian women get their noses pierced on the right nostril to wear nose ornaments like a nose-pin or a nose-ring.

8. A *kibalanumā* is believed to be a kind of compass whose needle is so adjusted as to always point towards Mecca. Muslims carried it with them to be able to face Mecca while reciting the *namāza* (prayers). Other commentators interpret the word differently. According to one of them (*Mānasiṅgha*), it means a marionette (*kaṭhaputlī*). In this sense it would mean, in whatever direction the puppet is revolved it turns back to face the audience again. Another commentator (*Kṛṣṇakavi*), taking the word as *kavalanavī*, interprets it to mean a small magic bowl which was used in locating the culprit in case of a theft. The suspects were made to stand in a circle and the bowl placed at the centre. When a *mantra* (sacred charm) was recited, the bowl would start moving and go to everyone by turns, stopping only in front of the thief.

Most probably Bihārī meant the word to signify the magnetic needle which keeps Mecca-wards. Living in the age of the Moghul emperor, Shāh Jahān, he was quite familiar with Muslim customs. Lālā Bhagawāna Dīna, one of Bihārī's noted commentators, also accepts this interpretation. (BBL, p. 28)

The same thought finds place in other poets writing in Hindi or Sanskrit. Sūradāsa uses the simile of the magic bowl in describing how the beloved's gaze stays on her lover alone. Rasalīna uses the same example as Bihārī and says, 'the lover's gaze remains fixed on his beloved like the *kibalanumā's* needle' (*kibalanuma lauṁ dṛga rahaiṁ nirakha mīta kī or*).

The *Āryāsaptaśatī* (though giving different examples) expresses the same thought: 'As the quick moving finger touches each bead in a rosary and moves swiftly on to rest on the central bead (which is of the greatest import), so does the girl look on each youth by turns, and ignoring him, finally rests her gaze on you.'

9. The verse is a good example of Bihārī's condensed style of writing and is often quoted to illustrate this quality of his.

Similar is Kālīdāsa's description of Śakuntalā stealing a glance at King Duṣyanta (translation Monier Williams):

> She did look towards me, though she quick withdrew
> Her stealthy glance when she met my gaze;
> She smiled upon me sweetly but disguised
> With maiden glance the secret of her smiles.
> Coy love was half-unveiled; then sudden checked
> By modesty left half to be divined.

10. The word *hari* can mean either Kṛṣṇa or the sun. The translation takes it to mean the sun. In the alternative Rādhā's gestures could be taken to imply

'lover, you are always in my heart'. But that wouldn't be a good enough reaction on Rādhā's part, seeing her lover was even prepared to fall at her feet!

An *ārasī* is a kind of ring with a small mirror set in it, worn by Indian women on the thumb of their right hand.

Rādhā touches her breasts with the *ārasī* to signify that she will meet her lover when the sun has set and it is dark. The *ārasī* signifies the sun because Rādhā has 'caught' the sun's image in its mirror by turning it towards the sun. Putting the *ārasī* between her breasts, points out to the setting of the sun—and that is when she will meet Kṛṣṇa.

12. The verse has become famous because it is believed to have provided the occasion for Bihārī's writing the *Satasaī*. It is said that Jayasiṅgha, the ruler of Amber, got so enamoured of a young girl that he always remained in her company and neglected the affairs of state. So much so that he gave orders that if any of his officials came with state matters and disturbed him in his dalliance, he would be sentenced to death. For a year things went on like this and the rajah's secretaries managed somehow to carry on the administration. But soon a very important issue came up and it became essential to take the rajah's orders for it. The secretaries sought Bihārī's advice, and the poet thought of an ingenious way to set right the erring ruler. He wrote out the verse on a bit of paper and concealed it in the basketful of flowers which used to be taken each day to the king's bedroom to be spread on the royal bed. Early morning when the flowers had withered, the rajah found something scratching him. It was the slip of paper on which Bihārī's verse was written. When he read it, the impact on him was so great that he realized his fault and henceforth began to look after the kingdom. He summoned Bihārī to his durbar and asked him to send more of his couplets, promising to give a gold *mohur* for each as a reward. Bihārī wrote about seven hundred verses (*sata*=seven, *saī*=hundred) and that was how the *Satasaī* got its name.

13. Normally it is the huntsmen of the city who hunt for deer in the forests. But in this case it is the other way around. The deer-like eyes of the *nāyikā* shoot arrows at the young men of the city so that they themselves become victims of the hunt of love!

A woman's lovely eyes are often compared to those of a deer by Hindi and Sanskrit poets.

Kānancāri means 'stretching up to the ears'. It's not that the woman's eyes are that long. Indian women paint a dark line to make their eyes seem longer. *The Bride's Book of Beauty* has the following observation about this : 'The size of the eyes is increased by drawing a short, fine pencil mark outwards from the corner of the lids where they join.' (BAH)

A similar idea is expressed by Bhavabhūti:

> Her pupils widening behind long lashes
> told of the admiration she felt.
> My heart, poor thing without defense,
> was captured, cut up and swallowed,
> and is now lost for aye. (SPI, p.141)

14. When someone casts a spell, it is believed its evil effect can be warded off by making an offering of salt and mustard in fire. By doing so the spell rebounds on the person who cast it. The eyes contain salt tears and so metaphorically Kṛṣṇa has made the *nāyikā's* eyes salty, i.e., has turned her spell against her. This is the significance of the word *lone* (salt).

Sāje means 'adorned'. One of the ways of adding beauty to eyes is by applying lamp-black to the edges of the eyelids (see note to verse 479). *The Bride's Book of Beauty* has the following other tips for decorating the eyes : 'Also kohl, made of sulphide of antimony with Chinese or Indian ink blackens them, preserves them against the sun and air and changes them to moonstones, brilliant, glinting, and flashing fire. A simple method of increasing the eyes' depth is to make the lids blue with the juice of the wild plum.' (BAH)

16. For Kāma, see note to verse 463.

17. The translation follows Lālā Bhagawāna Dīna's version (BBL, p. 120). Some commentators take the second *lāi* (not *lāī,* which means have brought) to stand for 'a passage dug by thieves for entering a house' instead of the alternative interpretation meaning 'the fire (of love)'. They interpret the concluding part of the couplet as 'now love has stolen through your eyes like a thief digging a passage for himself, and have set your heart aflame'. Bhagawāna Dīna's reading of the verse seems to be more meaningful and so it has been adopted in the translation.

18. *mukti* meaning 'emancipation', 'liberation' or 'release' is the state conceived by Hindu philosophy in which the soul (*ātman*) becomes one with the Absolute (*Brahman*).

Jagannātha Dāsa Ratnākara, one of Bīharī's renowned commentators, thinks these words should be taken as spoken by the *gopīs* (cowherd girls) to Ūdhava (Kṛṣṇa's friend and counsellor). His interpretation is: 'On hearing Ūdhava speak to them about *mukti* (emancipation), the *gopīs* said "If this emancipation you speak of does not provide a way to meet Kṛṣṇa, we have no use for it. If we can be united with him in hell, we do not fear going there for it".'

Other critics read in the verse the doctrine of the *dvaitas,* i.e. those who believe in a god with form (Īśvara), and consider emancipation to be the soul's dwelling in heaven with god. If this interpretation is accepted the sense would be: A worshipper of god with form, says to one who believes in a formless god (to refute his doctrine), 'If emancipation does not provide a way to obtain the beloved personal god, it is fit to be shunned. If one can find him even in hell, it were better to go there and undergo hell's torments for union with him.'

These interpretations seem to be unnecessary. Usually Bihārī mentions Kṛṣṇa by any of his numerous names when the verse is meant to refer to him. In this he does not. The simple interpretation is that *sājan* and *piya* here mean the lover (*nāyaka*) and the girl (*nāyikā*). She wishes to convey her intense love for him through her companion.

19. *naṁdakumāra* means 'son of Naṁda' (*kumāra:* son), i.e. Kṛṣṇa. In the *Āryāsaptaśatī,* the Sanskrit poet, Ācārya Goverdhana conveys a similar thought:

> Tidying her hair
> with neck bent and
> her tresses massed
> on her face,
> even then somehow
> she manages to glance
> through them at you.

20. *devar* means the younger brother of a woman's husband. Hindi poets often depict the *devar* as being enamoured of such a woman particularly when she is a newly-wed wife and he is unmarried.

The *Gāthāsaptaśatī* expresses a similar idea:

> Even though her brother-in-law
> lusts for her,
> that virtuous woman
> suffers silently
> and does not tell her husband,
> lest his tempestuous nature
> may create a split in the family.

21. *tribalī* means the triple folds appearing on a woman's belly, above her navel. These are considered to be one of the signs of beauty according to Hindi and Sanskrit love poets. Describing a Padminī, the lotus-eyed woman (a woman

of the most beautiful kind), Kalyāna Malla mentions three folds crossing 'her middle, about the umbilical region'. (ARA, p. 114)

ali ki oṭ hvai means 'eluding her companion'.

The literal meaning of *oṭ* is 'screen, shelter, or concealment'. Some commentators have therefore taken this to mean, 'The *nāyikā* hid behind her companion and peeped at her lover, herself unseen by him'. But that wouldn't explain why the *nāyikā* bared her midriff region by going through the pretence of raising her hand and shifting her sari up to cover her head. Obviously she did that to hide her love-affair from her companion. In that case her companion could not be an accomplice, which one would have to believe she was, if she acted as a screen for the *nāyikā* to gaze at her lover.

23. *syāma raṅga* has a double meaning. It means 'the love of Kṛṣṇa (he is also called Śyāma, *raṅga* meaning 'love'), or it can be taken as 'black colour' (*śyāma* meaning 'black' or 'dark', and *raṅga* meaning 'hue'). Kṛṣṇa is believed to be of dark complexion. The strangeness lies in the fact that although the *nāyikā's* mind is drenched in black colour it comes out white! This is meant metaphorically of course. The idea is that love of Kṛṣṇa does not result in agitation but is satisfying and pure.

Some commentators take the verse as relating to a devotee of the god Kṛṣṇa, but since Bihārī is essentially a love poet, it would be more appropriate to interpret it as being for the *nāyikā.*

Poet Jasavantasiṅgha similarly says:

Wonderfully,
her red-dyed lovelorn mind
mingling with Kṛṣṇa.
instead of becoming darker
emerged white
shorn of all its dross.

25. Accompanied by her women companions, the *nāyikā* (who is apparently a milkmaid) is out selling curd. Her lover, the *nāyaka,* meets her on the way and in the impetuosity of his passion catches hold of her. She frees herself and addresses her impatient lover in these words. She chides him for appearance's sake because of the presence of her companions, but very subtly signifies her consent also by throwing a hint to him to come secretly to her house when she will satisfy his longing.

Some commentators have interpreted the couplet thus: 'You are shamelessly stopping me on the way. Don't you understand that it's love-making I desire, while you are asking me for useless things instead, like curd and milk! Why don't you take me somewhere, like to the woods, so that we can make love? If we start doing so here my reputation will be ruined.' (BSR, p. 114) But this interpretation does not seem to be appropriate because the *nāyikā* is out with her companions (milkmaids usually went in company), and she could hardly make her intentions so clear to the *nāyaka* in their presence. In that case she would be what she accuses him of being, i.e. shameless!

26. The *nāyaka* here is most probably Kṛṣṇa (though the poet does not say so specifically), and the *nāyikā*, Rādhā. The idea behind the mingling of the cows is that Rādhā surrenders herself to Kṛṣṇa's love. The moment she sees him she falls deeply in love and says, 'I make no distinction between you and myself. My cows are yours.' Love springs between them in a moment spontaneously.

27. *gaunā* means the ceremony held at the time the bride goes to her husband's home for the first time. Child-marriages were common in Bihārī's days. Girls were often married when they were only about six or seven years old. But they went to their husband after attaining puberty, and when they did, there was a ceremony to celebrate the occasion. This was known as the *gaunā*.

The words *bātaiṁ calīṁ* ordinarily means 'mention was made', i.e. the *nāyikā* (who had been married) and was now grown up would be going to her husband's home. While talking among themselves one of her companions happened to say that the date of her departure had been decided (this would be determined after consulting the almanac and picking out an auspicious date). But some commentators have stretched the words to mean 'the girl's *gaunā* was postponed for some future date' (taking the word *calīṁ* to mean *calāimāna*, i.e. 'unsettled'). In that sense the girl is happy to learn that she isn't to go to her husband, and the reason is that she has a secret lover. Going away to her husband will mean parting from him. It is true Bihārī often narrates illicit love too, but here the intention does not seem to be to describe an intriguing girl (known to Hindi poets as a *parakīyā muditā*) who prefers a lover to a husband. Such a girl, if she can carry on a secret affair, would be clever enough to hide her feelings of happiness on learning that she isn't to part with her lover. The girl described in Bihārī's verse seems to be an artless one (known as a *svakīyā*). Her companions must have been tutoring her about the pleasures of sex (as they are often believed to do in Hindi love poetry) and the girl is happy to be able to enjoy those pleasures now.

The interpretation taken in the translation is supported by Lālā Bhagawāna Dīna as well as by other commentators. (BBL, p. 139) Dr Śakuntalā Pāñcāla also gives the meaning of *calīṁ* as 'having started', 'begun', and not as 'unsettled'. (BBP, p. 191)

30. For *khañjana* see note to verse 479. It is a kind of Indian wagtail. Bihārī has particularly chosen a *khañjana* as the trapped bird because the eyes of a beautiful woman are likened to those of the *khañjana* by Hindi poets. Here the *nāyikā's khañjana*-like eyes are trapped by the birdlime of the *nāyaka's* glances.

31. The *nāyikā* here is perhaps Rādhā and the *nāyaka* is Kṛṣṇa. Kṛṣṇa is represented as wearing a tiara or coronet, putting on a yellow dress, a garland of flowers round his neck, and holding a flute on which he plays.

32. The verse here refers to Kṛṣṇa, and the *nāyikā* is Rādhā, his beloved, or some other cowherd girl whom he has bewitched. The *nāyikā's* companion is upbraiding her for looking at him again and again thus inviting people's censure. But the *nāyikā* is helpless because dark-complexioned Kṛṣṇa has charmed her by his beauty. The verse contains the *nāyikā's* reply to her companion.

33. The *nāyikā* has been gazing at the *nāyaka* for a long time and her companions get apprehensive that people might start noticing her behaviour. So they try to persuade her to come away: 'You've been gazing at him long now, and that ought to be enough. Now let's go.' The verse gives the *nāyikā's* reply. Some commentators take the *nāyaka* to be Kṛṣṇa, but there is nothing in the verse to indicate this.

34. Some commentators have taken the words to be spoken by a go-between (*dūtī*) to the *nāyaka* when he asks her to arrange a meeting between him and the *nāyikā*. Ratnākara would have them spoken not by a go-between but by a companion of the *nāyikā* to whom the *nāyaka* makes the request. Bhagawāna Dīna takes them as spoken playfully by the *nāyikā* herself when the *nāyaka* asks her to come with him to gather flowers from the arbour. 'You really want to make love I know' she quips him, 'on the excuse of gathering flowers from the arbour'. This appears to be the most likely interpretation. The *nāyaka* here is Kṛṣṇa because he has been called Hari, which is another name for him.

The episode of King Bali is told thus: Bali was a good and virtuous demon-king (*daitya rajah*) who, through his penance defeated Indra, king of the gods, and extended his authority over the three worlds. The gods prayed to Lord Viṣṇu who took the form of a dwarf, Vāmana, and asked Bali for three steps of land as charity. Bali thought of course that this was a mere trifle and readily agreed. Having been given the boon, the 'dwarf' stepped over heaven and earth in two strides, but spared Bali the nether regions because of the king's kindness to Prahalāda (Bali's grandson and Viṣṇu's devotee). Kṛṣṇa was an incarnation of Viṣṇu, hence the connection between him and Vāmana.

36. The *nāyikā* has been love-making in the forest with the *nāyaka* (who here is Kṛṣṇa because of the mention of the coronet). By chance her companions see her emerging from the forest with her lover and question her about it. She gives them this story. The acrobat of her trumped up version has to be described as wearing a coronet because Kṛṣṇa, whom her companions have seen, wore it. Hindi and Sanskrit poets often make their *nāyikā* trump up a story to hide their amours. Poet Maṅḍana describes a situation in which a *nāyikā* cleverly clears herself with her companions when they happen by chance to see Kṛṣṇa embracing her:

I had gone to draw water from the Yamunā
when suddenly black clouds arose.
I hurriedly put the pitcher on my head
and started climbing the river bank
when I tripped and was about to fall;
but Kṛṣṇa, who was there just at that moment,
caught me in his arms
and steadied poor me.

38. The *nāyikā* is praising the *nāyaka's* attractive eyes which enslave her mind in spite of herself. Expressing a similar idea, poet Bhikārīdāsa says:

Lover, the fascination of your eyes
is beyond words;
even when one is careful
they steal away
the wealth of the mind.

42. Kṛṣṇa was born in Mathurā and was taken to Gokula to be brought up by Yaśodā and her husband Naṅda among the cowherds at Vṛndāvana in the Braja country. Vṛndāvana was the scene of his love exploits with the cowherd girls. Later he returned to Mathurā. The couplet here is spoken by one cowherd belle to another about Kṛṣṇa after he had gone away from Vṛndāvana. She nostalgically recollects his presence at the places where he used to make love to her and her fellow cowherd girls.

45. Poet Matirāma has a similar thought:

What can I do friend?

Ever since I've seen Kṛṣṇa
my mind is not in my control;
acting as a broker
Kāma has sold me to him!

48. Poet Matirāma expresses a similar idea:
They're playing blind-man's-buff,
and as soon as her lover
covers her eyes with his hands
she guesses it's him.

49. The *nāyaka* sees his girl in a thick crowd, perhaps a fair. Fearing that some of her friends may guess their secret love, she does not look at him, but softly whispers something which he can't make out. The incident keeps preying on his mind and vexing him. Maybe, he thinks, she meant to tell him where he could meet her for love-making, and since he failed to catch her words he is deprived of the pleasure.

50. *phirakī lauṁ* means 'like a *phirakī*'. A *phirakī* is a round piece of leather or wood with two holes in it. By passing a string through these holes and pulling it alternately this way and that, the disc moves round clockwise and then anticlockwise. Poet Deva has a similar idea:
She fears to glance on him freely
from her casement
and restlessly wanders
from window to window
like a revolving *phirakī*
to have a glimpse of him.

53. What the poet wants to say is that the girl's ankles are so shapely and beautiful that her lover can't take his eyes off them even for a moment.

54. A *pāil* is an anklet with tiny bells attached to it. When the girl wearing her *pāils* moves, the bells make a melodious tinkling sound.

55. *sāhas* means 'boldness', 'pluck' or 'courage'. The implication is that the *nāyikā* glances again and again at her lover, braving censure or public opprobrium, but can't even then fathom the depth of his beauty, which shines with a new light every time she looks at him. It is like a swimmer who, because of dangerous sea animals like crocodiles etc., can't get across the river. The *nāyikā's* eyes are likened to the swimmer, and the sea creatures to the people who are there to criticize the girl who shamelessly gazes on her lover.

56. The reference is to the abduction of Rukmiṇī by Kṛṣṇa. Rukmiṇī was the daughter of the rajah of Kundulpur. Kṛṣṇa wanted to marry her and she too was in love with him, but her brother, Rukma, persuaded her father to wed her to Kṛṣṇa's rival, Śiśupāla. Rukmiṇī sent a message to her lover, asking him to come to her aid. Kṛṣṇa arrived while the preparations for the wedding were going on. But meanwhile his old enemy, Jarasandha, a demon, had also come along with his army of demons. This dismayed Rukmiṇī, but her fears were soon dispelled when Kṛṣṇa arrived. Soon after, Balarāma, his warrior brother, along with his band of soldiers, also reached there. On the wedding day, Rukmiṇī, guarded by Śiśupalā's soldiers went to worship the goddess at the local temple on the outskirts of the city. Kṛṣṇa appeared suddenly and, surprising Śiśupāla's soldiers, lifted her into his chariot and sped away.

60. The incident referred to in the verse is one of the episodes of Kṛṣṇa's romantic exploits with the cowherd girls. The girls, having discarded their clothes, were bathing naked in the river Yamunā. Kṛṣṇa came quietly, and gathering all their clothes, climbed up a tree. The disconcerted milkmaids, covering their breasts and private parts with their hands, came out of the water and beseeched him to return their clothes. Instead of doing so the mischievous lad asked them to raise their hands and pray to the sun god, so that their breasts, which they had hidden, may be exposed to his view. The girls, who were pretending to be angry (they were not really so because they were eager to show their lover their shapely bodies!) could not help smiling at his ingenious device to see them entirely nude.

61. *surati* means 'memory' or 'remembrance' and *su rati* 'the recollection of his blissful love-making' (*su*= 'beautiful' or 'sweet', *rati*= 'love' or 'love-making'). An interpretation of *su rati* made by one commentator as 'not for a moment', taking *rati* or *ratti* to mean 'a little', seems quite unnecessary. (BBB, p. 160) Firstly it would leave us only with the 'memory of Kṛṣṇa' (while Kṛṣṇa would assuredly be remembered by the girl for his love-making too), and secondly the first line already conveys the sense that Kṛṣṇa's remembrance never leaves the *nāyikā.* Its repetition in the second line would be superfluous.

62. Some commentators take the words of the couplet to be spoken in reply by a virtuous wife to her companion who tries to transfer her love from her husband to another man. But such a situation is rather unusual in Hindi poetry. If the woman is so faithful to her husband, her friend would surely know it. She would hardly make an effort to divert the woman's affections. Yet another interpretation is that the words are meant to be the reply of a firm believer in a

certain religious creed, whom her friend is trying to convert to another faith. (BSS, p. 219) This, however, seems even less likely.

65. The *nāyikā* (who is a village milkmaid) is churning curd to convert it into butter and buttermilk. The process in the Indian villages was to mix water with curd and then churn it with a wooden stick having a flower-shaped end which stirred up the curd and water. The curd was churned with water gradually added to it. So the girl has two earthen pots, one containing the curd and the other water (which she will mix in it). Her lover's coming so excites her that she begins churning the water instead of the curd, and that too with the flower-shaped end of the stick upwards and the plain end downwards!

69. Bihārī's comparison is ingenious inasmuch as the hawk is known to fly rather low, but when it spots a prey, it goes high up—much higher than its victim—and then suddenly swoops down to catch the bird in its claws. The verse depicts the poet's close observation of the habits of birds of prey.

70. The joining of the hands is one of the important ceremonies observed in a Hindu marriage. The bride's father ceremonially places the bride's hand on that of the bridegroom. This is called *pāṇigrahaṇa* (*pāṇi*='hand', *grahaṇa*='taking hold of' or 'holding'). The equivalent words used in the verse are *hathalemaiṁ* (*hathale*='the *pāṇigrahaṇa* ceremony', *maiṁ*='in').

kuśa grass is a kind of grass used by Hindus in religious ceremonies. The marriage is complete only after the bride and the groom take seven rounds of the fire with their garments knotted, and this comes last of all. The standing of the hair and perspiration—both signs of sexual longing—are likened to the *kuśa* grass and sacred water respectively, both of which are used in the ritual.

72. Some commentators (including Lālā Bhagawāna Dīna) take *pīṭhi die* to mean 'turning away (from the world)' i.e. 'becoming disinterested', and interpret the verse as follows: 'Seeing the splendour of your body through your casement, he has got disinterested in everything else. Caring for you alone, his glance is always fixed on your window.' (BBL, p. 99) An argument given in favour of this interpretation by one commentator is that it is not possible for the lover to wake up the whole night, and even if he does so how can he hope to see his girl in the dark through the casement? (BSR, p. 218) But this does not seem good enough to reject the other interpretation (of Ratnākara) adopted in the translation. The intensity of the *nāyaka's* love would be enough to keep him awake nightlong, hoping to see his girl. Besides, she might be having a lamp burning in her room, and might keep her window open because of the summer's heat. The night, when the girl would be in *déshabillé*, must be

providing a better opportunity than the day to have a more intimate sight of her beautiful limbs!

73. Pauraṇic tales means stories from the *Purāṇas* (Hindu scriptures) written in verse interspersed with various dialogues and observations. They contain many mythical stories of gods and goddesses. The *nāyikā's* lover is a youth who earns his living by reciting the *Purāṇas* to audiences interested in them. In the course of this he relates an incident of illicit amour. A woman, who is his mistress, is also present in the audience, and she gives him a flirtatious smile when he is relating it, but the youth does not wish the secret to be out, and forces back his own smile. An observant woman in the audience however, cleverly guesses the truth and tells her friend about the incident.

76. *Phāga* is the Hindu festival of Holī which is held in the bright half of the *Phālguna* month (February–March). It is celebrated by sprinkling coloured water on one another and also by applying coloured powders on the face. Red powder made of a farinaceous material is known as *gulāl*. If, while smearing it on a reveller, a little of it accidentally gets into the eyes it can cause a great deal of pain and smarting.

78. The *rasa maṅḍala* or *rasa* dance is one in which men and women dance together, holding each other's hands. The *lahācheha* is that stage of this circular dance when it gathers speed and the dancers whirl round very swiftly. The *rasa* dance of the *lahācheha* kind is believed to have been accomplished by Kṛṣṇa's delusive power. Archer has the following description:

> The cowgirls in pairs joined hands and Kṛṣṇa was in their midst. Each thought he was at her side and did not recognize him near anyone else. They put their fingers in his fingers and whirled about with rapturous delight. Kṛṣṇa in their midst was like a lovely cloud surrounded by lightning. (AL, p. 43)

79. The couplet expresses Rādhā's grief on Kṛṣṇa's departure from the Braja country (Vṛndāvana) for Mathurā. The river reminds her of Kṛṣṇa, firstly because of its dark waters (Kṛṣṇa was also dark-hued) and secondly because the river bank was the scene of their amorous sports.

Some commentators, like Lālā Bhagawāna Dīna, interpret *kharhauṁ hauṁ* as 'seething' or 'churning', and take the couplet as spoken by Ūdhava (Kṛṣṇa's friend) to Kṛṣṇa. (BBL, p. 221) In that case the sense would be that Rādhā's hot tears are so copious that where they fall they make the waters boil! But that would be too fanciful an interpretation.

82. *pīt-paṭ* means 'yellow garment' (*pīt*='yellow', *paṭ*='garment'). Kṛṣṇa is usually shown as wearing a yellow dress.

84. *rahaṁṭa-gharī:* a *rahaṭa,* sometimes called a Persian wheel, is a contrivance in villages used by cultivators to draw water from a well. A number of bucket-shaped pots are strapped on to a leather band which moves along an axle so that each pot goes below the water level, gets filled, and moves up. The water is emptied outside and taken by a pipe to the fields for irrigation. Thus each pot keeps on drawing water from the well as it moves up and down on the leather strap. A pot may be scooping up water at one moment, another emptying it, a third dropping below the water level and yet another pot getting out of it. In the same way, says the poet, the girl's eyes keep brimming with tears, shedding them, swimming with tears, and drowning in them.

88. The slayer here refers to Kāmadeva, the Hindu god of love, who strikes his victims with his flower-tipped arrows and makes them slaves to love. (see note to verse 463)

91. For *gulāl* see note to verse 76 *ante.*

93. The strangeness of love lies in its having contrary results. Ordinarily it is things which entangle with one another that break. In love the lover's eyes are entangled but what breaks are family ties. In a society in which marriages were arranged it is obvious that the secret love of the *nāyaka* and the *nāyikā* would invite censure from their families, and they would disown them. Again, if a string snaps, the only way to join the two bits is to knot them together. Here, however, love springs in the genial minds of the lovers but it awakens jealousy in the hearts of evil-minded folk who grudge their good fortune. Thus love's string is tied in the minds of lovers but the knot finds place in the minds of those who are envious of them.

Poet Rasanidhi has a similar thought:

Say how does it happen
that the eyes are entangled
but 'tis the minds that are tied?
In love's land I've seen strange things!

And at another place he says:

Strange are love's ways,
one thing is broken
quite another joined,
and the knot put on a third!

103. Some commentators think the couplet is meant to convey a taunt to the *nāyikā* by the woman go-between: 'You've been entrusting me with messages of love to convey to your lover, but now that you are sure of his love you've unceremoniously dropped me!' But most probably the poet's intention was just to make a comment on the limited utility of such go-betweens.

kalābūt is a word of Persian origin (*kālabud*). In constructing arches a temporary support of mud, plaster, or bricks, was usually given till the arch became strong enough to stand by itself. Then the substructure was removed.

109. *loṭ* or *tribali* means the three folds or wrinkles appearing on the belly above the navel of a woman which are considered to be a sign of beauty. See note to verse 21.

Certain commentators, including Ratnākara, read *lauṭ* for *loṭ* in the couplet (*lauṭ* means 'turning back'). They interpret it as follows: 'Seeing her lover on the way the *nāyikā* raised her hand to pull down her veil. This caused her blouse to shift up and to hide her bare midriff from him, she hastily turned back. This gesture of his beloved filled the *nāyaka* with delight.'

The interpretation, however, seems unlikely. Hindi poets seldom show their lovers charmed with a woman's back but the lovely folds on her belly are quite another matter. The turning back of the *nāyikā* would disappoint her lover rather than captivate him!

110. The translation follows the interpretation of Lālā Bhagawāna Dīna (BBL, pp. 15–16). The *nāyaka* has come disguised as the barber's wife (who customarily visited rich households to settle the hair, apply lacquer dye to the feet, massage the body etc., of the lady of the house). He starts settling the *nāyikā's* hair. His make-believe is perfect but the thrills his touch send through her body arouse her suspicion.

A different interpretation is given by Ratnākara and others. According to these commentators the *nāyikā* sends her companion to deliver her lover a message. The lover, who is enamoured of the lovely messenger, makes her stop for a while and (perhaps after making love to her during which her tresses open out) settles her hair himself. He does it in the same manner as he has been arranging the *nāyikā's* hair. So she guesses at once that her messenger is having an affair with the *nāyaka*.

This interpretation is also possible, but it does not account for the thrill felt by the *nāyikā* from the caress of the hands of the disguised *nāyaka*. The hands would be able to excite her desire only if they were the *nāyaka's*.

113. According to popular belief the crow has two eye-sockets but only one pupil, and this keeps moving by turns from one socket to the other. In the same way, imagines the poet, the *nāyaka* and the *nāyikā* have only one soul between them which keeps both alive.

114. The *nāyaka* and the *nāyikā* met each other, and when she looked at him ardently he fell in love with her and began to yearn for her. When the *nāyikā's* companion conveyed this to her, the *nāyikā* answered her in these words.

119. *prasāda* ('holy offering partaken of by a devotee') has no suitable equivalent in English. When Hindu worshippers make offerings of flowers, flower garlands, sweets etc., to the deity of a temple, the temple priest gives them a part of the offering, or some other thing offered by another devotee, as *prasāda*. This is reverentially taken by the worshippers. If it is a flower garland, as in this case, the worshipper wears it round his neck, or puts it away in some suitable place.

By some chance the garland which the priest gives as *prasāda* to the *nāyikā* (who goes to worship in the temple) is the one which the *nāyaka* had previously on his visit made an offering of. The *nāyikā* recognizes it and thrills with joy to feel her lover's garland round her neck. The priest, who is unaware of their romance, thinks it is because of her excess of devotion to the deity!

123. *mehṅdī* is the henna plant known as *camphire* in Palestine and *hennah* in Iran. Pliny calls it 'the cypress of Egypt'. It is commonly grown in India. When young, it has smooth twigs which later become thorny. It blooms throughout the year with flowers of delicate fragrance, but is at its best in the summer and rainy seasons. The shrub is particularly valued for the red dye yielded by its leaves when crushed into a paste and dampened. Indian girls apply the paste to their nails, palms and feet (often in lovely patterns) and allow the paste to dry. The paste is then washed off leaving a red dye on the spots to which it was applied.

The *nāyikā's* ardour (due to her lover being near her) makes her perspire, and the paste which is in the process of drying gets soaked in her sweat! So her companion asks her lover to go elsewhere for sometime to allow the paste to dry and colour her nails.

125. For *gulāl* see note to verse 76.

126. Obviously the balconies of the lovers adjoin each other and are separated either by just one partition wall in between, or their houses are so close that the walls along their balconies are almost each to each. The second possibility is

greater because if there are two separate walls close together (with a little space in between) the lovers would have to lean forward to be able to kiss.

127. *Pūs* is the tenth month of the Hindu calendar, corresponding to December–January—the coldest part of the Indian winter.

Some commentators make out that the *nāyikā* perspires just because of the thrill she experiences on thinking about her lover. But seeing that it is the coldest part of winter, the more likely meaning is that she has come after vigorous love-making, and it is that which has made her perspire.

128. The Holī festival is celebrated by spraying coloured water on one another through syringes. The objective is to make a person soaking wet. Normally after that he is spared, as then the water can hardly drench him more. But in this case, just as the lovers' greedy glances can't stop even after love's surfeit, the revellers go on sending jets of coloured water on each other, even though they are fully soaked!

129. The reference is to Kṛṣṇa who is of a dark complexion. He visits his girl, perhaps on the sly. On one of these occasions her companion happens to see him and marks the disturbed state of her friend, who is so much in love with Kṛṣṇa that the very sight of him sends shivers of excitement through her. Her friend is surprised to see her thus. The girl tries to hide her true feeling by making her believe that she is trembling not because of uncontrollable passion but because of sheer fright at seeing the dark stranger in her house!

131. A *tilak* is a vertical mark made by a powder or paste on the middle of the forehead. It can be a sacerdotal mark or (as here) put on by women for adornment.

132. Some commentators, like Ratnākara, take the words as spoken by the *nāyaka*: 'That fair girl smiled and spoke to me artlessly. And now I am ever longing to hear her speak so again.' The translation follows Lālā Bhagawāna Dīna's version (BBL, p. 128), and has been preferred because it seems to be more expressive.

136. *cora-mihīcanī* (blind-man's-buff) is a game in which six or seven persons (both boys and girls) take part. One of them, 'the thief', is blindfolded and the others hide. The 'thief' then removes the cloth-band from his or her eyes and runs about searching for them. Those who are hiding try to run quickly and touch the *khuṭavāṁ* (the place where the 'thief' is blindfolded). If the 'thief' can touch the player before the player reaches the *khuṭavāṁ*, that person becomes the 'thief'. Thus the game goes on.

The game provides several opportunities for the *nāyaka* and the *nāyikā* to embrace. When he takes his turn as 'thief' she comes forward to blindfold him standing close, so that her breasts are pressed against his back. When they touch each other in the game, they have a hurried embrace. If some other player becomes the 'thief', they go and hide together and hug to their heart's content. And if either the *nāyaka* or the *nāyikā* is the 'thief', they get together (unseen by others), under pretence of searching, and embrace for a brief moment.

138. The *nāyikā* is going along with her companion when she suddenly sees the *nāyaka* coming her way. She stops all at once and begins to gaze longingly at him. Her companion, who is unaware of the secret love between them, questions her about this strange behaviour.

140. *cutakī* is a long tapering rope made of hemp and shaped like a woman's braid of hair. In training a horse this is given a snap several times near him so that he is impelled to run. At the same time the rider restrains him by pulling the reins. So the horse is prevented from moving forward and keeps prancing up and down. This forced prancing is called *khūṁd.*

143. *cakor* is the Indian red-legged partridge which, according to poetic belief, eats fire and is enamoured of the moon at which it keeps staring fixedly. The *nāyaka* has been showing indifference to the *nāyikā,* and her companion suggests she should find another lover. But the *nāyikā* tells her in clear words that her love for the *nāyaka* is too deep to be switched on to another man.

144. *nakh-ruci-cūran* literally means 'the powder of the nails' beauty'. Thugs used to exercise their magic powers and prepare a powder from dead men's nails. When this was sprinkled on the victim he would be spellbound and helplessly follow the thug, who took him to a lonely spot and robbed him.

Certain commentators, like Lālā Bhagawāna Dīna, omit this couplet.

145. The terms *tāla, tāna, swara* and *rāga* are from Indian music, the basic principles of which are quite different from European music. Indian music is based on melody, western music on rhythm. Various combinations of notations are known as *rāga* (the basic modal pattern), and though there may be many *rāgas,* each one follows a fixed pattern which can't be violated.

tāna means 'a tune', *tāla* 'musical measure' and *swara* 'notation'.

147. A *vaidya* is a physician who practises the *āyurvedic* (Hindu) system of medicine.

149. Some commentators, including Lālā Bhagawāna Dīna, read *tilaka* for *tilaku,* taking it to mean 'a vertical beauty mark'. The girl's beauty mark is

likened to an arrow, so that the verse reads, 'That young woman, her forehead adorned with an arrow-like beauty mark, glanced at me for a moment, and like a flame of fire, turned away from her casement.' The translation (which follows Ratnākara's version) takes the word as *tilaku* meaning 'a moment'. The idea is that the girl peeped out of her casement for a moment, and ever since the *nāyaka* is bewitched by her beauty. (BBL, p. 36 and BBP, p. 223)

The effect of the girl's sight on the *nāyaka* is a significant factor which has been missed in Bhagawāna Dīna's version, and so that of Ratnākara has been preferred.

nāvak sara is explained by Bhagawāna Dīna as follows: 'This is a kind of tiny arrow which is shot through a cylindrical device on the bow. In fact this cylinder is known as a *nāvak*. But by implication it has come to mean "a small arrow or a dart".' (BBL, p. 36)

150. According to the text the girl, who may be Rādhā or some other cowherd girl whose lover is Kṛṣṇa, addresses these words to her right arm. But seeing it is unusual to address a limb, this has been avoided in translation.

The throbbing of a woman's right arm, or of the right side of her body, is considered a good omen according to Indian superstition. As a reward for throbbing, the girl promises that she'll use only her right arm (the bringer of bliss) when she clasps Kṛṣṇa to her bosom.

155. *Bhṛṅgī kīt* (*kīṭ*='insect') is a kind of insect of the wasp variety about which it is popularly believed that it catches other tiny insects and carries them to its hole. Then it keeps buzzing round them ceaselessly. Just by looking at the *bhṛṅgī* all the time, the shapes of the tiny creatures are transformed and they all become *bhṛṅgīs*!

160. For the incident of the lifting of Goverdhana mount see note to verse 438.

161. Some commentators (e.g. Bhagawāna Dīna) interpret 'O thorn! By getting into my feet you saved my life; for I was dying for his caress, and just then he came that way, and holding my foot fondly in his hands, took it out.' (BBL, p. 104) It's more likely, however, that the *nāyikā* was dying of grief because of mistakenly feeling that the man whom she loved was not interested in her. That could have caused the kind of brooding sorrow that might have taken her life. She couldn't have died merely because her lover had not petted her for so long. In that case his touch could have revived her with pleasure, but surely not saved her from dying! The translation, therefore follows the version of other commentators like Dr Bhāṭī and Śrī Rākeśa. (BBB, p. 383 and BSR, p. 483)

162. The *nāyaka* and the *nāyikā* were going to worship in the local temple, where shoes were not allowed. So they went barefoot. The path by which they went was rough and littered with gravel on one side and smooth on the other. Out of love for her, the *nāyaka* left the smooth path for his beloved to walk on, and himself took the rough one. Seeing that the sharp gravel was hurting his feet, she beckoned to him to walk on her side of the path. But he found her gesture so charming that he kept straying to the gravelled path again and again just to hear her go on repeating it!

164. An *ārasī* is a mirror-set ring which a Hindu woman sometimes wears on the thumb of her right hand.

171. The *nāyaka* and the *nāyikā* are celebrating the Holī festival in which the revellers throw fistfuls of *gulāl* (red farinaceous powder) on each other. (see also note to verse 76)

179. Gokul is the country district near Mathurā. The home of Kṛṣṇa's foster-parents, Devakī and Vasudeva, it was the scene of Kṛṣṇa's amours with the milkmaids.

182. The verse lends itself to at least three different interpretations. Rādhā has had a tiff with Kṛṣṇa, and has kept herself aloof for sometime. She refuses to be reconciled with Kṛṣṇa. Two of Rādhā's companions are speculating on the chances of reconciliation. The different interpretations are as follows: The love of these two is everlasting. They will certainly make up because both of them belong to noble families. Rādhā is the daughter of the great Vṛṣabhānu, and Kṛṣṇa brother of the illustrious Balarāma. The second version is: They can never love each other for long, for Rādhā is the daughter of the Sun (who's particularly fiery when he is in the Taurus zodiac) and Kṛṣṇa brother of the raging Śeṣanāga (whose incarnation Balarāma was believed to be). Yet another interpretation is as follows: It's better that their love ceases, for it can't be of the tender kind. Aren't they beasts! For is not Rādhā the sister of a bull (i.e. a cow), and Kṛṣṇa no less, as he's the brother of a bull (i.e. a bull)!

These different interpretations emanate from the varied meanings of some of the words in the couplet, viz:

cirajīva—(a) 'not joined in any way' or in other words 'always joined' (b) 'not joined at all'.

vṛṣabhānu—(a) 'daughter of the mighty Vṛṣabhānu' (b) 'daughter of the Sun in the Taurus zodiac' (c) *vṛṣabha anujā* (*vṛṣabha*='bull', *anujā*='sister') 'sister of a bull'.

haladhar ke bīr—(a) 'brother of the powerful Baladeva' (b) 'brother of Haladhar (Śeṣanāga)' (c) 'brother of a bull' (*hala*='plough', *dhar*='bearer of' i.e. 'one who is yoked to a plough', or in other words 'a bull').

Śeṣanāga or Śeṣa is King of the serpent race (*nāgas*) and of the infernal regions (*pātāla*). He has a thousand heads which forms the canopy of Viṣṇu. Sometimes he is shown as supporting the world or holding on himself the seven hills. When he yawns earthquakes occur. He is believed to have been incarnated in Balarāma, Kṛṣṇa's brother.

The translation follows the second interpretation for the following reasons: Being of noble lineage can hardly have much effect on lovers' tiffs, so the first version seems unlikely. The love of Rādhā and Kṛṣṇa, considered divine by devotees, can't be brought to the level of bestiality, even in an attempt to humour. One would never expect that of a Kṛṣṇa devotee such as Bihārī, even though this interpretation has been accepted by some commentators, notably Bhagawāna Dīna. (BBL, pp. 3–4) Thus the third version too is unacceptable.

184. Some commentators take *manamohana* to be Kṛṣṇa, which seems unnecessary because *manamohana* means 'he who captivates the heart' (*mana*='heart', *mohana*='captivating'). Even though Kṛṣṇa is also known as Manamohana, the other explanation interpreting the word as just a bewitching lad seems to be more appropriate here.

186. *loṭan* is another word for *tribalī*, the triple fold forming above the waist and below the navel, when a woman bends her body. (see note to verse 21) The *Gāthāsaptaśatī*, too, speaks of such a woman gathering flowers:

> That roguish lad
> keeps following the woman
> who's picking blossoms in the garden,
> pretending to ask her
> the price of the flowers,
> when all he wants
> is to gaze at her bosom
> beneath her raised hands!

187. The gifts exchanged by the lovers through a messenger denote their infatuation. The significance of the rose is 'My heart is imbued with your love as inseparably as the pigment colouring this rose'. The betel has the same significance, viz. 'My heart, too, is coloured with your love like the colour of this betel'. Lovers often sent such symbolic presents to each other through messengers or friends.

189. *besari motī—besara* or *nath* is a gold ring with one large pearl, worn by Indian women on the left nostril. The ring passes through a hole bored in the nostril, and the pearl rests on the woman's lips because the ring reaches down to them.

The *Abhijñānaśakuntalam* says in a similar strain: 'O black bee! I am still wondering if this girl (Śakuntalā) will accept me, and you are fearlessly savouring the nectar of her lips!'

190. *beṁdī* is an ornament worn by Indian women. It is suspended by a string which runs along the parting of the hair and hangs on the forehead. It is set with gems and diamonds. The planet Mercury (believed to be the son of the Moon), is usually assigned the colour green. But according to Indian astrology Mercury acquires the quality, colour and nature of the planet in whose orbit it is moving at that time. Since it is depicted as being 'in the lap of Moon' it wouldn't be wrong to take its colour as white (as Bihārī has described it). In fact this shows the poet's intimate knowledge of astrology.

The *nāyikā*'s companion also cleverly hints that if the *nāyaka* visits his beloved at this time, he will get the utmost pleasure, for when Mercury is in the House of the Moon, it is considered to be an auspicious moment. The time will not only be favourable to love-making, in all probability the union might lead to the birth of a son. Mercury reposing in the lap of his father, the Moon, is suggestive of that.

Love-Making

192. Some commentators give '*garab*' its literal meaning, i.e. 'arrogance', suggesting that the *nāyikā* has played the man in love-making. The contrary emotions of 'shyness' and 'arrogance', 'indolence' and 'longing', they feel, convey this. But perhaps this would be reading more in the lines than what the poet meant.

193. Poet Amaru describes a similar situation:

> When, touching the knot of her brassiére,
> her lover said 'O woman of languorous eyes,
> when you take these off you look lovelier',
> her eyes beamed with the pleasure to come.
> Seeing her so
> her friends smiled
> and gladly went away.

In the *Kṛṣṇacarita* (Exploits of Kṛṣṇa) there is the following passage: 'When her companions saw this (i.e. signs that the two wanted to make love), they started going out one by one, hand on mouth to conceal their smiles. The flame of the earthen oil lamp also began to quiver with the breeze raised by their sari ends, as though it too was about to close its eyes and depart!'

196. Among the many forms of kissing described by Vātsyāyana, there is one called the 'clasping kiss'. This is when one of the two (either the man or the woman) takes both, the upper and lower, lips of the other between his or her own (KS, p. 37).

The woman has been making love, and her lover has bruised her lips during love-making so that they have become suffused with blood. In order to hide this from her companion she chews a number of betels whose red spittle seems to colour her lips red. But soon the betel-juice fades away and her friend becomes wise to her love-making.

Describing the lips of Padmāvatī after her night of love-making with Ratnasena, her companion says:

> Your lips have been moistened
> by those of your lover
> and appear as though you've
> chewed betels! (Malik Muhammad Jaisī, *Padmāvatī*)

197. Some commentators interpret the verse in the sense that the rope of the swing broke, and just then the *nāyaka* happened to be there. They censure Bihārī for making his *nāyaka* so callous as to harbour thoughts of love-making when his beloved is in danger of her life! One of them, for example says: 'This couplet has crossed the bounds of propriety. Love has become in it obscenity. The *nāyaka* is out and out a voluptuary and there is not even human sympathy in him, to say nothing of true love. The *nāyikā* has fallen from the swing, and her life is in danger, and here is this unfeeling lover of hers who can think only of assuaging his lust!' (BSR, p. 90)

There is nothing, however, in the verse to warrant such an explanation. The relevant words are *parī parī-sī ṭūṭi*. Here the first *parī* is an adaptation of the Hindi *paṛnā*, which means 'to drop' as well as 'to fall down'. Thus the sense would be 'dropped off'. There is no hint of the breaking of the rope or of an accident. Then the comparison to a fairy nymph dropping from the sky (*parī-sī ṭūṭi*) confirms the sense of the *nāyikā*'s jumping off the swing of her own free will. Perhaps she is swinging just gently and gets off and runs to meet her lover, maybe stumbling somewhat before he steadies her. The rest is of course instinct.

198. *kiṅkinī* is a band of silver or gold Indian women wear round the waist. A number of tiny bells are attached to it, which tinkle with the movement of the waist.

mañjīra or *nūpur* is an anklet, also with small bells on it. It is worn as an ornament round the ankles, particularly by a newly-wed girl.

paryau joru—when two wrestlers fight, each one is said to be the *joṛā* (match) of the other. When one of them is flung down by the other on the wrestling ground they say 'The victor's *joṛā* has been flung down'. Love-making is here likened to a wrestling match. The victorious *nāyikā* has, so to say, flung down the *nāyaka* and is astride him.

viprīt rati (love-making when the woman is on top) is mentioned by various Hindu erotic writers like Vātsyāyana (KS, p. 54), Kalyāna Malla (AR, pp. 240-1) and Paṇḍit Kokkoka (*Rati Rahasya*).

Poet Bhavabhuti describes a woman taking the man's role in love-making:

When the anklet has grown still
the girdle's sound is heard.
It's ever when the lover tires,
the mistress plays the man. (SPI, p. 158)

Another Sanskrit poet, Ajñāta, says in the same strain:

The sound of her anklets has ceased
now only her girdle bells jingle,
it's evident he's exhausted with love's task
and so she plays the lover.

199. The oil-lamp here means a shallow open receptacle with a cotton wick, burning in mustard oil.

A Sanskrit poet has a similar thought:

'Sweetheart, let me play the mistress, you the lover.'
To this she answered 'No' and shook her head;
but slipping the bracelet from her wrist to mine,
without the use of words she gave consent. (SPI, p. 157)

200. *binduli* or *bindī* is a round mark of vermilion powder made by a married woman on the middle of her forehead. The lovers have been adding a little bit of variety into their love-making. The *nāyikā* has worn her lover's clothes, and he hers, also adorning himself as a woman would. She was on top and he beneath. Afterwards the *nāyaka* apparently forgot to wipe off the vermilion mark from his forehead. In the morning the *nāyikā*'s companions see him like

that and they guess their secret. But the *nāyikā* keeps on denying it. One of her companions, therefore, points out (in the verse) the futility of her denial.

Some commentators feel that the verse can be explained by just assuming that the *nāyikā* has been playing the lover's role, and it is needless to bring in the exchange of clothes (as Ratnākara and others do). One commentator, who does not favour Ratnākara's view, reasons out that the vermilion mark has appeared on the *nāyaka*'s brow simply because when the *nāyikā* (who's on top) has bent down to kiss the *nāyaka*, their foreheads have met, and the *bindī* mark has left a similar smudge on his brow, which he has forgotten to wipe off. (BSR, p. 127) But in that case (1) Why should it be assumed by the girl's companion that the *nāyikā* has been on top? The smudge could have been there even if they had been love-making in the normal manner. Whether it was the *nāyikā* who bent down to kiss the *nāyaka* or the other way round, the result would have been the same. (2) If the exchange of clothes etc., explanation is to be discarded, one would expect a *bindulī* mark on the *nāyikā*'s brow *in addition* to the smudge on the *nāyaka*'s brow. But the verse does not point to this. (3) Quite often instead of vermilion powder a light metal (now plastic) disc is firmly fixed on the same spot. Maybe it is this. The *nāyaka* would have put it on when he dressed up as a woman, but just forgot to remove it.

202. The *nāyikā*'s pride could either be due to her being able to get such enjoyment from her lover as her co-wives were not able to, or because she has triumphed over him in love-making.

203. *rada-chada* means 'marks made by the teeth in biting'. Hindu erotic writers recommend the love-bite as one of the acts of love-making (KS, p. 43; AR, pp. 219–21). The Sanskrit poet, Vallaṇa has a similar thought:

> Your lower lip is a ruby
> despiteitsflaw,
> there is no need, sweet innocent,
> to hide it with your hand. (SPI, p. 162)

208. *A prauṛhā* is a woman of the most wanton kind. She is always eager for love-making and wishes to be with her lover day and night. She does not care for what people might say about her behaviour, and is utterly shameless. She gloats over the love-marks made by her lover on her body during love-making.

An *apauṛhā* or *navoṛhā* is a newly-wed girl inexperienced in the ways of love. She has been described by the poet, Matirāma as 'an extremely shy and quiet girl, who does not readily come to her lover's arms'.

Lālā Bhagawāna Dīna's interpretation of the verse is slightly different. He does not picture the newly-wed girl as intoxicated. It is in the *nāyaka*'s eyes, which are intoxicated by her beauty, that the more wanton and desireful for love-making she becomes. (BBL, p. 77) But that does not explain why a newly-wed girl should start behaving in this way. Her being tipsy could, on the other hand, be reason enough.

210. In other words, when the *nāyaka* pulled off his sweetheart's clothes to undress her for love-making, she bashfully closed her eyes.

213. Hindu gods are often represented with their consorts. Viṣṇu (the Preserver) is shown seated on a lotus with his spouse, Lakṣmī, beside him, or reclining on a lotus leaf. Śiva (the Destroyer) is represented with his consort, Pārvatī, whom he once embraced so passionately that they 'merged into a single androgynous being called Ardhanārī'. (HWB, vol. 2, p. 193) Śiva is sometimes shown as 'Ardhanārīśvara (Hermaphrodite Lord), fused halfway into the form of his spouse Pārvatī, or shown as a half-male, half-female figure in sculpture and painting, exhibiting male elements along the right side of his body, and female elements on the left side'. (HWB, vol. 1, p. 43)

'Śiva embraced Pārvatī's bosom alone. But that won't satisfy the *nāyikā,'* her messenger tells the *nāyaka.*

214. Lālā Bhagawāna Dīna interprets the verse as though the *nāyikā* had dreamt that her lover had clasped her hand through the hole in the wall. But if Bihārī meant it to be love-making in a dream, the hole in the wall would be unnecessary. The lover could very well have embraced his girl as she slept. The partition wall need not have come in the way at all!

216. The woman described is a newly-wed who has got over her shyness and who has begun to respond to her husband's love somewhat. She is what Hindi poets call a *viṣrabdhanavoṛhā nāyikā.*

218. The woman is evidently a newly-wed who has not yet got over her shyness. Or maybe she is a bashful girl whom her lover is trying to win over in the *Kāma Sūtra* manner: 'When a girl accepts the embrace, the man should put a *tambula* or a screw of betel-nut and leaves in her mouth, and if she will not take it, he should induce her to do so. . . . At the time of giving this *tambula* he should kiss her mouth softly and gracefully without making any sound.' (KS, p. 72)

221. Some commentators (among them Lālā Bhagawāna Dīna and Devendra Śarmā 'Indra') have interpreted the verse in a question–answer form. (BBL, pp.

143–4; BSS, p. 320) According to them the *nāyikā* asks the *nāyaka*, 'By what is it disproved that even a little untruth creates unpleasantness?' The *nāyikā* answers 'When a woman says "no! no!" at the commencement of love-making.' According to Devendra Śarmā the question–answer takes place between the *nāyaka* and the *nāyikā*'s messenger.

It may true that *kaun bāt pari jāi* ('By what is this evident?') in the first line of the verse, may suggest this. But on the other hand it is most unlikely that the *nāyikā* or her messenger would give such an answer, or that the *nāyaka* would ask them such a question. Hence the question–answer form has not been adopted in the translation. Other commentators too (like Dr Deśarājasiṅgha Bhāṭī and Śrī Rākeśa—BBB, p. 405; BSR, p. 507) do not explain the verse in this way.

224. The *Gāthāsaptaśatī* has a thought much on the same lines:

After love-making
the ignorant
newly-wed,
wondering how her breasts
came to be scratched,
tries to wipe off the mark,
washit
and rub it off!

Another Woman

226. The verse is about a married woman. Someone tells her that her husband has made love to another girl. She readily believes it and starts sulking. Her companion hastens to reassure her. There can be two interpretations to the words of the girl's companion, of which the first one seems more likely.

(i) You are far lovelier than the girl who you suspect is carrying on an affair with your husband. Your beauty is like that of the rose bud, while she is like the bud of a *madāra* (the swallow wort plant) which is not at all attractive. So how can you expect him to prefer her to you?

(ii) A black bee never hovers round the bud of a *madāra* plant. In the same way your husband cannot abandon propriety and make love to any woman other than his wife.

pātarī kāna kī would be equivalent to the Hindi idiom *kāṇa kī kaccī*, meaning 'accepting without question', i.e. 'overcredulous'.

227. The woman who says these words is what Hindi poets call a *prauṛādhīrā khaṇḍitā nāyikā*, i.e. a woman who, even though being married, has a lover. Here the woman, who is an expert in love-making herself, is quick to discern the tell-tale signs of the *nāyaka's* having dallied with another woman. The *nāyaka's* mistress has brushed his eyebrows with lips stained with red betel-juice and so left red spots on them. He has kissed her on the eyes and got smudges of lamp-black on his lips. Red lacquer dye is applied by Indian women to their feet in order to beautify them. The *nāyaka* has beseeched his mistress to let him make love by falling on her feet, and that's how he has got red stains on his forehead. In the *Kāma Sūtra*, Vātsyāyana advises the lover to do this if every other thing fails to persuade a girl for love-making, 'for' he says 'it is a universal rule that however bashful or angry a woman may be, she will never disregard a man's kneeling at her feet.' (KS, p. 72)

230. The *nāyaka* has stained his forehead by falling at the feet of the woman begging her to let him make love. (see note to verse 227)

231. The *nāyikā* has sent her messenger, obviously a beautiful girl, to call her lover. But the *nāyaka* finds the girl so irresistible that he thinks it a better idea to make love to her instead. In the intensity of his passion while love-making he bites her cheeks. The marks are noticed by the *nāyikā* and she taunts the messenger with these words.

tarivana or *karṇaphūla* (*karṇa*=ears, *phūla*=flower) is, as the name denotes, a flower-shaped ornament worn by Indian women on the lobes of the ears. It is of gold with jewels set in it and has a screw-like pin which passes through the hole in the ear and is screwed on to a small round conical piece behind.

Some commentators interpret the verse as being spoken by the *nāyikā's* companion to her, praising the beauty of her ear ornament: 'O dear friend, your lover got so entangled between your golden ornament and your cheek's luster and teeth's glimmer, that he lost his senses and his gaze was unable to reach your charming face.' But the words used in the verse, *caukā cinha* ('teeth marks') clearly indicate the love-bites on the messenger's cheeks. Vātsyayāna mentions such teeth marks inflicted during love-making: 'All the places that can be kissed are also places that can be bitten, except the upper lip, the interior of the mouth, and the eyes.' (KS, p. 42) A Sanskrit poet, Māgha, says:

Well may you hide her scratches with your cloak
and cover with your hand the bitten lips;

but how suppress the perfume that fills all the four directions
accusing you of adultery. (SPI, p. 162)

kapol-duti (lustre of the cheeks)—Hindi poets describe a beautiful woman's cheek as being 'bright and lustrous'. The women of Sthaṇavicāra, for example, described by Bāṇa had such bright cheeks that they 'gave perpetual sunshine'. (*Harśacarita*, translated by M.R. Kāle)

232. For co-wives, see note to verse 475. A similar thought is expressed in the *Vikrama-Satasaī:*

Are you not ashamed, lover,
to take back your heart
which you had given me,
to give it to another?

233. Kāmadeva or Kāma, is the Hindu god of love. (see note to verse 463) He does not use a catapult but shoots flower-tipped arrows from his bow whose bowstring is a line of bees. Here he seems to undertake the comparatively clumsier task of using a catapult to force the unfaithful lover back to his beloved! The lines should not be understood, however, as meaning that Kāmadeva really lets off a volley of stones from a catapult. What the poet means is that as someone may shower stones from a catapult and so confound a wild elephant, and cause him to turn around, so Kāma influences the mind of the faithless lover and brings him back to his beloved. The comparison has been brought in because (i)the marks made by small stones discharged from a catapult would be about the same shape as those made on the *nāyaka's* bosom with the pearls of the woman's necklace, (ii)an elephant keeps roaming about the forest unrestrainedly and the *nāyaka* too seems to have no restraint on his lust.

234. For *caukā* see note to verse 231.

235. Commentators have two different explanations for this verse. Ratnākara and others believe it to be spoken by the *nāyikā's* woman friend who is eager to prevent any misunderstanding between the lovers. When the *nāyaka* comes home with red betel-juice marks showing on his cheeks, where the woman whom he has been secretly making love to, has kissed him, the *nāyikā* gets annoyed. Her friend speaks these words to her in an attempt to remove her suspicion. At the same time she throws a hint to the *nāyaka*, as much as to say, 'Don't be a fool. Go and wash away the tell-tale signs of love-making from your cheeks.'

On the contrary some commentators think the *nāyaka* is not at fault. It is really the flash of rubies in his ear ornaments falling on his cheek which make them seem reddish (men also wore such ornaments). The *nāyikā* is needlessly suspicious, and in her jealousy mistakes the reflection as streaks of red, which she thinks have been caused by another woman's betel-juice-stained lips. Her companion removes this unfounded suspicion. Yet other commentators think the reflection falling on the *nāyaka's* cheeks is not that of the rubies in *his* ornament but of the ornament worn by the *nāyikā* who is sitting near him.

Ratnākara's interpretation seems more likely. If the lovers had been together all the time (and the *nāyaka* would not have come from outside) the question of the *nāyikā's* suspecting him could just not arise. If at all she thought the streaks on his cheeks were marks of betel-stained lips, it would be *her* lips, not those of another woman. As for the question whose ear ornament it is, more likely it is the *nāyaka's*. The ruby could then have shone against his cheeks (the two—the gem and his cheeks) being close together. It would be difficult to imagine the rubies being reflected on his cheeks from some distance. Indeed this could be possible only if the lovers were sitting in a close embrace. Bihārī's verse clearly shows that the *nāyikā* is angry, and surely an angry woman could not be sitting with her arms around her lover!

239. The polygamous *nāyaka* and his wives are diverting themselves with 'water sport', a favourite pastime those days. When women sported in the water they were often joined by their husband or lover, and they playfully splashed water on each other amusing themselves in a tank or a pond in various ways. The sport provided a good opportunity for flirting, and the women in the process showed off their bodies.

240. A *nāyaka* who brazenly deceives his girl by making love to another woman, and then cunningly tries to hide his wrongdoing, is called a *śaṭh nāyaka*. The man described in the verse is one of this kind. The *nāyikā* is a *khaṅḍitā*. Such a woman is greatly grieved when she notices marks of love-making made on the limbs of her lover by some other sweetheart of his. The *nāyikā* wittily pays back her faithless lover in his own coin!

244. Probably the lover here is Kṛṣṇa, though the verse does not specifically say so. Kṛṣṇa (which literally means 'dark') is often represented with a bluish hue. Hence the comparison here with water in a sapphire bowl. In describing the art of love-making, Hindu classics on erotics mention the making of nail marks by the lover. (KS, p. 39; AR, p. 221)

Some commentators, like Bhagawāna Dīna, think the couplet signifies that the *nāyaka* had made love to the woman with her on the top (BBL, p. 167). But the nail marks could have very much been made on his body even if he had been on top and his mistress below.

245. The *nāyaka* has two wives, the *nāyikā* who speaks the words, and another, her co-wife. The *nāyaka* has arranged to be with them by turns. When the turn of the co-wife comes, he goes instead to another woman with whom perhaps he has been carrying on an affair for some time (and whom he is likely to wed also in the near future). When the *nāyikā* learns about this, she is swayed by contrary emotions. These are explained as follows:

She feels glad because her husband has slighted the co-wife, of whom she is jealous, but sorrowful because when (as she anticipates) the *nāyaka* marries the woman he has been having an affair with, there'll be another co-wife who'll become a formidable rival. If the *nāyaka* did not go to the co-wife, why didn't he come to me, instead of going to his secret beloved? This thought makes her angry. She is amused because the *nāyaka* did not consider her co-wife worthy enough to have company with. She is pleased to think that the *nāyaka* never gives *her* a go by, and always comes to her when it is her turn. The *nāyikā's* vexedness is because she feels that now that the *nāyaka* has found a new girl, he may in preference to his girl, give her a miss too when *her* turn comes.

249. Lālā Bhagawāna Dīna has given an alternative interpretation reading the words *jau guahi tau* ('if you consider me at fault') as *jyauṁ gunahī tyauṁ* ('as a wrongdoer would be imprisoned'). This is as follows: 'One cannot achieve salvation by a million deceitful words. Only by keeping the image of the god for ever in one's eyes as securely as a goaled wrongdoer is kept in prison, can one get it.' (BBL, p. 125)

However, since Bihārī is primarily a poet of love, it seems it was not his intention in this verse to convey a kind of spiritual message. The other interpretation which seems more likely, has been adopted in the translation.

250. *dacchina piya,* literally '*dakṣiṇa* lover', is a *nāyaka* who has many co-wives, but has vowed to give his affection to all equally. Our *nāyaka* is one of this sort, but apparently he has found a mistress next door with whom he is so infatuated that he doesn't ever make love to any of his co-wives.

Ratnākara thinks the words of the couplet are spoken by a woman messenger to the *nāyikā* and interprets them thus: 'That young man who was hitherto enamoured of other women, has now abandoned them, and cares only for you. If he remains away from you even for a day it seems like a year to him.' (BSR, p. 217) Bhagawāna Dīna has other interpretations. In one he takes *dakṣa* to mean 'clever', and believes the faithless *nāyaka* has only one wife, not many. The woman messenger tells him: 'O clever youth, being entangled with a wicked woman, you have abandoned your rightfully wedded wife. Have you forgotten your marriage vows? See, your wife is so grieved by your being away that a day seems like a year to her!' His other interpretation is that the faithless youth gives preference to one of his co-wives as against the other. A companion of one of the neglected wives tells him 'O youth, though you have vowed to give equal attention to all your co-wives, you neglect the straightforward and good natured ones and bestow all your love on the one who is a rogue! The others feel your absence so much that each day seems like a year to them.' (BBL, p. 196)

Though these interpretations can also be accepted, the one most likely has been adopted in the translation. The meaning of *bāsari* is 'a house' or 'the wall of a house'. A *ghar* (house) is also known as *bākhar* in Indian villages. This fits in most with the interpretation adopted.

251. The verse has been taken by some commentators just to convey the sense that things (or persons) of one kind go with each other, like betel-juice with lips, both being red, and lamp-black with eyes, both black. But this interpretation would be too facile. The other one seems more likely, viz. that the *nāyaka* has been making love to another woman, whom he has kissed on the eyes (hence the lamp-black on them), and by whom he has been kissed (hence the red betel-stains on his eyebrows). This interpretation follows that of Dr Deśarājasingha Bhāṭī. (BBB, pp. 184–5)

The last three lines of the verse (as given in the translation) are to be taken as implied.

252. The word *syāma* indicates that the lover here referred to is Kṛṣṇa (Śyāma is another name for him).

A *hammām* (a word of Arabic origin) is a public bathing place which is kept heated to give a hot bath which cleans up all the pores of the body, removes tiredness, and gives the bather a tingling sense of well-being.

traya tāpa means 'the three kinds of warmth' (*traya*='three', *tāpa*='heat'). Here it signifies the girl's heat of passion, heat of the desire of her expectation, and the heat of her separation (i.e. the longing caused by being parted from her lover for a long time).

Some commentators have a spiritual explanation for the verse. According to them it refers to a devotee of Kṛṣṇa who is bearing the three kinds of sorrows (*traya tāpa* meaning in this sense the triple sorrows of the body ailments, those of divine agency like misfortunes, deaths etc., and those caused by nature, for example, natural calamities, cyclones, earthquakes and the like). The devotee bears these sorrows in the hope that the god, Kṛṣṇa, will take pity on him and come to give him salvation. In this sense the verse would mean: 'I have harboured the three kinds of sorrows in my heart (as one would prepare a *hammām*) in the hope that (like a bather is tempted to come to a *hammām* to get comfort), Kṛṣṇa may one day come and redeem me.'

The greater probability is that the poet did not mean to introduce a spiritual element, for the words of the couplet clearly have an erotic import.

256. *bhau pyārau prītam tiyan manau calat pardesa*—When a woman knows that her husband will soon be leaving her and going away on a long journey, she becomes all the more affectionate towards him. The co-wives realize that now that the newly-wed girl has blossomed into youth, their husband will always be with her, and will hardly pay them any attention. So for them it is like as if he were away on a voyage!

257. Viṣṇu, one of the gods of the Hindu Trinity, is believed to be the Preserver of the Universe. Lakṣmī is his consort. Śiva is another of the gods of the Trinity, who is the Destroyer (the third, Brahmā, being Creator). Śiva is represented as bearing the crescent moon on his forehead. The words of the *nāyikā* in this couplet should be taken as spoken in a sarcastic sense. The fact that the *nāyaka*'s mistress has scratched his forehead with her nails in the fervour of passion, shows she is not adept enough in the art of love-making. An experienced woman would have scratched his bosom instead of the brow, though according to some erotic writers the brow is not forbidden. Vātsyāyana says: 'The places that are to be pressed with the nails are as follows: the arm pit, the throat, the breasts, the *jaghana,* or middle parts of the body, and the thighs.' But he adds, 'Suvarnanabha is of the opinion that when the impetuosity of passion is excessive, then the places need not be considered.' (KS, p. 39)

258. Tīja is celebrated as a festive day by Hindu women in honour of Pārvatī, daughter of Himāvata (the Himalayas), who, by her severe austerities, won Lord Śiva as her husband. Married women celebrate the Tīja festival for the well-being of their husbands.

Here the co-wives of the *nāyikā* have become jealous of her because even though they have worn fine dresses and ornaments, and she continues to wear a dirty sari, she outshines them in loveliness. Secondly, the *nāyikā's* sari is rumpled and soiled with her husband's perspiration because he has been making love to her the whole night, and she is too tired to change her dress or adorn herself. Finally, the *nāyikā's* reluctance to change the sari soiled with her husband's perspiration shows that she wishes to continue wearing it in order to keep the fond memory of their love-making. This demonstrates the affection of the *nāyikā* for her husband, and the co-wives regretfully realize that it is she who is his favourite.

261. Commentators have given different interpretations to this verse. According to Lālā Bhagawāna Dīna it is an observation by the *nāyikā's* companion on the deep love of the *nāyikā* for the *nāyaka*. She says: 'The ruby necklace on her bosom makes it seem that the love she bears for him has overflowed her heart and spilled outside.' (BBL, p. 58) Another commentator, taking the verse to be about the *nāyaka's* illicit love-making, thinks that he has not forgotten to take off the necklace, and that the beads in it have merely left marks on his bosom because of his having embraced his mistress too tight. (BSR, pp. 273–4) The commentator says it can be imagined that if the *nāyaka* had exchanged clothes and ornaments with his girl to take the woman's role, he would forget to hand back her necklace after having made love. But *chalakat bāhir* 'spills out', shows that it is a red ruby necklace. Besides, however hard the *nāyaka* embraced his mistress, the necklace couldn't have left marks which remained for so long. And, if it did come in the way of love-making then it would have been the most natural thing to discard it. Incidentally, according to Hindi poetic convention, which assigns various colours to emotions, love is believed to have a red hue.

266. *harā hara-hāru* means 'the garland of Lord Śiva'. Śiva, the Destroyer and one of the gods of the Hindu Trinity, is represented as having a serpent coiled round his neck. In other words the expression means 'a serpent'.

268. *sūran* is a kind of edible tuber. It tastes good when properly salted and cooked in oil, but if it is not cooked to perfection it causes the throat to itch and is difficult to eat.

The *nāyaka* has been making love to another woman and is trying to conceal his infidelity by lying to her. The couplet contains the *nāyikā's* reaction to his dissembling words.

271. *Nirguna māla* means literally 'stringless beads'. The beads can't, of course, be held together without a string, but when the lovers clasp each other tight, it is only the beads which leave an impression on the *nāyaka's* bosom, not the string. Hence the poet calls them marks of 'stringless beads'.

273. The girl whose lover has gone away is a *madhyā nāyikā*. Such a girl is young, shy and comparatively inexperienced in love-making. She feels the absence of her lover and desires him back, but is not much grieved because of her weak sexual longing and soon gets used to it. On the contrary the young girl's neighbour, who is her sweetheart's secret love, is a *prauṛhā nāyikā*. A *prauṛhā* is brazenly wanton. So her lover's absence torments her much more than it would a *madhyā*.

The young girl's happiness in seeing her woman neighbour more tormented than herself may be due to jealousy. Or may be because she is glad that the woman—whom she now knows to be her sweetheart's mistress—being more attractive, will persuade the *nāyaka* to come back soon. She herself is reluctant to convey her longing to him, being of a bashful type. Yet a third reason for her happiness may be that she knows she'll soon accustom herself to her lover's absence, but her neighbour will be suffering with grief every moment!

Lālā Bhagawāna Dīna comments on the couplet's singular charm and considers it to be unique in Hindi love poetry because, firstly, it expresses the feelings of two opposite types of *nāyikās* in the same verse and, secondly, it is a happy combination of the sentiments of humour and love (*hāsya* and *śṛṅgāra*).

278. In this verse Bihārī has used the names of a number of flowers with great ingenuity, some of them in a double sense. These are as follows:

(i) *apaṭaiyata* (also called *iśkapeṁcā*), is a variety of jasmine. The word also means 'to cling to'.

(ii) *mo garaiṁ* means 'my neck', while *mogarā* (or *mugarā*) is also the name of a flower—another variety of jasmine with fragrant yellow flowers.

(iii) *so na ju hī* means 'I am not that (girl)'. If the words are read as one, it would be *sonajuhī*, the name of yet another kind of jasmine with fragrant yellow flowers.

(iv) *campaka* or *campā*, to which the complexion of the *nāyaka's* mistress is compared, is a lovely evergreen tree, five to six metres in height, with fine foliage. It yields in April delicately fragrant yellow flowers with single axils of leaves.

(v) *gullālā*, to which the *nāyaka's* red sleep-starved eyes are compared, is a flower of deep red colour.

282. The translation follows Ratnākara's version. There are slight variations in those of others. Dr Deśarājasiṅgha Bhāṭī and Śrī Rākeśa read *cit sakucat* (or

sakucit) kat lāl instead of *kat sakucāvat lāl,* and interpret 'Lover, if you really love these girls (with whom you get infatuated), why do you feel ashamed when someone speaks about them?' (BBL, p. 338 and BSR, p. 421) Lālā Bhagawāna Dīna, who also reads the controversial words as *kat sakucāvat,* considers the couplet to be spoken by the *nāyikā* to her faithless lover. She says 'Your false amours will make my companions feel that I do not really love you and so you are forced to go to other girls, or that I am inexpert in the art of love. This will put me to shame in their eyes.' (BBL, p. 176)

284. *darakat nāhiṁ* means 'it does not crack or break open' (referring to the pomegranate). When pomegranates are about to get ripe on the tree, they are covered with a cloth-bag tied round them. This is to protect them from birds etc., and also to speed up the ripening process. But quite often the warmth of the sun heats up the cloth jacket so much that the pomegranate inside becomes over-ripe and cracks.

guna or *guṇa* usually means 'good qualities' or 'merit'. Here it is used sarcastically in a bad sense to mean 'faults' or 'vices'.

288. *guṛhal* is a flower with large petals and a long stamen, often of a red or a white colour. According to popular superstition if it is grown in the garden or placed in a vase in the house it causes strife in the family.

The *nāyikā's* companion very cleverly compares the *nāyikā's* sulking to a permanent guest. A guest normally comes for a short while only. Just so, sulking should be short-lived. But the *nāyikā* has kept on feigning indifference for too long. Her companion subtly hints to the *nāyaka* that he should now apologize for his fault and make up with the *nāyikā.*

291. The words *saina na bhajai* have been variously interpreted by commentators. Some, like Dr Deśarājasiṅgha Bhāṭī and Śri Rākeśa, believe it means 'staring fixedly' (BBB, p. 373; BSR, p. 470). Others, like Lālā Bhagawāna Dīna, Lallūjī 'Lāl' and Devendra Śarmā 'Indra', think the expression means 'does not get on the bed'. (BBL, p. 179; BSL, p. 87; BSS, p. 298); The translation follows the latter interpretation. The meaning of *saina* has been given by Dr Śakuntalā Pāñcāla as 'lying on the bed' (BBP, p. 326), and so *saina na bhajai* should signify 'refuses to get on the bed'. Śrī Rākeśa has given two reasons for not accepting this interpretation, (i) That it's not possible for the mark to be distinguished on the bedsheet, and (ii) How can it be supposed that the *nāyaka* has made love to another girl in the *nāyikā's* own house, without her knowledge? A braid mark however, can be quite easily noticed on a bedsheet which has been slept upon. It would be rumpled at that

particular place. As regards the second point, the woman may have been made love to in the *nāyaka's* house (not in that of the *nāyikā*). It was quite usual for a girl's messenger or a go-between to bring her to her lover's house (see verse 613). The profligate lover here has forgotten to take the simple precaution of changing the bedsheet!

296. Ratnākara's interpretation is a little different. According to him the woman at whose feet the *nāyaka* fell to implore her for love-making, is sore about his having spoilt the pattern of the red lacquer dye on her feet (the dye must have been still wet). So she has her revenge by playfully kissing him on the eyes so that his eyebrows may get stained in red!

Ratnākara's interpretation is certainly imaginative, but it is unlikely that Bihārī meant the verse to convey this. In other couplets too the poet has described the crimson eyes of a lover who has been making love all night, and this one is probably in that sense. Some commentators, as for example Dr Deśarājasiṅgha Bhāṭī, would have it that the red streaks on the *nāyaka's* eyes are because of his girl having kissed them with her betel-juice-stained lips (BBB, p. 385). But in that case it would be the eyebrows, for even if it supposed the girl was so clumsy as to leave betel stains on her lover's eyes, he would have immediately washed them off. Betel-juice in the eyes would certainly make them smart! The translation, therefore, follows Lālā Bhagawāna Dīna's version (BBL, p. 178), which appears to be more rational.

298. Ratnākara gives a different interpretation to the verse. According to him the words are spoken by a wise person and refer to a wealthy man, or to an ill-advised king, or to an ignorant or impotent person: 'However greatly distinguished I become, I can't rise in the estimation of the king who does not prize persons of merit. My good qualities might increase, like hair which keeps on growing, but his appreciation won't, as the eyes can't be made larger than they are.' (BSR, p. 505). Or it may be a woman with a similar complaint, viz. that however attractive she makes herself, it can hardly make any difference to her lover who, being impotent, can't give her any enjoyment.

These interpretations, however, appear to be too fanciful, and the simpler and more obvious one followed by other commentators (including Bhagawāna Dīna, BBL, p. 117) has been adopted in the translation.

299. Different interpretations of the verse have been given. According to some commentators the words are meant to be spoken by the *nāyikā*, who has sent her woman messenger with a message for her lover, but the faithless lover has found the charming messenger to be good to make love to! Others take the

couplet to be meant for the *nāyikā* who has made love, but who tries to hide this from her companion. Then there are those (like Devendra Śarmā 'Indra') who believe that it is a description of the *nāyikā* given by her woman companion to the *nāyaka* to tempt him to make love to her while she is flushed with wine. (BSS, p. 291) Another commentator (Girijādatta Śukla) takes it just as a description of the woman's beauty heightened by her being drunk. Yet others, like Bhagawāna Dīna, think it is a description by the *nāyikā's* companion of the *nāyaka's* beauty, increased all the more by his being drunk with wine. (Dīna reads *mad chakī*, 'drunk with wine' for *madana kī* 'like that of Kāmadeva'. BBL, p. 155)

None of these versions, however, seem appropriate. Most commentators have used the word *madana* (meaning Madana or Kāmadeva, the Hindu god of love, famed for his beauty). So the drink aspect is ruled out. Besides, the 'body glistening with perspiration' can be explained by love-making rather than by inebriation. The comparison to Kāmadeva implies that the verse is meant for a man. If it was for the *nāyikā*, she would be likened to Ratī (Kāmadeva's wife) who is believed to be the epitome of beauty. Considering all these factors, the verse has been interpreted as a kind of taunt by the *nāyikā* to the *nāyaka*, when he comes home with signs of his nightlong, clandestine love-making.

303. *beṁdī* or *biṁdī* is the round beauty mark Indian girls put on their foreheads. It may be painted (usually red) or be just a dab of vermilion.

ghanasyāma (Ghanaśyāma) is another name for Kṛṣṇa.

The Woman Offended

305. One commentator (Padmasiṁgha Śarmā) has given a novel interpretation. According to him the *nāyaka* repeats his fault knowingly because the first time he had taken the name of the other woman the *nāyikā* had got angry, and her anger itself lent her charm. Now he wants to see the same captivating expression on her face again, and so deliberately mentions her rival's name to make her jealous.

The theme of another woman whose affair with the *nāyaka* makes the *nāyikā* jealous, is often taken up by Hindi poets, and the *nāyaka* is shown as straying from the course of true love! In fact erotic writers seem to permit sexual relations with a woman other than one's wife. Gonikaputa says that sex with the wife of another man too may be indulged in, to accomplish some end, for example gaining the favour of a woman's husband. According to Kalyāna Malla 'if a man is so madly in love with the wife of another that he feels he would die without having her, he may, in order to save his life, have sexual intercourse with her once, but never again!' Vātsyāyana too is of the same view. Paṇḍit Kokkoka has a similar remedy for a woman who cannot live without her lover. If such be the case, the lover may oblige her once so that her life may not be lost. But he should not keep on encouraging her!

307. *hahā*—means 'to beseech most humbly'. Dr Śakuntalā Pāñcala gives the meaning of *hahā* as follows: 'When one entreats another in the Braja country with the greatest of humility he uses the word *hahā* or *hāhā* in doing so.' As for example, '*hahā* dear friend, I touch your feet, please agree to this,' etc. The *nāyikā's* companion speaks on her behalf of as well as for other friends of the girl who have been persuading her to make up with the *nāyaka*.

310. The *neem* is a tree found in India, about six to ten metres high, with glossy leaves and fragrant white flowers. It is believed to have medicinal qualities and people use its twigs for cleaning their tongues. It bears a small capsule-like fruit which is extremely bitter.

320. *soṁṭha* is dry ginger which has a pungent taste. In the fields where it grows, sometimes by chance a hard root springs up which is sweet to taste, but if one of these is mixed with other bits of dry ginger, of which chutney is made, it tastes sweet but causes nausea and vomiting, because the sweet root is poisonous.

The *nāyaka* has come after love-making with another woman and the *nāyikā* is sulking. Her antagonism is perfectly justified. In fact it is the *nāyaka* who ought to be apologetic, but in a male-dominated society perhaps he thinks he has a right to keep a mistress!

327. *Māgh* (January–February), the eleventh month of the Hindu calendar, is one of the coldest months in India.

329. An arrow-cage (*sarapañjara*) was a big cage of arrows used in ancient times to imprison a heinous criminal. Spear-like arrowheads were fixed all around its walls. When the prisoner was caged in this, the sharp points would pierce him from all sides even if he moved a little. It was thus a sort of a torture chamber.

330. The translation follows Lālā Bhagawāna Dīna's version (BBL, p. 328), who reads the third word in the first line as *mana* meaning 'heart'. Other commentators read it as *muni* ('sage') and interpret the couplet as follows: 'Desire for love-making arises even in the hearts of sages in the rainy season,

and abandoning their penance they long to embrace women, as dark clouds eager to caress the earth. Therefore leave your sulking, dear lad, and go to your beloved.' (BSR, p. 379) Bhagawāna Dīna's interpretation seems to be simpler and preferable.

The Indian rainy season (that comes as a relief after the heat of summer) is delightful and invigorating and favourable to love-making. Besides, it is the season when, because of the pathways being flooded with rain, travel is not possible. So lovers remain together and enjoy themselves. In view of this it is unnecessary to bring in the sages too!

331. *Agahan* is the ninth month of the Hindu calendar corresponding to November–December. It is specially tempting to lovers because of the extreme cold, when they would like to lie cuddled up close together.

For Kāma see note to verse 463.

332. *mādhurī* is a Spanish jasmine which has a sweet fragrance.

Lālā Bhagawāna Dīna has an interesting comment on this verse. He says: 'The words can be taken to be an observation on spring by the poet himself; or of the *nāyikā's* companion spoken to her (in which case it is to remove her feigned indifference); or of the *nāyaka* for the *nāyikā* (an expression of his longing for her); or spoken by the *nāyikā* to the *nāyaka* (in which case it is to prevent his going abroad by telling him how passion-stirring spring is). The verse would be in a suggestive sense if considered as spoken by the woman messenger to a wayfarer about to go on his journey, or if taken as a message for her lover given by the *nāyikā* to her messenger, and in a figurative sense if considered as spoken to a black bee by a woman conceited by her beauty. Thus the couplet is capable of many interpretations.' (BBL, p. 235)

333. A *jurāfā* is believed to be an animal inhabiting Africa. It always lives with its mate and if the two are separated, it dies.

344. Poet Amaru describes a similar situation:

> Lying on the same bed
> their backs each to each
> not speaking or answering
> the lovers were eager to make up
> yet restrained by pride:
> but the moment they looked behind
> their sidelong glances met
> and laughing uproariously
> they fused in a tight embrace.

346. A *lauṅg* is a nose ornament worn by Indian women. It is a clove-shaped pin, usually of gold, and decks a hole which is made in the left nostril. It's called a *lauṅg* because that is also the word for 'clove'.

Cloves have a bitter taste. So the *nāyaka* tells the girl that the clove-shaped ornament of her nose gives him the feeling that she is showing bitterness towards him.

Meeting

347. The verse can also be taken as meant for a gardener, interpreting *bārī* as meaning *osarī* or *pārī*, 'a ditch around a tree for watering it'. Then the meaning would be 'O gardener, water the plants in your garden and keep them from withering, for then they are sure to bear fruit.' (BBB, p. 32) But the entire implication of the verse would then be lost. So the alternative meaning which follows Lālā Bhagawāna Dīna's version (BBL, p. 183) has been adopted in the translation.

348. The *agastya* tree is a soft-wooded tree about twenty to thirty feet high, with pale green leaves. It flowers in early autumn, bearing white flowers tinged with red.

The *nāyikā* has promised to meet her lover on the second night of the bright lunar fortnight, when the moon goes down, near a particular *agastya* tree. But she has forgotten about the assignation and fails to turn up. Her lover sends a messenger to see what holds her up. The messenger finds the girl sitting in the company of the village elders and so cannot openly convey the lover's message. She does it by overt hints as in the verse. The mention of the new moon and the *agastya* tree reminds the girl of the time and place of her meeting, and she hastens to meet her lover without any of the elders knowing about it.

Some critics, following the interpretation of Lālā Bhagawāna Dīna, have taken these lines to be spoken by the *nāyikā's* companion to the *nāyaka* in praise of her friend's beauty, comparing the loveliness of her face to the new moon. (BBL, p. 246) But the wordings of the verse clearly show that the moon is likened to the lone *agastya* flower, not to the girl's face. The translation, therefore, follows the version of other commentators, like Deśarājasiṅgha Bhāṭī and Śrī Rākeśa. (BBB, p. 75; BSR, p. 84)

The lone blossom on the *agastya* tree recalls Wordsworth's lines:

> Fair as a star, when only one
> Is shining in the sky.

349. Poet Keśavadāsa speaks of four kinds of meeting—in person, by seeing the portrait of the beloved, hearing her voice, and finally seeing her in a dream (*Rasikapriyā*, chapter 4). Another Hindi poet says much in Bihārī's manner:

Heavy with sleep, my eyes closed
and in a moment my lover came in a dream;
but as I made to clasp him, I awoke,
and he was no longer there.
Other women, friend,
miss the bliss of love-making by remaining asleep,
I missed it alas, by waking!

350. *mālatī* is a dense creeper which yields fragrant flowers. The *tamāla* is a tall sturdy evergreen tree which grows on hillsides, and in some places along the banks of the Yamunā river.

The *nāyikā* has wisely chosen the *mālatī* bower as the meeting place. It is unfrequented (or else black bees would not swarm there), cool, inconspicuous and easy to locate. Women went to the riverside usually to fetch water, so her going is not likely to attract any undue attention. Besides, the branches of the fragrant *mālatī* creepers twining round the *tamāla* tree-trunks provide an ideal setting for making love.

Some commentators, like Lālā Bhagawāna Dīna, have taken the verse merely to signify that the *nāyaka* should seek the shade of the *mālatī* bower mainly to avoid the sun's heat. (BBL, p. 156) But surely, the *nāyikā* would not date her lover merely to give him relief from the sun!

351. It is usual for lovers in the villages to meet secretly in fields, particularly in those in which the plants grow high and dense. The *nāyikā*, who is secretly meeting a lover is worried because most of the crops have been harvested, and there is no place where she can meet her lover unseen. Her confidante reminds her that the *arahar* crop is still unharvested. *Arahar* is a cereal crop which grows a little above a man's height, with dense green leaves, and so provides excellent cover. Hemp and sugarcane are usually harvested in winter by about November, and cotton by March–April. But *arahar*, which is sown in July–August, is harvested in June (the Indian summer end). Therefore, it is the last to be cut.

352. There are three pickings of cotton, the first in *Kuār* (September–October), the second in *Agahan* (November–December) and finally in *Caitra* (March–April), after which it is cut and the fields lay bare. The girl who is picking cotton in the field for the last time (i.e. March–April) bemoans that after the cotton has

been harvested, the plants will be cut away leaving her no cover to meet her lover as she used to before. (see note to verse 351 *ante*)

Some commentators interpret *sāiṁ* as meaning the girl's husband, but here it would better fit in as signifying the grief felt by the girl.

353. A *kos* is two miles.

354. By placing her hand on her bosom and then on her head the *nāyikā* conveys the following message:

(i) You are enshrined in my heart. I'll certainly meet you as you want me to. The Hindi expression *śirodharya hai* (*sir*='the head', *dhār*='to be held by') means 'worthy of respect'. Hence the girl's putting her hand on her bosom and then on her head signifies 'I respect what you (seated in my heart) say'.

(ii) I swear by the Lord Śiva I will meet you at midnight.

(iii) I will meet you on the third night of the dark fortnight in the arbour between the two hills.

(iv) I'll meet you in the Śiva temple on the Yamunā bank.

(v) I'll not forget my promise to meet you, but I'll meet you after sunset.

356. *Aświn* or *Kuār* is one of the months of the Hindu calendar corresponding to September–October. The night of full moon in that month is the *śarada pūrṇimā* night (*śarada*='early winter', *pūrṇimā*='the full moon'). The moon then shines with the greatest brilliance. According to popular belief amongst Hindus it rains nectar then!

The *nāyikā* has a date with her lover but it has apparently slipped her mind. When she does not come, her lover sends a messenger to remind her. The messenger cleverly does so by pointing out to the loveliness of the full moon, thereby hinting at the rendezvous where she has agreed to meet her lover.

Some commentators, like Bhagawāna Dīna and Dr Deśarājasiṅgha Bhāṭī, interpret the couplet differently: 'When *śarada's* full moon is in the sky, girls will of themselves be filled with longing and be impelled to go to their lovers. Then, of course, dear girl, you can't help shaking off your arrogance and meeting him. So why not win his love by doing so now, of your own free will?' (BBL, p. 136; BBB, pp. 161–2) But the words *karati na kyauṁ cit ceta* in the first line, meaning 'why don't you remember?' clearly indicate that the messenger is trying to remind the *nāyikā* of something. So the alternative interpretation does not quite fit the context. The translation follows the interpretation which has been adopted amongst others by Śrī Rākeśa. (BSR, p. 197)

361. The translation follows the interpretation of Lālā Bhagawāna Dīna. (BBL, p. 238) Some commentators, however, do not introduce the romantic element

and take the couplet merely to be a description of the intense darkness created by the thick clouds. But Lālā Bhagawāna Dīna's version is more in keeping with the spirit of the *śṛngāra rasa* poetry, and hence has been preferred.

Some critics blame Bihārī for being inaccurate in mentioning the ruddy goose in the rainy season. This bird, they say, does not appear in the rains at all. The argument is a hair-splitting one, because even though the bird hibernates elsewhere in the rainy season, it was customary for bird lovers to keep caged ruddy geese, or tame them. Quite possibly they wandered about in the gardens of royal courts. Another objection taken is that the words used are *lakhi cakaī cakavāna*, i.e. 'seeing the male and female ruddy goose together as well as separated'. How can the birds be seen at all in the darkness? Bhagawāna Dīna explains this by taking the word *lakhi* to mean 'understand' or 'give attention to'. It is believed that the pair get separated in the night and call each other in a characteristic plaintive voice. So any one who listens carefully to the ruddy goose calling out to his mate can detect the plaintiveness in the voice, thus realizing that the two are separated. Also, since they are apart in the night only, he can know by the bird's call that it is night time.

362. *campā* is a fragrant yellow flower (see note to verse 278), often threaded into garlands.

Separation

370. 'Gust-shaped talks'. When the *nāyikā's* companions begin to talk about her lover who has gone abroad, the separated girl is comforted. Such talks are likened to gusts of winds which bring relief to the girl tormented by parting from her lover.

A Sanskrit poet, Amaru, says about a parted woman:

The moon seems hot,
sandalwood paste burns her;
each night seems a thousand years
and the lotus garland
is like an iron chain!

373. Poet Rasanidhi also uses the simile of the kite. His *nāyikā* says, 'My mind keeps flying like a kite, the string of which is in my lover's hands.'

378. This verse does not find place in the collection of Lālā Bhagawana Dīna. The allusion is to the *Rāmāyaṇa* in which the story of Rāma is told. His wife, Sītā,

was taken away by Rāvaṇa, the ten-headed demon-king of Laṅkā, and was captive there till Rāma rescued her after a fierce fight in which Rāvaṇa was killed. According to mythology, Rāma, who was an incarnation of Viṣṇu, had put the real Sītā in charge of the fire god, Agni, when he realized she would be carried away by Rāvaṇa, and had created her shadow. When this 'shadow'-Sītā was rescued from the demon-king, she was cast into the fire, and the real Sītā handed back by Agni, to whose charge she had been given. Thus it was not, as most believe, that Sītā was 'purified' by the fire, but that it was the ever pure Sītā being handed back to Rāma by the fire god. Maybe that's why Bhagawāna Dīna omits this verse.

379. In Bihārī's days thugs would tempt a child with a piece of *guṛ* (unrefined sugar) and take him away to some distance from his home. They would then rob him of his jewellery (which children customarily wore).

380. *Causara* has been taken by some commentators to mean a heavy garland of flowers or pearls. But it seems more likely Bihārī meant a particular kind of four-stringed flower garland, which women of those days wore to keep cool. Dr S.S. Pāñcāla also gives this meaning in *Bihārī Śabda-Kośa.* (BBP, p. 196)

382. A *ghuṁghacī* is the seed of a type of creeper. It is a small, hard, oval seed of brilliant red colour with a tiny black spot on it and a white dot inside the black. Attractive in appearance it can be threaded into a garland. The *nāyaka* places the garland 'laughingly' around the *nāyikā's* neck because it is a mere trifle, but all the same it must have looked nice on the beautiful woman! She treasures it as a gift from one whom she greatly loves.

Bihārī very subtly and appropriately refers to the *ghuṁghacī* garland. The seed of this is also used to preserve camphor. If some of the *ghuṁghacī* seeds are placed in a container of camphor then the camphor will not easily evaporate and is preserved. Thus the garland of *ghuṁghacīs* on the *nāyikā's* bosom keeps her camphor-like soul from going away.

383. Some commentators take the words to be meant for the separated *nāyaka.* But this seems unlikely as the parted girl is more the subject of Bihārī's love poetry than the separated lover.

384. Here the dual aspect of Kṛṣṇa is pointed out—as a lover and as an incarnation of Lord Viṣṇu. He is the woman's lover as well as the protector of her life, so the *nāyikā's* friend says, 'Apart from hastening to your beloved and removing the sorrow of her separation, you have a duty as lord and preserver of life to save her from death.' Death is said to be a blessing in the sense that it

will remove the extreme suffering of the parted girl, which has become unbearable now. Compare Shakespeare's:

> Fly away, fly away breath;
> I am slain by a fair cruel maid. (*Twelfth Night*: II.iv.54–5)

386. *barī* can mean both 'burning' and 'raving'. Some commentators, like Ratnākara, interpret it as 'burning', implying that the girl burns in the grief of separation. But the *juru* or *jara* in the next line, meaning 'fever' would apply more to 'raving', for it is in high fever that one begins to rave. So *barī* has been taken to mean 'mumbling incoherently while in the high fever of separation'.

387. *sudarasana* has a double meaning here (i) a powder (*chūrṁa)* given as medicine to cure fever, (ii) *suṁdara+daraśana* (*suṁdara* meaning 'charming' and *daraśana* meaning 'presence') i.e. 'charming presence'. The verse shows Bihārī's acquaintance with the āyurvedic (Hindu) system of medicine.

391. *bali* or *balihārī* literally means 'I die for you'. There is no exact equivalent for this in English. The *nāyikā's* confidante says to the *nāyaka* in a bantering sort of way 'dear lad, you are so dear to me that I can lay down my life for you, go and see to what state the *nāyikā* has been reduced through separation from you'.

The idea behind going on the quiet is that if the *nāyikā* comes to know of her lover's arrival, the great joy of meeting him will revive her and conceal her state of misery.

392. The *vīṇā* is an Indian stringed instrument somewhat like the *sitār*. *Malhāra* is a tune in Indian music, which if played or sung expertly, is believed to cause rainfall. *Pūs* is one of the months of the Hindu calendar, corresponding to December–January, the height of the Indian winter. Journeying was almost impossible in the days in the rainy season (July–August) because there were very few roads, and the village pathways would be impassable. So people set out in winter (summer's heat made the journey difficult). Although it does rain a little in the winter in India, it is not so much as to be a hindrance for travel. The *nāyikā*, however, wonderfully makes the rain pour heavily in winter by playing the *malhāra* tune!

Poet Rasikeś has a similar idea. Describing what a woman does on learning that her husband has planned to go abroad in the *Pūs* month, he writes:

> Hearing her friends say
> her husband would go abroad in *Pūs*
> that clever lady thought out a way.

She brought out her flute,
and praying to god,
played on it the *malhāra* tune.

393. Ratnākara has given a different interpretation. According to him the *nāyikā*, unable to bear the sorrow of separation, is dead, and the *nāyaka* is sorrowing over it. His confidant consoles him in these words: 'It was better for her to die than to bear the intense sorrow of her separation. By her dying at least the grief of one of you is no more, or else both of you would be plagued by it. You, being a man, will be able somehow to endure the shock of her death, but it would have been a torture for that tender girl to endure the sorrow of her separation.'

But perhaps Bihārī never intended to make his *nāyikā* die in this manner. It would be as though the heroine in a story died almost in the beginning! Besides, Bihārī's *Satasaī* is mainly a work of love poetry, and so the atmosphere of gloom created by the *nāyikā's* death would be out of place.

394. The translation follows Bhagawāna Dīna's interpretation which appears to be more appropriate than others who read *braja* for *jaga* in the couplet. According to them the concluding part of the verse means 'No one should venture out in Braja as the fire has spread throughout the city.'

The fire of separation is considered to be strange because normally a spark is caused by the striking of two hard things, as for example two stones, but here two soft things have caused it, viz. the eyes of the *nāyaka* and the *nāyikā*. Again the fire has its origin in one place, but it burns in another—the *nāyikā's* heart, when usually a fire blazes only at the place where it is caused.

397. For Kāma see note to verse 463.

400. The *Gāthāsaptaśatī* has a similar idea:

I have not been able to rearrange yet
my braid's ruffled hair,
and you are thinking of leaving again,
O heartless lover!

402. The *nāyikā's* lover has gone abroad. Even though there is no news of his coming, the heaving of her bosom and the flickering of her left eyelid make her believe that he might be arriving. So she hastily puts on a new dress to welcome him.

The flickering of a woman's left eyelid is considered to be a good omen. The changing of the dress has particular significance, for the *Kāma Sūtra* says that during the absence of her husband a woman 'should wear only her auspicious ornaments' (KS, p. 90), and remain dressed in ordinary clothes. But it seems the *nāyikā* transgresses Vātsyāyana's directive about how to meet a husband on his homecoming, inasmuch as he says in *Kāma Sūtra*, 'And when her husband returns from his journey, she should receive him at first in her ordinary clothes, so that he may know in what way she has lived during his absence. . . .'

403. Hindu cosmogony believes the cosmic unit of time to be a *kalpa,* which is just a 'day' of Brahmā, the Creator. This 'day' is equivalent to 4,320 million years! (Reckoned in terms of the Christian year). Brahmā creates the universe in the morning of his 'day', and at 'night', heaven and hell as also the created world, all return to chaos.

The idea being that even the few minutes her lover takes in greeting his friends before coming to her, seem unending to the *nāyikā*—so great is her longing to unite with him.

404. To the girl parted from her lover, even the cool moonbeams seem like the sun's rays. The lady of one of Vākkūta's verses similarly addresses the moon complaining: 'Shoot not your fire-shooting rays, O moon.' (SPI, p. 179)

405. Lālā Bhagawāna Dīna has given an alternative interpretation also (reading the words *jau guahī tau,* 'if you consider me at fault' as *jyauṁ gunahī tyauṁ,* 'as a wrongdoer would be imprisoned'). This is as follows:

> One cannot achieve salvation by a million deceitful words. Only by keeping the image of the god with form ever in one's eyes as securely as a gaoled wrongdoer can one get it. (BBL, p. 123)

However, since Bihārī is primarily a love poet, it seems it was not his intention in this verse to convey a spiritual message. The other interpretation which appears more likely has been adopted.

407. *khas* is the fragrant root of a grass which has a cooling effect. In Bihārī's days (and sometimes even now), curtains of *khas* were hung on windows and fixed on doors in the unbearably hot Indian summer months. The curtains were drenched with water and the hot winds blowing through them caused evaporation, thus cooling the room.

The winter month, *Māgh,* is the eleventh month of the Hindu calendar (corresponding to January–February) when it is exceedingly cold.

408. Commentators have given different interpretations for this verse. The translation follows Bhagawāna Dīna's version (BBL, p. 209). Others take the

couplet as being spoken by the *nāyikā's* woman messenger to the *nāyaka* who has gone abroad. According to other commentators the *nāyaka* was in love with the *nāyikā's* woman neighbour as well. The *nāyikā* came to know of their secret affair, and almost every day there would be a row. He had in fact gone away to escape from this unpleasant situation for some time. The *nāyikā's* messenger comes to him and speaks to him of the *nāyikā's* condition, but cleverly conveys to him also the grief of his other love, thus throwing him a hint that he should return at least for the other woman's sake.

Bhagawāna Dīna's interpretation seems to be the simplest and most direct, and has therefore been adopted. The others are too fanciful and stretch the point too far.

409. *tithi aum* or the *avam* lunar day. According to an astrologer's almanac, the lunar day is fixed in relation to the rising of the sun. If a particular *tithi* is fixed for a certain lunar day, that will subsist even though another *tithi* may actually begin a few hours after the rising of the sun on that day. And if on the day after that yet another *tithi* begins according to the almanac, that *tithi* will remain even if actually the previous one is still continuing. Thus the *tithi* which subsists from after the rising of the sun on the first day to the time the *tithi* (as in the almanac) of the second day starts, is as though it had no existence, because it is not counted as a *tithi* for either of the two days.

414. *Māgh* (January–February) is among the coldest months of the Indian winter. *lū* is hot scorching wind that blows in the day during the hottest month of the Indian summer (June).

419. The *jawāsa* is a thorny plant which grows on the banks of rivers. When the rain falls its stems and leaves shrivel up. The root, which is in the ground, however, gets firmer.

423. Draupadī, daughter of Drupada, king of Pāñcāla was married to all the five Pāṇḍu princes. Of these the eldest, Yudhiśthira, had a gambling match with his cousins, the Kauravas, in which he lost everything including Draupadī, whom he staked in the last bid. So she became a slave and Duryodhana asked her to sweep the room. On her refusal, Duhaśāsana dragged her by the hair before all the chieftains and insulted her. He even started pulling her sari to bare her and thus dishonour her in the assembly. But Kṛṣṇa came to her rescue and miraculously caused her sari to become more and more long. Duhaśāsana got tired of pulling folds after folds of the sari, for it seemed to have no end, and at last gave up in despair and shamefacedly went back to his seat. The incident is narrated in the famous Hindu epic, the *Mahābhārata.*

427. Duryodhana (literally 'hard to conquer') was the eldest son of Dhṛtarāśtra and leader of the Kaurava princes in the great *Mahābhārata* war. Towards the end of the battle, on the eighteenth day, after his side had been utterly defeated by the Pāṇḍavas, he fled and hid himself in a lake, for he had the power of remaining under water without being affected by it in any manner. He was discovered after a great deal of difficulty and incited to come out through taunts and sarcasms to fight with Bhīma (one of the Pāṇḍava brothers). The incident is related in the *Mahābhārata*.

The idea of the analogy is that as Duryodhana hid in the waters, being untouched by it, so the *nāyikā's* lover resides in her heart and yet is not moved by the grief caused by separation.

428. *āṭhauṁ jāma* means *āṭhoṁ pahara*. A *pahara* was the unit of time before clocks came to be used. There were eight *paharas* (*āṭha*= 'eight') in the day and night of twenty-four hours, and each *pahara* was three hours. Hence *āṭhaum jāma* means all the twenty-four hours, i.e. 'day and night'.

430. *seṁhuṛa* is a kind of cactus (swallow wort). If letters are written on paper with the juice of the plant, they are invisible. But if a little heat is applied to the paper on which they are written, they get revealed and can be read.

433. For *lū* (hot winds) see note to verse 414. The Indian summer follows a brief spring.

Some commentators take the couplet to be just the poet's observation, not words spoken by the *nāyikā's* companion to her. However, the import remains the same either way.

435. *maulasirī* (or *vakula*) is a beautiful tree with a thick spreading crown and dark green glossy leaves. In March it bears pale green fragrant flowers which are often threaded into garlands.

Commentators have given various interpretations to this verse. Mānasingha takes it to be meant for Rādhā. Others, like the writer of the *Rasacandrikā,* and Prabhudayāl Pāṇḍeya, say that the garland itself seemed to be thrilled with love on contact with the *nāyikā's* neck! Ratnākarа́ would have it that the *nāyikā* appeared so splendid with the garland round her neck that it seemed she herself had become a lovely garland! But these interpretations seem too fanciful, and so the more obvious and direct one has been adopted in the translation.

437. *Caitra* or *Caita* is the first month of the Hindu calendar corresponding to March–April when it is neither too hot nor too cold and the nights are pleasant. The full moon of *Caitra* has an ethereal beauty.

438. The incident referred to is the lifting of Mount Goverdhana by Kṛṣṇa. It was customary to offer Indra, god of the firmament, sweets, rice, saffron, sandal and incense once in the year. When the cowherds were getting ready for this annual offering, Kṛṣṇa asked them to worship instead the Goverdhana hill, and promised that if they did so the spirit of the mount would show itself. He then assumed the form of the spirit and himself received the offerings. This enraged Indra, who ordered the clouds to rain in torrents for seven days and nights. Faced with the deluge the cowherds were terrified, but Kṛṣṇa calmly raised the hill, supporting it on his little finger, thus protecting them from the flood waters. Indra was baffled, and realizing Kṛṣṇa's supremacy, came down from the sky and offered his submission.

pralaya—Hindus reckon cosmic time in terms of *yugas* (ages), of which there are four, viz., Kṛta, Tretā, Dvāpara and Kali (the one in which we are living). These *yugas* have a period of 12,000 celestial years (a celestial year being equal to 360 ordinary years). Thus the *yugas* extend to 4,320,000 years (called the period of *mahayuga* or *manwatara*). Two thousand *mahayugas* (or 8,640,000,000 years) make a *kalpa*. At the end of the *kalpa* the world is dissolved and then recreated. This dissolution is called *pralaya*.

Some commentators interpret the verse in a devotional light: 'When powerful Indra, out of wrath for being denied his customary worship, caused torrential rain which seemed to bring the world's destruction before its due time, Kṛṣṇa protected the milkmaids and the cowherds of Braja by lifting the Goverdhana mount.' Though this is a more direct interpretation, it appears to be too facile, as it would be a mere mention of one of Kṛṣṇa's many episodes. Besides in another verse (686) the poet has made a direct reference to the incident. He would hardly have two verses having an identical meaning.

The other interpretation which Bhagawāna Dīna and other commentators have adopted is more expressive and is in keeping with the spirit of Bihārī's love poetry, and so this has been preferred in the translation. (BBL, pp. 6–7)

442. *aragaja* is a kind of yellowish perfume made from sandalwood, saffron and camphor, which is applied by Indian women to their bodies. The *nāyaka*, who is abroad, has sent this perfume as a gift of love to the *nāyikā* through her companion.

443. Some commentators think the *nāyikā* has died due to the grief of separation and the parrot has memorized the pathetic words she spoke at the moment of her death. But this interpretation is both unnecessary and unlikely, for in Hindi love poetry the parted woman may become insensible, emaciated,

feverish and may approach death, but she never dies! In fact the *nāyaka's* timely arrival has saved the *nāyikā* and all is well again. But her sorrowful words remain on the tame parrot's tongue as a reminder of the past agony of separation.

445. The words *uṛyau usās samīra* in the text signify an idiomatic expression in Hindi (*usās ke samīra se hṛdaya kā uṛanā*) meaning 'the heart soaring aloft on the wind of her sighs', in other words 'she's agitated'. A kite can't fly if singed or wet, but the parted woman's heart burnt by separation's fire and drenched by her tears, keeps aloft on the deep sighs of her sorrows.

446. Some commentators give a slightly different interpretation: 'Those who can bear the grief of separation from their sweethearts in this exciting rainy season and yet stay alive, are truly immortal!' The translation follows Bhagawāna Dīna's version. (BBL, p. 241) The word *amar* literally means 'immortal', but it would be too much of an exaggeration to say that a man would become immortal either if he had had the bliss of union with his loved one or if he had withstood the grief of separation from her. Hence the word has been translated as 'long life'.

452. Indian houses are built differently from those in the west. There is usually an inner courtyard and verandas with rooms opening in to them. After these, towards the front there may be other rooms and then a kind of parlour or roofless space, and finally a big door opening out to the lane or a street.

456. *nirāsa=nīra+aśan* (*nīra*='water' or 'rain'; *aśan*='he whose life depends on') means the Indian sparrow-hawk, a bird which according to poetic convention keeps alive by drinking only the raindrops which fall when the moon is in the fifteenth lunar mansion (the raindrops are believed to generate pearls). The *papīhā* or *cātak*, as the sparrow-hawk is popularly called, appears in the rains and, perched usually on the twig of a mango tree, calls aloud '*pī*! *pī*!' in a plaintive voice.

459. *kema kusuma* means the *kadamba* flower (*kusuma*='flower'). The *kadamba* tree has ovate-oblong glossy leaves with solitary bunches of flowers in a ball-like form at the end of its branchlets. The flowers are of a dull yellow colour and mildly fragrant, and appear at the beginning of the rainy season. The tree is associated with Kṛṣṇa.

460. Kṛṣṇa used to make love to Rādhā and to the milkmaid girls in Gokul—the scene of his early life, his favourite haunt being the bank of the river Yamunā. After killing the tyrant, Kaṅsa, Kṛṣṇa left Gokul and went to Mathurā, the place

of his birth. This cast a gloom over the milkmaids whom he had loved and who were deeply enamoured of him. One of them is bemoaning her sorrow in this verse.

The verse is somewhat unconventional inasmuch as here just those things give pleasure to the separated milkmaid, which pain a woman parted from her lover, viz. the shade of the thick woods and the gentle fragrant breeze. This is rather unusual in Hindi love poetry in which all pleasant things (even pleasant associations with the loved one) cause grief to the woman whose lover has gone away.

Beauty

463. Kāma or Kāmadeva (*deva*='god') is the Hindu god of love. He is lord of the *apsaras* (heavenly nymphs). His bow is of sugarcane and its bowstring is a line of bees. Each of the arrows he uses is tipped with a distinctive flower. He is shown as a handsome youth riding on a parrot. Nymphs attend to him, and one of them carries his banner—a fish (*maraka*) on a red background.

465. *khubhī* is an ear ornament shaped like a clove, worn by Indian women. *Manamatha* is another name for Kāma. See note to verse 463 *ante*.

466. The girl is a *śuklābhisārikā* (*śukla*='light', *abhisāra*='tryst'). Such a woman loves to dress in white and has a complexion 'fair as the yellow lotus'. (AR, p. 114) As the name *śuklābhisārikā* suggests, such a girl goes to meet her lover on moonlit nights.

467. *sonajūhī* is a variety of jasmine yielding yellow flowers, and *mālatī* is a dense climber which bears white, fragrant flowers.

468. Long eyes are taken by Hindi poets to be a mark of the adolescent girl. Girls would sometimes make a fine pencil mark outwards from the corners of their eyelids to make their eyes seem longer. Poet Vidyāpati writes of 'eyes stretching to the ears to whisper the message of adolescence'.

469. There can be two interpretations. If the meaning of the word *jhilamilī* is taken to be 'glimmer' the sense would be as conveyed in the verse translation. If it is taken to be 'ear ornament' it would be 'Her ear ornament glitters bewitchingly from beneath her thin dress, as though a *kalpa* tree branch and the leaves on it were reflected in the waters of the sea'. The former interpretation has been preferred because the comparison to a branch of the *kalpa* tree would be more appropriate for the girl's body than her small ornament. Unless the girl is beautiful, the glitter of her ornament would be of little account.

The *kalpa* tree (Wishing Tree) is believed to be a mythical tree growing in heaven, which fulfills all desires.

470. Thugs used to roam about the countryside in eighteenth century India. They would travel in the company of their victim for several days. Reaching a lonely spot, one amongst the gang would suddenly throw a rope or a cloth round the unsuspecting man's neck, and his accomplice would deftly catch the other end. The noose would be pulled tight while a third villain would seize the man and throw him on the ground, at the same time kicking him on some vital part. The noose tightened as the man fell. Resistance was impossible. The unfortunate victim would be robbed and his corpse thrown into some pit nearby.

cilaka cauṁdha—this is a poetic exaggeration. Starlight can hardly appear as bright as daylight. Here the poet imagines that the traveller, who is likened to the lovelorn *nāyaka*, suddenly wakes up in the bright starlight and mistaking it for daylight, resumes his journey. The thug (compared to the beauty of the girl) who is after him, finds this a good opportunity to put the noose (compared to the girl's smile) round his neck, and strangling him throws his body into a pit (here compared to the dimple on the *nāyikā's* chin).

471. The first *urabasī* in this verse stands for Uravaśī, a celestial nymph (*apasarā*) mentioned in the *Ṛg-Veda,* who was so ravishing that at the very sight of her, Mitra (Ruler of the day) and Varuṇa (Ruler of the night), while engaged in performing a sacrifice, emitted their seed. She is said to have approached Arjuna, the Pāṇḍava warrior, and the *Mahābhārata* describes her as 'challenging in beauty the moon itself'. The other *urabasī* (also called a *hamela*) is a necklace of gold coins or gold discs threaded together.

473. It is believed that a black mark, usually of lamp-black, put on the cheek or forehead of a child or of a grown-up person, will act as a protection against the evil eye. Here the black mark has just the opposite effect!

474. It is customary for Indian women to call for the wife of a barber to apply red lacquer dye to their feet, because of the expertize with which she does it. The manner in which she does it is as follows: She soaks a small cotton plug thoroughly with a thick solution of the dye. This she moves along the foot, gently squeezing out the dye from it. Here the barber's wife finds the *nāyikā's* heel so red that she mistakes it for the dye-soaked cotton and keeps on squeezing the heel itself!

475. A rich man of those days married several women, and it was natural that his co-wives were jealous of one another, particularly of the younger and the more attractive one, who became the husband's favourite. Poet Matirāma expresses a similar thought:

> The more the breasts of that youthful maiden rise
> the more are lowered the humbled eyes of her co-wives!

476. According to Indian astrological belief when the planets Mars, Saturn and Moon are in the same House there is bound to be heavy rain. Further Mars' colour, according to Indian astrology, is red, and that of Jupiter yellow. So the red auspicious mark on the *nāyikā's* forehead signifies Mars, and the saffron or yellow, Jupiter.

Indian women put *bindī* marks on their forehead. This is made from *rolī* powder, prepared from a mixture of turmeric and lime. A yellow saffron mark is also made to enhance beauty.

477. For 'black mark' see note to verse 473.

478. The literal meaning of *bepāi* is 'without feet'. The use here is purely metaphorical. The poet means that when the barber's wife saw that the lady's heels were as red as the dye she was about to paint them with, she found the job she came for as impossible as walking is for a man without feet! The expression is also significant inasmuch as the barber's wife realized that compared to the *nāyikā's* feet her own feet did not the least appear as feet ought!

479. *khañjana* is a kind of Indian wagtail. Hindi poets often compare women's eyes to those of a *khañjana* bird. The bird is often seen in India in autumn and winter. It has a black and white plumage and a rather long tail.

Collyrium (lamp-black) is used by Indian women to beautify their eyes. The *Kāma Sūtra* recommends it for enhancing the loveliness of the eyes. (KS, p.155) *The Bride's Book of Beauty* has the following note about it: 'A layer of collyrium or the soot of a lamp is applied to make the eyes dark and bright.' (BAH)

480. *Jeṭh* is the third month of the Hindu calendar corresponding to May–June. It is the year's hottest month.

Jagannātha Dāsa Ratnākara has a different interpretation. According to him the words are spoken by the *nāyaka* to his beloved in order to persuade her to stay on in his house so that he may have more of her company: 'Do not venture out, dear beloved, in the scorching heat of this hot *Jeṭh* noon when even the Shade rests under the forest trees and dare not leave the four walls of the house.' But this would be unnecessarily reading a romantic meaning in a verse which as a description of the heat of summer has infinitely more charm.

481. The *nāyikā* is offended because she has discovered that the *nāyaka* has come after disporting with another woman. So she angrily covers her face with her sari and will not look at him. Her companion tries to reconcile the two.

Hindi and Sanskrit poets often compare a beautiful woman's face to a lily or to the moon.

482. *raṁge tribidha raṁga*—means 'triple-coloured eyes', (*raṁge*='coloured', *tribidha*='triple'). In other words their black pupils, the whites, and the crimson hue taken on by them.

Some commentators take *sāyaka* to mean 'an arrow' thus interpreting *sāyaka sama* as 'like an arrow', but that does not tie up with 'triple-coloured'. So it is more appropriate to interpret the word here as 'twilight' or 'dusk' because that can explain why the poet speaks of the *nāyikā's* eyes of three colours (white, black and crimson).

The lilies are abashed because the woman's eyes outmatch them in beauty. The fishes hide themselves in the depth of the pond because they can't bear to see the eyes which beat them in beauty. Besides, even otherwise, at dusk fishes seek the inner layers of water, and lilies which have blossomed all day, close theirpetals.

483. *bar jīte* literally means 'won by might'. In other words the *nāyikā's* eyes are victorious over Kāmadeva's arrows, i.e. their glance is sharper than the arrows.

For Kāmadeva see note to verse 463. He is also called Kāma, and is the Hindu god of love.

Hindi and Sanskrit poets often liken a beautiful woman's eyes to those of a deer.

484. The words *aṅga aṅga naga* literally mean 'the gems of the ornaments worn on each limb'. It might seem surprising that Bihārī describes his *nāyikā* as laden with so much of jewellery. But in those days ornaments were worn in plenty. According to Malik Muhammad Jāisī, a fifteenth century poet, women ought to wear ornaments for the ears, nose, neck, forearm, waist and feet (*padmāvata*).

dīpasikhā sī deha—this literally means 'her body glowing like the flame of a lamp', and could be interpreted to mean either 'Her body appeared to be like the flame of a lamp because of the numerous ornaments she wore', or 'the radiance of her body was like the flame of a lamp'. The two expressions (*aṅga*

aṅga naga jagamagāta and *dīpasikhā sī deha*) are entirely separate and do not qualify each other. Hence the second explanation would be more rational and this has been followed. It should be remembered that a lamp here means just a shallow earthen oil-lamp (there was no electricity then). The flame of such a lamp would not give much light anyway. Besides, Hindi and Sanskrit poets (with poetic exaggeration of course) conceive of a woman's beautiful body as having a shine like that of gold or moonlight (see Bihārīs own verse number 466).

485. The comparison to double-tinted silk (*tāfatā raṅga*) is very appropriate here. *Tāfatā* cloth woven of warp and wool of varied colours, acquires different tints when seen from particular angles. Just as childhood and youth blend in an adolescent girl. She has not abandoned her childhood ways completely, but youth influences her thoughts and manners, and brings about marked changes in her growing body.

487. Mainās are a hill tribe of Rājasthān who are dacoits and highway men. For Kāma see verse 463.

488. *gardarāne tana* ('youthful body'): the word *gadarānā* is usually used for a fruit, meaning its pre-ripening stage. The word is appropriately used here for suggestively describing the rustic girl who has crossed adolescence but not yet reached womanhood.

hūṭhyau dai—hūṭhyau is from Hindi *aṁgūṭhā* meaning 'the thumb'. A rustic girl in the village often stands with her palms closed into her fists, placing her hands on her hips, mocking someone or making coquettish gestures. This is called *hūṭhyau* in Brajabhāṣā, the language in which Bihārī wrote.

aipana is made by grinding turmeric and grains of rice finely and making it into a paste by adding water. A mark of this paste made on the forehead is a kind of adornment for women.

490. The *campā* tree bears very fragrant, pale yellow and rather silky flowers. A golden complexion is prized, and Hindi poets often liken a beautiful woman's body to the *campā* flower.

491. For Kāma, the Hindu god of love, see note to verse 463. His banner is a fish on a red ground, and therefore the comparison of Kṛṣṇa's fish-shaped ear ornament to Kāma's standard. Some commentators think that Kṛṣṇa's ear ornament has been likened to Kāma's flag on the gateway because some girl has found a way into his heart through the ears, i.e. he has been won over by the praise of her beauty heard from her friends or messengers. But such does

not seem to be Bihārī's import. Nowhere in the verse is there any indication that Kṛṣṇa has been attracted to any particular girl. The implication rather seems to be that thoughts of love and love-making are now arising in his heart. The comparison to Kāma's banner can be explained by the fact that the ornament is above the 'city of Kṛṣṇa's heart' on which the god of love has established his rule. So the banner flies aloft as though the ears, where the ornament is, are the roof over the gateway of that city.

492. Some commentators interpret the verse to mean that the angry *nāyikā*, looks lovely even when she is in a rage. But this appears unnecessary, nor is it implied by any word of the couplet. Most probably the poet just means to emphasize the captivating loveliness of the girl. She need not be angry to look beautiful.

The girl puts on a horizontal beauty mark which is made above the eyebrows, parallel to it, dipping down to a small arrow-like curve to touch the bridge of the nose.

493. Normally the moon which shines with the sun's borrowed light, fades away when the sun comes out. But here the rising of the sun makes the moon shine out more. The implication is that the ornament's glimmer does not throw the beauty of the girl's face (which is like the moon) into the shade, but increases its beauty.

ṭīkau is a round ornament studded with gems which an Indian woman wears on her forehead.

496. *Jeṭh* is the Indian summer month when the heat is most intense, and the days are long. (see note to verse 480)

498. *sīṁk* ('a nose-pin') is a clove-shaped ornament worn by Indian women on the nostril.

For *campā*, see note to verse 490. The expression 'alighting for once' needs an explanation. According to convention, in Hindi poetry a black bee may sit on a lotus but not on a *campā* flower. It can't be assumed that a poet like Bihārī was unaware of this. Perhaps what he is expressing is that the beauty of the *nāyikā* is so greatly enhanced by the nose-pin she wears and the sapphire glimmering in it, that men are intoxicated by it, and forget what is proper and improper; just as the black bee alights on the *campā* flower unaware that it is not a flower from which he is accustomed to suck nectar.

499. *jala keli* ('water sport') was a favourite pastime of women. Nobles and nabobs often had swimming-pools in their palaces in which the women of their harems disported.

501. The *nāyikā* is wearing a nose-ring (*besara*) with a pearl in it. The pearl casts a reflection on her lips, which the simple-minded girl, takes to be lime, and tries to wipe off again and again with the end of her sari. Seeing this her companion addresses her in these words.

A *besara* or *natha* is a big gold ring with a large pearl threaded at one end, worn by Indian girls, particularly those newly-wed. Lime is mixed with catechu paste and applied to betels which Indians chew. It is also made up into a ball with tobacco and eaten. The *nāyikā* mistakenly thinks some of the lime has got stuck on her lips and again and again wipes them with the corner of her sari.

502. The girl's messenger cleverly manages to convey to the *nāyaka* by this hint that the girl has been drinking, and so it's the right moment for him to go to her. With a drink or two she would lose her shyness and be more inclined for love-making.

503. Some commentators take the word *sādī* ('plain') as *sārī* ('sari'). But this is not quite appropriate, as then it would imply that the growing girl's breasts can be seen through her sari and the perfumed bodice. Such an interpretation is wholly unnecessary and confusing. Perhaps the girl wears her sari so that it does not cover her bodice at all. The translation follows Bhagawāna Dīna's version. (BBL, pp. 50–1)

505. *kusuma* is a red flower.

506. *maulasirī* (also called *vakula*) is a beautiful shady tree with a thick, spreading crown. Its leaves are glossy and of a deep green colour, and it yields pale fragrant flowers in March.

507. *anavaṭa* is an ornament shaped like a ring, often with gems set in it, worn by Indian women on the toe. The idea is that the toe ornament of the *nāyikā* glitters as brilliantly as the sun.

tarivana (also known as *karṇaphūla*) is a flower-shaped ornament worn on the earlobes by women. It is a kind of ear-pin with the outer portion set in gems in the form of a flower (*karṇa*='ear', *phūla*='flower').

508. The expression *keli taruna* is used in a double sense. The first *keli taruna* means a banana tree (*keli*='banana', *taruna*='tree'). The second one means 'give the pleasure of love-making (to her lover)', *keli* meaning here 'love-

making' and *taruna* 'a youth'. As the banana tree is perfectly smooth and straight, a woman's thighs are often compared to it by Hindi and Sanskrit poets.

Kāma is here spoken of as Brahmā the Creator (*bidhi maina*). This is because as the god of love, Kāma's work is only to make people fall in love. Creation is really the job of Brahmā (one of the gods of the Hindu Trinity). Here the girl's thighs, which please her lover, are *made* out of Beauty, and shaping something like that involves creation. So Kāma and Brahmā both have been mentioned.

512. *beṁdī* is a kind of flower-shaped ornament worn by Indian women. It rests in the middle of the forehead, and is suspended by a string tied to the braid, and runs along the parting of the hair. A real flower may sometimes replace the ornamental gold or silver one.

514. A *cakor* is the red-legged partridge found in India. According to convention in Hindi poetry, it is believed to be enamoured of the moon which so captivates the bird that it keeps gazing at it ceaselessly. When poets speak of the intensity of love they liken it to that of the *cakor* for the moon.

515. Hindu women keep the fast of *karvā cautha* which falls a week after the *Duśerā* festival (in October). The fast is kept for the longevity of their husbands' lives, and is observed very strictly, for the fasting women do not even drink water till the moon has risen in the sky. In order to see whether the moon is up or not they climb their balcony, so that the fast may be broken at the appointed time. If it is broken before, they will not earn the merit conferred by the fast, and its purpose will be defeated.

516. The fast mentioned here is the *karvā cautha* (see note verse 515 *ante*). The *aragha* (religious offering) is made to the moon by pouring water by the women who observe the *karvā cautha* fast. That ends the exacting fast, and after that they get down from their rooftops to eat.

518. *beṁdi* (not to be confused with *beṁdī*, the forehead ornament, mentioned in verse 512) stands for *biṅdi*, the round beauty mark adorning an Indian woman's brow (see note to verse 476). This may be of many different colours, (or sometimes multicoloured).

519. *saṅkrauna*—when the sun, after completing its path through one sign of the zodiac and in passing into another crosses the dividing line between the two, it is called the time of *saṅkrānti*. The period when it is passing across is considered auspicious.

taruna is the period in a girl's life when she has completed her fifteenth year and entering her sixteenth. The *kisora* period is when she is yet a child (between eleven and fifteen). Some commentators read *tarani* for *taruna,* and take the word as meaning *sūrya* (the sun), in the sense that 'the sun of the girl's beauty is crossing her fifteenth year', which is the dividing line between childhood and youth. (BBL, p. 12; GBS, p. 10; also Kṛṣṇa Kavi and Mānasiṅgha)

520. The face-seeing ceremony is one which follows the advent of the new bride in her husband's home. All the adult members of the house (men as well as women) give her money or presents as gifts when they see her face for the first time.

523. *śarada* night is the night of the full moon of the *Aświna* month (September–October) when the moon shines with the greatest brilliancy.

525. *guñjana* is another name for *ghuṁghacī,* for which see note to verse 382.

The swallowing of the forest fire is one of the incidents in Kṛṣṇa's life. Archer relates it as follows:

> At midnight there is a heavy storm and a huge conflagration. Scarlet flames leap up, dense smoke engulfs the forest and many cattle are burnt alive. Finding themselves in great danger, Nanda, Yaśodā, and the cowherds call on Kṛṣṇa to save them. Kṛṣṇa quietly rises up, sucks the fire into his mouth and ends the blaze. (AL, p. 35)

Some commentators give an ingenious interpretation, reading in the verse something more than a description of Kṛṣṇa's beauty. According to this, a girl loved by Kṛṣṇa has promised to meet him at a certain spot, but due to some reason cannot do so. Kṛṣṇa comes back disappointed, and wearing a garland of *guñjana* seeds purposely passes by the girl who is sitting in the company of elders of the village. The girl feels very sorry, and in this couplet tells her confidante that the *guñjana* garland on Kṛṣṇa's bosom is to indicate to her that the separation-like forest fire which he had swallowed is now emerging, i.e. he is greatly grieved by not finding his beloved at the agreed place.

The simpler interpretation, however, has been incorporated in the translation, and this is the one by Lālā Bhagawāna Dīna. (BBL, p. 3)

527. Some commentators believe the couplet contains the words spoken by the *nāyikā's* companion to hasten her to keep her appointment with her lover whom she is to meet. The *nāyikā* is getting delayed because she begins to wear all her ornaments. Her companion fears she will be late and her lover will go away disappointed. So she gives this subtle hint, which is also a compliment, to her friend. But the couplet can be taken to be just in praise of the *nāyikā's* superb beauty, and the romantic slant does not really seem necessary.

Others have taken the couplet to express Bihārī's views about poetry—that good poetry needs no ornamentation (*alaṅkāras*). It subsists on its natural simplicity. This too appears fanciful, and in fact is quite in opposition to Bihārī's verses in the *Satasaī* which abound in ornamentation of language and figures of speech.

532. *aṅgarāga* is a scented paste made of musk, sandalwood, saffron etc., used as a kind of cosmetic by women to heighten the beauty of their limbs. The *nāyikā's* innate beauty is so great that instead of increasing it, cosmetics only spoil it.

533. Some critics take the couplet to be spoken by the *nāyikā's* companion urging her to make haste in order to meet her lover with whom she has an appointment. She tells her not to delay by wearing ornaments or else she'll get late. But there is no reason why such an interpretation need be given. More likely she is just praising the *nāyikā's* beauty.

When a mirror gets rusty and loses its silvery surface, the mercury coating behind, which is of a yellowish colour, begins to show up. This is a rather dull reddish yellow, very much inferior to the bright lustre of gold ornaments.

534. The holy rivers Gaṅgā (whose waters are clear) and Yamunā (which is bluish due to its depth) meet at Prayāga (Allahabād), where they are believed to join the subterranean Sarasvatī. This meeting point, held very sacred by Hindus, is known as Triveṇī ('the triple braid'). Here the white finger of the *nāyikā* is likened to Gaṅgā and the blue sapphire in her ring to the Yamunā.

535. *pacatoriyā*—In Bihārī's time a very thin cloth was made in India, so thin that a sari made of it would weigh just about five grams! It is this particular kind of sari which is mentioned here (*paca*='five').

jalacādara—In the arbours of princes and nobles of Bihārī's age, one would often come across a thin stream of water falling from a height (a kind of artificially created waterfall). A row of oil-lamps would be lit and placed behind this. The glowing lights seen through the water gave a picturesque effect. This was known as a *jalacādara* (*jala*='water', *cādara*='a mantle' or 'sheet').

536. *Māgh* (January–February) is among the coldest months in India, when the sky often remains overcast and the sun can be very dimly seen beneath the clouds.

For *cakor* see note to verse 514.

537. In all probability Bihārī wrote these lines simply to bring out the *nāyikā's* irresistible charm, but commentators have assigned various fanciful reasons for

the unsuccessful attempts of the painters to paint the *nāyikā's* portrait, as follows: (i) The painter is so stunned by her beauty that he can only gaze and gaze and his hands refuse to move, (ii) He is so overcome with her loveliness that he begins to tremble with excitement and his fingers can't remain steady, (iii) He starts perspiring when he sees such an incomparably beautiful girl and drops of his sweat falling on the canvas smudge it, and (iv) The girl's beauty is so wonderful that it keeps changing and increasing each moment, so that what he paints can never really represent her!

538. For *gulāl* see note to verse 76.

539. In the *Phāga* (Holī) festival, it is customary for youths to give presents to girls who have played Holī with them. (see also note to verse 76)

Some commentators depict the *nāyikā* in this verse as being a dancing girl. The *nāyaka* has gone to see her dance, and she charmingly pulls at his garment, insisting on being given money as a reward. He purposely puts her off because he is overcome by the coquettish manner of her asking and wants to see more of that. But the word *phaguvā* (or *phāga*) has a definite association with the Holī festival. So this interpretation is not quite suitable.

540. Rāhu is believed to be a *daitya* (demon) and the cause of eclipses. He is supposed to seize the sun and the moon and swallow them, thus obscuring their rays. Here the black hair of the *nāyikā* is likened to Rāhu, the red mark on her brow to the sun and her face to the moon. As her hair is spread on her brow and hanging down her face, the poet imagines it's Rāhu swallowing up both the sun as well as the moon, thus causing an eclipse of both at the same time. It is believed that the most appropriate time for love-making is when the sun has not completely set and the moon has just risen.

Some commentators, including Bhagawāna Dīna, have put it the other way round. The sun and the moon combining have courageously caught Rāhu, the troublemaker. (BBL, p. 19)

But according to tradition it is Rāhu who swallows the sun or the moon. Besides, the reason given by Bhagawāna Dīna for taking this view is not good enough. He says *chabi deta* in the verse means 'gives loveliness', and when Rāhu swallows the sun or the moon, they grow dimmer. So how can their loveliness increase? It seems the words *chabi deta* are meant in a general sense, i.e. the scattered hair and the beauty mark of the girl look lovely. The words need not be tagged on to the second line.

542. *kapūramaṇī* is a brilliant yellow stone to which a dry blade of grass or a straw is attracted in the same way as iron is attracted by a magnet.

543. The *nāyikā* is grieved by the separation from her lover, who lives nearby towards the east of her house. Her companion goes on the roof to see the moon rising on the second night of the bright fortnight of the lunar month, perhaps to break a fast she has undertaken. By chance her gaze falls on the *nāyaka*, who is standing on his balcony. She hastens to the *nāyikā* to tell her of this so that she may also go up her own balcony and see her lover.

The moon of the *nāyaka's* face is unique inasmuch as it is on the east (for the *nāyaka* is standing on the balcony of his house which is on the eastern side of the *nāyikā's* house), while the moon of the second night of this fortnight rises on the west. Also, ordinarily the sight of the moon (being associated with romance) increases the grief of parting, but here the moon of the *nāyaka's* face will allay it.

545. The translation is based on Ratnākara's interpretation and has been preferred because of its greater expressiveness and being more along the lines of love poetry. A simpler interpretation is given by Bhagawāna Dīna and others, as follows: 'About midnight, somehow the breeze which had remained stagnant the whole day, started, and gently brushing against my breast cooled me, driving off the daylong heat'. (BBL, p. 247)

551. *bichiyā* is an ornament, shaped like a ring, worn on the toes by Indian women. It's not heavy at all, but here the poet imagines that the *nāyikā's* rosy feet are so delicate that her toes, being overburdened by the ornament, seem to be squeezing out the red lacquer dye she has applied to her feet!

552. Śiva, the Destroyer, one of the gods of the Hindu Trinity, is represented as wearing a crescent moon on his brow. So Kāma, the love god, seems to try and outvie Śiva by decking himself with hundreds of moons.

Kṛṣṇa is represented in Hindu mythology as wearing a crown of peacock feathers.

555. A *damṛī* is an eighth part of a pice, while a rupee contains sixty-four pice. In Hindi numerals a curved oblique mark placed on the right side of a figure signifies that it should be counted as rupees. If the curved mark is not there the figure represents so many pice.

562. For *khañjana* see note to verse 479. Some commentators take the couplet to be a description of autumn, likening it to a beautiful girl, for, with autumn come the lotuses, the *khañjana* birds and, of course, the moon. But the general trend of the verse shows it is to emphasize the girl's beauty rather than that of autumn.

563. The *dupahariyā* flower (also known as *bandhujīva* or *bandhuka*) is a red flower which blossoms in the rainy season.

564. Bhagawāna Dīna interprets the couplet somewhat differently, though the import is the same. His reading is: 'Sugar cane, honey and nectar remain desirous of talking to her' (in other words her speech is so sweet that they get their sweetness from that only). (BBL, pp. 115–6) The translation follows the simpler interpretation given by other commentators.

567. The waters of the Yamunā river are deep and so take on a bluish hue.

573. The *palāśa* (also known as *ḍhāka*) is a common forest tree bearing many flaming scarlet-orange flowers in February–March. It flowers in a leafless condition and the flowers have black calycycles.

575. Bhagawāna Dīna believes (with justification) that the verse is not Bihārī's and ought not to be included in the *Satasaī*. (BBL, p. 269) Other recensions have, however, included it, and so it has been incorporated in the translation. The *nāyikā* could be a village belle.

577. The comparison of lovely eyes to a wagtail, black bees, fish and deer is conventional in Hindi and Sanskrit poetry.

580. Brahma or Brahman (to be distinguished from Brahmā the Creator) is a Vedāntic concept meaning the invisible Reality which is of the same nature as the soul (*ātmā*). The idea often comes up in the Vedānta and particularly in the philosophy of Śankara, the renowned Indian philosopher. In the philosophy of Śankara, known as *advaita,* Brahman, sometimes conceived as being consciousness bliss (*sat-cit-ānanda*), is believed to be unseen, and comprehensible only by wisdom and by the authority of the *Vedas* (Hindu scriptures).

581. Brahmā is the Creator, one of the gods of the Hindu Trinity.

582. Commentators interpret the word *mutaharu* differently. Lālā Bhagawāna Dīna takes it to be 'the front part of the face'. (BBL, p. 252) Others, like Dr Deśarājasingha Bhāṭī, take it as 'that portion of the wrap or sari which hangs down the head'. (BBB, p. 420) The latter interpretation has been adopted in the translation because it sounds more reasonable. The poet has already said that the girl souses her face with water (*mumha pakhārī*), and to say again that she washes the front part of her face is mere repetition, which one would not expect from a poet of Bihārī's stature. Besides, this interpretation has also been taken for *mutaharu* by Dr S.S. Pāncāla in *Bihārī's Language.* (BBP, p. 292)

584. *murāsā* (also called *karṇa-phūla* or *tarkī*) is a flower-shaped ornament worn by Indian women in the ears, either as a clasp, or more often (and always in old times), by being screwed on a pin through pierced earlobes. It may be set with pearls, or sometimes with gems.

585. The lane in which the two are going is streaked with moonlight, so that at some places it is dark and at others bright. Where it is dark, Kṛṣṇa's form, which is of a dark hue, merges with the darkness, and only Rādhā can be seen. At other places Rādhā, who is fair and of a golden complexion, merges with the moonlight, and only Kṛṣṇa is visible.

586. *bindi* is the round beauty mark Indian women put in the middle of their foreheads.

Some commentators take the couplet as a description of the *nāyikā* coming from her bath, and interpret *silasile* as 'wet' (meaning thereby that her hair is still damp and so looks lovelier). (BBB, pp. 428–9) But wet hair can hardly be said to be attractive. More likely it means *phulela,* i.e. 'oil scented with the attar of fragrant flowers'. (BBL, pp. 59–60) Thus *silasile bāra* (or *bāla*) would mean 'hair glistening with perfumed oil'. Bhagawāna Dīna suggests an alternative meaning also if the verse is taken as spoken by the woman messenger of the *nāyikā* who says: 'Go to her, for she eagerly awaits you, looking lovely in simple adornment.' (BBL, p. 60) But this interpretation is unnecessary and there is nothing in the wordings of the couplet to warrant it.

592. Lālā Bhagawāna Dīna takes *bhāji* to mean 'fleeing' (BBL, p. 20), but that does not appear to fit in with the sense. The moon loses its brilliance in an eclipse, and so fear of the demon, Rāhu (who is believed to cause the eclipse by swallowing the moon), is more likely to make the moon keep its brilliance in Mars' safe custody rather than just run away! The translation follows Ratnākara's version, which takes *bhāji* to mean 'separated from' not 'fleeing'.

akhat or *akṣat* means 'consecrated grains of rice'. These are applied to the middle of the forehead. The *nāyikā* has been to the local temple, and the priest has put the rice grains on her forehead. When she comes home she applies the red *bindi* (round beauty mark) on the same place. She puts the *bindi* on the rice grains because it would be improper for her to remove the holy grains for putting her beauty mark there. The rice grains shine against the background of the red *bindi*, hence the comparison of the moon's brilliance hid in Mars (which is believed to be of the colour of blood, see note to verse 696).

Ordinarily when the moon is in the orbit of Mars it is considered to be an auspicious moment. That's why the *nāyikā's* messenger tells the *nāyaka* to go to his beloved, for at this time she will give him the greatest pleasure in love-making.

595. Perhaps the rose petal got stuck to her cheek when she slept or lay in her bed. It was customary to strew rose petals or tender flowers on the bed.

The translation follows Bhagawāna Dīna's version reading the word as *gāla* ('cheek') (BBL, pp. 40–1). Some commentators read it as *gāta* meaning 'the body'. (BSR, p. 539 and BBL, p. 437) But even though the rose petal can't be easily distinguished because of its similarity to the *nāyikā's* tender and rosy skin, it must have been *seen* as a rose petal! And it would be far easier for the *nāyikā's* friend to notice it on her cheek than on her limbs (which would be hidden by her dress).

596. For *campā* see note to verse 490.

597. *cīṁkā* is a kind of net of ropes or other material, suspended from a roof. It was the old system to keep earthen pots containing curd, butter and eats, away from the reach of cats, mice and so forth.

The *nāyaka* finds his beloved placing a pot of butter in the *cīṁkā*, and is so enraptured by her raised arms (revealing part of her breasts and waist because of her dress moving up), that he wants her to remain like that always. Compare this with Keats's *Ode to a Grecian Urn*:

Fair youth, beneath the trees, thou canst not leave
Thy song, nor ever can those trees be bare;
Bold Lover, never, never canst thou kiss,
Though winning near the goal—yet, do not grieve;
She cannot fade, though thou hast not thy bliss,
For ever wilt thou love, and she be fair!

598. *sunakirabā* or *sunakīrā* (also known as *bhaṁbhīrā*) is a winged insect which appears in the rainy season in large numbers. It has shiny wings with the dull gleam of mica. The village woman sticks one of these wings on her forehead in place of the usual *biṁdī* (beauty mark).

Wisdom

599. *pīnasa* is a nasal disease known to the Hindu *āyurveda* system of medicine, in which the patient loses his sense of smell.

It is believed the lines were composed by Bihārī, after the death of Jayasiṅgha, his royal patron, when he ceased to be honoured in the royal durbar because the rajah's successor had no taste for poetry.

605. *dhatūrā* is a thorny berry. It is a kind of poison, but just a little of it produces intoxication. Its other name is *kanaka*, which is also the word for 'gold' in Hindi.

606. See note to verse 605 *ante*.

608. *moṣu* (*mokṣa*) means liberation or salvation. It implies freedom from rebirth in the world of suffering and a union of the soul with god, and is the highest acme of Hindu spiritualism.

609. For *ghuṁghacī* see note to verse 382.

612. For *guṛahala* see note to verse 288. It is a very common flower, red in colour, but without scent.

615. *Jeṭh* (May–June) is the hottest month in India, while *Māgh* (January–February) is the coldest.

Some commentators give a different interpretation. According to them the *nāyaka* has had a tiff with the *nāyikā* and abandons her for his co-wife. The co-wife feels proud of having won his favours, and seeing her so, her companion tells her: 'O foolish woman, don't feel puffed up on getting your husband's love. You've won it only because he has quarrelled with the *nāyikā.* As soon as he'll get fed up with you, you'll seem good no longer and another woman, for whom he'll forsake you, will be pleasing to him; just as the shade seems pleasant in the hot summer *Jeṭh* month, but troublesome when the winter month of *Māgh* comes.' (BBB, p. 213; BSR, p. 257) This would be reading more into the couplet than what perhaps Bihārī actually meant. The more obvious interpretation (following that of Bhagawāna Dīna, BBL, p. 187) has been preferred.

617. It is believed that the stem of a lotus flower lengthens with the increase of water in the lake, so that the lotus always remains above its surface.

619. The *madāra* is the swallow wort plant. Both the *madāra* and the sun are known as *arka* in Hindi.

620. *amāvasyā* is the last day of the dark half of the month, when the night is pitch dark.

621. The Mārwāṛ country is a desert area, where it is very difficult to get water. But watermelons grow there of themselves in the sandy soil.

Jeṭh is the hottest month of the Indian summer corresponding to May–June.

624. 'Scorning glances' needs explanation. There is a pun on *hara* (the last word in the second line). The word means 'a necklace' or 'garland', and also 'defeat'. Thus onlookers exclaim '*hara*! *hara*!' i.e. 'defeat! defeat!' when the garland flaunts itself on the girl's raised breasts.

626. Some commentators take the couplet as advice to keep a friendship. Lālā Bhagawāna Dīna, for example, gives the following interpretation: 'If you want the brilliance of your friendship not to fade, and to prevent animosity from entering your friend's mind, do not let the dust of your authority settle on it (i.e. do not lord over him).' (BBL, p. 267 and BSR, p. 311) But this interpretation seems rather farfetched and, so, the other simpler one (BBB, p. 262) has been preferred.

628. Some critics think the verse expresses Bihārī's disgust at the profligacy of the courtiers in Jayasiṅgha's court, but it seems to be just a general observation.

629. The Hindu scriptures are the *Vedas* and *Smṛtis*. *Vedas* (root *vid*='know'), the foundation of Hindu religion, are hymns written in Sanskrit. There are four *Vedas—Ṛg, Yajur, Sāma* and *Atharva*.

Smṛti 'what was remembered', ordinarily meant only the *dharma-śāstras* (law books). Manu, the ancient Hindu law-giver says 'By *Śruti* ('direct revelation') is meant the *Veda* and by *Smṛti* "the institutes of law"'. In its wider sense, however, *Smṛti* is said to include the *Ramāyaṇa, Mahābhārata,* and the *Purāṇas.*

633. The *śrādha* fortnight is the period in the year when Hindus make ceremonial offerings of food to their ancestors. It is customary to put aside a little of the offering for a crow to eat.

634. For '*śrādha* fortnight' see note to verse 633 *ante*. If the crow does not itself come to take the food offered, he is persuaded to do so by getting away a little distance and beckoning to him.

635. Some commentators take the lines to refer to the *nāyikā* whose lover has gone away to a foreign country. The idea is that, as the spring comes again bringing back the roses to the rose bush, her lover will return to give her bliss. (BSR, p. 347) Others think they may refer to a talented person who does not forsake his royal patron in the latter's bad days, hoping that things will take a turn for the better. (BBB, p. 285) But most probably the lines are meant to be a general observation of the poet. (BBL, p. 270)

637. Washermen, labourers and potters, use donkeys for transport—washermen for taking bundles of clothes to be washed, labourers for carrying the mud they dig (most houses have mud walls in Indian villages), and potters to transport their finished earthen pots for sale.
644. According to Indian astrology when the spots on the moon grow less or disappear, it means some disaster like a deluge or a calamity, which may cause the end of creation (*pralaya*) is about to take place.

649. The translation is based on Ratnākara's interpretation. Lālā Bhagawāna Dīna interprets the verse differently. According to him the words are spoken by the *nāyikā* to her erring husband who is in the habit of going out and spending a lot of time with his mistresses. She points this out, and her apologetic husband promises not to go out any longer. But she does not believe him, and says: 'You may resolve not to go out, or give a thousand excuses protesting your innocence, but I will not believe you, for a man's nature cannot change.' (BBL, p. 270) The interpretation may be ingenious, but appears to be unnecessary, because in all probibility the poet is just making a general observation.

650. *cola* is a kind of wood, pieces of which when placed in water and put on the boil for some time, yield a kind of fast dye. The dye is so permanent that if a cloth is dyed in it, the colour will never fade.

652. Ratnākara has taken the verse in a different sense. According to him it is addressed to a person who has become vain because he is treated with honour by a king: 'Why are you swollen with vanity because you are honoured in the king's court? Don't you know there are other monarchs mightier than him, before whom he bows and at whose feet he falls?' (BBL, p. 425) The language of the verse, however, and the specific mention of Kṛṣṇa's peacock feather, and particularly of Rādhā is a clear indication that the verse is meant for Kṛṣṇa (who is conceived of as wearing a crown of peacock feathers).

653. The day after the Divālī festival (the festival of the lamps) is celebrated in India, in the *Kārttika* month of the Hindu calendar (October–November), the worship of *goverdhana* or *godhana* is held. In villages cultivators make figures of *godhana* (conical in shape) out of cowdung (a cow is considered sacred among Hindus) and worship them by offering flowers etc., and by also putting vermilion marks. After the worship concludes the cow dung figures are left lying where they are, and so are often trampled under the hooves of stray cows, buffaloes, bullocks and other animals.

Devotion

654. This forms the opening verse of the *Satasaī* and, as is usual with Hindi poets, is in the form of an invocation. Such invocations are of three kinds. The first kind seeks a blessing from some god or goddess. The second kind is one in which the writer salutes his guru or some divinity. The third kind tells the reader about the subject matter and the object of the work. Bihārī's invocation is a combination of the first and third, because it seeks the blessings of Rādhā, Kṛṣṇa's consort, and also indicates that the author is writing about the loves of Rādhā and Kṛṣṇa, a theme common in Hindi love poetry of the *Śṛṅgāra rasa* kind. (see Introduction)

bhavabādhā—According to Hindu belief there are three kinds of sorrows. These are (i) *ādhyātmika,* sorrows like diseases and mental anguish, originating from the sufferer himself; so called because these rise from the *ātmā* (self), (ii) *ādhibhautika,* caused to the sufferer by other living creatures like beasts, reptiles, birds and so forth. These are called *ādhibhautika* because they arise from *bhūtas* 'created beings', and (iii) *ādhidaivika,* suffering resulting from supernatural forces like the ill-effects of stars, planets, evil spirits, ghosts and the like. Since these sorrows are caused by *daivas* or *devas* (gods) they are called *ādhidaivika.* Here the poet uses the words *bhavabādhā* (*bhava*='world', *bādhā*= 'impediments', i.e. sorrows) apparently in a general sense to include all kinds of sorrows.

ja tana kī jhāīṁ paraiṁ—there can be three interpretations to these words according to the various meanings of *jhāīṁ paraiṁ* (viz. 'falling of the shadow of', 'thinking of' or 'having a glimpse of'). These are:

(i) Rādhā, whose very shadow captivates Kṛṣṇa, bestow your blessings on me.

(ii) I seek the blessings of that Rādhā, by meditating on whose form dark-shaped sins and sorrows are destroyed. (Śyāma is another name for Kṛṣṇa, but it also means 'black'. Kṛṣṇa is conceived of as being 'dark-hued'.)

(iii) Rādhā is believed to have a yellowish complexion and Kṛṣṇa a bluish one. So when Rādhā's shadow falls on Kṛṣṇa, her lover, the yellow and the blue mingle and become green (*harita*='green', *duti*='splendour'). In other words the splendour of Rādhā's body increases when Kṛṣṇa is with her. Some critics think this shows Bihārī's knowledge of colours, for green results from the mixing of blue and yellow. The other (and more obvious) interpretation is that when Kṛṣṇa sees Rādhā he begins to sparkle with joy. The expression *harā-bharā* is used in the sense of being revived or refreshed. A drooping plant becomes *harā-bharā* when it is watered. Similarly here, when Kṛṣṇa sees his beloved Rādhā, his face begins to sparkle with joy.

Of these alternative interpretations, the simplest and most likely is the third, i.e. 'the very glimpse of Rādhā delights Kṛṣṇa'.

655. The incident of the elephant is from the Purāṇas. While an elephant was drinking water from a stream, a crocodile seized his foot and began to pull him into the current. The elephant could not free himself despite all his strength, and when only the tip of his trunk—just so much as a needle's eye—remained free of the swirling waters, he called on god. His prayer was heard. The crocodile died and the elephant was saved. It seems, says the poet, that after this god decided never again to come to the aid of his devotees!

The verse is in the form of a complaint or taunt addressed to god (known in Hindi poetry as *ulāhanā).* Many of Bihārī's devotional verses are couched in this form.

656. Some of the words in the verse have a double meaning. Thus *taraunā* means 'without salvation' (*taranā*='to get salvation'), and also 'a flower-shaped ear ornament worn by women'; *Śruti* means 'the *Vedas*' and also 'the ears'; *nāka-bāsa* means 'finding a place in heaven' and also 'being on the nose' (according to Indian poetical concepts the nose is given primary importance in the human body and the ears are hardly ever mentioned); *besari* means 'the vilest soul' and also 'a ring-shaped ear ornament worn on the nostril by Indian women'; *mukutana* means 'persons who have obtained salvation' and also 'pearls'.

Because of the double meaning of some of the words the verse can either be taken as emphasizing the superiority of devotion to god over mere recitation of the scriptures or knowledge, or meant to depict the splendour of the woman's ear ornament. This is one of the verses which shows Bihārī's supreme poetic skill. The devotional aspect has been preferred as it seems to be closer to the poet's intention.

657. Yama, the Hindu Pluto, god of Death, is represented with a fearful visage of green colour, wearing red clothes and riding a bull. He bears a ponderous mace, and a noose to secure his victims. The road to his abode is guarded by two insatiable dogs with four eyes and wide nostrils, and so the souls of those dying, hurry past them. In his palace called Kalīcī, he sits on his throne known as Vicārabhū and judges the souls of the dead as they are brought to him by his

messengers (*yamadūtas*), while his two chief attendants, Canda and Kāla-puruśa, stand by. As his porter, Vaidhyata, admits each soul, Citragupta, his recorder, reads out from his register, called *agrasandhānī,* the deeds performed by him in his life on earth. Yama then gives his judgment. The soul either ascends to the abode of the manes (*pitṛloka*) or is born on earth again in another form, or is sent to one of the twenty-one hells according to his guilt.

Nṛsiṁha or Narasiṁha is believed to be one of the incarnations of Lord Viṣṇu. He was half-man and half-lion. According to mythology, he emerged from a stone pillar to kill Hiraṇyakaśipu, a wicked demon-king. The demon had been tormenting his own son Prahalāda, who was Viṣṇu's devotee.

658. Although only the word *gīdahiṁ* ('vultures') is mentioned in the verse, the implied reference is to Jaṭāyu, who in Hindu mythology is the son of Garuṭa, Viṣṇu's vehicle, and the king of vultures. Jaṭāyu fought fiercely with Rāvaṇa, the demon-king of Laṅkā, when he was carrying off Rāma's wife, Sītā. He was mortally wounded, but managed to inform Rāma about Sītā's fate before he died. Rāma, along with his brother Lakṣmana, performed Jaṭāyu's funeral rites, and their ally Jatāyu attained heaven.

It was Rāma who redeemed Jaṭāyu, yet Bihārī mentions Kṛṣṇa (Murārī is another name for him). This is because he considered both of them as one, for both the gods (Rāma and Kṛṣṇa) are believed to be incarnations of Viṣṇu.

661. Rāma is the seventh incarnation of Viṣṇu. He was the eldest son of Daśaratha, a king of the Solar race, reigning in Ayodhyā. Rāma's story is related in the *Rāmāyaṇa* or *Rāmacaritamānasa.*

664. The verse could also be taken as meant to console the *nāyikā* whose lover has gone away. The *nāyikā's* confidante says, 'Friend, bear your grief cheerfully. When you hope for pleasure from him, do not resent the sorrow of parting.' But *sīsa caṛhai lai* ('accept with reverential resignation') would more appropriately refer to god, for the *nāyikā* can hardly be believed to have 'reverence' for her lover!

666. The Candra clan is a branch of the Yādavas. Kṛṣṇa's father, Vasudeva, king of Dvārkā, was of the Yādava race and his mother was Devakī.

The Braja country (Vṛndāvana) was the one where Kṛṣṇa was brought up amidst cowherds and milkmaids by his foster parents Naṅda and Yaśodā, and the scene of his amours with the milkmaids and Rādhā.

Commentators give an alternative interpretation to mean: 'O Kṛṣṇa-like Keśavarāma (Keśavarāi, Bihārī's father), you were born in a family of Brāhmins, and of your own accord settled in Braja. You are like Kṛṣṇa to me.

Relieve my sorrows.' This would be addressed by the poet not to the god Kṛṣṇa, but to his own father. (BBB, p. 82 and BSR, p. 92)

The alternative interpretation is unlikely because (i)The words *pragaṭa bhaye* mean 'appeared as an incarnation' and this could apply only to Kṛṣṇa, who is considered to be an incarnation of Lord Viṣṇu, (ii)It would seem presumptuous to pray to one's father to relieve him of sorrows. This would better apply to god, and (iii)Bihārī has petitioned Kṛṣṇa to relieve him of his sorrows in many other verses also. So this too most probably refers to Kṛṣṇa.

667. Hindus often paint (usually with sandalwood paste) sacerdotal marks on their foreheads or other parts of the body. The Śaivites (worshippers of Śiva) apply vertical marks, while Vaiṣṇavites (worshippers of Viṣṇu) apply horizontal marks.

669. In this verse the poet puts forth the *advaita* view according to which only the formless god (Brahman) exists as Truth and Reality, and the world of name and form (*nāma-rūpa*) is unreal. The idea is that the world is only a reflection of god.

670. Rādhā, in her divine aspect, is considered to be an incarnation of the goddess Lakṣmī and is worshipped accordingly.

Prayāga (Allahābād) is considered sacred, for here the holy rivers Gaṅgā and Yamunā meet the fabled subterranean Sarasvatī.

Kṛṣṇa, who is believed to be of a bluish complexion, is likened to the deep waters of the blue Yamunā river, while Rādhā, who is fair, to the clear Gaṅgā waters. The two came together in the Braja country, and so the woods of Braja where they made love are said to have the sanctity of Prayāga.

672. *barana* or *varṇa* means literally 'class' (not 'caste'). Rādhā and Kṛṣṇa are not of the same *varṇa* in the ordinary sense of the word, for in reality Kṛṣṇa belonged to a royal family of Brāhmins and Rādhā was a cowherd girl. They are said to be of the same class here because they complement each other (see verse 654 '*jā tana kī jhāiṁ paraiṁ syāma harita duti hoi*'), or maybe, as Bhagawāna Dīna says, because their names are almost identical—Kṛṣṇa is also called Śyāma, and Rādhā Śyāmā. (BBL, p. 4)

locana jugala aneka literally means 'many pairs of eyes', i.e. the divine couple can be seen only by one who has 'many pairs of eyes'. The idea is that their divine glory cannot be comprehended by human eyes. When Arjuna, Kṛṣṇa's disciple, wished to see his divine form, Kṛṣṇa told him, 'You cannot see that by your human eyes, so I will give you divine eyes to see it.' It was only then that Arjuna saw Lord Kṛṣṇa's divine form. (*Bhagavad Gītā,* XI)

673. Hari is another name for the god, Viṣṇu, whose incarnation Kṛṣṇa is believed to be.

674. For *moṣu* (or *mokṣa*) meaning 'liberation', see note to verse 608.

675. A *vaijayantī* garland is a particular kind of garland which the god, Kṛṣṇa, wears. It is made of five different colours of flowers. The word *māla* ('garland') means here the *vaijayantī* garland worn by Kṛṣṇa.

679. The reference is to the *Rāmāyaṇa.* Rāma's wife, Sītā, was carried away by Rāvaṇa, the demon-king of Laṅkā. Rāma took the assistance of the monkey-god and, with an army of monkey warriors, waged a war on Rāvaṇa and rescued Sītā. The problem was how to bridge the intervening ocean between Laṅkā and the mainland to take the army across. This was solved by Nala and Nīla, who were experts in building bridges. But they could only do so with Rāma's divine help. The monkeys hauled big stones and dropped them into the ocean. By Rāma's grace they miraculously floated on the water, and a bridge was soon built.

680. *tribhaṅgī lāl*—playing on his flute, Kṛṣṇa stands with his body waving in three undulations. So he is called *tribhaṅgī* (*tri*='three', *bhaṅga*='waves').

Translator's comment—Bihārī of course meant the verse to convey his deep devotion for the god. He is eager that Lord Kṛṣṇa should dwell in his heart. So he is willing, even at the risk of being called wicked, to make his heart crooked. Kṛṣṇa's askew form will easily be contained in such a heart for 'a square peg in a round hole' will not be easily put together. But the couplet could also be taken to mean that it is generally straightforward men who undergo suffering in the world. If god inhabits the heart of a simple and virtuous man he gives him sorrows, while in the crooked heart he's at ease!

683. Some commentators give an alternative meaning: 'If one considers god as having qualities, god becomes more distant to him. But if he is thought of as formless he is all-pervading, and being then able to reside in a man's heart comes closest to him, as a kite given string flies higher, but pulled, comes near.' (BSR, p. 340) However, Bihārī being a devotee of god in his form as Kṛṣṇa, whose attributes he has described in a number of couplets, will hardly get into the controversy of whether god is with or without form. The other interpretation, which seems to be more direct and appealing and applies equally to the worshipper of god with form as well as to the believer in a formless god, has been incorporated in the translation.

686. See note to verse 438.

687. The Braja country, which surrounds Mathurā, was the scene of Kṛṣṇa's early life. The verse brings out the divine aspect of Kṛṣṇa.
690. For the reference to the lifting of the Goverdhana mount see note to verse 438.

Bhagawāna Dīna has given an alternative interpretation also from the angle of love. The *nāyikā* is pretending to be angry and her companion urges her to make up with her lover. She tells the *nāyikā:* 'See, the dark clouds rising in the sky fill hearts with longing. Abandon your indifference and make love to your attractive lover who is fond of disporting in the woods. Clasp him to your rising hill-like breasts.' (BBL, p. 134) Such an interpretation is possible because some of the words in the couplet have dual meanings. These are (i) *manamohana,* which means 'Kṛṣṇa' as well as 'the *nāyaka* who captivates the heart', (ii) *ghanasyāma,* which means 'Kṛṣṇa whose form is as charming as the dark clouds' and 'dark clouds', (iii) *kuñjabihārī,* meaning firstly, 'Kṛṣṇa who sported with milkmaids in the forest', and secondly, 'the *nāyaka* who is eager to make love in the woods', (iv) *giradhārī,* meaning both 'Kṛṣṇa, who lifted the Goverdhana mount' and 'one who is endowed with rising hill-like breasts' (*giri*='a hill').

The devotional sense is, however, more suitable because of the reference to the various incidents in Kṛṣṇa's life. This is also favoured by most of *Satasaī's* commentators.

691. The Kali age or Kaliyuga is one of the four *yugas* (ages) of the world's existence, according to Hindu cosmogony. It is the last of the *yugas* (the one in which, it is believed we are living) in which righteousness and virtue are at their lowest ebb.

In Praise of Jayasiṅgha

693. *lākhana kī fauja* cannot be interpreted as 'an army of lakhs' because the mention of 'lakhs' twice in the couplet would be a poetic defect which a poet of Bihārī's standing could not be guilty of. Lākhana was most probably a chieftain or a little-known prince, for there is no mention of him in contemporary accounts of Bihārī's times. The *Ma'āsir-ul-umrā* mentions a warrior Lakkhī, who was a *mansabdār* in the Nizāmsāhī Rāj, and *deshmukh* of Sandhkher in Daulatābād. He was Sivājī's maternal grandfather. When Shāh Jahān, the Moghul emperor, was ruling, Jayasiṅgha was sent to accompany Khānjalān Lodhī in his campaigns in the south of India. Maybe Jayasiṅgha encountered

Lākhana during one of these. Or possibly he may be a Jāṭ warrior with whom Jayasiṅgha fought. The Mahāvan Jāṭs of Agra were powerful in Shāh Jahān's time, and the emperor had sent Qāsim Khān, whom Jayasiṅgha accompanied, to subdue them.

695. *darapana-dhāma* (*darapana*='mirror', *dhāma*='house' or 'place') means 'the hall of mirrors'. Jayasiṅgha, who was Bihārī's royal patron, used to sit in the hall of his palace (known as *śīśamahal, śīśa*='mirror, *mahal*='palace') at Āmergaṛh when he gave audience to the public. The walls of this hall were studded with tiny, round mirrors. The mirrors were so placed that each one would reflect the figure of the rajah when he sat on the throne. Shāh Jahān himself had such a hall of mirrors in his palace at Agra.

696. The planet Mars, which gets its name from the Greek god of war, Ares, whom the Romans identified with Mars, is believed to be of blood-red colour. The poet's use of the simile is particularly appropriate because Jayasiṅgha's face shone red, showing both his zeal to fight the warriors in war and also his anger towards them.

697. The verse actually reads: 'O hawk, do not, under the influence of someone else, kill innocent birds for the advantage of others, for in doing so you do not gain any merit, and your labour goes to waste.' But this by itself would not convey what the verse really endeavours to express. In a veiled manner, the poet seeks to criticize his royal patron, Jayasiṅgha, for fighting with the Rājpūts for the benefit of the emperor, Shāh Jahān, whose vassal he was. Hence mention has been made in the translated version of Jayasiṅgha and Shāh Jahān as well.

698. Under orders of his father Shāh Jahān, Auraṅgazīb, was sent at the head of an army to attack Balkh. Jayasiṅgha was also sent along with him. The Moghul forces were trapped and surrounded, but Jayasiṅgha very cleverly and with great valour, managed to rescue them and brought them safely to Kābul.

699. Adhāsura was one of the many demons sent by Kaṅsa the tyrant usurper of Mathurā to kill Kṛṣṇa, his divine rival. The demon swallowed the cowherd folk along with all their cows, but Kṛṣṇa ripped its belly open and saved them.

700. *patina rākhi cādara curī—cādara* is a 'wrap' or 'shawl' and *curī* or *cūrī* means 'bangles', while *rākhi* is 'kept' or 'preserved'. If a Mohammedan dies his widow ceases to cover herself with a wrap; while in the case of the death of a Hindu, his widow breaks her glass bangles as a sign of widowhood. Thus by bringing the trapped soldiers from the Balkh battle, Jayasiṅgha 'preserved' the

cādaras of the Mohammedan wives and the *cūrīs* of the Hindu women. In other words he saved them from being widowed.

701. Jayasiṅgha was Bihārī's royal patron. He was delighted with one of the poet's couplets (see note to verse 12) and commissioned him to write others, giving a gold piece (*mohur*) for each one written (see Introduction). Later Jayasiṅgha made Bihārī his court poet.

Diverse tastes—*The Satasaī* contains various kinds of verses on diverse themes such as love, love-making, separation, human beauty and the beauty of nature, wisdom and so forth. So the poet calls it a 'book ministering to diverse tastes and fancies'.

Miscellaneous

702. The verse has a personal angle inasmuch as Bihārī had to live in his in-laws' house at Mathurā for sometime in his youth. Perhaps this verse is an expression of his feelings about the treatment given to him there.

An alternative interpretation is also given by some commentators as follows: 'A woman can't show indifference and keep away from her lover for long in the winter month of *Pūs*. Her indifference is as shortlived as the welcome a man gets when he stays too long with his in-laws.' (BBB, pp. 125–6)

Pūs is the month of extreme winter corresponding to the month of December–January according to the English calendar, when the days are shortest.

706. *chāyāgrāhini* literally 'catcher of the shadow' (*chāyā*='shadow', *grahaṇa*='catch' or 'seize'). The reference is to Siṅghikā or Chāyāgrāhinī, who was a female demon living in the ocean near the island of Laṅkā. She had the power of catching a living being by his shadow. Once the shadow came in her clutches the man (or animal) died and she would devour him. Hanumāna, the monkey-god, Rāma's messenger bound for Laṅkā, came across her while he was flying over the ocean (he is believed to be the son of the Wind god). The demon attacked him, but he was able to kill her. The incident is mentioned in the *Rāmacaritamānasa* of Tulsīdasa.

708. Some commentators, including Bhagawāna Dīna, read the word *kahalāne* ('restless' or 'agitated with heat') as two words *kaha lāne*, which in the dialect of Bundelakhaṅḍa means 'why?' or 'for what reason?' (BBL, pp. 236–7). Thus they think the first line of the couplet poses a question and the second one is its

answer. The explanation given is that an artist presented a painting to Jayasingha, Bihārī's royal patron, in which a peacock and a snake, a lion and a deer, were resting together without caring to prey on each other. The rajah asked his courtiers why such creatures had been painted together. No one could answer him except Bihārī, who gave him the reason for this in the second line of the couplet.

This ingenious explanation, however, seems to be unnecessary, for the interpretation of *kahalāne* as 'oppressed by the heat' is good enough, and fits in very appropriately in the context. The direct meaning has, therefore, been incorporated in the translation.

709. According to popular belief the male and female ruddy geese stay together in the day, but part at night, each of them going to the two extreme ends of the pond. From there, they call to each other plaintively all through the night. So the longer winter nights keep them separated for longer. On the other hand lovers are happy because the longer nights provide them more opportunity for love-making.

710. The idea here is 'When you are in Rome do as the Romans do'. The cultured girl has no need to put on airs because she is sure of herself. But if she does not behave affectedly as the women in the village do, they'll laugh at her and not take her as one of their own.

711. The astrologer was happy because he knew he would get rid of his wife's lover soon, for according to the horoscope the man who fathered the child would die soon after. And of course he was happy to know it was not *he* who was to die! Astrology has a great following in India, and it is believed that if one's horoscope has been correctly cast at the time of birth, then the future events in the life of that person can be accurately foretold.

712. Elongated eyes, pointed at the corners, are considered very attractive in the Indian concept of beauty.

APPENDIX

Key to the Verses

The serial number of the verses as in the text is given in the first column and the number in Ratnākara's arrangement in the second.

Serial number in text	*Number in Ratnākara's arrangement*	*Serial number in text*	*Number in Ratnākara's arrangement*	*Serial number in text*	*Number in Ratnākara's arrangement*
1	5	26	128	51	206
2	9	27	134	52	207
3	10	28	139	53	208
4	12	29	144	54	212
5	15	30	147	55	213
6	18	31	154	56	215
7	27	32	157	57	216
8	30	33	158	58	218
9	32	34	159	59	219
10	34	35	160	60	224
11	36	36	162	61	227
12	38	37	166	62	232
13	45	38	174	63	239
14	47	39	177	64	242
15	50	40	178	65	245
16	58	41	179	66	246
17	66	42	182	67	247
18	75	43	193	68	249
19	78	44	194	69	257
20	85	45	195	70	259
21	88	46	196	71	262
22	118	47	198	72	263
23	121	48	200	73	264
24	123	49	202	74	265
25	126	50	205	75	272

76	280	119	470	162	606
77	290	120	472	163	610
78	291	121	480	164	611
79	292	122	493	165	612
80	293	123	500	166	613
81	294	124	502	167	616
82	302	125	503	168	617
83	305	126	505	169	618
84	307	127	508	170	623
85	309	128	514	171	633
86	316	129	515	172	634
87	320	130	517	173	636
88	325	131	518	174	638
89	336	132	522	175	639
90	349	133	523	176	645
91	352	134	524	177	646
92	356	135	527	178	650
93	363	136	530	179	652
94	368	137	531	180	658
95	372	138	533	181	663
96	373	139	534	182	667
97	374	140	542	183	678
98	375	141	543	184	688
99	382	142	545	185	697
100	384	143	547	186	698
101	386	144	550	187	702
102	397	145	552	188	705
103	399	146	554	189	706
104	406	147	557	190	707
105	407	148	564	191	709
106	417	149	570	192	23
107	422	150	572	193	24
108	423	151	574	194	76
109	424	152	577	195	84
110	436	153	582	196	96
111	443	154	583	197	99
112	444	155	586	198	129
113	447	156	589	199	130
114	450	157	592	200	137
115	452	158	598	201	155
116	454	159	599	202	183
117	460	160	601	203	214
118	468	161	605	204	319

205	324	248	240	291	587
206	354	249	250	292	591
207	369	250	260	293	600
208	387	251	267	294	603
209	463	252	281	295	607
210	464	253	286	296	608
211	465	254	287	297	609
212	466	255	289	298	640
213	494	256	296	299	653
214	571	257	297	300	654
215	594	258	315	301	657
216	627	259	323	302	662
217	630	260	332	303	700
218	632	261	339	304	29
219	642	262	346	305	49
220	643	263	348	306	72
221	644	264	365	307	107
222	651	265	379	308	108
223	655	266	380	309	132
224	665	267	383	310	197
225	683	268	393	311	233
226	14	269	394	312	243
227	22	270	410	313	256
228	33	271	446	314	273
229	65	272	449	315	279
230	79	273	456	316	310
231	82	274	458	317	314
232	83	275	467	318	337
233	97	276	482	319	343
234	100	277	498	320	360
235	113	278	499	321	364
236	115	279	507	322	370
237	122	280	511	323	404
238	136	281	520	324	409
239	153	282	528	325	412
240	168	283	540	326	415
241	169	284	546	327	416
242	184	285	551	328	453
243	185	286	555	329	476
244	186	287	558	330	484
245	187	288	565	331	495
246	199	289	569	332	496
247	211	290	579	333	497

334	509	377	64	420	358
335	536	378	74	421	378
336	539	379	77	422	395
337	548	380	86	423	400
338	559	381	89	424	402
339	562	382	90	425	405
340	566	383	98	426	408
341	568	384	110	427	414
342	604	385	114	428	445
343	631	386	119	429	455
344	649	387	120	430	457
345	675	388	124	431	475
346	685	389	125	432	485
347	19	390	140	433	488
348	92	391	142	434	510
349	116	392	146	435	513
350	127	393	148	436	516
351	135	394	150	437	519
352	138	395	163	438	521
353	145	396	164	439	525
354	149	397	170	440	526
355	176	398	172	441	529
356	231	399	175	442	535
357	253	400	203	443	537
358	254	401	217	444	549
359	459	402	222	445	553
360	469	403	223	446	563
361	486	404	225	447	585
362	544	405	230	448	593
363	560	406	234	449	595
364	578	407	244	450	596
365	656	408	266	451	615
366	684	409	275	452	622
367	704	410	277	453	625
368	37	411	278	454	635
369	39	412	283	455	659
370	48	413	284	456	660
371	54	414	285	457	667
372	56	415	298	458	669
373	57	416	308	459	672
374	60	417	317	460	681
375	62	418	328	461	703
376	63	419	329	462	2

463	3	506	204	549	403
464	4	507	209	550	413
465	6	508	210	551	418
466	7	509	220	552	419
467	8	510	229	553	420
468	13	511	236	554	440
469	16	512	248	555	442
470	17	513	252	556	448
471	25	514	258	557	462
472	26	515	268	558	473
473	28	516	269	559	477
474	35	517	270	560	478
475	40	518	271	561	483
476	42	519	274	562	487
477	43	520	288	563	490
478	44	521	295	564	504
479	46	522	299	565	512
480	52	523	304	566	532
481	53	524	306	567	538
482	55	525	312	568	556
483	67	526	318	569	567
484	69	527	322	570	573
485	70	528	326	571	576
486	73	529	327	572	580
487	87	530	330	573	597
488	93	531	333	574	603
489	95	532	334	575	614
490	102	533	335	576	626
491	103	534	338	577	628
492	104	535	340	578	629
493	105	536	342	579	647
494	106	537	347	580	648
495	109	538	350	581	664
496	112	539	353	582	666
497	133	540	355	583	670
498	143	541	359	584	673
499	152	542	362	585	674
500	165	543	385	586	679
501	173	544	388	587	680
502	180	545	389	588	682
503	188	546	390	589	686
504	189	547	392	590	687
505	190	548	398	591	689

592	690	633	434	674	261
593	691	634	435	675	301
594	693	635	437	676	361
595	694	636	438	677	371
596	695	637	439	678	391
597	699	638	441	679	401
598	708	639	451	680	425
599	59	640	461	681	426
600	94	641	474	682	427
601	111	642	481	683	428
602	117	643	491	684	471
603	131	644	584	685	501
604	151	645	590	686	541
605	191	646	619	687	561
606	192	647	620	688	581
607	228	648	624	689	621
608	235	649	637	690	641
609	237	650	668	691	661
610	255	651	671	692	701
611	276	652	676	693	80
612	282	653	694	694	156
613	303	654	1	695	167
614	311	655	11	696	226
615	313	656	20	697	300
616	321	657	21	698	710
617	331	658	31	699	711
618	341	659	41	700	712
619	351	660	51	701	713
620	357	661	61	702	171
621	366	662	68	703	251
622	367	663	71	704	344
623	376	664	81	705	345
624	377	665	91	706	433
625	381	666	101	707	479
626	396	667	141	708	489
627	411	668	161	709	492
628	421	669	181	710	506
629	429	670	201	711	575
630	430	671	221	712	588
631	431	672	238	713	692
632	432	673	341		

PENGUIN CLASSICS

The House of Ulloa Emilia Pardo Bazán

The finest achievement of one of European literature's most dynamic and controversial figures – ardent feminist, traveller, intellectual – and one of the great 19th century Spanish novels, *The House of Ulloa* traces the decline of the old aristocracy at the time of the Glorious Revolution of 1868, while exposing the moral vacuum of the new democracy.

The Republic Plato

The best-known of Plato's dialogues, *The Republic* is also one of the supreme masterpieces of Western philosophy whose influence cannot be overestimated.

The Life of Johnson James Boswell

Perhaps the finest 'life' ever written, Boswell's *Johnson* captures for all time one of the most colourful and talented figures in English literary history.

The Metamorphoses Ovid

A golden treasury of myths and legends which has proved a major influence on Western literature.

A Nietzsche Reader Friedrich Nietzsche

A superb selection from all the major works of one of the greatest thinkers and writers in world literature, translated into clear, modern English.

Madame Bovary Gustave Flaubert

With *Madame Bovary* Flaubert established the realistic novel in France; while his central character of Emma Bovary, the bored wife of a provincial doctor, remains one of the great creations of modern literature.